A Shot
of Sultry

MACY
BECKETT

sourcebooks
casablanca

Published by Sourcebooks Casablanca, an imprint of Sourcebooks, Inc.
P.O. Box 4410, Naperville, Illinois 60567-4410
(630) 961-3900
Fax: (630) 961-2168
www.sourcebooks.com

Printed and bound in Canada.
WC 10 9 8 7 6 5 4 3 2 1

This one's dedicated to you, reader.
Thanks for visiting Sultry Springs!

Chapter 1

BOBBI GALLAGHER'S MAMA USED TO SAY MEN WERE like one-ply toilet paper: transparent, disposable, and only good for one thing. Ironically, it wasn't until Mama overdosed and Bobbi went to live with two men that she finally understood what a healthy relationship looked like. And while she didn't share her late mother's hatred of the male sex, she couldn't understand why young women—like the radiant bride in her viewfinder—were so eager to torch their freedom by getting married.

Grasping one cool, titanium tripod leg, Bobbi rotated her Sony Camcorder to capture the bride and her father as they swayed on the polished, twelve-by-twelve, parquet dance floor. Too bad the old guy didn't teach his daughter there was a vast world beyond husbands and babies. She gradually zoomed in on the dad's tear-streaked face, figuring she could edit the footage set to some cheesy background music, like that "Butterfly Kisses" song.

God, was this what her life had come to? Creating sappy video montages? She'd wanted to make a difference in the world—to let her films speak for those without a voice. If her friends from UCLA could see her now…

"Nice ceremony, dontcha think?"

Flinching to attention, Bobbi glanced over her shoulder at an elderly woman in a skintight, black spandex dress hemmed just above the knee. She looked like a cougar version of that little old lady from the Tweety Bird cartoons—right down to the wire-framed bifocals teetering on the tip of her nose.

"Beautiful," Bobbi said with a manufactured grin. "I think they'll be really happy together." According to statistics, they'd be divorced within five years and fighting over who kept the dog, but she kept that to herself.

"Back in my day, folks didn't bother with all this poppycock." Granny-on-the-prowl raised her glass of gin toward the sea of white-draped tables that flanked an open bar. "They left church and drove straight to the motel." Waggling her brown, penciled-on eyebrows, she whispered, "To bury the weasel."

"Oh, uh…" *Don't picture it! Don't picture it!* Damn. Too late. "I should probably get back to—"

"Hey, you look kinda familiar." Granny paused and wrinkled up her already wrinkled forehead. "Do I know you?"

Whirling back to the camera, Bobbi used her hair as a curtain and scratched her nose, an old nervous habit she'd never managed to break. "Nope. I'm from Inglewood, not LA." Six months ago she'd been all over the local news like a bad rash, but she'd given herself a little makeover since then, bleaching the signature hot pink streaks from her blond hair, then asking Papa Bryan to dye everything red and give her the same boring, asymmetrical bob as all the suburban soccer moms.

"Hmmm. I know you from somewhere. Maybe—" Suddenly, Granny stopped and sniffed the air. "Hot diggety! The buffet's open!" And then she was gone,

shuffling through the crowd and elbowing anyone care-
less enough to get in her way.

Talk about saved by the smell. She'd have to do a
better job staying out of sight, maybe back up and film
from the room's periphery. The daddy-daughter dance
ended, and Bobbi tapped the pause button and then
made her way to the ladies' room while guests feasted
on the artery-clogging buffet offerings.

Once inside the toilet stall, a handmade sign caught
her attention: *Please don't flush paper towel's. Thank's!*
Oh, Judas Priest. Apostrophe abuse drove her nuts, and
she knew she wouldn't be able to relax until she rescued
that poor sentence. Fortunately, she kept a bottle of
Wite-Out in her purse for just such an occasion. After
covering the errant marks with correction fluid, she
smiled and released a quiet sigh of relief, then waited
for the restroom to vacate before fixing all the other
signs too.

She returned to her post to shoot some footage of the
cake, especially the couple's iced blue monogram and
the delicate, pink, spun-sugar roses that adorned the top
layer. The sweet scent of buttercream icing flooded her
nostrils, causing her stomach to rumble in response.

"Taping weddings now?" said a man's nasally voice.
He laughed—an obnoxious ahr-ahr-ahr that sounded
like a barking seal—and added, "Oh, how the mighty
have fallen."

Bobbi froze and clenched her teeth. She didn't have
to turn around to know that thick Brooklyn accent
belonged to Garry Goldblatt, trash-media mogul and
creator of the sickening *Chicks Gone Crazy* series,
where drunken college coeds with daddy issues bared

their breasts and ditched their dignity for a few fleeting seconds of "fame."

Their paths had crossed several times since they'd first met six months ago at the Golden Calf awards... the night her work had won for best documentary. That was before she'd placed her trust in the wrong person and lost everything: career, reputation, spirit. Garry was right—she'd fallen from the stratosphere straight into the depths of wedding bell hell.

"Got a nephew with a bar mitzvah coming up," he teased. "Want that gig? I can put in a good word with my sister."

"I'm working, Garry." What a lie. Bobbi would deliver the best damn wedding video anyone had ever seen, but it wasn't work, not to her. "Go away."

"Actually," he said, ignoring her request, "I'm glad you're here. I was gonna call you on Monday."

Bobbi left the camera running and turned to face him, scanning his short, bulbous frame, bald head, and the bushy, black tufts peeking out from beneath his nostrils. Garry had always reminded her of Humpty Dumpty. After the fall. Squaring her shoulders and lifting her chin, she asked, "Why?"

"Got a proposition for you."

"Don't waste your time. I'm not taking off my top."

He flicked a glance at her C-cups for a moment, appraising her like a jeweler might inspect a diamond through his loupe. "Pretty decent rack, but that's not what I had in mind."

"What, then?"

"*Chicks Gone Crazy* earned me some serious coin, but reality TV's trending now, and I'm getting in while it's still hot. I started a new series called *Real Life, Real Love*. I wanna focus on what it's like to be young and single today—playful, sexy stuff, but clean enough to air on my network before nine. Here's the thing," he whispered, leaning in and bathing her in his sour scotch-breath. "The competition's focused on the metropolitan market, but they're ignoring a huge demographic that I intend to swoop in and snag. The hicks."

"Hicks, as in…"

"The rural community. My first project's called *Sex in the Sticks*, and I want you to shoot it."

"Are you serious?" Bobbi took a step back and tried to gauge whether Garry was jerking her around. She wouldn't put it past him—the man had some serious brass berries and a moral compass that pointed due south.

"Serious as a tax audit. I don't dick around when it comes to business, Gallagher."

"Why me?"

"I saw your piece on child migrant workers. A little long and boring—actually, it dragged worse than my grandpa's balls—but you got a knack for getting people to spill their guts, and you catch raw emotion like nothing I've ever seen. *Sex in the Sticks* isn't the respectable, politically correct shit that usually wets your panties, but it beats this"—he hooked his thumb toward the wedding cake—"don't you think?"

Slimy bastard or not, the man had a point. Besides, it wasn't as if she had other offers. Nobody—not even her closest "friends"—returned her calls these days. She ran her tongue over the smooth surface of her front teeth and began to take his proposition seriously. "What's involved, exactly?"

"Simple. I'll hire the crew, and I'll front you a few months pay. Looks like you need it. Go to the middle of nowhere—we're talking Podunk, cattle-rustling, bull-riding, sheep-fucking, redneck country—find a couple of sexy, single cowboys, and follow them around while they go looking for love in all the wrong places. At the end of the summer, edit the footage into four or five one-hour segments. If I like it, I'll pay you twice your old salary to produce *Real Life, Real Love*."

Great leaping Buddha, that was six figures—curvy figures too—with enough cash up front to pay off the bills that had piled up since she'd been sacked. Working for Garry wouldn't salvage her reputation within the industry, but it would get her foot back in the door. And with that kind of salary, she could squirrel away enough money to make an independent documentary in a couple of years—and do it right this time—which *could* bring her back from exile. Realizing her dream wasn't dead, just dormant, made the inside of Bobbi's chest bubble with effervescent hope. She even knew the perfect place to film *Sex in the Sticks*.

"It could work," she said, careful not to betray her excitement and give him all the power, "if I stayed with my brother in Texas for the summer."

"I didn't know you had a brother."

"Neither did I until a couple years ago."

"Whatever." Garry's eyes followed a well-endowed bridesmaid as she swished past in her strapless taffeta gown. "I don't care where you go as long as it's remote."

"Not to worry," Bobbi said with a small laugh— the first to escape her lips in months. "I know just the place."

—∿∿—

A storm was coming. Trey Lewis felt it in his bones—literally. Ever since the accident two years ago, when he'd barely survived a twenty-foot nosedive off old Mr. Jenkins's roof, Trey's femur throbbed like a giant's heart whenever a new weather system rolled in. He tipped his head back and shook a tiny waxed paper envelope of BC Powder onto his tongue. The bitter taste of crushed aspirin made him shiver, but nothing worked faster than this stuff.

Running his fingers through his damp, freshly washed hair, he escaped the scorching Texas sun and pushed open the door to Shooters Tavern. It was five o'clock on the button—respectable drinking time—and he needed a cold Bud like nobody's business. And since his best friend, Luke Gallagher, owned the place, and Trey had helped him renovate it, all his drinks were on the house. For the next hour, at least. Trey was about to drop a bomb on Luke, and his free suds would be history after that.

For the last decade, Trey had supervised the construction crew for Helping Hands, Luke's nonprofit group. They'd done some great work over the years, but having a best friend for a business partner—butting heads over everything from concrete to contracting—had started to affect their friendship, and it was time to move on. Besides, he'd applied to have his military record expunged in exchange for accepting a civilian contracting job in Dubai. He'd known a couple of guys who'd done it already, and it had opened up a world of opportunity for them. It might even get his dad speaking to him again.

The soothing scents of hops and sawdust and the sounds of laughter punctuated by clacking cue balls greeted Trey like an old lover, and even though his eyes hadn't adjusted to the darkness yet, he made his way blindly to his favorite seat. He'd worn that path thin over the years, and he knew it by heart. Hoisting onto his bar stool—the one with his name carved on the underside—Trey smiled and sighed as his butt cheeks molded perfectly into the leather-covered cushion.

"Bud," he told the bartender, a brand-new redheaded boy who didn't look old enough to drink. Probably some college kid visiting his folks for the summer.

"Bottle or draft?" asked the boy in a voice that cracked on the last note.

"Draft. Always draft." Trey shoved a couple of bucks tip across the polished bar and swiveled around to check out the place.

He could see now, all the way to the pool tables in the back where his buddy, Colton Bea, the county's youngest deputy, was hustling a bearded, potbellied biker type. While the clueless mark bent over the pool table setting up a shot, Colton pretended to ride the guy's ass from behind, pumping his hips, rolling his eyes in mock ecstasy, and making wild O-faces. Yep, that was Sultry's finest, right there.

If Trey leaned a little to the left, he could see into the new room he'd helped Luke add on last summer, where a shiny, new mechanical bull had just taken up residency. It was all the buzz among folks in three counties, but Trey had no desire to straddle a piece of machinery designed to launch his *cajones* into his throat, so he returned his attention to the neglected Bud in front of him.

That first pull of ice-cold draft mingled with the leftover aspirin coating Trey's tongue, and he grimaced before taking a few quick chugs to wash it down. "Hey, kid," he said, wiping his forearm against his mouth and nodding toward the flat screen mounted on the wall. "Put on the Cubs game, will you?"

But the redhead wasn't listening. Hell, he looked lobotomized the way he stared, slack-jawed, at something near the front door. When Trey darted a glance in that direction, he understood why.

"Hot damn," he heard himself whisper.

"You ain't kidding," the bartender said.

But Trey wasn't listening. His gaze fixed like carpenter's glue on a different redhead, one curvier than the road to hell and twice as hot, who'd just wheeled a travel suitcase in the front door. She was a California girl—he'd bet his last brewski on it—big city, not beach. Coastal girls were laid back; they wore ponytails, denim cutoffs, and not much else. "Laid back" and this lady didn't exist on the same plane.

Looking like she'd just stepped off some edgy designer's runway, she planted her mile-long legs apart, standing ramrod straight and gripping her hips with manicured hands. A sleeveless pink top clung to the swell of her breasts—C-cups, Trey had a knack for these things—while a thin, white belt cinched her tiny waist. Her fiery-red hair was cut long in the front, short in the back, and not a single, pin-straight strand looked out of place. "California" paced a small circuit by the door and scanned the room, probably waiting for her eyes to adjust to the darkness. Since she couldn't see him ogling, Trey took in her strappy, high-heeled sandals,

then worked his way up her long, tan legs to her black
shorty-shorts, which encased the most delicious pair of
thighs he'd ever seen in his life—thick and tight and
so smooth he could almost feel her velvet skin against
his palms.

Double damn! Trey was a thigh man, through and
through. When he wrapped a woman's legs around
his hips, he wanted to feel soft flesh, not bone, and he
wanted between California's luscious thighs more than
he wanted the Cubs to win the World Series. Well,
not quite that much—a man had to keep his priorities
straight—but enough to fight off every other drooling fool
in the bar that night. Trey didn't know California's name
or how long she planned to stay in town, but one thing
was certain: he'd take her home tonight or die trying.

Ignoring the ache in his leg, he hopped down from his
bar stool and ambled slowly toward the door, appearing
in no hurry. California glanced up and her eyes widened,
revealing warm, green irises that reminded Trey of the
undersides of leaves when the sun shone through them.

"Need some help with your luggage?" Trey nodded
toward her suitcase.

For several seconds she said nothing, just rubbed
the tip of her cute button nose. Finally her full, red lips
curved into a smile that would kick the wind out of any
man's lungs. "What's your name, cowboy?"

Cowboy? Trey was from Chicago, but whatever.
He'd play along. "Trey," he said, smiling and making
sure to flash his dimples, those surefire, panty-removing
gifts from God. "How 'bout you?"

California's lips parted in awe—a classic case of
dimple daze. "I'm Bobbi. Are you single?"

Wow, she didn't waste any time. Holding up his left hand to showcase the absence of a wedding ring, he said, "Yes, ma'am."

"Totally single? No girlfriend?"

"No girlfriend." His ill-fated relationship with Trish, the cocktail waitress at Shooters, had ended over a year ago. "I'm all yours, darlin'."

"Great!" She scratched her nose again and smiled wider. "Let's get together later and chat."

Score! Thank you, baby Jesus! This was shaping up to be the easiest lay ever. That was, until a new voice joined the conversation.

"Well, now, Trey," Colton Bea said in his slow drawl, "who's your friend?"

Trey felt his back stiffen. Colton was poaching tail, a direct violation of the Bro Code.

"I'm Bobbi," California answered while looking Colton up and down, seeming pleased with what she saw. Not surprising since the crazy, cockblocking bastard had inherited the lethal combination of russet skin and jet-black hair from his Cherokee mama and blue-green eyes from his Scots-Irish daddy. All the local girls flopped onto their backs like trout when Colton walked by. "Are you single?" she asked him.

"Oh, yeah." Colton used his index finger to tip back his Stetson. "You're safe with me, honey. I'm a lawman."

"Only because his granddaddy's the county judge," Trey retorted. "Don't you have someplace to be, *Colt*?"

"Wonderful." California clapped her hands together and leaned forward, just enough to give Trey a peek down the front of her blouse, where the curves of her voluptuous breasts strained to escape the confines of her black lace bra. *Triple damn!* "I have to meet someone real quick, but then we should all get together. I have a proposition for you gentlemen."

Good Lord, what kind of kinky shit was this girl into? Trey didn't care how hot she was, threesomes were off the menu, especially when another dude was involved. The risk of crossing swords was too high. Plus, nobody liked boldly going where their friends had just gone before.

Colton raised his black eyebrows and gave a shrug that said *I'm up for it.* "I'll be right over there, honey," he said, tilting his hat toward the pool tables. "Just holler when you're ready."

"Hey," she said to Trey when Colton had walked away. "Can you tell me where to find Luke Gallagher?"

Oh, snap. Now everything made sense. Before Luke married his childhood sweetheart, June, he'd avoided relationships in favor of cheap, one-night stands. From the stories Luke had told, it sounded like most of the women he'd slept with were straight-up freaks, like this one. He knew Luke had come a long way and busted his butt to get June to marry him, and Trey wasn't about to let some old booty call ruin things for his buddy.

"He's probably home," Trey said, knowing full well Luke was in the back office. "With his *wife.* What do you want with him?"

"I'm his sister."

Trey couldn't help but laugh. This chick had moxie; he'd give her that. "Nice try, darlin'. Too bad you're talking to his best friend. I happen to know Luke's an only child." California was undeniably sexy as hell, but it was time to take out the trash. "Why don't I give you a ride back out of town?"

"No, really." Her posture stiffened and she folded both arms beneath her breasts. "He's my half-brother."

"Give it up, lady. Luke's done with skanks. Now, how about that ride?"

"Wha—" A crimson flush crept up her long, slim neck, past her cheeks, and all the way to her hairline. "You can take that ride and shove it up your—"

"You're leaving here one way or the other." Trey pushed open the front door, grabbed her suitcase, and tossed it out onto the gravel parking lot. "You gonna come peacefully?"

"You sonofabitch! Who the hell do you think—"

Then Trey did what any good friend would do: he hauled her meddling, home-wrecking ass out of there. Leaning into her midsection, he hoisted California over one shoulder, clamped a hand over her sweet thighs, and carried her into the muggy haze. Squinting against the sunlight, he walked toward his Chevy pickup while the screeching hellcat pounded her fists right into his kidney.

"Goddamnit!" he hissed, stumbling from the pain. Someone had taught this girl to fight. He slapped her hard on the backside—enjoying it a little too much— and she screamed like he'd just appeared outside her shower with a butcher knife.

"Hey!" Luke's familiar voice yelled from behind. "What's going on out here?"

"Luke! Get this asshole off-a-me!" California cried, laying it on thick with the damsel-in-distress act.

"Just go back inside," Trey said, giving Luke a pointed look. "I got this."

Luke fell back a step like he'd taken a bucket of water to the face. "What the hell're you doing to my sister?"

"Your what?" Stupefied, Trey let California slide to her feet while blinking in shock at his oldest friend. "You never told me you had a sister."

"Yeah. I've been meaning to…"

"Well, ain't that some shit." Trey guessed he should apologize to California. But when he glanced at her again, it was only to see her closed fist hurtling toward his eye.

Chapter 2

THE JOLLY GREEN GIANT, CLAD IN HIS SIGNATURE leafy toga, flashed a toothy grin at Bobbi from the bag of frozen Niblets molded around her fist. *Ho, ho, ho*, he seemed to say. *You should've gone for the balls.*

Of course, the overgrown sprout was right. Daddy Bruce had taught her to hit a man's soft parts—she'd known better than to attack the face—but when that caveman, Trey, had walloped her on the ass, her temper had choked out all rational thought.

Gritting her teeth, she tentatively stretched and flexed her fingers while jagged barbs skittered beneath the surface of her frostbitten skin. Had she broken her hand? She sure hoped not, because her health insurance had vanished right along with her job, and she couldn't afford an out-of-pocket trip to the ER. Heck, she barely had enough cash to get through the summer, and that was assuming Luke agreed to let her stay.

She peeked up through her lashes at her big brother, seeing her own green eyes narrowed beneath a mop of brown hair. He gave a disapproving shake of his head and settled behind the most disorganized desk she'd ever seen, its nicked, mahogany surface barely visible beneath piles of paperwork, loose receipts, Coke cans, and old pizza boxes that reeked of stale onions. The room's dingy, wood-paneled walls seemed to close in around her, and a charged silence rippled the air, reminding her of many past visits to the principal's office. Just like old times, side-by-side with another bully who'd mistakenly pegged her as an easy target.

She squirmed on the oak seat and slid a glare at Trey, wishing she could knock the smirk off his annoyingly exquisite lips. The burning imprint of his hand still raked the surface of her skin, throbbing with each thump of her heart. And the worst part? There wasn't a single mark on the jerk. He'd dipped his chin at the last second, so her fist had connected with the top of his hard, blond head, instead of her original target. A dirty trick, but damned clever. She couldn't help admiring his quick reflexes.

"Sorry, buddy," Trey said, watching her with those turquoise eyes, but talking to Luke. "What was I supposed to think? She was trying to set up a devil's three-some with me and Crazy Colt."

"*What?*" Luke tipped back in his chair and grabbed the desk for support. "Jesus Christ, Bobbi!"

"In your dreams!" This guy made jumping to conclusions look like an Olympic event. Bobbi stood, pointing one frigid finger at Trey, while the bag of corn plunked to the floor. "I said I wanted to talk!"

"She asked if we were single." Trey ignored her protest, moving to sit on the edge of Luke's desk and crossing his long, jean-clad legs at the ankles. "Then said we should get together later—she had a *proposition* for us." He tilted his head and lifted one brow. "What does that sound like to you?"

"Well?" Luke folded his arms and flashed a stern expression that clearly showed whose side he was on. So much for blood being thicker than water.

Closing her eyes, Bobbi sank back into her chair

and took a deep, cleansing breath. She felt control slipping though her fingers like a wet bar of Dial, and she wouldn't give the rednecks of Sultry Springs the satisfaction of saying she'd turned out just like her crazy mama. When she opened her eyes, she plastered on a grin and channeled the saccharine voice of a flight attendant. "Seems we had a miscommunication. I'm here to film a documentary, and I wanted you and that other gentleman to be a part of it."

"Where I come from, we call that porn, darlin'." Trey snickered and shook his head, sending a few locks of wheat-colored hair in motion across his forehead. "And I'm not into sharing my private fun with the world."

"It's not porn, you moron. I'm supposed to find a couple of single, rural guys and record their journey to find love. Kind of like a dating reality show. I thought you two would be a good fit."

And by "good fit" she meant dead sexy, but in totally different ways. First, the dark and dangerous bad boy, Colt. One hundred percent pure, wild mischief had danced across his features, and she knew he was trouble—with a capital T and that rhymed with B and that stood for bat-shit crazy—but her viewing audience would eat him up with a spoon and lick the bowl clean.

And then the golden boy, Trey, with his blond hair, Technicolor-blue eyes, strong, angular jaw, and a pair of dimples that went deeper than Aristotle. Although Bobbi wanted to push him into the path of an oncoming Mack truck, she couldn't deny he had a face that would tempt a saint and a body made for sinning—tall and lithe and bulky in all the right places. Even now it was hard to ignore his rounded biceps or the way his broad shoulders stretched that thin, white T-shirt within an inch of its life. From time to time, he'd reach down to massage one of his muscular thighs, which drew her attention to his jumbo-sized—*look away!*

Too bad the personality didn't match the packaging.

"But," she cleared her throat and reached down to retrieve her frozen veggies, "I can see that was a huge mistake. You're out of the running."

"Aw, shucks." Trey snapped his fingers and flashed a sarcastic smile. "How 'bout Colton?"

"I still want him."

"Might wanna rethink that. We don't call him Crazy Colt for nothing."

"You're serious?" Luke rubbed the stubble darkening his jaw. "This doesn't sound like…uh…your kind of thing."

"It's not." Luke knew her pretty well considering they'd only spent a couple of weekends together over the past few years. "I'm not going to lie," she lied, scratching her nose. "I only took this assignment so we could spend some time together. Wouldn't it be fun if I stayed with you for the summer?"

"Well, yeah, but why didn't you call first?"

Because she couldn't risk him saying no. Better to beg forgiveness than ask permission. "I wanted to surprise you."

"So let me get this straight." Luke pushed away from his desk and walked to a porthole-sized fish tank built into the wall. Three translucent, pink jellyfish flitted like tiny phantoms inside, and Luke tapped the glass as if to greet them. "You're gonna follow around strange guys like Colt while they go carousing and barhopping and trying to pick up women?"

"In a nutshell."

"Where's your crew?"

"My cameraman and sound boom guy fly in next week." And, God help her, Bong and Weezus would stand out like ink on a wedding dress in this tiny town.

"What about the rest?"

She shrugged. "There is no rest." In more ways than one. "It's a small project."

He turned, grabbing his hips while his brows reached for the sky. "So you're doing this with no protection?"

"Oh, come on, Luke." She stood and tossed the Niblets onto a Domino's box. "Don't start on me with that sexist crap. I spent a weekend with the Crip Queens, so I think I can handle a couple of good ol' boys."

Luke went quiet, returning his attention to the graceful jellies, while Bobbi glanced at his littered desk and wrestled the urge to sort through the clutter with her one good hand. It looked like a paper shredder blew chunks in here. How could anyone run a business like this? The Coors delivery receipt was so soiled with pepperoni grease she couldn't read the amount due, and sweet mother of God, someone's red thong was peeking out from beneath a pile of invoices. It probably belonged to his wife, but that didn't make it any less disturbing.

Eventually, Bobbi had to close her eyes. Just looking at the chaos made her feel all squirrely inside, and Luke probably wouldn't appreciate her going through his things. She'd do it another time, when he wasn't around. Maybe introduce him to the magic of accordion files.

"Wait." Luke's voice interrupted Bobbi's plans for staging an organizational coup. He spun on his heel and studied her in silence, narrowing one eye like he was trying to bend a spoon with his mind. Then his gaze danced a cha-cha between her and Trey, causing her tummy to sink. She didn't like the look of this.

"You can stay with me and June on one condition." Luke set his jaw in a way that said he wouldn't negotiate. "You have to use Trey as one of your subjects."

"*What?*" they both said in unison.

"Whoa, whoa, whoa, buddy." Trey held his palm forward. "Don't get me roped into this cluster. I don't want her following me around with a camera, and you know I don't do relationships—"

"No surprise there," Bobbi interrupted. "I'm not working with this barbarian. You saw what he did to me."

"I was about to apologize." Trey pushed off the desk and tapped one finger against his skull. "Right before you decked me."

"You broke my hand!"

"Oh, don't be a baby. Let me see." Before she could object, Trey lunged forward and claimed her fingers. After holding the ice pack for so long, the contrast of his hot grasp blazed a trail over her skin as he skimmed one callused palm over hers. She gasped, and Trey glanced up in alarm, softening his grip. But it wasn't pain that had made her breath catch. It was his hands—massive and powerful and even rougher than his personality— nothing like the smooth, manicured touch of the guys she'd dated back in LA. She suddenly felt very small, like Thumbelina cupped in his palm, and she yanked free.

"It's not even swollen," he declared with a dismissive wave.

While Bobbi cradled her fingers protectively against her chest, Luke clapped Trey on the shoulder.

"You're the only guy I trust to look after my kid sister."

"I'm not a kid." But her voice came out in a half-whine, making her sound like one.

"I dunno, buddy." Trey raked a hand through his hair. "Looks like she can take care of herself just fine."

Trey regarded her for a moment, and Bobbi nodded a silent thanks. Luke, however, wasn't having it.

"What if *you* had a sister?" he pressed. "Would you leave her alone with Colton? That SOB's got the sneakiest fingers in the county, and he's hornier than a four-balled tomcat. Any other loser she snags for this project will be just as bad."

Bobbi laughed at her brother. "If you're worried about my virtue, I'm afraid that ship's sailed. It circumnavigated the globe by now. I played my V-card at sixtee—"

"Stop!" Luke cupped his hands over his ears, and Bobbi half expected him to follow with *La-la-la-la, I can't hear you!* "I don't wanna know that."

Trey groaned and pinched the bridge of his nose. "Dude, ask me for anything else, just not this."

"Please." Luke dipped his head, giving his friend a pleading look, complete with wide, hound-dog eyes. "Do me a solid here."

A set of creases rippled Trey's forehead, and several emotions played across his face—mostly hesitation, but Bobbi detected more. A lot more, like panic. Her story radar beeped a red alert. Something was up with Golden Boy. "Ah, Jesus. I can't believe I'm doing this."

Luke took that for a yes. "Thanks, man. I owe you."

"Goddamn right you do." Trey heaved a sigh, and Bobbi took in his stiff shoulders and the muscles tightening the thick column of his neck. Interesting. The signature body language of a guy with something to hide. Her radar went from red alert to DEFCON 1. "I gotta talk to you," he said to Luke. Then, turning his blue gaze on her, he added, "In private."

No matter. She'd get it out of him eventually; she always did. Bobbi didn't know why she cared, but once piqued, her curiosity wasn't easily sated.

"Let's get back on track." Bobbi flexed her hand again, satisfied it wasn't broken after all. "I can't work with him. It'll come across on camera and kill the mood if he's not even trying."

Luke turned his back on her and began stacking pizza boxes. When he uncovered the thong, he shoved it casually into his front pocket as if panties crossed his desk every day. "Well, you better figure out a way to make it work or find another place to crash. That's final."

Bobbi chewed her lower lip, studying Trey as he kneaded his thigh and muttered curses under his breath. Even though he wasn't her type, she imagined he didn't have to sleep alone very often. If he'd take direction, she should be able to hook him up with some nice little Texan—a country girl who thought God gave women small feet so they could stand closer to the stove—someone who wouldn't mind Trey's sand-papered hands or his brutish attitude. Nodding at him, she conceded, "Okay, but you have to try. Even if it's just a summer fling."

"Fine." He shrugged one shoulder. "But I'm not gettin' busy on camera, and I'm not gonna lie and say I'm looking for something serious."

"You mean you actually *talk* to women instead of throwing them over your shoulder and hauling them back to your cave?" She stood and grabbed her purse from the edge of Luke's desk. "I need to touch base with Colt." And clear things up if he'd made the same crazy three-way assumption.

Luke walked her to the door while Trey stepped aside. "Listen," Luke said, "I need a minute with Trey. You go on and handle your business, and I'll meet you out front and take you home."

"I've got a rental, so I'll follow you."

"A rental? For the whole summer?" Luke shook his head. "That'll cost a fortune. We'll drop it off on the way to my place, and you can use Bruiser, June's old car."

Bobbi picked a piece of lint from her hot-pink blouse and feigned indifference, but on the inside, she shimmied her hips in a wild victory dance. The money she'd save might be enough to repay Papa the retainer fee he'd leant her. As for the rest of her legal fees, that would take more time. Like a lifetime. "You sure she won't mind?"

"Nope. We were about to donate it to Goodwill 'cause no one else'll have it. It's not pretty—"

Trey laughed without humor. "Uglier than a lard bucket full of toads. You won't get carjacked, that's for sure. But it's the Chuck Norris of hatchbacks. The thing won't die."

"I'm not picky." As long as it got her from point A to point B, she didn't care what the beater looked like. With one last glance into Trey's sea-blue eyes, she chirped, "I'll be in touch, Golden Boy. Get yourself in the mood for love."

"I gotta call June." Luke slammed the door behind Bobbi. "Think she'll be pissed?"

Trey stood toe-to-toe with his best friend and scanned his face—crooked, twice-broken nose, wide jaw peppered with dark whiskers, high forehead permanently creased from too much scowling—and searched for any similarities to the redheaded goddess he'd claimed as his sister. Aside from the eyes, Trey didn't see the resemblance. More importantly, he wondered how the hell Luke had gone ten years without mentioning her. His buddy had always been an overly private man, but damn, why would he keep something like this a secret?

A tiny seed of doubt took root and sprouted in Trey's mind, spreading like kudzu over a vacant lot. Maybe their friendship wasn't as tight as he'd thought. He'd always felt at home in Sultry Springs—assumed folks like Luke had made him part of the family—but what if he'd only seen what he wanted to see? What if he was just another Yankee outsider to them, even after all these years? In that case, leaving town would be a whole lot easier than he'd anticipated.

"I dunno. Got any more sisters comin' to visit?" Trey asked. He took two giant steps toward Luke's desk and snatched the bag of corn, knocking an empty Coke can to the floor in the process. "Maybe a brother? Secret compound of wives on the side?" Bending low, he tugged open the mini-fridge door and chucked the corn inside.

"You're mad." It wasn't a question.

"Here's what I don't get." Trey plopped into Luke's chair. "You didn't trust me enough to tell me you had a sister, but now you expect me to spend the whole friggin' summer keeping her out of trouble." Shaking his head, he dug both thumbs deep into his thigh, where a slow warmth flared up the length of his femur. "You know how hard that's gonna be? She's smokin'. She'll draw every horn-ball from ten miles around."

"Hey!" Luke lifted his chin, along with one index finger. "Don't talk about her like that."

"You're something else, you know that? What's your problem—why didn't you tell me?"

"I had my reasons."

"Yeah? Let's hear 'em."

Luke's jaw tightened and he gazed into the wastebasket like the answer might've fallen in there, along with the crumpled tissues and banana peels. He hesitated a few times, and when he finally spoke, he kept his eyes trained on the garbage. "You know about my mama."

Yeah, Trey knew. When Luke was twelve, his mom had gone out to finish her Christmas shopping. Only she'd passed Toys"R"Us and kept driving till she hit California. Miss Pru—June's grandma—had taken Luke in, and she'd raised him like her own son.

"Bobbi was only three or four then," Luke continued. He cleared his throat. "Mama took *her* when she skipped town, and after she died, Bobbi went into foster care. I just found her a few years ago."

"Okay?" Trey didn't understand what any of this had to do with keeping Bobbi a secret. "Does June know?"

"Of course." Luke bent to retrieve the fallen Coke can and tossed it into the recycling bin. "June lived right next door with her grandma. She remembers Bobbi from when we were all kids."

"Wait a minute." Was Trey the only guy in the county who hadn't known about this? If he hadn't felt like an outsider before, he sure did now. "If it's no secret, why didn't you tell me?"

"Why does it matter? You know now." Luke slashed one hand through the air like a samurai to declare the topic closed. "What's next—you wanna hold hands and go on TV and talk about our feelings? Enough of this crap."

Trey delivered a burning *fuck you* glare and clutched his leg. That slow warmth had sparked a flame inside his bones, and he sucked in a sharp breath while fishing another BC Powder from his pocket.

He needed to head out before things got ugly. Not only had Luke ticked him off, but the aspirin wasn't doing the trick, and his temper boiled even hotter when pain set in. The stubborn ass in front of him was still his business partner, for the next few months at least, so it probably wasn't a good idea to let things escalate to fistfighting. Even though that's exactly what they needed—one good brawl to break the pent-up tension and start fresh.

"I better check on your sister. If I know Colton, he's bending her over the pool table while we're back here bullshitting." Grasping his leg, Trey stood. "Anything else I can do for you?" The question was just a sarcastic jab, and he didn't expect the response that followed.

"Yes."

"What's that, *buddy*?"

Luke stood too. Bracing both hands against the desk, he leaned forward and shot laser beams into Trey's eyes. "Keep it in your pants."

"What?" He couldn't have heard that right. "Are you screwing with me?"

"I saw you watching Bobbi when she was in here."

Luke's green eyes simmered, his grip tightening around the desk's ledge.

Of course Trey'd watched her. He'd perched right there on the edge of his friend's desk with a front row view of Bobbi's succulent thighs, and when she'd gone all pouty and folded her arms, it had pushed up her breasts and given him a peek down the front of her top. Who in his right mind wouldn't have taken a gander at that? "Jesus, that's no crime. She's a fine-looking woman, and I—"

"Don't pull that shit. I know you. But you don't know her, or all the stuff she lived through with our nutjob mama. Sometimes I think I got the best end of the deal, getting left behind. She's damaged. Fragile—"

"The lump on my head disagrees with you." Fragile his ass. Luke had more wool over his eyes than a mammoth. The dupe hadn't even picked up on his sister's lies. She had an easy tell: scratching her nose. Bobbi might've come up hard, but she seemed stronger for it, and her brother was seriously deluded if he thought she needed a savior. Hell, Trey was the one who needed protection. She'd balled that little fist and jabbed fiercer than Tyson.

"I'm not gonna argue this."

"You got nothing to worry about," Trey assured him. Even if Bobbi had the sweetest thighs this side of the Pecos, she was wound so tight she practically squeaked when she walked.

"I want your word. I know I'm not the easiest guy to get along with, but I've always thought of you like a—" Luke stopped just short of *brother*, and Trey felt it like a cold shot to the chest. "Just don't bang my sister."

"Don't worry." Trey crossed the small office and threw open the door. "No chance of that happening."

Chapter 3

BOBBI TOOK THE LIBERTY OF CRANKING UP THE RADIO, letting John Denver's "Rocky Mountain High" replace the awkward silence inside Luke's truck. Instead of objecting, her brother relaxed his death grip on the steering wheel and hummed along with John in obvious relief.

Their visits had always started like this: neither of them knowing what to say to the other once they'd exhausted all the small talk. They'd already rehashed Luke's wedding a dozen times, and when they'd stooped to discussing Sultry County's recent humidity level—*It's like breathing underwater, I swear to God, Bobbi*—she knew it was time to quit trying so hard and just shut up. It was a sobering reminder that despite their common last name, their relationship didn't go any deeper than what she shared with the bag boy at Ralph's Marketplace. If anything, she knew more about that kid than her own flesh and blood.

An empty can of Mountain Dew rolled against her sandal and she kicked it aside, turning her attention out the window, where leaves, weeds, and crops blurred past at sixty miles an hour. The landscape was greener than she'd expected—rows of cedars and oaks that backed up to alternating fields of high cotton and soybeans. She hadn't set foot here since Mama'd left town all those years ago, and she'd always imagined Texas as a dust bowl, dry and brown and dismal. Her mental pictures couldn't have been more wrong. In fact, the lush scene kind of reminded her of California's wine country, only flatter.

"That's my place, just up ahead." Luke turned onto a gravel road and nodded at the windshield. "Built it myself, just me and Trey." His face shone with boyish pride, and it coaxed a smile to Bobbi's lips.

But her smile faded and the breath caught at the top of her lungs when Luke's property came into view.

On the surface, there was no reason for her to feel gut-punched over the sight of four walls and a roof. It was a cute, modest home—a gray, two-story colonial with a wide, welcoming, wraparound porch—but the damned thing looked eerily like her old dollhouse, the one she hadn't seen since she and Mama had snuck out of their apartment in the middle of the night to avoid six months back rent.

One of Mama's boyfriends had bought the dollhouse for two dollars at a yard sale, probably to keep Bobbi entertained while he and Mama spent all afternoon boffing and getting high in the back room. Though the house had only come with a few pieces of mismatched furniture and a one-armed doll, Bobbi had spent each day fantasizing that she lived there instead of a grimy, roach-infested shoebox with a bunch of dopers. She hadn't thought of that toy, or that hellish time in her life, in ages, and the memories churned up a cocktail of sick feelings, which she promptly pushed away and locked down tight.

But just before snapping the padlock on those emotions, a chunk of jealousy broke free and floated to the surface. "This is where you grew up?" She pointed to the placid pond in the front yard, encircled by hydrangea bushes in full bloom that exploded with pink and yellow blossoms. She hoped Luke hadn't detected the bitterness in her voice.

"No." He pointed beyond the trees to an equally beautiful location in the distance. "Over there with June and her grandma, Pru. You can't see the house from here. It's about a five-minute walk."

Nice. While she was evading slumlords, he was munching apple pie in Mayberry.

"And there's Bruiser, your car for the summer," Luke said, pointing to an ancient, lavender sedan that, from a distance, appeared tie-dyed.

At first Bobbi had been too fixated on the house to notice the old clunker, but she couldn't take her eyes off it now—it held her entranced in its fugly spell. As they drove closer and parked beside it, she realized the streaked, faded look had been achieved via spray paint. How had Trey described it? Uglier than a bucketful of assholes or frogs or something like that. Either way, it fit, but she'd suck it up and drive the purple people-eater if it meant repaying her debt to Papa. She didn't like feeling beholden to anyone, not even her dads.

"Awesome," she managed to choke out. "Thanks again."

While climbing down from the truck, Bobbi pulled in a deep breath, filling her nose with the odd mixture of honeysuckle and stagnant water. She stretched her arms high and lifted onto her toes, letting the sunlight kiss her cheeks. At nearly seven, the sun still dominated the sky, but its rays warmed the tops of her shoulders instead of scorching them like it'd done when she'd left the airport at noon.

She'd just turned to ask Luke for help with her

luggage when the screen door flew open, slamming against the wood siding. Then a curly-haired brunette appeared, squealing with glee and balling her fists like a kid on Christmas morning. This must be June. Every part of Bobbi's new sister-in-law bounced with enthusiasm—heels, hair, boobs—as June skipped down the porch steps and came barreling at Bobbi with outstretched arms.

Bobbi braced for impact, widening her stance and digging her three-inch heels into the gravel. The running hug didn't disappoint, though it did knock her back a couple of inches. A mass of vanilla-scented curls tickled Bobbi's chin, and June's arms locked around her and squeezed like albino boa constrictors. In response, three loud pops sounded from Bobbi's spine.

"Oh, sorry!" June pulled away, her fair cheeks flushing scarlet. "No extra charge for the chiropractic adjustment." Smiling, she chewed the inside of her cheek as her brown eyes overflowed with adoration. Bobbi couldn't help but like her immediately. "It's just…" June darted a glance at her bare feet. "With everything Luke's told me, I feel like I already know you. And I've always wanted a sister."

Bobbi came dangerously close to unraveling, and she had to fight to maintain a calm expression while her heart warmed and swelled to the size of a cantaloupe. She'd always wished for a sister too. When she was young, back before she'd understood how wrong it would be to bring another child into their screwed-up home, she'd begged Mama to "go to the hospital and buy a baby." But as much as she wanted to return June's sentiment, she couldn't get the words out. Instead, she turned her face to the breeze and blinked her welling eyes until they dried.

"It's been ages since I've had any girl time," she said. Not very sisterly, but it was the best she could do. Clearing the thickness from her throat, she took a moment to study her new relation, admiring June's cherubic face and the golden-brown ringlets that brushed her shoulders. She had a classic hourglass figure, but with a disproportionately wide rear end, which Luke couldn't stop watching. Just proof that the way to a man's heart was through a big, round ass. Too bad Bobbi didn't have one of those. In the genetic grab bag of life, she'd gotten stuck with fat thighs instead.

"We're going to have so much fun this summer," Bobbi added. "I can't wait to—"

And then, in true guy fashion, Luke opened his mouth and ruined the moment. "I'm gonna sprout ovaries if you two don't quit this mushy girl crap." He wrapped one arm around his wife and pulled her hard against him, then ruffled her hair playfully as he teased, "Besides, who needs a sister when you've both got me?"

June perched her chin on Luke's chest, and the two shared a look so intimate it made Bobbi feel like the mother of all third wheels. She'd filmed a lot of weddings, but she'd never seen a couple gaze at each other quite like this—as if the rest of the world had fallen away, and they existed in their own parallel dimension. The look of two people wholly, irrevocably in love. The way no man had ever looked at her.

It hadn't occurred to Bobbi before now how awkward it could be sharing a home with newlyweds. Though the wedding had taken place almost two years ago, the honeymoon clearly wasn't over.

The sound of gravel crunching beneath tires drew the lovebirds' attention to the road, and Bobbi glanced over her shoulder to watch a red Chevy pickup park beside Luke's Ford. She caught a glimpse of gray hair through the passenger window, but the sun's glare blinded her before she could identify anything more.

"It's Grammy Pru," June explained. "When she heard you were back, she couldn't wait to see you again."

"Good news travels fast." Typical small town. "Oh, and look." Bobbi pointed at Trey, who'd hopped down from the driver's seat and jogged around to open the elderly woman's door. "Golden Boy too."

"You already met Trey?" June asked, sounding disappointed. "I was going to introduce you." As in, *I wanted to play matchmaker*. No dice, sweetie.

Luke chuckled as he dipped his mouth to June's ear, no doubt to relay the story of how Trey's hand had already "met" Bobbi's rear end.

With heat rushing into her cheeks, no, not *those* cheeks, Bobbi glared at Trey. But then he did something that softened her stone heart and left her puzzled. Gently, he cupped the grandma's shoulder with one hand and guided her down from the truck with the greatest of care. Though the old lady was built like a brick house—seriously, she had to be six feet tall with hands the size of frying pans—Trey linked their elbows and placed her massive palm atop his forearm like a wedding usher and escorted her to where everyone stood at the foot of the porch.

How very chivalrous. How very un-Treylike.

"Well, ain't this a nice surprise?" Amazon Granny wore a floral muumuu and a thin-lipped smile that didn't quite reach her eyes. Though her hair was pulled into a bun tighter than a Hollywood face-lift, she kept tucking imaginary strays behind her ears while unapologetically staring Bobbi down. Unlike June's unconditional acceptance, it seemed Granny had decided to withhold judgment—make sure Bobbi hadn't come to town with dishonorable intentions toward her long-lost brother. "Little Bo Gallagher," she said. It sounded like a cross between an accusation and a challenge.

"Bobbi," she clarified in a cool voice. She should be used to the scrutiny by now—she'd never felt like she fit in—but she'd expected a little more acceptance in her own hometown.

"Bo?" Trey asked with a smirk.

"Mmm-hmm." Pru nodded, narrowing her eyes at Bobbi's strappy heels. "It's what her mama used to call her."

This was news to Bobbi.

"So, wait." A crooked grin brought Trey's dimples out in full force, and Bobbi's heart quivered of its own volition. "Bo and Luke?" He chortled to himself. "Got a cousin named Daisy? If so, take me to her right now!"

Luke's brows formed a dark slash over his eyes as he explained to Bobbi, "Mama was a big *Dukes of Hazzard* fan."

This was also news to her. From what she remembered, Mama was a fan of opiates, Junior Mints, and dickheads—in that order. She'd never watched shows. Instead, she'd used the television as an electronic babysitter, always tuned to *Sesame Street* or whatever program had kept Bobbi out of her hair. And until the truancy officer had shown up, the TV had been Bobbi's teacher for a few years, since dressing a child and walking her to the school bus was too much trouble for Mama.

"The Duke boys were moonshiners, like my daddy." Luke rubbed the back of his neck and took a sudden interest in his steel-toed boots. "She quit watching after he died."

"*Your* daddy?" Trey asked, obviously wondering why Luke hadn't said *their* daddy.

"We're both bastards with different dads," she said. "That okay with you, Golden Boy?"

"Jesus, it was just a question."

"Language, Trey Lewis!" Pru smacked his upper arm.

"Sorry, ma'am." He placed a hand over his heart. "Good thing I've got you to pray for my soul." He was clearly teasing, but when Trey flashed that easy smile, Pru forgave him with a grandmotherly pinch of his cheek.

Bobbi rolled her eyes, and Trey caught it, giving her a not-so-innocent grin. One that said all the praying in the world wouldn't wash away the sins he wanted to commit with her. She knew that look—it was the same one she'd seen on his stunning face at Shooters when he'd introduced himself, and her stomach had dipped into her shorts then just like it was doing now. Biting her lip, she dropped her gaze and studied her red-polished toenails.

"We should probably fire up the grill before the storm sets in," Trey said.

Bobbi glanced at the endless, blue sky, where a single cotton ball of a cloud hovered above. "What storm?"

Shaking his head, he laughed dryly. "Oh, it's

coming." Then he limped—wait, limped?—to Luke's truck to retrieve her luggage. He clearly favored his right leg, something he hadn't done a few minutes ago. If he'd hurt himself, she didn't want him towing her fifty-pound suitcase.

"I can get that." She teetered across the gravel on her sandals, but Trey waved her off and hauled the bag toward the house as easily as carrying a lunch box. For a few stunned seconds, she watched his bicep muscles bunch beneath his snug shirtsleeve until he tipped open the screen door and disappeared inside. She shook her head, criticizing herself for getting worked up over a few silly muscles, and followed.

An icy blast of air-conditioning frosted the bare skin on Bobbi's arms, and she rubbed her hands together while her eyes adjusted to the dim lighting. The clunk of Trey's heavy work boots echoed up the steps, which seemed presumptuous at first, but as Luke's best friend, it made sense that he'd know the way to the guest bedroom.

The place still had that new house smell—paint, varnish, plaster—and two unpacked cardboard boxes in the foyer confirmed the newlyweds hadn't quite settled in yet. But judging by the gleaming hardwood floors and meticulously aligned chair railing, Luke and Trey were skilled builders who'd put a lot of love into this home.

June smoothed two fingers over the goose bumps puckering Bobbi's arms. "Luke keeps it colder than a witch's heart in here. It's the only thing we fight about." She leaned in and waggled her eyebrows. "Cover me while I go change the thermostat."

June dashed away, and a few moments later, Trey

returned down the stairs. He motioned for Bobbi to join him, and when she did, he lowered his voice and said, "Top of the stairs, last door on the right. It's the smallest room in the house, the paint's the color of dried puke, and the sun'll wake you up every morning at six, but it's farthest from the master bedroom." He pressed his lips to her ear, brushing her with his soft mouth as he whispered, "Trust me, that's the one you want. This one time, I crashed upstairs…"

Bobbi got chills on her chills. She pretended to listen as Trey told some story about having to spend the night here, but the tickle of his warm breath had switched her headlights to full-beams, and she had to sneak a peek at her blouse to make sure her bra was concealing the evidence. Thankfully, it was. She scratched her nose, figuring it had been way too long since she'd gotten lucky if a little whisper action affected her like this. Good thing she'd remembered to pack BOB, her Battery-Operated Boyfriend. With three speed settings and a seven-inch core of rotating ball bearings, she'd forget the caress of Trey's lips and the heat of his breath in no time.

"…screamed louder than a freight train." Glancing over her shoulder, he clumsily changed the subject when Pru walked within earshot. "And that's how I know a storm's coming."

Right on cue, thunder boomed from outside and shook the walls. "Impressive," Bobbi said, meeting his blue gaze. "Got any other magical powers?"

A wicked grin curved his lips, and Bobbi warned, "Don't answer that." Eager to put some space between them, she hurried into the living room but stopped short, skidding to a halt before she'd fully crossed the threshold. "Oh my god," she whispered in shock. "Mismatched furniture."

A plaid sofa in burgundy tones clashed with two easy chairs, one blue, one brown, while a distressed, white, shabby-chic coffee table displayed an assortment of remote controls on a silver tray like they were finger sandwiches instead of gadgets. She shut her eyes, but all she could see was that damned dollhouse.

"They're just starting out," Trey said critically while brushing past her into the room. "So what if they can't afford new furniture?"

He didn't understand, and Bobbi had no intention of explaining for his benefit. "They don't have a one-armed doll lying around, do they?"

Settling in the brown leather chair, Trey studied her in silence for a moment. "No, but they've got a three-legged cat."

Not an exact match, but close enough to make her feel like she'd stepped into the *Twilight Zone*. Wasn't there an episode where someone lived inside a dollhouse? Yeah, she remembered now. A guy named Charley had obsessed over one of the miniature figures inside the house until he wound up becoming one himself. Only Bobbi didn't want to be inside the replica of her favorite childhood toy. She didn't even want to remember it.

All those emotions she'd locked down tight began bucking against the vault, demanding release, and Bobbi's pulse raced as tiny beads of sweat broke out on her upper lip. Darting a glance around the room, she identified the only visible source of chaos—an overflowing, disorganized shelf of DVDs and video games—and she made a beeline for it. Then Bobbi knelt on the floor and did the only thing that made her feel calm when life was out of control: she put things in order.

Hmm. How should she sort the movies— alphabetically or by genre?

"What's she doin'?" Pru asked, as she crossed the small room and lowered onto the couch with a groan.

Alphabetically, for sure, starting with *All the President's Men*.

"Don't ask me," Trey replied. "She's a strange bird. A pretty bird, though."

Bobbi had a bird for Trey, and she showed it to him in the form of her middle finger.

"Well, that wasn't very nice," he said with a smile in his voice. "Bo wanna cracker?"

Ignoring him, she slid *Bill and Ted's Excellent Adventure* next to *Big Love, Season 1*.

"Folks tend to get cranky when they don't eat," he continued. "Or when they're tired. Or when their favorite lipstick gets discontinued. Is that what's got you in knots, Bo Peep?" He used a mock lispy voice to tease, "Revlon quit makin' your perfect pink?"

She pointed a Blu-ray at him, but before she could tell Trey where to stick his hypothetical lipstick, lightning flashed, followed by deafening thunder, and the house went dark. Rain and hailstones mingled to pelt the roof in an oddly soothing percussion, and she took a deep breath, refusing to let Trey bait her.

"Oh, sugar." June sashayed in, holding a tall glass of something Bobbi couldn't identify in the feeble sunlight filtering from the far window. "Now the stove's out too. I was going to make a frozen pizza since we can't use the grill." She offered the glass to Bobbi. "Sangria? It's my specialty."

"Yes!" Oh, hell yes. Bobbi brought the cool glass to her lips and tipped it back, savoring the tangy blend of fresh juice and sweet, magical booze. It was the best sangria she'd ever tasted—not too tart, not too syrupy. She'd forgotten June was a bartender, and now she understood the reason behind Shooters' success. Well, that and because it was the only bar in three counties. But June would blow the competition away if she had any. "You're the best sister-in-law I've ever had."

Giggling, June lit a couple of jar candles and brought them to the coffee table. "Then maybe you'll let me borrow some of your clothes. I love your outfit."

"Oh, thanks. One of my dads designed it." And since Daddy Bruce made all his samples in her size, she received a free, designer wardrobe each season. Sometimes, just once in a while, it didn't suck to be her.

"One of your *dads*?" Trey asked, then instantly held both palms out and clarified, "Don't get your panties in a bunch. I'm only askin'!"

Luke joined the party, kneeling at his wife's feet. "Yeah, Bobbi was adopted by a gay couple. I met 'em when I was looking for her a few years back. They're really good guys."

Bobbi grabbed one candle and scooted closer to the shelf to resume her work.

"Huh," Trey said. "Is the other dad a hairdresser?"

She whipped her head around, red locks slapping her in the eyes. "Way to stereotype, Golden Boy."

"Jesus!—oops, sorry, Miss Pru—I mean, goddamn! Why do you try so hard to be offended all the time?"

"Quit your blasphemin', Trey Lewis!" Pru was a few inches too far to swat the blasphemer from the sofa, so she grabbed a nearby *Sports Illustrated*, rolled it up, and cracked him over the head.

"Ow!"

"I don't have to try very hard when you're around," Bobbi objected, though it wasn't the first time someone had accused her of being overly sensitive when it came to hot-button social issues. Her most recent ex had nick-named her the Liberal Loco, one of the many reasons he was an ex.

"You've been pissy with me for something or other since you came to town. Your ass is tighter than a clam with lockjaw."

"Dude," Luke warned.

"Okay, okay. Sorry, Bo Peep." While she sat there with her mouth agape, Trey leaned forward, resting his tanned forearms on his knees. "So, what *does* your other dad do?"

Narrowing her eyes until Trey was barely visible through tiny slits, she gritted her teeth and muttered, "He's the best damn stylist in Inglewood."

Trey smirked and relaxed against the chair, folding both hands behind his head in smug satisfaction, while June tried to cut the tension by suggesting they adjourn to the kitchen to make sandwiches for dinner.

Bobbi followed, but only to refill her glass. She'd decided to drink her supper tonight. While alphabetizing June's spice rack—seriously, why would anyone put the cinnamon next to the rosemary?—she turned Trey's words over in her mind. *Your ass is tighter than a clam with lockjaw*. That wasn't true. Just because she liked things neat and orderly didn't mean she was uptight. She knew how to have a good time. Sure, this year had been rough, and she'd cried more than she'd laughed, but that didn't make her a Debbie Downer. That bonehead, Trey, didn't know her. They were practically strangers.

She mentally repeated her own words until she started to believe them.

Over the next few hours, she refilled her glass again and again, until Trey's teasing and Amazon Granny's critical stares and memories of her one-armed doll began to drift from her consciousness like dandelion seeds floating away on the breeze. After her fifth sangria, those pesky spice labels wouldn't hold still long enough for her to read them, so Bobbi staggered to the kitchen table to make a sandwich. But someone must have pulled the chair out from under her, because she wound up on the beige linoleum *beneath* the table. Ah, what the hell. It was comfy down here. With a soft giggle-snort, she curled onto her side and tucked both hands under her cheek like a pillow. Right before passing out on the kitchen floor, she heard one last echo of Trey's voice and opened her eyes to the blurry, tan tips of his Timberlands.

"That's some sister you've got, buddy," he said. "It's gonna be a long-ass summer."

Bobbi awoke several hours later, head stuffed with cotton and her stomach churning like the San Francisco Bay at high tide. Groaning, she rolled to the side and squinted at the digital clock on her nightstand. Midnight. That was it?

She pushed to her elbows, wondering how she'd made it into bed. A glance at the floor revealed her sandals parked neatly beside her suitcase, and Bobbi was pretty darned sure she couldn't have managed unbuckling those tiny straps in her inebriated state. June must've helped, poor girl. This wasn't the kind of first impression Bobbi'd wanted to make on her new sister-in-law. She'd have to repay June somehow, maybe surprise her with one of Daddy Bruce's new fall designs. But right now, Bobbi had more urgent matters to attend to.

She knew from extensive, firsthand experience that the only way to avoid a hangover was to drink twice as much water as alcohol. If she snuck downstairs and chugged a gallon, she'd be up all night peeing, but it'd be worth it in the morning. Slowly, she lowered one foot to the hardwood floor, then the other, bracing herself against the mattress when her brain spun a pirouette inside her skull. Whoa, how many times had she refilled that glass?

On wobbly knees, she felt her way out of the bedroom, down the dark hall, and then clung to the handrail while descending the stairs. A soft glow emanated from the kitchen, along with hushed voices, and Bobbi peered into the room to find June and her grandma sitting at the table sharing a slice of pecan pie and working a Sudoku puzzle.

June glanced up and waved with her fork. "Hey. Glad you're up and about. Luke was worried about you. How're you feeling?"

Pru didn't say a word, just raked a concerned gaze over Bobbi, probably deciding the acorn hadn't fallen far from the Gallagher family tree.

"I'm fine," Bobbi said with care, barely managing to keep the slur out of her voice. "Just thirsty." Lifting her chin, she walked to the sink in slow, measured strides and filled a glass with water from the tap. She felt the weight of June and Pru's eyes on her as she downed the glass and refilled it two more times, and she wished they'd finish their dessert and go to bed, selfish as that sounded. Because if there was a magical way to explain why she'd rolled into town unannounced for the first time in twenty years, then proceeded to get hammered and pass out on the floor, she didn't know how.

"Why don't you join us?" June used one foot to push out the chair across from her at the table. "I was just telling Grammy how excited I am to have you here for the whole summer."

Right. More like how worried she was about having a boozehound for a housemate. Bobbi brought her glass to the table and took a seat. She had to say something—she couldn't let them assume she'd carried on her mother's pathetic legacy—but what?

"Uh, listen," she began clumsily. "About before...I don't want you to think..." As desperately as she tried, she failed to shake the apology off her tongue.

"Gotta be hard." Pru speared a pecan with her fork. "Comin' back here after all this time, 'specially when everyone knows you, but you don't remember 'em. Dontcha think, June?"

Bobbi knew what Pru had just done, and she silently thanked her with a small grin.

"Oh, yeah." June's eyes widened as she caught on, and she nodded a little too emphatically, curls bouncing around her face. "I moved to Austin after high school and didn't come home for almost ten years, so I know the feeling."

"Really?" Bobbi leaned forward, folding her arms on the table. "Why?"

Grandmother and granddaughter shared an uneasy glance, and June admitted, "We had a little falling out."

Bobbi couldn't help it. Her story radar bleeped another red alert, and the prying words came tumbling forth. "Ten years for a little falling out?" Bringing a hand to her heart, she gasped at her own rudeness. "I'm sorry. That's none of my business."

"You're family." June said it without hesitation, and after Pru tilted her head and scanned Bobbi for a moment, she nodded in agreement. "My business is yours too."

While June told the story of her parents' death and how Pru's rigid upbringing had pushed her away, Bobbi marveled at how effortlessly her new sister had accepted her as part of the family. Just like that, with no background investigation or even a quick-n-dirty credit check. How'd she do it? How'd she know Bobbi wasn't an axe murderer, or considering her mother's reputation, a junkie conspiring to rob her blind? After what'd happened with the Smyth documentary, Bobbi didn't even trust a vagrant to squeegee her windshield without the proper credentials, and no one in California welcomed a stranger into their home for a Coke, let alone a summer.

"Well," Bobbi said when June had finished, "I'm glad it all worked out. My brother's a lucky man."

June averted her gaze and twirled a lock of hair. "I'm pretty lucky too."

"Luck had nothin' to do with it," Pru declared, claiming the last bite of pie. She shoveled it into her mouth and spoke with one cheek full. "The Good Lord knew what He was doin'."

Either way, a guy's taste in women said a lot about him. Bobbi didn't know her brother's political affiliation or even his favorite sports team, but the fact that he'd chosen June—a kindhearted childhood playmate—over some melon-boobed Stepford wife told her he was a good man.

Too bad the same couldn't be said about his taste in friends.

Chapter 4

"HEY, GOLDEN BOY," BOBBI WHISPERED IN TREY'S EAR. "Wake up. I need you."

When Trey felt the warm, wet tip of Bobbi's tongue flick his earlobe, his eyes shot open and he sat bolt upright, fisting his cotton sheet in one hand and covering his heart with the other. With his pulse racing, he scanned his bedroom, seeing nothing but a pile of unfolded laundry atop his dresser, but then Bobbi cleared her throat in a teasing *ahem*, and he jerked his head toward the sound.

"Hot damn," he breathed.

There she was, kneeling beside him on the bed, wearing a black satin bra, matching panties that laced up the front with pink ribbon, and a smile that oozed dirty, dirty sex. Either he'd died and gone to the Playboy Mansion—aka heaven—or he was dreaming.

"Lie down." She shoved him back against the mattress and straddled his chest, bringing those glorious thighs so close he could smell her cinnamon-scented skin. "I've got a big problem."

Yeah, he had a big problem too—nine inches of trouble growing stiffer by the second.

She dipped two fingers inside her bra and produced a tiny bottle of oil, then unscrewed the cap and poured its contents into her palm. She locked eyes with him while bringing her hands together and rose onto her knees, rubbing that oil all over her thighs. His erection went from standard wood to ball-clenching steel, and he lifted his hips in a desperate need for friction—anything to ease the pressure. But again and again, she teased him, moving just out of reach, until he feared the tension mounting between his legs might actually kill him.

Never breaking her seductive gaze, she bit her lip and moaned as she massaged herself, those long, glistening, red-polished fingers kneading deeper into her flesh with each stroke.

"See?" She pointed just below the lacy crotch of her panties to a patch of dry skin. "I keep missing a spot." Sliding her fingers up and down the length of his chest, she begged, "I need your help."

She didn't have to ask twice, especially since this was a dream. His promise to Luke only extended to the physical realm. In the filthy recesses of Trey's subconscious, he could ride her ten ways from Sunday. But when he tried curling his hands around her hips, they slipped off her oily skin and bounced against the mattress. He reached out more than a dozen times, never able to grasp her.

"What's wrong?" She furrowed her brow. "Don't you want to touch me?"

Yes! he tried to say through frozen lips, but apparently, he'd gone mute too.

As he failed to give Bobbi what she needed, she grew more impatient, finally sighing and moving off the bed. "Never mind. I'll ask Colton to do it." She padded out of the room while he silently screamed for her to stay. With a shrug, she called over her shoulder, "I'll bet *he* knows how to use his hands."

When Trey awoke, it was to the most painful morning wood he'd ever experienced, and at twenty-eight years old, he'd had more than his fair share of boners. Squinting against the sunlight, he glanced at the tent he'd created beneath the sheet. Hell, that was no ordinary tent—it was a friggin' Ringling Brothers Big Top. You could fit a clown car under that dome.

The reason behind the blue-balling nightmare was obvious. Last night he and Luke had carried Bobbi upstairs and tucked her into bed. Poor thing had been scratching her nose and chugging sangria for hours and couldn't even take off her own shoes, so he'd stayed behind to unfasten her sandals. All alone with the unconscious redhead, he'd stared at her long, tanned legs—especially those thighs—and felt a compulsion to touch her that'd had his fingers trembling like an alcoholic's.

Of course he hadn't laid a hand on Bobbi. Even if he'd had Luke's blessing to roll her in the hay, he still wasn't a pervert who molested women in their sleep.

But he'd looked. A lot.

The phone rang, and he decided to let the answering machine get it so he could take care of his raging hardon. But when he heard, "Trey? It's your mother. Pick up. I know you're there," he unhanded his johnson and swore loudly. He didn't know a man alive who could spank the plank to the tune of his mother's chiding.

Groaning, he rolled to the side and answered the phone. "Hey, Mom." He cleared the huskiness from his throat. "It's the butt crack of dawn. Somebody better be dead."

She got right to the point. "Your father's leaving me."

"What do you mean?" He sat up, rubbing one eye

with the heel of his hand. "Like for an assignment?" Dad had retired from the army ten years ago, but he still took the occasional contracting job.

"If by 'assignment' you mean spending time with his latest whore," Mom said coolly, "then yes."

Trey shook his head and fell back against his pillow. He had neither the time nor the inclination to get sucked into his parents' bullshit today. For thirty years, his asshole father had messed around, and for thirty years, Mom had pretended not to care. He didn't understand why she stayed with the old bastard—they had more money than God, and she'd get half of it if she left—but she'd always refused to call it quits.

"This is nothing new, Mom. He's not leaving you."

"He most certainly is, Trey Alexander Lewis." By the smooth tone of Mom's voice, you'd think she was discussing the latest sale at Nordstrom. He didn't expect her to say, "He had me served with divorce papers last night, right in the middle of my Bunco game, in front of all my friends."

He pushed to his elbows. "You're serious?" After all the years Mom had spent holding the family together and putting up with Dad's affairs, *he* was the one bailing? And to lower the boom in front of Mom's dice-tossing, chardonnay-swilling friends was a lousy way to handle it, even for a jerk like the Colonel.

"Why would I joke about this? It was mortifying. The whole city's talking about it."

He doubted anyone in Chicago gave a rat's ass about the Lewis divorce, but he held his tongue. For a woman like Mom, who calculated a person's worth based on how close he lived to the Magnificent Mile, being publicly jilted probably seemed like a fate worse than death.

"I'll try talking to him," Trey said, "if you want him back." Personally, he didn't see the point of staying in an unhappy marriage, and he'd never witnessed a happy one. Well, except for June and Luke, but what they had was an anomaly. "Why not let him go, Mom? Start fresh."

"*Fresh?*" Her voice was so cold he felt the frost from a thousand miles away. "I'm fifty-five! I gave all my fresh years to that bastard, your father, and by God, he should have to live with the stale ones now!"

"All right, all right. I'll call him, but I can't guarantee he'll answer."

And Luke wonders why I don't do relationships. Marriage is an institution, all right. For lunatics.

"Oh, he'll pick up. I told him your big news last week."

In other words, Trey was forgiven, now that he'd finally agreed to a civilian contracting gig to clear his besmirched military record. Dating all the way back to the Revolutionary War, each generation of Lewis men, and even a couple of women, had served in the U.S. Army—until Trey had ruined the family legacy with his other-than-honorable discharge seven years ago. Dad had barely said a dozen words to him since.

"Try not to worry, Mom. No matter what, you've always got me."

Apparently, that wasn't what she wanted to hear. She made a lame excuse about having to rush off to one of her social clubs and disconnected. Two hours later, Trey had the extreme misfortune of speaking with the Colonel. Both parents in one morning, never a good way to start the day.

"Mom's upset." Trey pressed his cell phone between his shoulder and ear while steering the Chevy onto the main road with one hand and fishing for his sunglasses with the other. "Says you're divorcing her. What's going on?"

"I'm divorcing her." Dad took a pull from his cigarette, taking his sweet time before exhaling. "The rest's none of your fucking business."

"It's my business when she calls me in hysterics." To the outside observer, Mom's display might've seemed controlled, but Trey knew any betrayal of emotion from her constituted a full-on meltdown. "After all the shit she's put up with over the years, you owe her—"

"I don't owe that woman a goddamn thing!" his dad barked, then muttered under his breath, "All the shit *she's* put up with? You don't know the half of it."

"Listen," Trey ground out through clenched teeth, "I don't know what she sees in you, but she wants to stay married. Why not scrape together some of that honor you're always talking about, and go back home?"

"Don't lecture me, you pissant. You wouldn't know *honor* if it bent you over and screwed you in the shower." He spoke the next words in a rush. "I've got a chance to start over with someone else, and I'm taking it. Worry about your own business."

The line disconnected.

Trey found his Oakleys and fisted them so tightly a plastic lens cracked.

"Ah, hell." He threw them aside and pulled down the sun visor, focusing his attention on the road before he killed someone. He should've known better than to waste his breath on that cold son of a bitch. Not only had he broken his favorite pair of shades, but he had no idea what to tell his mom.

Glaring at the asphalt, he sneered and mockingly repeated his father's words. "You wouldn't know *honor* if it violated you in the shower." To hear the old man talk, you'd think Trey had sold military secrets or poisoned his own men, when in truth, it'd been an honorable act that'd wound up getting him in trouble.

He and Luke had been stationed together in Germany, and Luke had married a local girl, Ada, who'd started cheating before the ink was dry on the marriage license. When Trey'd busted Ada with a captain from another unit, he'd done his best to get the jerk to back off, and it had ended in a public fistfight. The army'd given Trey the boot for striking a superior officer.

That didn't make Trey a dishonorable guy, damn it, but try telling that to the rest of the world, who couldn't see past the label on his discharge papers. Finding decent work was harder than winning the Nobel Prize when a guy had a mark on his record like that, which was exactly why he wanted it expunged. All he needed to do was complete two years of security detail in Dubai, and his OTH would be lessened to a general discharge. As much as he'd like to stay in Sultry Springs and run Luke's nonprofit, Trey wanted something more—maybe his own contracting business—and businesses were built on reputation.

He'd get his good name back if it killed him.

—⁓—

By the time he pulled up to the Sultry County Community Center, a tension headache gripped his temples in a vise, his balls felt heavy as watermelons, and he was in an all-around shitty mood. But thanks to the clear weather, at least his leg didn't hurt. Hanging Sheetrock was a lot easier when he wasn't gimping around with his bones on fire. He pulled on his Cubs ball cap, grabbed his cooler, and used one boot to push open the Chevy door.

"Hey, boss." Little Carlo Hernandez—otherwise known as Gopher—loped over to meet him, smiling from beneath shaggy, black hair that reached his jaw. Trey scanned the gangly boy, taking in the denim cutoffs that barely clung to his waist with a "belt" of discarded rope.

"I told you," Trey said, pointing at Gopher's knobby knees, "no shorts on the job site."

Shrugging, the boy shoved his hands in his pockets. "I only got one pair of pants 'n' they're dirty." His stomach growled loud enough for Trey to hear it five feet away. Jesus, did the kid's parents ever feed him?

"Here." Trey pulled out his wallet and handed Gopher a twenty. "Walk down to Richman's and bring back a couple dozen donuts for the guys. And for Crissakes, order some biscuits and gravy for yourself. Can't have you passing out on my watch."

The kid snatched the cash and made a run for it, probably afraid Trey would change his mind.

Most of the Helping Hands volunteers were parolees from the halfway house or folks working community service hours for misdemeanors. At thirteen, Carlo was the youngest crew member Trey'd ever supervised. He'd been on the job three weeks, ever since the sheriff had busted him painting "Hammertime" on half the stop signs in Sultry Springs. Trey had to admit he had a soft spot for the kid. Anyone who looked that happy to come to work every morning didn't have much to go home to.

Thinking of Carlo always made Trey wish he had the budget to rebuild the community center into something special, maybe a two-story fitness complex with basketball courts and a gym on the first level, so kids would have a place to burn off their energy. Instead, the simple, boxy structure reminded him of the junior high school and boasted only ten small rooms and a kitchen. Turns out aesthetics weren't as important to the county as low energy bills and cheap maintenance, so he'd given the board exactly what they wanted.

At least it was sturdy. He nodded appreciatively at the brick and stonework. Most of his guys were real yahoos, but a few had an aptitude for masonry, and they'd done a nice job finishing the front wall yesterday after he'd left. Speaking of which, it was time to quit eyeballing the place and head inside.

He'd just crossed the lawn and set his cooler on the front stoop when a sheriff's cruiser came hauling ass into the parking lot with lights flashing and sirens blazing. Its tires squealed louder than a *Deliverance* actor, spinning wildly and tainting the air with clouds of rubbery smoke until it skidded to a halt beside Trey's Chevy.

Shit, what now?

Figuring the sheriff had come for one of the workers, Trey darted a glance around the property to see which of his crew members had the guiltiest look on his face. He noticed Sean Flannigan discreetly toss a bag of weed into the bushes, but nobody took off running or voluntarily dropped to the ground.

When the cruiser's engine cut off and the driver exited

the car, Trey released a quiet sigh of relief. It was only Colton, that crazy SOB. He should've known. No other county cop drove like a drunken, blindfolded primate.

The good deputy tipped his Stetson at him, grinning like he knew something Trey didn't, then he ambled around to the passenger door and opened it, revealing a familiar pair of long legs. Damn. This day just kept getting better and better.

Placing one high-heeled foot on the pavement, Bobbi took Colton's outstretched hand and stepped into full view, wearing another pair of black shorty-shorts and a white top that left very little to the imagination. All at once, a dozen guys dropped their jaws and sucked in their guts, gawking at Bobbi in a way Trey didn't like one friggin' bit.

"For the love of God." Unbuttoning his shirt, Trey stormed over to Bobbi. "What the hell're you wearing?" After slipping his arms out of his sleeves, he wrapped the shirt around her shoulders and tugged it closed like a straitjacket while she gasped in shock. His knuckles accidentally brushed the hardened tips of her nipples, and he clenched his eyes shut, willing away another boner. "Half these guys are parolees, and you're waving a leg of lamb in front of a pack of starving dogs. What're you even doing here?" *With Colton, no less.*

She swept her gaze over the crew before it landed on Trey's bare chest and held there. Slowly, she pushed her arms into his shirtsleeves, never taking her eyes off him, and pure pride lifted the corners of Trey's mouth, especially when Bobbi swallowed hard enough to make her throat bob. He shouldn't care that she obviously found him attractive, but he did.

"Um." She glanced over his shoulder toward the cement mixer. "I need to do a preliminary interview with you two, and Colton was nice enough to offer me a ride."

Oh, he wants to give you a ride, all right. On his lap. "Well, how thoughtful of him."

At the mention of his name, Crazy Colt used one finger to lift a lock of Bobbi's hair to his nose, and before Trey knew what he was doing, he'd reached forward and smacked his friend's hand aside. Colton just chuckled in a way that said, *Game on, buddy.*

"Let's get outta this heat." Trey pointed to the front entrance, still doorless and draped in thick plastic. "Just watch out for nails. I'd hate for you to ruin that pedicure, Bo Peep."

He led them to the kitchen, the only space that wasn't littered with Sheetrock and sacks of plaster, and hopped up on the dusty Formica countertop. Colton took a seat on a parcel of Pergo boards, and Bobbi hovered in the doorway, hugging herself and frowning at the scraps of wood and debris on the tile floor. Knowing her, she probably wanted to sort the mess according to size and color.

"Okay." She pulled a tiny notebook and pen from her back pocket. "Since the documentary's about the rural dating scene, I want to get a feel for your types and a little information about your romantic history." She nodded at Colton, poised to take notes. "How about you? What do you want in a woman?"

He winked at her and drawled, "My schlong."

Trey stifled a laugh while Bobbi's fist tightened around her pen. "I'm serious."

"All right, honey. Give me a minute to think." A few

seconds later, he shrugged one shoulder. "Someone who puts the toilet seat back up when she's done?"

"And who knows when to leave," Trey added. "I hate it when they wanna spend the night."

"Amen to that, brother."

"Oh, come on." Bobbi slammed her notebook on the counter, then shifted her weight to one hip and folded her arms. Trey's shirtsleeves covered her hands, making her look like a kid in oversized pajamas. "Don't tell me you're both Peter Pans."

Trey shook his head. "I got nothing against growing up. I just don't believe in relationships—gave it a go twice, and it sucked both times. Monogamy's not natural."

"What sucked about it?" Bobbi asked. "One woman wasn't enough?"

"Actually, *they* cheated on *me*."

"Oh." She blinked a few times and turned to Colton. "How about you? Ever been in love?"

With those words, Colt froze. A dark cloud moved over his face, erasing his teasing smile. He pressed his lips together and got a far-off look in his eyes, and Trey knew he was thinking about Leah McMahon, the preacher's daughter. *Best thing that ever happened to me*, he'd said one night after half a bottle of whiskey. *And I screwed it up*. She'd left Texas years ago, and no one had heard from her since, not even her father. Colt never talked about her sober, and he didn't elaborate now either.

Eventually, Bobbi grew tired of waiting, so she asked Trey about his first love.

"Mindy Roberts," Trey volunteered. The memories didn't faze him anymore, so he didn't mind sharing.

"Hooked up with another guy and sent me a Dear John while I was in basic training."

"Ouch." She made a sour face. "What about the second girl?"

"That'd be Trish." Thank God she'd left her job at Shooters. She may have gotten their friends in the breakup, but he'd won the bar, and that's what counted. "She'd been crushing on me for years, and your brother kept bugging me to give her a chance. The whole thing was an epic bore, right up until the night I walked in on her riding the Heineken delivery guy like Seabiscuit. Believe it or not, I felt relieved when I caught 'em. Gave me an excuse to dump her without looking like a prick."

"Maybe you're connecting with the wrong kinds of women. What's your type?"

Curvy, uptight goddesses with thick thighs. "Don't have one."

"Hmm." Bobbi tipped her head, studying him. "You guys are completely transparent. You're afraid of commitment because you think everyone cheats," then pointing to Colton, "and this one's been hurt. Badly."

Whatever. If she wanted to buy into that psychobabble crap, let her.

"And what about you?" Trey pushed off the counter, landing on his feet with a thud that stung his right leg. "Why's there no ring on that pretty little finger?"

"Because I've got bigger plans for myself."

"Oh, yeah?" he asked. "Like following me around with a camera while I try to get laid?"

That hit the mark, just as intended, and Trey bit back a laugh. Pissing her off was too much fun. He loved watching the color rise in her cheeks, her breasts heave as she folded her arms beneath them, and those thighs jiggle when she planted her feet apart. He'd promised Luke he wouldn't screw Bobbi, but that didn't mean he couldn't screw *with* her. By the end of summer, maybe he could get her to loosen up a little.

Her green eyes practically glowed with fury. "This is just temporary, so I can spend some time with Luke." Then she scratched her nose, the little liar.

"Sure, Bo Peep."

"And stop calling me that."

"Sure, Bo-dacious."

She pulled in a deep breath and geared up for a good, old-fashioned bitching, but then Carlo came shuffling into the room with a box of donuts tucked under his arm like a football, and she missed her chance.

"Little Hammer," Colton said with a mock salute.

"Hey, pig."

Trey smacked Carlo upside the head. "Respect." The gravy drippings on the boy's shirt told Trey he'd eaten, but despite that fact, his stomach rumbled again. "Still hungry? You got a wooden leg?"

"Maybe worms," Colton said.

Glaring at the "pig," Carlo tossed the box of donuts onto the counter and plucked one out. He bit off a huge chunk and mumbled, "I ain't got no worms."

"Don't have any worms," Trey corrected and then clapped him on the back. "Check my cooler; I packed you an extra lunch. Then go around and get everyone's time sheets."

"Okay, boss."

As soon as Gopher's footsteps retreated out of earshot, Bobbi bit her lip and gazed at Trey with a crooked grin curving her mouth. He glanced over his shoulder to see who the hell she was smiling at because it couldn't be him, but he found no one.

"What?" he asked.

"Nothing." She fingered one button on the front of his shirt, but made no move to take it off and return it to him. Something flashed in her eyes—damned if it didn't look like approval—and she continued beaming while she told Colton to take her home.

Trey leaned against the door frame and stared at her legs as she clicked across the parking lot, wondering what had just transpired. Women. He didn't pretend to understand them.

She was a strange bird, all right, just like he'd told Miss Pru, but he hoped he dreamed of her again tonight. Minus the oil.

Chapter 5

BOBBI HAD MADE A FEW KEY OBSERVATIONS DURING her first week in Sultry Springs. She'd learned that grits, for example, tasted just like warm, buttered popcorn. When June's grandma had baked them with mild cheddar cheese and diced jalapeños, Bobbi'd had a foodgasm right there at the kitchen table. And speaking of Amazon Granny, she still watched Bobbi like a warden, but her smiles had warmed, softening her attitude into something akin to acceptance, which was wonderful...now if she'd only quit trying to recruit Bobbi for her dwindling church congregation.

Another important find, she'd discovered Blessed Brew, a quiet coffee shop in town, which had become her second home. Whenever June and Luke started nuzzling each other's necks and giggling, Bobbi fled the love nest before they embarked on another of their earsplitting sex marathons.

"Here ya go, hon." A teenaged redhead wearing frosted pink lipstick, bless her misguided heart, set Bobbi's breakfast order on the table. "Great dress, by the way. Where'd you get it?"

Bobbi handed the waitress one of Daddy Bruce's business cards and relaxed against the vinyl booth to sip her coffee. The wide front windows of Blessed Brew gave her a view of "the square," a small fountain flanked by park benches, right in the heart of Sultry Springs.

As she absently watched a young family toss pennies into the fountain, she reflected on her most important realization to date: she'd misjudged the rough-handed golden boy, Trey Lewis.

Oh, he still had issues, make no mistake—he got his jollies from irritating her, and don't even get her started on his fear of commitment—but he wasn't the chauvinistic simpleton she'd once thought. Over the past several days, she'd observed him on the job while Bong and Weezus had filmed preliminary footage, taking a special interest in the way he mentored young Carlo. That boy gazed at Trey with an unadulterated case of hero worship, which spoke volumes about Trey's true nature. Assholes didn't take the time to teach stinky teenage boys the precise way to tape and float drywall, patiently demonstrating the technique all afternoon, nor did they casually offer food and clothes in a way that didn't emasculate or offend.

And when it came to *her* clothes, Bobbi'd worn the skimpiest tops in her wardrobe to the community center each day, knowing full well Trey would remove his shirt, wrap it around her shoulders, and work bare-chested for the rest of the afternoon. Judas Priest, her battery-operated boyfriend had gotten plenty of play after eight hours of watching Trey's hard, sweaty body in motion. Too bad she couldn't indulge in a discreet summer fling with him, but it was the height of unprofessionalism to sleep with a subject, especially considering what'd happened the last time. If only Luke hadn't insisted his best friend participate in the documentary...

Bobbi's cell phone vibrated inside her purse, and she reached in to check the caller ID.

"Shit." Yet another text from that sleaze, Garry Goldblatt. She'd hoped he wasn't the kind to micromanage a project.

Sex in the Sticks going ok?

Fine, she replied, stretching the truth a wee bit. *Meeting w/crew in five minutes.*

Keep me abreast. Better yet, keep me two. :)

What a douche. She tucked the phone inside her bag and glanced out the window for any sign of Bong's white van. She needed a brainstorming session with her guys in the worst way.

It's not like she'd really lied to Garry—the project wasn't tanking—but she'd begun to worry how to capture two promiscuous commitment-phobes finding love, especially in a way that didn't bore the viewer. This wasn't like filming weddings. She needed drama, which was rooted in conflict, something that didn't seem to exist in the daily lives of her carefree bachelors. Bobbi figured she had a choice: dig up trouble or manufacture it, and she greatly preferred the former. Maybe it was time to find out what Trey had been hiding.

The cowbell hanging above the door gave a distorted tinkle, and she spotted Weezus and waved him over to her booth. Every single head in the café turned as her cameraman shuffled by in his oversized Birkenstocks—a nearly seven-foot-tall Asian guy with dreadlocks the color of ripe blueberries tended to have that effect—but he paid them no heed. Surely, he was used to the attention by now.

"Where's Bong?" she asked, gesturing for him to take the seat across from her.

"Parking the van." When Bobbi leaned around him to scan the half-vacant parking strip directly out front, Weezus clarified, "He didn't want to park too close to the sheriff's station, so he pulled around back."

She sniffed a little laugh. The courthouse and jail were both adjacent to the square, and she doubted the good deputies of Sultry County would like what they found in the glove box of Bong's van. Except for Colton—he'd probably confiscate the stash and smoke it himself.

A few seconds later, Bong jogged inside, drawing the eye of a few college-aged girls in line. At thirty, he still had that baby-faced, surfer-boy look, but he needed to shave his ridiculous, wiry soul patch. It looked like he'd dipped his chin in blond bean sprouts.

"Hey." He slid into the booth beside Weezus and pointed at Bobbi's bowl of grits. "What's that?"

Before she could answer, the waitress reappeared, keeping a safe distance, as if the guys smelled bad. Which they totally did. They'd been on some all-natural crystal deodorant kick, and it wasn't working. "Can I get you something?"

Weezus frowned at the menu's limited offerings. "Got any cage-free, organic eggs?"

"Or a Green Monster smoothie?" Bong asked.

Bobbi rolled her eyes. She loved working with this duo, but they were prima donnas when it came to food. "Right, because your bodies are such temples." To Dionysus, maybe. "Just bring some black coffee and a few cinnamon rolls," she told the girl, who nodded and hurried away.

While her two-man crew grumbled from across the

table, Bobbi got down to business. "Everyone knows there's nothing real about reality television. It's scripted and planned out beforehand, and any wild, unexpected stuff that happens is just a bonus."

They nodded in agreement.

"We need to figure out how to bring some drama to the table. Trey and Colton are too laid back, and picking up women won't be a challenge for either of them because they're gorgeous."

"Yeah, where's the tension?" Weezus asked.

"Exactly." Bobbi salted her grits and took a bite, closing her eyes to savor the buttery flavor. Not as good as Pru's, but still tastier than Wheaties, her usual breakfast of choice.

Bong stroked his pseudo-beard. "Once, I heard about this reality director who used to pay extras to stir up shit. Get them to start fights, things like that. What if we hired a pretty girl to get close to one of the guys, then paid someone to play her jealous husband?"

"I don't know." Bobbi turned her spoon upside down and held it in her mouth while considering the idea. She pulled it out, shaking her head. "That sounds so seedy."

"Well, we *are* working for Goldblatt..."

"True, but the last thing I need is another scandal." Her career would never survive it. "Let's try to keep everything on the up-and-up."

"Then I've got nothing."

Bobbi sighed. "They're both hard-core bachelors, and we've got them testifying to it on camera. What I'd really love is to show a one-eighty by the end of the project—have them both in serious relationships."

"I'm not much of a matchmaker," Weezus said.

"Besides, I don't see it happening with these two. I overheard Trey on the phone yesterday, and he said something about moving at the end of summer."

"Oh, yeah?" she asked, a spoonful of grits suspended an inch from her lips. "To where?"

He shrugged. "And Colton's crazy as a shithouse rat." Leaning in, he lowered his voice and disclaimed, "I don't know why a rat would hang out in a shithouse—I mean, they're really smart animals, and cleaner than most people think—but I heard some redneck say that in the Sack-n-Pay last night." Then he grabbed Bobbi's fork and helped himself to a bite of her breakfast. "Anyway, I agree with the Bonger. We might have to make our own mischief."

So, which was worse, handing in a finished product that was dryer than saltines in the desert, or risking her reputation again? "Okay, look into it, but don't pull the trigger yet. Let's take the guys out tonight and see how it goes."

"You're the boss."

The front door cowbell clunked again, and Pru walked in on the arm of an old man who looked uncannily like a balding Albert Einstein, minus the moustache. He stood at least ten inches shorter than his date, but he squared his shoulders and raised his chin proudly, seemingly unaffected by their height difference.

Bobbi waved at June's grandma, which seemed like the friendly, small-town thing to do, and the couple ambled over. When they got within smelling distance of Bong and Weezus, they backed up a few paces.

"Well, I'll be," the man said. "Tiny Bo Gallagher, all grown up."

"Bo?" Weezus asked with a snort. She kicked him under the table.

Pru patted her date's upper arm. "This is Judge Bea. He knew your mama."

At the mention of the word *judge*, Bong's backbone locked, and his gaze flickered everywhere but the old man's eyes.

"A little too well, I'm 'fraid." Bea spoke to her, but narrowed one eye at Bong. "She was a right regular customer in my courtroom."

"Oh, I've heard about you," Bobbi said, turning the subject away from her crazy mother. "You're Colton's grandpa." She remembered Trey insinuating nepotism had earned Colt his job on the force, and her interactions with Deputy Horndog left no doubt the accusation was true.

"Mmm-hmm." Now Bea turned his squinty pirate eye on her. "I hear he's gonna be part'a your TV show." The fact didn't seem to please him.

"That's right."

"Listen." He leaned into her crew's odorous cloud as far as he was willing to go. "Your brother's like family, but don't think I won't shut this thing down if I think you're makin' the town—or my grandbaby—look foolish. We clear?"

Grandbaby? Colton was in his early twenties, like her. Bobbi wondered just how much coddling and law-bending the good judge had done for his kin over the years. That alone could make for an interesting piece, but she forced herself to let it go…for now. "Crystal," she chirped with a forced smile.

"I'll be watchin'."

"Feel free," Bobbi said. "I've got nothing to hide." But that was a bold-faced lie, and from the wry grin on the judge's lips, he knew it.

After Pru and Bea excused themselves to a secluded table in the back, Bobbi sent Trey and Colton a text to meet her at Shooters at nine o'clock that night. As usual, Trey didn't respond—he believed texting was for teenagers—but Colt messaged back almost instantly.

Ok. Got a question 4u.

What?

r-u Irish?

Think so, she typed. *Why?*

Got any Cherokee in u?

No.

Let me know if u want some.

Damn, she walked right into that one.

———⚡———

Later that night, she and the crew set up inside Shooters, and since Bobbi couldn't afford special lighting for this project, June had thankfully agreed to keep all the overhead fluorescents on. The place was packed, and for the thousandth time, Bobbi wished she had an assistant to collect signed waivers from anyone appearing on camera and to corral drunken patrons out of the shot.

Weezus stood on a chair above the crowd, filming Colton as he slow-danced with a voluptuous brunette, and Bong extended the microphone above the couple on his "fishing pole," collecting what Bobbi hoped was spicy dialogue. It didn't matter that the jukebox had fallen silent half an hour ago. Colt and his flavor of the minute seemed all too content swaying to the tune of clacking cue balls, cheers, and laughter.

Bobbi glanced around for Trey, but she couldn't spot him in the sea of bodies. After nudging her way to the bar, she waited for June to finish an order before asking, "You seen Trey?"

"Yeah." June tossed some ice cubes into a martini tumbler and gave it a shake. "I think he's still in the office. Said he wanted to talk to Luke about something important." Lines of concern wrinkled her porcelain forehead. "Neither of them looked too happy when they went back there."

Interesting. "I'll go check on them," Bobbi shouted over the din, "and make sure they're playing nice."

In the five minutes it took Bobbi to inch to the back office, she collected several unsolicited phone numbers, not to mention half a dozen ass-grabs beneath her floral minidress. Not that she needed protection, but she finally understood her brother's insistence on having Trey on the project. The good ol' boys of Sultry Springs couldn't take a hint, especially after they'd sucked down a pitcher of beer.

The clamor faded once she reached the other side of the *employees only* door, soon replaced by muffled shouts coming from Luke's office. Bobbi tiptoed through the hallway until she reached Luke's door, but instead of playing referee, she pressed her ear to the oak and snooped. A bubble of guilt rose into her throat, but she swallowed it. After all, this was her job.

"...leaving me screwed!" Luke yelled. "You couldn't've told me sooner? What am I supposed to do?"

"I just found out a week ago. And besides, we both know a dozen guys who can take my place, so quit acting like I shot your dog."

"What's this really about?"

"I told you," Trey said with a razor's edge to his voice. "Clearing my record."

Bobbi perked up. Golden Boy had a record?

"That's bullshit. You finally caved to the old man, didn't you?"

"I don't give a damn if you believe me or not. Either way, I'm going." Trey snorted a humorless laugh. "Thanks for making it so easy."

With that, the door flew open, and Bobbi gasped, stumbling back against the wall. Luke came charging out and stormed right past her without the barest acknowledgment that she'd been eavesdropping. He clomped down the hall and out the rear entrance to the parking lot, slamming the heavy, steel door behind him hard enough for Bobbi to feel the floor shake through her ballet flats.

She placed a hand against the door frame and peered inside Luke's office, where Trey stared at the jellyfish floating in tranquil contrast to his rage. The muscles in his back strained the fabric of his T-shirt until she feared he'd rip the seams like the Incredible Hulk. Tentatively, she stepped inside and closed the door behind her. Trey whirled around, blue eyes ablaze in a way she'd never seen before. The heat from his gaze sparked a flame in the pit of her belly, and she instinctively backed away, pressing her spine to the wall.

"How much did you hear?" he asked, advancing on her one slow step at a time.

She held out a defensive palm. "Just enough to know you're leaving, and Luke's not happy about it."

Tilting his head, he studied her, no doubt weighing the plausibility of her story. Several seconds later, he nodded. "Fine. Go on, then. I'm not good company tonight."

She didn't move. "Where're you going?"

A charged silence followed, rippling the space between them, until Trey eventually heaved a sigh and muttered, "Dubai. When summer's over."

"That's a long way from home." The rigid set of Trey's jaw told her she was pushing her luck, but she pressed harder. "What's in Dubai that's so important?"

"You ask a lot of questions." He inched closer, reminding her of a tiger stalking its prey.

She shrugged one shoulder, maintaining a blank expression though her pulse quickened. "Occupational hazard."

"A civilian contracting job," he finally said. "Two years security detail for some bigwig developer who's working with the military."

He didn't seem excited about the venture. "Why? I thought you were happy here."

Trey smirked, flashing one dimple. "How 'bout this, Bo Peep. I'll show you mine if you show me yours."

Bobbi glanced away from his piercing glare and focused on her brother's desk. "What's that supposed to mean?" She pushed off the wall and skirted around Trey, then began absently sorting receipts. She couldn't think clearly enough to organize the mess, but Trey was making her nervous, and she needed to do something with her hands.

"It means," Trey said from behind, settling close enough to surround her in his delicious scent of sandalwood and sex, "I know you're lying to your brother." He swept her hair aside, brushing her neck with his fingertips, and whispered in her ear, "So what're you really doing here?"

Closing her eyes, Bobbi splayed both hands against the scattered paperwork to steady herself while the room spun. She hoped Trey hadn't noticed the goose bumps he'd brought to the surface of her skin. "J-just shooting this project, like I said."

He used his thumb to trace the chills along her upper back. He'd noticed, all right. She could practically feel the smug smile in his feather touch. "You're a terrible liar."

Without permission, her body backed against his, molding them together, his growing erection pressing her bottom.

Trey sucked a breath through his teeth. "What the hell're you doing?"

Playing with fire was what she was doing. "Nothing." Unable to stop herself, she ground against the thick bulge straining the front of his Levis. "We should get back to the bar."

"I told you," he said, low and gritty, as he grasped her waist and turned her to face him, "I'm not good company tonight."

Bobbi's breath hitched when Trey backed her onto the desk and stepped between her knees. His stone chest brushed her nipples, tightening them instantly. "I don't care," she barely managed in a whisper. "You have to s-suck it up and put on a happy face."

With one hand, Trey fisted her hair, tipping her head back. He pressed his lips to her earlobe and murmured,

"There's only one thing that's gonna put a smile on my face." In one rough motion, he took her breast in his palm and used his thumb to stroke its hardened tip, electrifying every nerve ending in her body. Bobbi clutched his back, and her mind flooded with sensual images of those muscles tensing and flexing beneath her fingers while he made love to her. She arched further into his palm and bit her lip to contain a moan. "Can you guess what that is?"

She nodded as much as his grip would allow, and with her heart thumping against her lungs, she yanked her dress up, wrapping one leg around his waist.

He released her hair and abruptly cupped the satin crotch of her panties, massaging with the heel of his hand until she groaned and fell back onto her elbows. "Oh god." She hadn't meant to say it out loud, but all the blood in her head rushed beneath his hand as he worked her relentlessly up and down.

"Move with me," he commanded.

She responded, arching her lower back, straining against him as he ground his palm in slow circles. Closing her eyes, she focused on the delicious tension mounting between her thighs, and for several long minutes, the only sounds in the room were her shuddering breaths and the soft rustle of skin rubbing satin. A tiny voice in the recesses of her mind told her this was wrong, but pure pleasure silenced it as she climbed higher and higher toward the peak.

"Look at me."

She allowed her lids to flutter open.

Still standing between her legs, Trey locked eyes with her and lightened the pressure, brushing his knuckles over the dampened fabric, teasing her until she felt swollen with need. Aching for more, she planted both heels on the desk and rose up to meet him.

"If I slipped off your panties," he said, fingertips swirling in *just* the right place, "and spread your gorgeous thighs nice and wide..." Gripping the desk with both hands, he fit their hips together, then rocked against her aroused flesh so slowly it made her eyes roll back. "I could make you come so hard you'd forget how to breathe, Bobbi."

Yes! She didn't know if she'd said it aloud, and she didn't care. Reclining flat on her back, she let her knees fall out to the sides and shamelessly begged with her hips.

"But," he said, "that'd be a real bad idea."

Oh god, no, it wouldn't. That'd be the best idea ever.

A distant door slammed—either the back entrance or the one leading to the bar, she couldn't tell—and Bobbi flinched, sharing one panicked glance with Trey as he pulled her to standing.

When Bong knocked once and barged right in, Bobbi was still pulling down her dress and fighting for oxygen, while Trey spun to face the wall—a wise idea considering his erection was probably visible from space.

"Oh." Bong's eyes widened. "Did I interrupt something?"

"No," she panted, finger-combing her hair. "What's up?"

Clearly, her sound boom guy wasn't fooled, because he gave a knowing grin and glanced at his checkerboard Converse slip-ons. "Colton wants to take us on a field trip."

"To where?"

"He won't say, but he promised we'd like it."

Bobbi didn't have a good feeling about this. Of course, circulation hadn't been fully restored to her brain. "What about the brunette?"

"They snuck into the bathroom right after you left. I think he's done with her now."

"Well, that was fast."

"Yeah." Bong stepped out of the office, winking at her. "People around here don't waste any time."

Bobbi caught his meaning, and her cheeks flushed. Though still throbbing below the waist, her senses had begun to return, and she couldn't believe what she'd almost done. If Bong hadn't interrupted them, she'd be on top of Luke's desk right now, spread-eagled with Budweiser invoices stuck to her bare ass, doing the dirty deed with one of her documentary subjects. What the hell was wrong with her? This was supposed to be her comeback project, not the final nail in her career's coffin.

"I'm sorry," she said to Trey, while smoothing the wrinkles from her dress. "I shouldn't have let that happen."

"Me too." Trey's voice was still thick with lust, but an added dash of guilt darkened his tone. "I was in a shitty mood, but that's no excuse." Still facing away, he cleared his throat. "Luke can't know about this. I'm supposed to be keeping you out of trouble, not... you know."

"Yeah, I know."

"So, we're okay, right?"

"Of course," Bobbi reassured him. She took a moment to steady her breathing and added, "I'm a professional."

Not that you'd know it from her behavior, but that was about to change. No more messing around. Nobody—not even the blond sex god at her side—would keep Bobbi from reclaiming her career and restoring her reputation.

She just needed her body to get the memo. Good thing she'd remembered to pack plenty of batteries.

Chapter 6

"THE SULTRY LADY. TEXAS-SIZED T&A," BOBBI READ aloud from the fluorescent pink sign atop their field-trip destination. Wonderful. Just when she thought strip clubs couldn't demean women any further, one rose to the occasion. She knocked on the Plexiglas divider to get Colton's attention. "Let me out."

Trey shifted beside her on the cruiser's backseat, gripping his knees hard enough to make his forearm tendons strain beneath his skin. She felt his pain. An hour had passed since their near-sex experience, and her pulse still throbbed uncomfortably right between her "gorgeous" thighs.

If I slipped off your panties and spread your gorgeous thighs nice and wide, I could make you come so hard you'd forget how to breathe, Bobbi. Even if she lived a thousand years, she'd never get those words out of her head. Trey hadn't said a thing the whole ride over, but she knew he was thinking about it too. It was the invisible elephant in the squad car. No, bigger than that. The invisible brontosaurus.

Colton opened her door and Bobbi stepped out, scanning the barely illuminated parking lot for Bong's van. He'd probably circled around back for an empty spot since Colt had claimed the last one in front of the two-story stucco building. A seductive beat drifted from the entrance to The Sultry Lady, punctuated by the whoops and whistles of what sounded like hundreds of men.

"I still can't believe a nice little town like Sultry Springs has," she made air quotes, "a gentleman's club." There was nothing gentlemanly about paying a desperate, young woman to grind on your lap.

"It's outside town limits," Colton said. "The county can't ban titty bars, thank the Lord, just regulate 'em."

"Is it always this busy?" she asked, moving aside to let Trey out.

Colton chuckled to himself and pulled off his Stetson. After raking his fingers through his jet-black hair, he tossed his hat into the cruiser. "Nope. You could say tonight's a special occasion."

Uh-oh. She didn't like the sound of this either. "Spill it now, or we're going home."

"All right, honey. Just calm down now." He made a *come here* motion, lowering his voice. "Can you keep a secret?"

"Usually," came her tentative reply. She and Trey moved closer, forming an awkward huddle.

"Not all of these cars belong to customers," Colt said. "The sheriff's been investigating prostitution rumors, and there's an undercover bust going down tonight. When the head guy gives the signal, they're gonna lock all the exits and sweep the private dance rooms. Should make an interesting episode for your show, don't you think?"

Bobbi straightened while a hesitant grin lifted the corners of her mouth. Finally, a lucky break. "To say the least. So, that's why you're here?"

"Nah." He smiled at Trey as if sharing a private joke.

"I'm just comin' around for my weekly inspection. It's a tough job, but I'm man enough to handle it."

Shaking his head, Trey hooked a thumb at his buddy and explained, "New law says the girls have to cover their nipples with latex, and this lucky bastard gets the job of making sure it's enforced."

"Lucky?" She gave Trey a narrowed sideways glance. "Since when is contributing to the sexual objectification of women considered a stroke of luck?"

Trey rolled his eyes. "Here we go."

Before she had a chance to school him on the negative impact of the sex industry on society, Bong called out from somewhere in the darkness. He jogged into view beneath the streetlight's glow and met them, panting for breath.

"Waste of time." He nodded toward the beefy linebacker standing guard at the front entrance. "They'll never let us take the camera inside. I tried something like this in Anaheim—"

"Don't worry," Colton said, "we're using the back door. I called in a favor from the co-owner." Smiling, he shifted his utility belt. "Found his homemade distillery while I was camping last summer, so he owes me big. Anyway, try to stay out of sight and ditch that microphone on a pole."

Bong considered a moment. "The smaller camera has a built-in mic, but the quality won't be the same."

Bobbi held up one hand. "For something this juicy, we'll deal with it."

"Juicy?" Bong asked.

"Don't advertise this," she said, "but they're busting up a prostitution ring tonight."

"No shit." They shared a glance, each, no doubt, recalling this morning's conversation about manufacturing drama. Catching their subjects inside a strip joint in the middle of a police raid was better than gold, and they both knew it. "Okay, then we'll go in the front and find a table with a wide view. I'll fit Weezus with a hidden mic and tell him to wear the strap-on."

That got everyone's attention.

"Not what you think," Bong said and jogged away.

Trey raised one blond brow, and while the three of them made their way to the back of the property, Bobbi explained that Weezus had crafted a strap-on apparatus similar to a Kevlar vest that concealed a small camera inside, and since he was already taller than 6'5", the added bulk looked natural on his Kong-frame. Like Bong had said, the quality would be rough, but the gritty effect might actually enhance the sense of danger on screen and make it easier to blur the faces of anyone who didn't sign a waiver.

When they reached the back door, Colton pounded a code with his fist that sounded just like the intro to "Ice, Ice, Baby," and a few seconds later, a portly man with a missing front tooth ushered them inside. Bobbi didn't doubt the validity of Colton's story, because this guy looked like the type to hide a still in the woods…maybe even utter the phrase, "You got a purty mouth, boy." She tried not to think too hard about his personal life as he led them to the dressing room.

From the way the girls bounced and giggled at the sight of Colton, you'd think he was a rock star. They left their individual vanities and lined up for inspection, thrusting their hard, fake cantaloupe boobs toward the deputy's face while issuing unspoken invitations with their eyes.

Unbelievable. He was like the Pied Piper for horny women.

A few girls tossed flirtatious glances at Trey, but he didn't notice. He'd averted his gaze, choosing to study his work boots instead of their nearly naked bodies, and Bobbi couldn't help admiring him for it.

While Colton took his time scrutinizing each latex-coated nipple, Bobbi turned her attention to the metal locker bank, which each dancer had embellished with photos and oversized name tags: Destini, Kandi, Brandi, Karli, Kourtni. It reminded her of the way girls in middle school used to decorate each other's lockers to celebrate birthdays or home games. She'd always envied those students. The only adornment Bobbi had ever found on her locker was a Gap ad with the words, "Get some new clothes, loser" scrawled beneath. As if living in poverty with an addict had been her first choice. When Mama'd died six months later, Bobbi had asked her dads to send her to a new school.

"Hey." Trey nudged her with his elbow. "I could use a drink. Let's go sit at the bar."

"Great idea." She snapped her fingers at Colt until she had his full attention. "Meet us out there when you're done."

He nodded, but as seriously as he took his job, it would probably take a while.

The scent of theatrical fog and the quintessential stripper song, "Closer" by Nine Inch Nails, greeted them inside the club. While Trent Reznor sang about getting closer to God in a really unconventional way, an emaciated blond in a glittery thong was doing creative but disturbing things to the pole on stage, captivating the audience seated at the tables below.

Bobbi spotted her crew in the back corner and gave them a wave as she climbed onto her bar stool.

"What're you having?" Trey asked, sitting so close their legs touched. He wrapped one arm around her waist and ordered a Bud draft.

"Vodka tonic." She glanced at his arm, then back to him. "What're you doing?"

"Sending a message."

"To?"

"All the dudes I saw watching you when we walked in the room." He pulled away just long enough to toss a twenty onto the bar before holding her again, tighter than before. "Marking my territory. Staking my claim. No one'll bother you now."

Snickering, the bartender opened a fresh bag of snack mix and shook it into a clean bowl. "He speaks the truth." He pushed the bowl across the lacquer bar and served their drinks before stepping away to help another customer.

"Lovely." At least he didn't pee on her. "How did I ever manage to fend off unwanted advances before you came along?"

"Probably by launching into some femi-nazi lecture."

"I hate that term. *Nazi* isn't a word you can just throw around, and it's completely inappropr—"

"Thanks for making my point." He took a chug of beer and licked foam off his upper lip. "More likely you'd sucker punch the guy, like you did to me."

"Yeah, well," she said as she squeezed a lime wedge

into her drink before taking a sip. "You had it coming. You smacked my ass. Hard!"

He held his mug just below his mouth, smiling as if replaying the memory. "Yes, I did. But if that didn't repel the poor bastard, you could always insult him like you did to June and Luke."

"*What?*" In her shock, she'd dribbled bittersweet tonic down her chin. "I never did that."

"You dissed their house." He released her waist and dug into the bowl of snacks, then handed over an extra napkin. "Their mismatched furniture, remember?"

"That had nothing to do with them." Blotting her chin, she struggled for a way to explain her reaction that night. She hadn't told anyone about the dollhouse—not even her court-appointed child psychologist—and never in a million years did she expect to say, "Their place reminded me of an apartment I lived in as a kid, and it stirred up some bad memories. That's all." It wasn't much in the way of confessions, but getting the words out felt strangely liberating.

Trey frowned around a cheek full of pretzel. "What kind of bad memories?"

"I dunno." Unable to hold his intense gaze, she used her swizzle stick to poke at the ice cubes inside her glass. "Feeling hungry and ignored. Not learning to read until fourth grade. Getting teased because I smelled bad and wore thrift store clothes. Teaching myself to fight before I could ride a bike. Take your pick."

He didn't say anything for a while, just traced a bead of condensation down the length of his beer mug and stared into the amber liquid like it revealed the secrets of the universe. Finally, he rested both forearms on the bar and said, "I'm doing it to clear my military record."

"What?"

"Going to Dubai. The army discharged me for striking an officer, but I can apply to have my record expunged after I serve out this contract. That's why I'm going."

"Oh." Now she understood—quid pro quo. He'd traded one uncomfortable admission for another. Her heart warmed, and Bobbi decided she liked Trey Lewis. "Well, good luck." She pilfered through the snack bowl and handed him a flawless, whole cashew. "I hope it works out for you."

"Keep this off the record though."

"Of course," she promised. "But why do you need it cleared so badly?"

He popped the cashew into his mouth while his chest shook with soft laughter. "Why are you really in town?"

"Oh, so it's my turn again?" No way was she spilling about the lawsuit. It was too embarrassing, and she'd divulged enough for one day. "I told you, I'm only—"

"Save it, Bo Peep. I knew you were full of shit from day one. You rub your nose when you lie."

"No I don't. I scratch my nose when I'm nervous."

"And when you lie. It's an easy tell."

"Really?"

He held up one hand. "I swear it on the Cubs."

"Huh." She touched the tip of her nose, hoping no one else had picked up on her habit.

Trey glanced over his shoulder to scan the crowd, then turned back to his Bud. "Wonder when the raid's going down. I've got an early day tomorrow."

"And you call *me* a strange bird," Bobbi said, raising

her glass at him. "Forget to take your Metamucil this morning?"

"My what?"

"You're a single guy at a strip club, and instead of getting a lap dance in a private room, you're grumbling that it's past your bedtime."

Smiling, he chugged the last of his beer, then wiped one hand across his mouth. "You offering? 'Cause we could find an empty room somewhere." When he glanced down at her thighs and licked his top lip, heat pooled in her lap, and she had to cross her legs to diffuse the sensation.

"Sorry. Left my sequined thong in my other bag."

"Damned shame."

Abruptly, the music stopped, and Bobbi rotated her stool toward the front entrance, where half a dozen armed, uniformed officers stormed inside and barred the doorway. A man's voice came over the speaker system, ordering, "Remain in your seats. I repeat: remain in your seats. The sheriff's department will release you momentarily." Plain-clothes cops rose from the crowd and made their way to the club's periphery, while the audience muttered in protest at being held hostage, especially when the dancer clicked offstage in her platform heels.

Here we go. She glanced at Weezus, glad to see he'd knelt on his table with a perfect view of the dozen or so doors to the exclusive dance rooms, where all hell was about to break loose. As long as Weezus's chest faced the action, he'd capture the mayhem on camera.

A scuffle broke out from one of the tables as a tall redhead pushed against a uniformed deputy. "You idiot!" the customer shouted, reaching into his back pocket. "Stand down!"

The deputy drew his gun. "Keep your hands where I can see 'em!"

"I'm a federal officer," the redhead protested. "You're interfering with an FBI investi—" Before the guy had a chance to produce his badge, another deputy tased him, and he convulsed wildly before crumpling to the floor.

At that, about twenty of the redhead's buddies— presumably other federal officers—jumped to his aid, swearing and shouting accusations. The undercover deputies jogged into the fray, demanding the feds "get down on the motherfucking ground!" and a full-on brawl ensued.

Her eyes found Weezus, who looked even happier than she was. "Thank you, God." Bobbi brought both hands together and turned her eyes to the ceiling as Trey pulled her against his chest in a protective stance.

"I don't like this."

She did. A bearded man who looked like a young Santa Claus just broke a beer bottle over the sheriff's head. The air was thick with testosterone and theater fog. The sounds of fists smacking flesh competed with grunts and squeaking shoes. You couldn't buy footage like this.

"I wanna get you out of here," Trey said, glancing at the blocked exits.

"Colton said we're locked in." She patted his bicep, trying to draw him out of bodyguard mode. "Just chill. Half the guys in here are cops. What's the worst that can happen?"

A chair came flying within inches of her head, and Trey jerked her aside just in time. Glaring at her, he set his jaw, while Bobbi placed a hand over her heart. No wonder he'd been contracted for security detail—it seemed reflexive for him.

"Okay," she conceded. "Maybe we should duck behind the bar."

When a glass shattered nearby, Trey shook his head. "Not good enough. Let's try the bathrooms."

Linking their fingers, he tugged her out of the main room. Once they made it halfway down the hall, he pushed against the men's room door, finding it locked. Bobbi tried the ladies' room, with the same result. A gunshot pierced the air, making her jump, and Bobbi's eyes automatically searched for a hiding place.

She spotted what looked like a small closet at the end of the corridor and sprinted to it with Trey on her heels. The door opened easily, revealing a dark, tiny space the size of a standing shower with electrical panels and several fuse boxes built into the walls. "Is it safe in there?" she asked.

"As long as you're not wet." He ushered her inside and followed, pulling the door closed behind him.

They stood face-to-face, pressed against one another as flashing green lights from a nearby modem cast Christmasy shadows beneath Trey's eyes. The cramped space was hotter than hell and crackled with electricity, and since the door didn't appear to lock, Trey held the handle while they listened to chaos unfolding from the hallway. The hollow beneath his throat pulsed rapidly. Both their breaths came in quick gasps for the next several minutes.

When another shot rang out, she squealed and buried her face in Trey's dampened chest. As much as she wanted to save her career, it wasn't worth dying for.

"Shh, it's okay." He stroked her hair, and despite the beads of sweat forming between her breasts, she locked both arms around his waist and plastered herself to every inch of him...including the steely length of his erection, perfectly aligned with his zipper. When she flinched, he incorrectly assumed it was out of fear, and tried soothing her. "You're safe," he whispered, trailing his fingers down her back. But she found herself wanting a whole lot more than comfort. Her heart sprinted, and all her stress and fear catapulted her libido into the stratosphere.

Trying to ignore the shouts outside, not to mention the warmth settling between her thighs, she pulled in a deep breath through her nose, savoring Trey's masculine scent. That only made things worse. Flashbacks of his teasing touch, his wicked words, his promise to leave her breathless, swirled in Bobbi's mind, and it didn't help knowing he obviously wanted her too. Closing her eyes, she focused on unsexy things, like student loans and attorney fees, but her thoughts always circled back to the memory of Trey's hand massaging between her legs.

She tried to be still, tried to ignore the urge to wrap her calf around Trey's hips and strain against him. Holding back took so much effort, she ended up fisting his T-shirt and clenching her teeth. Then Trey went and ruined everything. He pushed his bulge against her belly and swept one hand down the length of her backside.

In the distance, the bar had fallen silent, but Bobbi

barely had time to register the fact before Trey dipped his head and brushed his soft lips across her earlobe while simultaneously inching her dress upward. All rational brain activity halted, replaced by surging passion, and the outside world ceased to exist.

"You know," he whispered, "we could…"

"…finish what we started," she replied, reaching around to stroke him through his jeans.

A low groan vibrated his chest as he thrust to meet her hand. "Just this once."

"Get it out of our systems." It sounded reasonable to her. One quickie—nobody would ever know—and she could stop wondering how his rough hands would feel against her bare stomach, or how deliciously he'd fill her, long and thick and hard. Once she'd had him, she could finally quit obsessing and focus on her job. She tore at the button of his jeans and lowered the zipper. "Do you have protection?"

"No." His breath hitched when she slipped her hand inside his boxer briefs and curled her fingers around him. "I mean yes, but no sex. I promised your brother."

She started to object, but quickly bit her lip when he tugged the dress to her waist and nudged her legs apart. Slipping two fingers beneath her panties, he murmured, "I can still make you forget how to breathe…and make you see stars too." With a touch that could only be described as sinful, he stroked her halfway to ecstasy while she matched his rhythm, pumping with her fist. "I want to get on my knees," he whispered in her ear, "and hook your leg over my shoulder," he dipped his fingers inside her, just deep enough to bring a sigh to her lips, "and lick you till you scream my name."

Oh god. She longed for that too, in the worst way, but she wanted to leave him shaking with pleasure even more. "It's your turn first."

When he didn't argue, she sank slowly until she knelt beneath him on the concrete floor. Trey used both hands to brace himself against the wall, and she pulled him free of his briefs.

Unfortunately, that's when a sheriff's deputy threw open the door, caught Bobbi with her hand in Trey's pants—and proceeded to arrest her for prostitution.

As the official led her outside by her cuffed wrists— right past her gawking cameraman, who, naturally, got the whole thing on film—two things occurred to Bobbi. One: the sheriff hadn't arrested Trey. What a sexist double standard. Weren't they equally guilty of this theoretical crime? And two: if she didn't get her shit together right now, hooking would be the only job she'd ever be able to find. She had to figure out how to stay away from Trey and his siren call of sex. For real this time.

Well, just as soon as he posted her bail.

Chapter 7

TREY PROPPED BOTH ELBOWS ON THE SLATE COUNTERTOP and glared at his coffeemaker in an effort to coerce it into dripping faster. Stifling a yawn, he scrubbed his bleary eyes and groaned at the prospect of another twelve-hour day on the job with nothing fueling him but the stale Folgers he'd found at the bottom of the pantry. Until this week, he'd never been a coffee drinker—had seen caffeine addiction as a weakness—but he needed that sludge more than air today.

Between bouts of fitful sleep and waking "up" with a boner every few hours, these friggin' sex dreams were going to kill him, especially now that he knew the feel of Bobbi's slick heat and the softness of her palm wrapped around him. How was he supposed to spend the next two months around her with that memory tickling his johnson? Because he'd never, ever forget. Unfortunately, neither would Bobbi, which explained why she still wasn't speaking to him.

She wouldn't even let him apologize, and he felt awful. The worst part was that he hadn't been able to do anything to help her that night except fetch Colton, who'd ridden to the rescue and plucked Bobbi from the sheriff's paddy wagon like a knight in shining shit-kickers. She'd been so grateful to Colt, she'd kissed him everywhere but on the mouth—just a dusting of pecks, but it still hit Trey like a punch to the junk. He and Bobbi had skipped first base and gone straight to third, so she'd never kissed him, and it'd chapped his ass to see her lips smacking all over Colt's gloating face.

The phone rang, and Trey closed his eyes, taking a deep breath and filling his nose with the pungent scent of strong coffee. It was probably his mom, and he had no intention of picking up to hear the latest installment of *As the Divorce Turns*. In the most recent development, the Colonel had offered Mom seventy percent of their liquid assets in exchange for a quick break, but she'd refused and nearly given her lawyer a stroke in the process.

"Hey, asshole," Luke's voice grumbled from the ancient answering machine in the other room. "Pick up, so I can apologize."

Trey smiled despite his lousy mood. He answered the cordless phone in the kitchen. "Let's hear it then."

"Don't be a dick. I'm sorry." Luke paused to swallow, probably sipping his own coffee. "We cool?"

"Yeah, we're cool."

"Cool."

Trey suddenly appreciated how guys didn't need a twelve-step program to get over a fight like women did. He pulled a mug down from the counter and watched the last few drops trickle into his Mr. Coffee carafe.

"Hey," Luke said without a trace of resentment in his voice, another reason men were better company after a fight. "I need to talk to you about Bo."

Trey froze with his fingers clenched around the mug handle. "'Bout what?"

"Did something happen to her in the last few days?"

Before or after she got busted with my dick in her hand? "Not that I know of. Why?"

"She's acting weird. Rearranging shit and organizing the whole house. I went to grab some batteries out of the—"

"—junk drawer." Where every man kept the batteries.

"Right. But she moved 'em, along with my duct tape and box cutter."

"Dude, what sinister plans are you cookin' up this morning?" Trey teased.

"That's not the point. I can't find a damned thing in my own house. Plus, she's all jittery and being pissy with me."

"Probably that time of the month." Trey poured himself a steaming cup of liquid motivation while guilt gnawed at his gut. "Just keep your head down for a few days."

Luke considered on the other end of the line. "Yeah, maybe you're right."

"She's tougher than you give her credit for, buddy." Trey brought the mug to his lips and sucked a scorching sip, recoiling at the bitter taste. He'd made it too strong again.

"So, what're you gonna do with the house?" Luke asked, changing the subject. "When you leave?"

Trey walked into the living room and leaned one shoulder against the wall, scanning his humble furnishings, while a tingle of regret needled at his chest. It wasn't the Taj Mahal, but he had the basics: black leather sofa, oak coffee table, entertainment center, big screen TV, and a few withering potted plants. He'd come to Sultry Springs a decade earlier with nothing but a duffel bag and a temporary job offer, not expecting to settle in this tiny town. Didn't take long before he'd been able to afford a handyman's special—a fourteen-hundred-square-foot ranch right off Main Street—and he'd fixed it up slowly over the years, with his own two hands.

"Think I'll rent it out," he decided, hooking one finger through his denim belt loop. "Should cover the mortgage and taxes."

"Good." Luke cleared his throat, and Trey could almost see him glancing away to hide his discomfort. "You're more likely to come back if you don't sell the place."

"Maybe." But what tied him to Sultry Springs wasn't the property, it was the people, and Trey'd found himself starting to let go—picking fights with Luke, declining Miss Pru's dinner invitations, making excuses to stay home when his friends wanted to go barhopping in the city. After two years of distance from everyone, would he want to come back? He couldn't say.

A few quick knocks that sounded like the intro to Queen's "Under Pressure" rapped from the front door. Only one person used that code. "Gotta go," Trey said. "Colton's here." He craned his neck to check the time on the microwave. "At eight o'clock in the morning?"

"Probably to bum a condom for some chick he wants to bang on his backseat. You're keeping him away from my sister, right?"

No, not at all. Bobbi didn't mind spending time with Colton. It was Trey she held at an arm's length these days. "Doin' my best."

"Thanks, bro. I owe you one."

The guilt that'd been gnawing on Trey's gut ripped off a huge chunk in its razor-sharp jaws. Luke wouldn't feel so grateful if he knew all the dirty things Trey'd done with the woman he was supposed to be guarding from the perverts of Sultry County. He'd made Colton look like a choir boy.

After hanging up the phone, Trey opened the door to the good deputy, who nodded a greeting, linked arm-in-arm with a skinny blond guy in handcuffs. Clarification: a *naked* skinny blond guy in handcuffs—and high as a giraffe's eye to boot—twitching and darting glances at the empty space that separated Trey's house from the neighbor's.

"Thanks for thinkin' of me, Colt." Trey scratched his bare chest and tried to keep his gaze away from the perp's trouser snake. "But I gave up tweakers for Lent."

"It's not Lent, and you're not Catholic."

"For this, I'll convert."

Naked dude's eyes went wide. "I gotta gopher in the hole!"

"You gonna let me in?" Colt tore off his Stetson and used it to cover the guy's backside when Mrs. Ray gasped in horror from the sidewalk.

"Depends on what you want."

"To borrow a pair of drawers. I gotta take him in, but not bare-assed on my backseat. I *use* that seat, you know what I mean?"

Trey nodded. Colton probably spent more time in the back of his cruiser than the criminals did. "You pick him up around here?"

"Two doors down." Colt tipped his head, pleading with his eyes. "C'mon, man."

"Fine." Trey stood aside and ushered them in. "But don't let him sit down."

While Colt and the druggie waited in the foyer, Trey jogged to his bedroom for a clean pair of underwear, choosing a pair of striped boxers he'd never worn. He preferred boxer briefs—more support for his boys.

When he returned, Colt had already helped himself to a cup of joe.

"Here." Trey handed over the garment. "I don't want these back."

Colt took a sip and immediately spat it back into the mug. "Christ, you make bad coffee." He dumped it into the sink, then fished around for the handcuff's key. After finding it, he freed the naked guy's hands, leaving the open cuffs dangling from one wrist. He grabbed the man by his elbow, dragged him to the hallway bathroom, and shoved the boxers at him. "Put these on." Holding one finger in the perp's face, he added, "If you pull any shit, I'll accidentally tase you in the balls."

"I can smell colors!"

"Shut up." Colt slammed the bathroom door. "Goddamn meth-heads." Leaning against the wall, he crossed one booted foot in front of the other. "You hear about this speed-dating crap Bo's got planned for us tonight? Oh, wait—" he held up one hand and grinned. "She's not givin' you the time of day, is she?"

Trey tugged his brows low. "She'll come around."

"If I have my way, she'll *come around* my anaconda soon." He brushed one thumb against his lips, the smug, smirking bastard.

"Watch it, Colt." In bare feet, Trey took three massive steps and closed the distance between them.

"I can't wait to get her down on those pretty little knees. If she did it for you, she'll do it for—"

"Shut up!" Trey's blood rose, and his head flushed with heat. Without thinking, he balled his fist and punched his friend hard in the sternum, sending him stumbling back in the hallway.

"I mean it." Trey's heart pounded so loudly in his ears, he almost couldn't hear his next words. "Watch your friggin' mouth."

To his surprise, Colt didn't charge him or fight back. Instead, he flashed a wide grin that said he'd gotten exactly what he wanted. He picked up his fallen hat and rubbed his chest. "I knew it! You're falling for the Bodacious Gallagher."

"You crazy jackass." Trey shook his aching hand, still shocked that Colt had taken a blow to the chest to make a point, though it shouldn't have surprised him. "Just 'cause I won't let you talk smack about her doesn't mean—"

"You look at her like a preacher watching the collection plate."

"So what? She's gorgeous. I've seen you checking her out too."

"Not like that." Colt tapped one finger between his brows. "You get a big-ass wrinkle right here when you're lookin' at her."

Trey self-consciously brought two fingers to his forehead. "Yeah, well I've got a little wrinkle up there now, but that doesn't mean I wanna have your baby, Crazy Colt." He pounded his fist against the bathroom door. "Hurry up in there." Trey's company had officially overstayed their welcome. "I'm not gonna lie. I like Bobbi, but it doesn't go any further than that, so don't run your mouth to anyone about this, especially not Luke."

"Hey, no worries." Colt tossed his Stetson atop his head. "Discretion's my middle name. And since you don't have any feelings for Bo, you won't care if I sleep with her, right?" While Trey's back tensed hard enough to crack a vertebra, his friend delivered a challenge. "'Cause if you're not gonna make a play, I will."

"She's Luke's kid sister."

Colton shook his head. "She's a consenting adult. And if you're too stupid to go for it, then step aside and let someone else take a shot, Lewis."

"All right, I'll give it a try," Trey lied. "Now leave her alone." He had no intention of "going for it." Not only had he promised to stay out of her bed, but the timing sucked too. He'd spend the next two years in Dubai, and absence made the heart grow colder, not fonder. Mindy had barely lasted six weeks. But if this convinced Colton to back off, it'd make Trey's job of watching over Bobbi a whole lot easier.

"Good. Let me know if you change your mind." With a satisfied nod, Colt opened the bathroom door a crack and peeked inside. "Ah, son of a bitch."

Trey pinched his temples. "Do I wanna know?"

"That the perp handcuffed himself to your towel rack and pissed his new boxers?" Colt clapped him on the shoulder. "No. You're gonna want to bleach that floor though."

―∿―

"Hey, boss," Carlo mumbled around a massive chunk of turkey sandwich, "how come that pretty lady don't come 'round no more?" He shifted on the countertop, never able to sit still longer than two nanoseconds. "She got nice legs."

"She *has* nice legs," Trey corrected. Which was the understatement of the century. "Bobbi's got work to do…like us. Now watch." He pressed a strip of tape into the drywall seam, added a few smears of mud, and pulled his putty knife against it. "See? Nice and smooth."

"Sealed up tight," Carlo parroted.

"Exactly. I want you to be able to do this by the time your hours are served. If you can master stuff like this, you'll make three times the minimum wage while you're still in school."

"Can I come work for you?" Glancing at the half-eaten sandwich clutched in his grubby fingers, he added in a rush, "I wouldn't eat too much or cause no trouble."

All the excitement in the kid's voice made Trey feel like he'd swallowed a frozen bowling ball. "I know you wouldn't." He wiped off one hand and patted Gopher's back. "You're the best guy on my crew."

"So that's a yes?"

"I'd love to hire you, but you're still too young. Plus, I'm moving to the Middle East in a couple months."

At those words, Gopher's shoulders rounded forward. By the look on his face, you'd think Trey had just announced that Santa died. Well, not that a thirteen-year-old believed in Saint Nick, but still.

"Hey," Trey said, "I'm gonna tell my partner, Luke, what a great worker you are. I'll make sure he brings you on board next summer when you're old enough for part-time, okay?"

That didn't seem to help. Carlo widened his already wide, brown, puppy dog eyes. "But you're comin' back, right?"

Trey hesitated, then decided to tell the little guy what he wanted to hear, even though the answer might change. "Yeah, sure. In two years." That was a lifetime to a kid. Carlo will have forgotten Trey ever existed by then.

"Okay." Gopher nodded, inky-black hair brushing his jaw, and crammed the rest of his sandwich into his mouth. With one cheek bulging with food, he declared, "I'll wait till you're back."

"Nope." Trey shook his head. Carlo was a good kid, but he could easily get into trouble if left with too much time on his hands. "I want you working with Luke while I'm gone. By the time I get back, I expect you to know how to raise a barn." He elbowed Carlo in his bony ribs. "Besides, how'd you expect to get a girlfriend with no spending money?"

"Is that why the redhead don't come around?" Carlo picked up a putty knife and practiced his technique. "You didn't buy her nothin'?"

"*Anything*," Trey corrected with a sigh. "And she's not my girlfriend." He gave Carlo a sideways glance, sizing him up for the first time. With a little meat on his bones, he could be popular with the senoritas—not necessarily a good thing. "Come to think of it, stay away from the ladies for a while. They're trouble."

"Whatever you say, boss." Biting his lip in concentration, Gopher produced a flawless seam.

"Nice! I think you've got it."

Speaking of trouble, Trey's cell phone vibrated in his back pocket, and he retrieved it to find a text message from Bobbi. This was the only way she communicated with him now, probably because she knew he wouldn't respond.

Galley Cat bar @9pm. Speed-dating. Dress up.

Like hell. Enough of this immature bullshit. If she

wanted him to cooperate, she'd have to meet him in person. It took fifteen minutes and a little help from Gopher, but Trey eventually managed to send a simple *No*.

What do u mean NO?

Come on me and we'll talk.

Oh, snap. He'd meant to type "come to me."

Not funny, a-hole.

Sry. Come *here* and we'll talk.

No. Will c u at bar.

Damn it, what was her problem?

If u want me there, come talk. Switching off.

Trey had no intention of turning off his phone—it was the only way to reach him at the community center—but he ignored the seven furious follow-up texts Bobbi sent over the next half hour.

He'd just sent the crew home and given up on Bobbi when his phone rang. An out-of-state area code he didn't recognize flashed on the screen, and he almost didn't answer. Reluctantly, he pressed "talk" and prepared to deflect a sales pitch.

"Hello?"

"Thank God." It was Bobbi, and she sounded like someone had pissed in her Cheerios. "I haven't been able to get ahold of anyone."

"So, what does that make me, Bo Peep?"

"Shut up and come get me. I blew a tire about five miles from Luke's place, and the spare's ruined. Triple A can't come get me for hours, and it's a thousand degrees out here."

"I didn't hear the magic word."

Bobbi fell silent for several seconds, and Trey could almost see the steam rising from her pretty, red head.

"I've got six magic words for you. I'll tell Luke what we did."

Dang, she hit below the belt. "Be there in a few."

—⁓—

By the time he reached her, Bobbi's flaming, red locks clung to the sides of her face with sweat, and the front of her white blouse was so damp Trey felt like he was judging a wet T-shirt contest. She looked insanely hot, both literally and figuratively. He pulled onto the road's grassy shoulder and parked behind Bruiser, then left the engine and air conditioner running when he stepped out to meet her.

Bobbi stood from her seat on the rear bumper, brushing her hands against her jeans. She'd picked a bad day to skip the shorty-shorts. With her gaze trained on his boots, her full mouth pulled into a frown. "Thanks for coming. I didn't want to—"

"Go wait in the truck." Trey brushed past her, nudging her shoulder with his elbow on his way to the driver's door. "Before you get heat stroke." He found the lever to pop the trunk and returned to the rear of the car, where Bobbi still stood with a puzzled expression on her flushed face. "I mean it," he half growled. "And drink the Pepsi in my cooler. You're probably dehydrated."

"I already told you; the spare's no good."

"I wanna see for myself."

She nodded slowly and backed away, still refusing to make eye contact. Trey watched to make sure she followed orders before rooting around the trunk for a jack and the tire iron. He tossed them onto the grass and pulled out the spare, frowning at its cracked rubber. Holy dry rot. No way this thing would last the five miles back to Luke's house. When Trey bounced the tire against the ground, it gave a soft pop and lost what little air had been trapped there since the eighties, or whenever this ancient clunker had come off the assembly line.

Wiping his palms on a rag he'd found in the trunk, Trey jogged back to his truck and climbed inside with Bobbi. Even though two solid feet of bench leather separated them, she scooted away until her back hit the passenger door.

"You're right." He shut his door and gestured for Bobbi to fasten her seat belt. "I'll drop you off at Luke's and go pick up a new spare from Lloyd's Auto. While you're home, I want you to take a cool shower and drink plenty of water." He pulled onto the main road and repeated, "Water, you hear? No booze."

From the corner of his eye, he noticed Bobbi rubbing her nose, and he wondered if she was nervous, or getting ready to lie to him.

"What's wrong?" he asked.

Scoffing, she gave a barely perceptible shake of her head. "It'd be easier to tell you what's *right*."

"Talk to me." After shifting into overdrive, he tried patting her hand, but she pulled away.

"Judge Bea issued a temporary injunction barring me from filming anywhere in Sultry County. I've been summoned to his office."

Trey didn't know whether to whoop with joy or curse Bea's name, because while this project was an epic pain in his ass, he could tell it was important to Bobbi. "Guess that means I'm off the hook for speed-dating."

"For now."

"Well, for what it's worth, I'm sorry. And I'll help out any way I can."

"Thanks. Speaking of help, I assume you'll come get me when you're done with the tire so I can drive home."

"Nuh-uh." He didn't like the deep red staining her cheeks, and he wanted her to stay home and cool off awhile. "After I change the tire, I'll chain Bruiser to my Chevy and tow it."

"Why?" She turned her upper body toward him, right along with her warm, green gaze.

"'Cause I want you to rest."

"No, I mean why are you doing it?"

He shrugged. It wasn't complicated. "'Cause you need me to."

"People only do nice things when they want something." Leaning forward, she readjusted a vent to blow cool air on her throat. "So what is it you want?"

It took Trey a few extra seconds to form his reply. The air-conditioning had circulated Bobbi's scent throughout the cab, and even sweaty as a linebacker, she smelled good. Like sugared cinnamon. How'd she manage to make his mouth water after baking in the sun for so long? At the end of a typical workday, he smelled like roadkill.

"I get why you feel that way," he finally said. "From what you told me last week, it sounds like a lot of people took advantage of you as a kid. But I don't want anything." Glancing over, he added, "This is what friends do for each other."

"So we're friends now?"

"Sure, why not? I like you." He reached over and

tugged a lock of her hair. "And sometimes you even like me back."

She pushed his hand away. "No touching. We can be friends who don't touch."

That brought a smile to his lips. "How 'bout friends who touch over the clothes? That's the best kind."

"No deal, Golden Boy."

"All right, all right." He walked two fingers in her direction and stopped just short of her hip. "I won't touch you till you ask me to."

"*Until* I ask you to? You're pretty sure of yourself."

"Well, considering what's already happened…" Like that relationship doctor on TV always said, the best predictor of future behavior was past behavior.

"Don't get your hopes up." Bobbi took a swig of his Pepsi, and he took his eyes off the road long enough to watch her swallow. Even the way she drank was sexy as hell. "I'll never ask you to lay a hand on me again."

Sure you won't. Trey kept his thoughts to himself and grinned as they drove on—no need to poke the bear— but based on his passenger's rigid posture, she wanted his hands all over her right now.

God help them both; it really *was* gonna be a long-ass summer.

Chapter 8

JUDGE BEA LIKED FISHING BETTER THAN SEX. WHAT'D led Bobbi to this conclusion? A plaque hanging directly above his law degree, proclaiming *Ten Reasons Why Fishing is Better Than Sex.* Leaning forward in her leather armchair, she squinted to read number one on the list. A limp rod is still useful for fishing. Classy.

At least two dozen stuffed trout adorned the wall of Bea's chambers—their gaping mouths stretched unnaturally wide, eyes bulging and glassy, tails frozen mid-thrash—accompanied by hand nets and feathered lures that reminded Bobbi of eighties hair accessories.

The good judge exhaled a cloud of spicy-sweet smoke from across his desk and studied her over the pipe in his withered hand. Tired of playing conversational chicken, Bobbi took one for the team and spoke first.

"You're taking ten years off your life, you know." She nodded toward his pipe.

He took a few leisurely puffs. "Yep, I reckon. But they're the worst ten, so I figure I won't miss 'em."

"But what about your family? I'll bet they'll miss those years." She'd used the same argument to get Papa Bryan to quit smoking when she was fourteen. "Don't you think you owe it to them to quit?"

His bushy, white eyebrows pinched together, and he tapped a small heap of ashes into an armadillo ashtray that Bobbi hoped to God was a replica. Considering all the dead, mounted creatures in this room, the odds weren't in her favor.

"Well, the way I see it," Bea eventually said, "I gave 'em life, a fine home, plenty'a food, and a righteous upbringin'." Folding his arms, he nestled back into his seat. "Seems they owe me, not the other way 'round."

Tipping her head in acknowledgment, Bobbi traced one finger along a zebra print stripe on her skirt. "I guess that's one way of looking at it." Common sense told her to let it go, but she couldn't resist broaching the subject of Bea's favorite "grandbaby," the spoiled deputy. "I can tell you do a lot for your family, especially Colton. You ever worry you've done too much for him?"

If Bea ever decided to retire from the bench, he could make a sweet living playing poker. Aside from the slightest tightening of his lips, he betrayed no emotion. The casual observer never would've noticed, but it was all Bobbi needed to know she'd struck a nerve. She probed deeper. "He's got a wildness in him—the kind that comes from a lifetime of overindulgence. Don't you think it's time to let him stand alone? Be accountable?"

A wily smile uncurled across the judge's lips. "Jumpin' to a few conclusions, there, little Bo. This has nothin' to do with Colton, though I can't say I'm surprised to hear the boy's been showin' his tail."

"Then why the injunction?"

"It's you."

Now it was Bobbi's turn to summon her best poker face. "I haven't done anything wrong."

"No? 'Cause I did a little diggin', and your background's murkier than my favorite fishin' hole."

Bobbi's whole body flashed hot then cold. The judge

was bluffing—he had to be. She'd gone to great lengths to make sure the details of her scandal weren't readily available to the public, not even for someone with Bea's connections. She let out a breath. "I don't know what you've heard, but—"

"Nothin'." Bea kicked up his booted heels and rested them on the corner of his desk. "Pretty tight-lipped crowd you run with. You must'a had a good lawyer."

Not just good—the best. And she'd still be making payments to Jacob Corkwell, Esq., when her hair turned gray, and she started sporting Depends.

"All I know," he continued, "is you got sued by the folks at Smyth when you accused 'em of unfair labor practices. After that, the trail goes cold, and that's more suspicious than a rap sheet. People with nothin' to hide, hide nothin'." He folded his hands atop his belly. "So if you wanna get the injunction lifted, you better start talkin'."

How much information would it take to satisfy his curiosity? She decided to start small. "I made an innocent mistake, and I paid for it. In the interest of protecting my reputation, I fought to keep things quiet. That about sums it up."

"Wrong answer. Try again."

Bobbi caught herself scrubbing her nose with the back of her wrist, so she tucked both hands beneath her thighs. "Look, I can't have this getting out."

"I'll keep it confidential. Gentleman's honor."

"I don't know…"

"I swear it." There was no indecision in the judge's tone. The promise in his gaze bolstered Bobbi's confidence. Though she didn't know Judge Bea from Bea Arthur, she believed him.

"Okay." She nodded slowly and took a deep breath before exhaling. "A reliable source, who made me swear to keep his name anonymous, approached me with proof that Smyth had bought—" she leaned forward, locking eyes with Bea "—not just hired, but actually *bought*—migrant workers from Asia. Allegedly, Smyth was keeping them in a barracks on the job site, but it was hard to verify because the place was locked down tighter than Fort Knox."

With a wave of his hand, Bea encouraged her to continue.

"Like I said, it was a reliable source, someone I'd known and trusted for years, so I was a little lax in verifying the documents and the photos. To make a long story short, my source wanted to bust Smyth so badly, he cut corners and forged some of the documents, and I had no idea." She laughed dryly at her own ignorance. "I probably could've found the evidence myself if I'd slowed down and taken the time to investigate."

"I think I see where this is goin'."

"After I launched the documentary, the company sued me for libel, and we settled out of court." She'd owe the bastards at Smyth for the rest of her life, but at least she'd insisted on a gag order under the settlement terms, so they couldn't breathe a word about her embarrassing screw-up. All the outside world knew was that she'd been sued and pulled the documentary. "For what it's worth, Smyth was guilty. I just couldn't prove it."

"And that's slander."

"So sue me." A nervous giggle rose to her lips. "Sorry. Bad joke."

"Well, hell, Bo. Is that it?"

"What do you mean, *is that it*? I can't get financing for a new documentary, so I'm stuck filming Garry Goldblatt's garbage just to pay my debts." Correction: to make a tiny dent in her debts. "I've sunk from filming award-winning social commentaries to following around two bachelors while they hook up with sleazy women. And even if I nail this project, it's no guarantee anyone'll take me seriously again. Not to mention all those migrant workers—I don't know if they were freed or just shuffled somewhere else. Isn't that enough?"

"I figured you'd done somethin' more…well…illicit, like blackmail or extortion. Why're you tryin' so hard to hide this from your family?"

Bobbi gave a soft snort and folded her arms. "Because everyone in this town assumes I'm some kind of shady criminal, just like my mother. You proved that."

"Now, hold up, there." Bea lifted one hand in supplication. "You were actin' fishy—stayin' away twenty years without a word, then showin' up with no good reason. That's what made me suspicious, not your mama's history. And everyone makes mistakes, 'specially Luke. Your kin won't think any less of you 'cause you messed up."

"Don't be so sure. We barely know each other."

"You gotta trust 'em with your flaws."

Easy for him to say—he didn't know the extent of her flaws. He'd grown up here in this virtual Eden with Luke and June. None of them knew what it was like to pick pockets while they were still in diapers, which, embarrassingly enough, had been until the age of four for Bobbi. Add "potty training" to the list of tasks too demanding for an addict.

"Remember, I told you this in confidence," she said, turning her thoughts away from neglect. "So, can I start filming again?"

"S'pose so." He dropped both feet to the floor and opened a manila file folder. Unlike Luke's desk, the judge's was organized and free from clutter, each office supply neatly encased in plastic the way nature intended. While he scribbled his signature on her new license, a sudden gleam sparked behind his eyes and he smiled, transforming his countenance so completely Bobbi couldn't help smiling in return. "If you're lookin' to tape a *real* love story, I'm proposin' to Prudence at the church barbeque tonight. Five dollars a plate." Still beaming, he blotted his signature. "Keep quiet though. It's a surprise."

That wasn't the kind of love Garry was looking for—too much small-town purity and not enough drunken wardrobe malfunctions—but Bobbi didn't give a damn. "That's better than speed-dating any day. I wouldn't miss it."

~~~

Since Bobbi had no place to be and the fierce summer sun had given the town a reprieve today, she decided to take a stroll down Main Street, where the air was thick with the scents of cedar trees and grilling hamburgers. At eleven in the morning, it was a little early for the lunch crowd, so the only sounds competing with her clicking heels were the flap of nylon flags overhead and snippets of Mexican folk music drifting on the breeze from the *Hallelujah!* dance studio on the corner. A wide banner stretching between two streetlights promised free hot dogs and fireworks at the Fourth of July parade next week, while wooden signs and green awnings clamored for her attention, boasting the best prices in Sultry Springs and enough religious literature to save a legion of souls.

Funny how the crumbling, rust-colored brick added to the town's charm—quaint and whimsical as opposed to run-down. That same aging brick composed the urban shops back home, but with a dilapidated effect that drove shoppers to the shiny, new strip malls on the outskirts of the city.

"Mornin'." A middle-aged man in coveralls nodded as he passed her on the sidewalk.

She returned his greeting with a smile and paused in front of the Sultry General Store. Shielding her eyes from the glare, she peered through the shop window, noting Texas-themed knickknacks, T-shirts, and an assortment of cowboy hats. Papa and Daddy didn't usually go for kitschy souvenirs, but the mental image of them in matching Stetsons had her gravitating through the door with a grin on her face.

Twenty minutes later, she left with gifts for her dads, a jar of Brimstone Barbeque Sauce for Luke, a homemade lemon pound cake for June, and a copy of *The History of Sultry Springs* for herself.

"Traffic" had picked up a bit in her absence, with four cars and two pickup trucks idling at the only red light on Main Street, and about two dozen clerical workers from the courthouse had filed out in search of lunch offerings. Bobbi wasn't hungry, but an iced mocha latte sounded good, so she headed to the coffee shop and took a seat at one of the bistro tables on the sidewalk. She'd just plunked her shopping bags into a nearby chair when she heard a familiar voice from behind.

"Hey, boss, it's that lady with the hot legs."

"Shh!" an even more familiar voice scolded. "Girls don't like hearing stuff like that."

"Why not?"

"You gotta pretend to like 'em for their personality."

Bobbi turned and glared at her new friend—the one she couldn't allow herself to touch. "Actually," she told the boy at Trey's side, "it's because women are more than just pretty faces or nice legs or big breasts. They're more than the sum of their parts. They're *people* with feelings and ideas, and they want to be respected. You remember that, and—"

"—and," Trey interrupted, "you'll score like Michael Jordan." After a moment of thought, he added, "But remember to keep it wrapped."

Bobbi balled her fists against her hips. "Don't teach him stuff like that!"

"Safe sex?"

"No! The scoring part."

"He knows I'm kidding." Trey ruffled the boy's hair and asked him, "What've I told you about the ladies?"

"Leave 'em be," Carlo said with conviction. "'Cause you can't get your hand pregnant." He pursed his lips for a second. "I guess your hand won't give ya an STD, either."

"Smart kid," Trey said to her, nodding at his young apprentice.

While she stewed in silence, Trey slid an appreciative gaze over her body, starting at her sleeveless blouse and ending at the tips of her four-inch, peep-toe heels. A slow grin lifted the corners of his mouth and brought both dimples out to play, leaving behind a pool of tingly heat low in Bobbi's abdomen. She glanced away from his stunning face, but the sight of his broad shoulders and the steely contours of his chest didn't help matters. Maybe they needed to be friends who didn't look *or* touch. Hell, who was she kidding? They couldn't be friends at all.

"Well, um." She glanced at his boots. At least those were safe. "I don't want to keep you."

"It's cool." Carlo shoved both hands in the back pockets of the jeans she'd seen Trey give him a couple of weeks ago. "We're just pickin' up some—"

"Nah, Gopher," Trey said. "*I don't wanna keep you* is code. It really means 'leave me alone.' Let's give Miss Gallagher some peace."

The boy's face fell, and Bobbi felt it like a kick to the stomach. "No," she objected, gesturing to the two free chairs at her table, "I'd like you to stay." She leaned forward and told Carlo, "You can't listen to everything Mr. Lewis says. He was raised by wolves."

"Werewolves, actually." Trey didn't waste any time taking a seat. "You order yet?"

Bobbi shook her head. "I'm just having an iced—"

"—mocha latte. Got it." He leaned forward to grab his wallet and handed Carlo a few bills. "Order the lady's drink, and get whatever you want. I'll have a Coke." After mini-Trey loped into the café, his mentor began rifling through Bobbi's bags. "Did some shopping, huh? Nice hats. Didn't take you for a Stetson girl."

"They're for my dads." She smacked his hand away.

"Did you just touch me, Bo Peep? I feel so violated right now." He waggled his blond brows. "Does this mean I get to touch you back?"

His sinful expression stole her breath. God, his eyes were so blue—even more so outdoors, like the color of Saint John's Bay in the Caribbean. When he looked at her like this, all wicked and full of mischief, her heart quivered almost painfully. In all honesty, she could see herself falling for this man if she wasn't careful. Maybe it was time to get serious about matching him with the perfect country girl, even if only for the summer.

Those cerulean eyes darkened, scanning her face as if searching for something he'd lost. "I was just kidding. I wouldn't do anything you don't want me to. You know that, right?"

"Of course. Sorry. I zoned out for a second." The urge to scratch her nose was so strong she had to sit on her hand to tame it.

"Good. You scared me for a minute." He leaned back, crossing his long legs at the ankles. "How'd it go with the judge? You met with him this morning, right?"

"Yep. The show will go on."

"Great. Speed-dating, can't wait." Trey's flat tone contradicted his words.

"Not tonight. We're going to the church barbeque instead."

That didn't seem to ring his bell either. "What'd the judge want? He didn't find out about that crazy shit at the club, did he?"

"No, thank God." She brought one hand to her heart. "Or thank Colton." Irritating man-child or not, he'd really saved her bacon that night.

Trey muttered something she couldn't quite interpret.

"Anyway, Bea ran a background check on me and wanted to clear up some things."

"Like what?" When a few seconds passed without reply, he used the toe of his boot to nudge her ankle and tempted her with another quid pro quo. "C'mon, Bo. I'll show you mine if you show me yours."

"Maybe I don't want to see yours." They both knew she was full of it, as the Cheshire grin on Trey's dimpled cheeks attested. After pretending to think it over, she said, "Okay, but you have to tell me the *real* reason you took the contracting job."

"Deal." He said it without hesitation, and Bobbi couldn't help envying the ease with which he laid himself bare. Trusting her with his flaws, as Bea had said. Even having just spilled her guts an hour earlier, it took a few tries to get her words flowing again.

But she did. She told him everything, and he didn't judge or scoff or belittle—he just listened, nodding encouragingly and gazing at her in a way that made her feel supported instead of pitied. By the time she finished, she felt ten pounds lighter.

"So this source," Trey asked, "were you involved with him?"

Bobbi considered a moment. "Not really."

"There's no such thing. Either you were, or you weren't."

"We weren't, but I wanted to be." Unable to sit on her hands any longer, she reached up to scratch her nose. "We were in the same journalism program at UCLA, but we didn't hang out in the same circles, know what I mean?"

"Sure."

"He knew I'd always had a crush on him—it's not like it was some big secret—but it wasn't weird between us. We kept in touch after graduation and worked together on a few projects, so when he came to me with this story, it didn't raise any red flags." Looking back, she could see how Derek had used her own feelings against her, how he must've known she'd gobble up his lies like chocolate-covered cherries if it meant earning his respect…and a moment in his arms. "Anyway, he's not a bad guy—"

"Whoa." Lurching forward, Trey jabbed his index finger at her. "Don't you dare defend that little prick!"

"He had good intentions."

"Bullshit! If his intentions were so pure, he would've filmed the thing himself and ruined his own career instead of manipulating you into doing his dirty work." Trey raked a furious gaze over her from head to toe, shaking his head at her naiveté. "And let me guess— because you kept his name out of it, nothing happened to the bastard, right?"

Bobbi glanced down at her skirt, seeing Derek's tear-streaked face instead of zebra-striped cotton. "Not officially, but he felt awful. He took off for a sabbatical in—"

"Jesus, Bo, you're doing it again." Trey scooted his chair closer and used his thumb to gently raise her chin. His eyes softened. "This guy was no idiot. He knew what he was doing, and he doesn't deserve your loyalty." Cupping her face, he used that same rough thumb to stroke her cheek, and Bobbi couldn't bring herself to push him away this time. "What's his name?"

She hesitated. Despite what'd happened, she'd promised him anonymity. Bobbi wanted to hold onto what little journalistic credibility she had left. "I can't tell you."

"Then how am I supposed to track him down and beat his ass?" A teasing smile flitted across his mouth. "C'mon, he's a criminal."

"Doesn't matter." She leaned half a fraction into his palm, much more than she should've done. Funny how the touch she'd once considered brutish now seemed so strong and comforting. She shouldn't crave it, but she did all the same. "A confidential source is—"

"Horseshit, that's what it is." With an eye roll, he released her cheek and took her hand in the barest grasp, just skin brushing skin. "Go on and keep his secrets if you like playing the martyr, but I wanna hear you say he's a dick."

She scrunched her forehead, not quite sure where this was going. "He's a dick?"

"Yeah, but say it with feeling."

She glanced over her shoulders to make sure no kids or nuns were within earshot. "He's a dick."

"Weak." He discarded her hand with a critical wave. "You sound like his doormat, but hey, maybe you're into that."

"I'm not a doormat."

"Then stop standing up for the asshole who tanked your career and buried you in debt."

"Fine." Bobbi's pulse rushed. It'd been a long time since she'd allowed herself to dwell on what'd happened, because the damage was done. Nothing could be gained from playing the woulda-coulda-shoulda game. But she couldn't believe how good it felt to say, "His first name's Derek, and he used me, and he's a total dick."

"Nice." Nodding in approval, Trey folded his arms.

"I'll just have to knock the bejeezus out of every man named Derek till you tell me his last name."

A giggle worked its way free from her throat. "No dice. I shouldn't have told you his gender, let alone his first name. What is it about you that sucks all the professionalism right out of me?"

"I dunno." Heat flickered behind his eyes like a match striking flint. "Want me to suck you somewhere else?"

"Absolutely not," she lied, then closed the subject. "Okay, your turn. Why's it so important to clear your record? Looks like you're doing fine to me."

He shrugged one broad shoulder. "An OTH isn't as serious as a dishonorable discharge. You get one of those, and you'll spend the rest of your life asking folks if they want fries with that. But it's still a mark on my record, and it's something employers look at. Then they start asking questions, and I have to explain why I decked an officer. Sometimes they believe me, but most of the time they don't."

"Why'd you hit him?"

"Because he was screwing my best friend's wife."

"Oh." She'd heard about Luke's first wife, but not much. Only enough to know it was a short and miserable marriage. "But you have a stable job, right?"

"Sure, but I want more than just a stable job. I want a career, maybe my own business. Then there's my family." Trey wrinkled his nose like he smelled something foul. "That's a whole separate disaster. How much you wanna hear?"

"Hey, I showed you mine, so..." She tipped her head to drive the point home.

"All right. This won't be pretty."

And it wasn't. The more Trey revealed about his family, the less "pretty" it sounded. On the surface, Trey'd had the kind of upbringing she'd ordinarily envy—the only child of an upper class family, with a well-respected father and an old-school domestic goddess for a mom. But there was no soft marshmallow center when it came to the Lewises. If Trey's parents were a candy bar, they'd be filled with sterling—shiny on the outside, but hard enough to break a tooth on the inside.

She was still shaking her head when Carlo strode to the table with a cardboard cup holder in one hand and a Chernobyl-sized chocolate chip muffin in the other. She took the drinks from him while he plopped into the empty chair.

"So," she asked Trey, pausing to take a sip of sweet iced coffee, "your dad's talking to you now? You think you can salvage that relationship?"

Trey laughed—darkly at first, then in deep chuckles that shook his chest. "No. Not after what he did to my mom." She'd just opened her mouth to ask him to elaborate when Trey cut her off with an impish wink. "You'll have to strip down and bare something new if you wanna hear that story."

"Hey," Carlo objected around a mouthful of muffin. "I thought you said she wasn't your girl."

Trey paused, fingers clenched around a plastic Coke bottle while his cheeks flushed. "She's not."

"Looks like it." Carlo threw an accusing glance at his boss. "You said ladies were trouble."

"That's right, I did." Trey lifted his bottle toward Bobbi in an abrupt farewell. "Which is why we're gonna leave Miss Gallagher alone and get back to work."

The weight of disappointment tugged at Bobbi's stomach, but Trey was right. Heck, Carlo was right too. The fact that she didn't want them to go meant she'd wandered into dangerous territory, land mines and booby traps and all. Whatever she and Trey had—label it chemistry, infatuation, or friendship—was bad news.

"I should get to work too." Bobbi stood and gathered her shopping bags, then bent low to bring herself eye level with Carlo. "I'm so glad I ran into you, though."

The boy wasn't listening. It appeared he'd chosen to gaze down the front of her blouse instead. His brown eyes widened, brows disappearing beneath shaggy hair, while his lips parted in awe.

"Whoa," he breathed.

Oh, brother. Like mentor, like pupil. And they had the nerve to call *her* trouble.

Chapter 9

BELIEVE IT OR NOT, BOBBI HAD NEVER SET FOOT INSIDE a traditional church. Sure, she'd tagged along with a friend once or twice to a hippy-dippy, new age service in an elementary school cafeteria, but that didn't count. It was nothing like the Holy Baptism by Hellfire Church, a gleaming, white clapboard building with arched stained glass windows and a majestic steeple stretching toward the heavens.

Bobbi's mama hadn't exposed her to religion, unless you counted repeatedly screaming *God, yes!* from the bedroom, and her dads had always described themselves as "spiritual, but not religious," whatever that meant. Growing up, they'd spent Sunday mornings sleeping in and enjoying Papa's banana-walnut pancakes with no prayers of thanks to God, Allah, Buddha, or the like. And because her friends—well, the people she used to consider friends—were so young, none of them had married yet, not that anyone in her circle would opt for a wedding officiated on hallowed ground. A sunset ceremony on the beach was more their style.

Beneath a mammoth, white tent on the vacant lot behind the church, at least a hundred God-fearing tee-totalers swilled Kool-Aid instead of beer, while beef barbeque broiled on an industrial-sized grill near the parking lot. Clearly, the action was out here—including half of Sultry Springs, her star bachelors, the crew, and two freelance cinematographers she'd hired for the occasion—but Bobbi couldn't stop darting glances at the vacant building to her left. For reasons she couldn't understand, she wanted to wander inside and explore the halls, touch the glossy wooden furniture, see what she'd missed all those years…if anything.

Maybe she could slip inside for a few minutes. Surely no one would mind. She stood on tiptoe and spotted Judge Bea and Pru chatting with a portly, bald man who'd introduced himself earlier as "Pastor Mac." Based on the judge's relaxed posture, he wasn't ready to pop the question any time soon. Even if Bobbi missed it, she'd given the crew detailed instructions on what to do—focus one camera on the happy couple, the others on Colt and Trey's reactions. A tiny needle of doubt pricked at the back of her mind. Bong and Weezus followed directions without fail, but she didn't know much about the freelancers, beyond their hourly rates. Best to follow up with them one last time before making her escape, then keep it brief—in and out.

She skirted around the crowd and found Colton leaning against a cedar tree about ten yards from the festivities. Instead of sweet-talking some young Baptist out of her panties, he stared at the clipped grass, arms folded, body tensed in a way that told everyone to leave him the hell alone, including Ron, the hired cameraman hanging by idly.

"Hey," she said, glancing between them and gesturing toward the tent. "The party's over there."

Ron raised one shoulder in a defensive shrug. "I tried getting him to mingle, but—"

"Not happening." Colton lifted his chin and stared

blankly into the congregation. Though barely audible, his voice was harder and colder than a glacier. "You're lucky I'm even here."

Whoa. What'd happened to her carefree skirt-chaser? Bobbi didn't know what was eating him, but her instincts told her not to nag. "Okay, no pressure. Just do what feels right." She turned to Ron and gave him a pointed look. "Remember what I said before?"

"Yep."

"Keep the camera rolling. I'd rather cut an hour of footage than miss the big moment."

Ron nodded with the signature tight-lipped grin of a man unaccustomed to taking commands from a woman. She didn't give a damn if Ron silently cursed her as long as he captured Colt's expression when his grandpa proposed to Pru. She had a feeling Colt wouldn't jump for joy at the news, and she planned to follow up with a quick, casual interview to tie in his pessimistic views on commitment.

She left them and went in search of bachelor number two, which didn't take long. All she had to do was follow the sound of obnoxious female giggling. Bobbi grabbed a plastic cup and filled it with cherry Kool-Aid while observing Trey, who sat atop a wooden picnic table with his booted feet resting on the bench. He'd dressed for the occasion in khakis and a turquoise button-down shirt the exact shade of his smiling eyes. At least six young women—including Bobbi's second freelancer, a busty blonde nearly as tall as Trey—hovered close by, each taking turns laughing at his jokes and vying for his attention. This should have made her happy, so why did she have the sudden urge to break something…like half a dozen pretty faces?

The camerawoman, whose name suddenly eluded Bobbi, tipped her head back in laughter, bringing one hand to her breast and resting the other on Trey's forearm, where she slipped her fuchsia nails beneath his rolled-up shirtsleeve. Bobbi's ribs tightened and her cheeks flushed red hot. Oh, hell no. She did *not* shell out hundreds of bucks for the idiot to hang all over Trey like this. Sticky liquid sloshed against her fingers as she slammed the cup beside the punch bowl. Shaking her dripping hand into the grass, she stalked toward her subject and his fan club.

Trey's eyes lifted and locked with Bobbi's, and his face illuminated so dramatically you'd think she'd flipped a light switch inside his head. His smile widened, gaze brightened, dimples deepened, and for a long, foggy second, she forgot why she'd charged over here in the first place. She stood entranced, struck dumb by the heat muddling her brain. Fortunately, the blonde at her side cleared her throat and broke the spell.

Bobbi whirled toward her, hands clenching into fists. "Taking a smoke break?"

"I don't smoke." Charlotte—yes, that was her name—smirked and quirked one pencil-darkened brow.

Channeling all her frustration into a laser beam glare, Bobbi stepped close enough to pick out the freckles half-concealed beneath Charlotte's makeup. Her voice dripped icicles when she said, "Then the break's over, isn't it?"

That wiped the smug grin off Charlotte's lips. She backed away and retrieved her camera from behind Trey's ass.

"I'm going inside for a minute," Bobbi said. "I want

that camera rolling and on his face," she pointed in Trey's direction without risking a glance at him, "the whole time. *Capisce*?"

Charlotte gave a tight nod, much like that of her misogynistic counterpart, and Bobbi turned on her heel and marched away before she said something she'd regret later. She strode toward the back door, acknowledging June and Luke with a waggle of her fingers as she passed them and kept going. The inside of her chest felt like an overwound clock, propelling her limbs faster and faster until she grasped the door handle and threw it open, charging inside.

She paced around the dim lobby for a few minutes, burning off anxiety like diesel fuel. When her pulse began to slow, she stilled her feet and took in her surroundings. Rolling her shoulders, she pulled in a deep, cleansing breath, noting the pleasing scent of Lemon Pledge. She tipped her head, listening for voices or movement, but heard nothing aside from the distant hum of a fan and forced air through the vents. The lobby held little of interest, just a bulletin board adorned with handmade flyers, a table displaying pamphlets, and several folding chairs, so she crept toward the heart of the building to the sanctuary doors.

With her fingertips pressed lightly against the cool oak, Bobbi hesitated, unsure of what to expect beyond this threshold. Would she sense a holy presence? Find comfort here? Experience a life-changing epiphany? She wasn't even sure if she believed in all that. For no discernible reason, her heartbeat quickened and she nearly turned and walked away. Just as she took a step back, someone pushed open the main door, and she spun around to find Trey squinting at her in the darkness.

"You okay?" he whispered.

"Yeah," she whispered back. "What're you doing here?"

"I could ask you the same question. I'm checking on you…but why are we whispering?"

She let out a nervous laugh as he clunked over to her in his Timberlands. After glancing up and down the vacant hall, he asked, "You lookin' to confess your sins, or commit some more? 'Cause I can help you with the second one."

"Neither."

"Then what?"

She bit her bottom lip and dropped her gaze to the hem of his khakis. "You'll think it's weird."

"Hey." Using one finger, he lifted her chin, then promptly pulled away and observed the no touching rule. "You *are* weird, but that's what I like about you. What's up?"

"Promise you won't laugh?"

Raising one hand, he mimicked the oath she'd made yesterday. "Scout's honor."

"I've never been inside a church before, and I wanted to see what it's like."

"Never?" His voice rose an octave. "Didn't they have a funeral for your mom?"

She shoved her hands into the back pockets of her jeans. "No. There was no one around to organize it. Her next of kin told the state to cremate her body. They asked if I wanted the ashes, but…" Shaking her head, she trailed off with a shiver.

"Well, I'm sorry it played out like that. You probably could've used some closure."

"Oh, I got it. In spades. The courts made me go to therapy, paint pictures, write good-bye letters, stupid stuff like that. I guess it helped, but I didn't like it at the time. I wasn't very cooperative."

Trey flashed a sarcastic smile. "You don't say."

"Don't look at me like that." She gave him a playful nudge with her elbow. "I'm not hard to get along with."

"Tell that to what's-her-name, the camera lady pouting outside. She turned ten shades of red after you tore her a new o-ring."

"Yeah, well, she deserved it. I didn't hire her to feel you up."

That elicited a mock gasp. "Jealous, Bo Peep?"

"You wish." Jealousy had nothing to do with it. Bobbi expected a certain level of professionalism from her crew, and Charlotte hadn't delivered. That was it, nothing more.

With raised brows, he inclined his head as if to say *Yep, I do wish*. He reached for the small of her back, but thought better of it. "Oops, almost touched you." Withdrawing his hand, he pushed open the door to the sanctuary, gesturing for her to step inside. "Ladies first."

"They won't get mad?"

"If they do, I'll take the blame. Those sweet little church ladies love me."

Bobbi didn't doubt it. So far, she couldn't think of anyone in Sultry Springs who didn't love Trey's easy smile and his deceptively innocent, dimpled cheeks. They had no idea how devilishly he behaved in the dark or how wickedly he could use his hands to turn a *no* into a *yes!* in under ten seconds. Come to think of it, maybe sneaking in here with him wasn't the best plan.

"Go on." With a gentle shove, he made the decision for her, then followed inside and let the door whisper shut behind him. "There's a light switch somewhere around here…" He groped the wall until he found what he was looking for and flipped on one dim row of bulbs above the pulpit. "This is it." Hands on his hips, Trey scanned the sanctuary along with her.

The room was smaller than she'd expected, and it didn't look anything like the lavish churches she'd seen portrayed on TV, with their two-story ceilings, linen-draped altars adorned with golden goblets, and faces of saints carved into the stone walls. Instead, this space felt simple, but in a good way, like a lone wildflower hand-picked by a child compared to a regal orchid in a florist's shop. The soft glow emanating from above the pulpit revealed three rows of glossy pews, and Bobbi could almost feel the polished wood against her bottom. She imagined how the fabric of her jeans would slip and slide over the seat, and a sudden urge to experience the sensation urged her forward.

"Let's sit for a minute," she told Trey, who didn't object.

Much like her visits to the movie theater, she deliberated until she eventually settled on a creaky pew in the middle-most spot. She scooted back and forth a few times to see if the seat was as slick as she'd thought. Her jeans clung to the bench, which disappointed her for some strange reason.

"So," Trey said, studying her with a mixture of amusement and confusion, "was it everything you dreamed of and more?"

She ignored his question. "You attend services here?"

"Hell, no." He laughed, gripping his thigh and

lowering onto the bench beside her. "I've only been here for a couple of weddings. Do I strike you as a church-going kinda guy?"

Leaning away, she made a show of appraising him, though she already knew the answer. "Guess not."

"I'm no missionary," he murmured with an evil gleam in his gaze, "but I can make you see God."

Bobbi rolled her eyes and tried to contain a snicker. "So far, we've got," she said as she ticked items off on her fingers, "see God, see stars, and forget how to breathe. You make some lofty promises, Golden Boy."

"Sure." He reached one arm behind her and rested it along the seat back. "But I deliver."

"Sure you do."

Leaning in close enough for her to feel the warmth rolling off his body, he whispered, "Oh, ye of little faith." Then, poising his lips a hairsbreadth from her ear, added, "Try me. But I'd have to touch you. You just say the word, and I'll give you a laying on of hands that'll have you speaking in tongues."

Refusing to shut her eyes and lean into him like her body begged her to, she scooted an inch in the other direction. "You're as bad as Colton." Which gave her an opportunity to change the subject. "And speaking of, he's in a shitty mood tonight. What's his deal?"

"Ah, that would be the pastor's daughter. They had a thing in high school, and he never got over it. I guess being here stirs up too many old memories."

"No way." That didn't sound like the Colton she knew, who probably didn't recall the names of half the women he'd screwed. "You mean he actually has a heart?"

"Of course." Trey delivered a look that shamed

her. "He might be a jackass, but he bleeds just like everyone else."

After her guilt died down, she asked, "So, what happened?"

"I dunno. That was before my time in Sultry Springs. She left town, and he doesn't like to talk about it."

That explained Colt's promiscuity—better to sleep with a different woman every night than to risk his feelings again by getting attached. The pastor's daughter must've done a real number on Colt. Maybe Luke knew the story. She made a mental note to ask him later, then turned her gaze to the rear of the sanctuary.

"Where's the confessional?" she asked. "And shouldn't there be more candles?"

"Unh-uh." Trey shook his head. "That's a Catholic thing. Same goes for holy water."

"Oh." Now she felt stupid for asking.

"But you can confess to me," Trey said with a light nudge. "Ready to tell me why you wanted to come in here so badly?"

Bobbi reached forward and plucked a hymnal from the shelf attached to the back of the next pew. Absently, she flipped through, pretending to scan the song selection.

"C'mon," he encouraged.

She had to consider his request awhile, because honestly, she didn't know the answer. Maybe it had something to do with her dysfunctional home, gazing out the window at other kids dressed in their Sunday best—even if it was only jeans and a faded polo shirt— while she sat alone in front of the television with nothing but a box of Cheerios to keep her company. Or maybe she'd reached a point in her life where she'd started to question her beliefs. Didn't that happen to everyone in their twenties?

"Okay," she decided. "But you confess to me first. What's going on with your parents?"

"You drive a hard bargain."

"Whatever." She smoothed one finger over the hymnal's gold embossing. "You open up easier than a flower at sunrise."

"Not for everyone." He took the volume from her hand and set it beside him. "I haven't even told Luke about this."

Shifting on the bench, she met his gaze. "Why not?"

"My mom's always hated Luke, and she's made no secret about it. She blames him for the discharge." He shrugged. "So it's not like he's gonna care that my dad's putting her through the wringer."

"I'm sure that's not true. If he's a good friend, he'll care about her for your sake." Of course, she didn't know her own brother well enough to judge his capacity as a friend, which didn't say much about her capacity as a sister. "What's your dad doing?"

"The short answer? Dumping my mom after she stayed with his cheating ass for thirty years."

"Ouch."

"You're not kiddin'. He'd always messed around—I overheard one of their fights when I was in junior high—but just a bunch of flings when he was stationed away from home. Never a long-term mistress or anything like that. Till now."

"Let me guess—he's replacing your mom with a newer model?" Bobbi remembered a conversation she'd had with Trey a couple of weeks ago, when he'd said all his girlfriends had cheated. Add his father's infidelity to the mix, and it was no wonder he believed monogamy was unnatural.

"Yeah, he wants to marry some thirty-year-old he met last winter. But my mom won't let him go. She's dragging out the divorce, probably hoping he'll change his mind before it's final. I keep trying to convince her to start fresh, but she won't listen, just keeps calling every single morning to bitch about what an asshole my dad is. As if I don't already know."

"She shouldn't be putting you in the middle."

"Yeah, but she's too embarrassed to talk about this stuff with her friends, so if it makes her feel better to dump it on me, I can take it...most days." He flashed half a grin. "Lately, I've been letting her vent on my answering machine."

Bobbi broke her own rule, reaching up to pat Trey's shoulder. "I'm sorry."

He trapped her hand with his own, then brought it to rest against his muscular thigh while he toyed with her fingers. "It's for the best, even if Mom can't see that right now. Life's too short to waste one minute on a bastard like the Colonel." He pulled a deep breath through his nose and exhaled in a huff. "But enough of my dirty laundry. It's your turn."

"Already?"

"Spill the deets, Bo Peep."

Leaning back against the solid wood, Bobbi relaxed her fingers and didn't object when Trey laced his in-between. His grasp was too warm and comforting to resist, and besides, it didn't get much more chaste than hand-holding inside a church sanctuary. She was totally safe…as safe as any woman could be in Trey's hypnotic presence.

So, why *had* she insisted on exploring the church? "Curiosity aside, I think it had something to do with this little girl who lived in my old apartment building. Her name was Nina."

"A kid?" Trey asked, not following her logic. "Did she try to convert you, or something?"

"No. Just listen."

"Sorry." He nodded for her to continue.

"I'd knock on her door all the time to ask if she could come over, but her mom always had some excuse to say no, and she never invited me in." Looking back, Bobbi couldn't blame Nina's mother. What kind of parent let her kids roam the halls of a slum or hang out in a druggie's apartment? "Anyway, it was just Nina and her mom—her dad wasn't in the picture—but every Sunday, her grandpa picked them up in his blue minivan, and they'd all go to church together. They were broke, everyone in that complex was, but they still looked nice in their Sunday clothes. Nina had these glossy, white gloves and a tiny Bible the size of half a sandwich. She'd hold her mom's hand, and they always looked so happy together."

"Unlike you and your mother."

"Exactly. So I think somewhere in the back of my mind, I associated church with happy families, and I wanted to see what I'd been missing." Bobbi's chest felt heavy, and she released a breath. "You know, Nina's mom never let us play together, not even one time."

"Well, that wasn't very Christian of her." Trey

wrapped his arm around her shoulders and pulled her close, placing a kiss atop her head. She pressed her cheek to the side of his stone chest and gave herself permission to savor the hug, just for a moment. Closing her eyes, she squeezed their linked fingers together and inhaled him—warm and woodsy and masculine. His body shook with stifled laughter, his voice husky. "I'll play with you any time you want, and you don't need my mama's permission."

A wide smile spread across her mouth as she pushed him away, freed her hand, and regained a few cool inches of distance. "No, thanks. You don't play fair."

"This is true."

Bobbi chafed her palms against her upper arms, feeling suddenly chilled after leaving Trey's heated embrace. The man was like a furnace. Figuring they should leave soon, she swept one last gaze over the pulpit, imagining the pastor gripping its edges, delivering a message of hope or comfort.

"You know," she said, "it's so peaceful in here. I wonder what the services are like."

A deep, tight voice from behind answered, "Long and boring."

Gasping loudly, Bobbi jerked around to find Luke glaring at Trey in a way that raised the hair on the back of her neck. She brought a hand over her pounding heart and wondered how long he'd been standing there. "What's your problem? Don't sneak up on me like that!"

"I didn't sneak. I opened the door and walked right in." Luke spoke to her, but never took his eyes off Trey, who maintained a cool expression despite the tension expanding his already broad chest. The two locked eyes in charged silence, communicating something she wasn't privy to. "You were too distracted to hear me," Luke said darkly. Then he turned his cold stare on her. "Bea's lookin' for you. Says 'it's time,' whatever that means."

"Oh!" Instantly forgetting Luke, she grabbed Trey's forearm. "Let's go. Hurry!"

Without giving either man time to ask why, she pushed past them and darted outside. When Trey caught up, she clutched his wrist and towed him over to Colton, who'd moved beneath the white tent to hear Judge Bea's speech, already in progress. All the attendees had gathered around, Dixie cups in hand, held in rapt attention as Bea spun a tale of meeting Pru for the first time when he'd rear-ended her car at a stoplight.

Bobbi had cut it close—seriously close—but at least Ron had followed instructions and kept the camera trained on Colt's face. Signaling for Ron to get Trey in the shot too, she stepped back and studied Pru's beaming countenance, her blue eyes alight in the darkness, wrinkles playing across her cheekbones as she smiled at her beau. That was the face of a woman in love—and one who knew a proposal was underway. Apparently, her soon-to-be fiancé wasn't very good at keeping secrets.

"So, anyhoo," Bea said with a dismissive wave, "it might'a taken a few decades, but she finally warmed up to me, and we became friends. And when my Martha passed..." Softly, he gazed at Pru and cleared the thickness from his throat. "Well, Prudence wouldn't let me fold up 'n' wallow in bed all day. She kicked my bony ass—" raising bushy, white brows, he turned and apologized to the pastor "—uh, hauled me outta bed, forced me back into the world of the livin', and

gave me a reason to wake up every mornin' after that."
Holding his chair in support, he lowered to one knee as
the crowd gasped in delight and broke out in excited
whispers. "Prudence, I dunno how many more years the
Good Lord's gonna give me, but I wanna spend 'em all
with you. Will you marry this crazy old man?"

Pru didn't hesitate to say, "Yes," holding out her
oversized right hand for Bea's ring as her late husband's
band remained on the left. Bobbi felt a tiny prickling of
envy for the couple. What were the odds of finding true
love twice in a lifetime, like they'd done?

In that moment, she couldn't deny wanting what Pru
and Bea had. What her dads had too—someone to watch
her with warm eyes and a soft smile from the other side
of the room, someone who thought her flaws were sweet
and quirky instead of annoying. She wanted a man to
look at her the way Luke gazed at June, so thick with
worship it forced her to avert her eyes every time. Too
bad all the good guys were taken. Or gay. Releasing a
quiet sigh, she searched for June and Luke in the crowd.

June grinned through streaming tears as her husband
held her tightly from behind, resting his chin atop her
head. That tiny prickling of envy surged inside Bobbi's
breast, and she had to shift her glance to Trey and Colton.
It appeared they understood her pain. Both had shoved
their hands into their pockets, toeing the dirt with their
boot tips, clearly conflicted and questioning their life
choices, though neither man would ever admit to it.

Colt was the first to break the silence in their sad little
group. "Well, I'm happy for the poor, old bastard." He
gave a begrudging shrug. "If he wants to spend his golden
years tied down like that, I'm not gonna talk him out of it."

Nodding in agreement, Trey added, "Bet he doesn't realize this'll cut back on his fishin' time. He'll have to get permission from the ball-n-chain now."

"Right," Colt said. "Tag along to Bible study and shit like that."

"Better him than me."

"You said it, man. I'm not throwin' away my freedom for any woman."

"Never works out anyway."

Bobbi held her tongue, but she couldn't help thinking the gentlemen didst protest too much. After casting one final, longing gaze at Sultry County's newest betrothed, she turned to Ron, ready to shut down filming for the night. To her surprise, he'd fixed his lens directly on her.

She rushed over to him and held up one hand to block the shot. "What're you doing?"

"You should've seen the look on your face," Ron said from behind his camera. Switching off, he lowered the equipment to the ground before massaging his shoulder. "If raw emotion's what you're going for, then—"

"I didn't hire you to film me."

"Hey." He flashed his palm. "I saw an awesome shot, and I took it. No biggie. Just cut what you don't want to use, but at least have a look before you decide."

The decision was already made. Bobbi knew what Ron had captured on film, and she had no interest in seeing her own loneliness and regret reflected back in crisp, digital display. She told him to find Weezus to transfer the film data, then paid him and sent him on his way, swearing never again to trust a freelancer. If she wanted something done right, she'd have to do it herself.

Story of her whole friggin' life.

Chapter 10

IT WAS THE FOURTH OF JULY AND HOTTER THAN Satan's ball sack. A relentless sun ruled the sky, ravaging parade-goers with its nuclear rays and wilting even the most energetic children into their lawn chairs, where they waved pint-sized American flags with all the enthusiasm of the undead. Trey lifted one shoulder to wipe a bead of sweat from his cheek, but two instantly formed in its place, convincing him to give up the fight. So much for the mild summer they'd enjoyed for the past month. And though you couldn't tell from the clear, blue sky, another storm system was rolling in, causing Trey's femur to flare like brushfire.

The unnaturally red hotdog he'd just bought would probably tear up his chest when heartburn kicked in, but he crammed half of it into his mouth anyway. Tart mustard crossed his tongue, followed by the salty, smoky flavor of one hundred percent pure beef byproducts. He closed his eyes to savor it—the taste of summer in the good ol' US of A. Could a guy even get a hotdog in Dubai? He honestly didn't know.

Oppressive heat, earsplitting bottle rockets, greasy food, and warm beer. Trey slouched. He was going to miss all this.

Clutching his thigh, he lowered carefully and settled on the curb, stretching his legs into the street five feet from the marching band, who'd been playing "Louie,

Louie" on a continuous loop for fifteen minutes. A pair of long, tanned legs strode into view to his right, attached to white flip-flops, and even though Trey knew every inch of those gams, he traced their smooth curves with his gaze, starting with Bobbi's slender ankles and ending at her succulent thighs. Sweet Jesus, he was going to miss those too.

She crouched beside him, using a stick to lift a half-shriveled earthworm from the sidewalk to the shaded grass. Despite the pain in Trey's bones clamoring for attention, a smile lifted the edges of his mouth. He'd never seen anyone attempt to rescue a creepy-crawly before. "You're just prolonging the inevitable." That worm was a goner.

"We'll see." She opened his cooler and reached inside, then cupped a palm full of melted ice and sprinkled it over the creature's parched carcass. Wiping her damp hand on her denim shorty-shorts, she joined him on the curb. "They're resilient."

"Like someone else I know." A woman who'd over-come a childhood filled with neglect, but hadn't allowed it to harden her—she had a warm heart and a touch that made his blood simmer. He'd sure like to lay her in the grass and drizzle ice water over her body, and it must've shown on his face, because she held up one finger in warning.

"Don't look at me like that. I want you to look at Sarah like that."

"Who's Sarah?"

Scoffing, she recoiled as if horrified. "The girl you liked from speed-dating!"

"Oh, the one with the cute little nose? I didn't say I liked her. I said she wasn't too bad."

"Well, she's right over there," Bobbi said as she pointed across the street to a spot he couldn't see through the crowd, "waiting for you, and I want results this time."

He shot her a questioning glance, squeezing his aching thigh between his thumb and forefinger.

"Colton's giving me all kinds of great material," she explained, "but I'm getting nothing from you." Tiny lines wrinkled her forehead, and she bit out the next words quickly. "Just do me a favor, and get to first base tonight." Dropping her gaze, she added, "On camera, or it doesn't count."

Something about her request pissed him off. Maybe it was the casual way she'd demanded he kiss another woman when the lips he wanted to feel against his own were the pink pair currently pouting in front of him. "That's really what you want?"

She danced around his question. "It's like you're not even trying."

Right, because he wasn't. The only woman in Sultry Springs who raised Trey's flag these days was the one person he couldn't have.

Luke had sensed it. After busting Trey in the sanctuary with his arm around Bobbi, Luke had pulled him aside and delivered a stern warning. *Back off. There're hundreds of hot chicks in the county, and you can have any one you want. Just not my sister.* But the problem was Trey didn't want anyone else. Asking him to pursue Sarah was like giving a kid a taste of German chocolate and then forcing him to feast on Brussels sprouts. He'd tasted Bobbi's sweetness, and it'd left him wanting more.

He observed her closely when he conceded, "Fine. And since I haven't been trying, I'll make up for it tonight. I'll show you a kiss so hot it'll melt your camera."

Her jaw clenched tight enough to crack her face in half like an egg, and she gave a silent nod. It was all Trey needed to know she wanted him too. A warm sense of satisfaction settled deep in his gut and kicked up its heels. He had no intention of leading Sarah on with a meaningless kiss, but Bo didn't need to know that. Let her stew awhile.

An awkward minute passed before she pointed to his thigh. "What's wrong? I notice you favor that leg sometimes."

"Fell off a roof a couple of years ago and broke it." Among other things, like his ribs, spleen, and pride. "It only bothers me when the pressure changes."

"My God, it's a wonder you survived."

Trey pulled a frosty Bud from his cooler and held it against his thigh. He rolled it back and forth over his tensed muscles, replaying the memory of that day and laughing despite the pain. "You could say I was distracted at the time."

"What happened?"

"Your sister-in-law was hitting on me."

"*What?*" Every muscle in Bobbi's torso seemed to lock, forcing her ramrod straight on the curb. Her head whipped around, and red tendrils of hair slapped her blushing cheeks. "As in June?"

"Yep. *Joooonbug* was servin' hours for a misdemeanor—got busted skinny-dipping with your brother. Anyway, she was cleaning out old Mr. Jenkins's gutters, and I was up there laying shingles. If I remember correctly," which he did, "she wanted to come over to my place and mix up some drinks." He waggled his brows. "To ply me with booze and get lucky."

Bobbi's pretty mouth gaped so widely Trey noticed she still had her wisdom teeth. "I can't believe she wanted *you*." In a flash, she touched his bicep. "I don't mean it like that. It's just, the way she looks at my brother—"

"You're right, Bo Peep." Trey barely had time to pat her hand before she pulled away. "It wasn't me she wanted. That's why I shot her down." Then he'd lost his balance and fallen twenty feet to the hard, unforgiving ground below. It was a miracle he'd walked away with so few injuries. Of course, he hadn't literally walked away—more like ridden via ambulance to Sultry Memorial.

"Oh, I am *so* calling her out on that at supper tonight. I can't wait to see the look on my brother's face."

"Might not wanna do that." Trey glanced at his jeans, now damp from the beer can. Figuring an ice-cold Bud would probably do him more good from the inside, he popped the top and took a deep pull, then wiped his mouth against the back of his hand. "Luke's pretty touchy when it comes to me and the women in his life. He's already riding my ass about getting too close to you."

She chewed on her bottom lip, eventually declaring, "It's none of his business."

"He means well." Besides, common decency said you didn't fool around with a buddy's wife, mom, sister, or ex. Trey'd violated the Bro Code, and he already felt lousy enough without Luke piling on the guilt. "Just leave him be."

"Fine, but can you take something for it?" She nodded at his leg.

Trey had a feeling she wasn't referring to BC Powder. "I can, but I won't."

"Too macho for pain meds?"

"More like too paranoid." After the accident, Trey'd spent two weeks in the hospital pumped full of opiates, feeling all warm and bubbly until the haze wore off. He knew the power of those drugs, and nothing should make a man feel that good unless it had a pair of breasts attached to it. "I've seen too many guys get hooked." Tough guys too, like the old, gritty Veterans of Foreign Wars marching in misaligned formation right in front of him. Life had dealt Trey his fair share of shit, but at least his pain was manageable, unlike some members of his old unit who'd had the misfortune of driving over an IED in Iraq a few years earlier.

From his peripheral vision, he noticed Bobbi watching him instead of the parade. She flicked a few glances between him and the vets and asked, "Does it bother you that you can't march with them?"

Of course it did, every damn year, like an annual reminder of his shame. "No."

"Has anyone ever thanked you for your service?"

What a strange question. He set his hotdog and beer atop his cooler and met her gaze. "Sure." Once, when he'd traveled in uniform from New York to Germany, a flight attendant had taken him into the plane's kitchenette and thanked him with her mouth, quite generously too. But he kept the details of that story to himself. "That was a long time ago, and I was only in the army a couple—"

"Thank you."

"Jesus, Bo, don't do that." He didn't want her pity. Gritting his teeth, he lifted the hem of his T-shirt to blot the sweat from his face. "There's more than enough sunshine out today. I don't need it blown up my ass."

She scooted so close, the tips of her soft breasts brushed his arm. "I think what you meant to say was *you're welcome*." Then, pressing even harder against him, she curled one hand around the back of his neck and kissed him on the cheek, those soft lips brushing the sensitive skin close to his ear and heating his body in a way that had nothing to do with the fierce July sun. Trey hadn't seen it coming, and before he had a chance to fill his lungs with her luscious scent of sweet cinnamon or wrap an arm around her slender waist, she pulled away.

Bringing two fingers against his cheek, he tried to hold on to the sensation while turning to face her. "Wanna thank me again? Maybe in French this time?"

She laughed and pushed to standing. "Save it for Sarah. I'm heading over there to prep her and talk to the crew. Meet me in—" she glanced at her bare wrist "—like fifteen minutes?"

Sarah. At the mention of her name, Trey let out a disappointed breath. Under any other circumstances, he'd jump at the chance to score with the pretty blond, but not now. Now it felt like work. "Do I have to?"

"Yes, and you have to like it. Or fake it really well." Hands on her hips, she scanned him from head to toe. "And wear that straw cowboy hat I saw in your truck last week. It's hot."

"It's all right. I'm used to working outside."

One corner of Bo's mouth lifted in a seductive smirk.

"That's not what I meant." She turned and jogged across the street, just ahead of the Shriners, and Trey shamelessly ogled the rhythmic jiggle of her thighs. God bless America. Watching her sensuous movements had made his pants too snug in the front, so he shifted his gaze— and his junk—to the left and mentally recited the Cubs' starting lineup.

Deciding to wear that battered, old cowboy hat more often, he crammed the rest of his hotdog into his mouth and gathered his cooler and half-empty beer. He checked on Bobbi's worm, happy to see it burrowing into the rich soil, and then he headed across the vacant courthouse parking lot to his Chevy.

He'd just set the cooler in his truck bed when his cell phone vibrated against his left butt cheek. He plucked it from his back pocket and checked the screen. *Dad calling*. The temptation to let it go to voice mail was strong, but Trey couldn't remember the last time his father had initiated a phone call. In the end, curiosity and perhaps a childish need for acceptance won out.

"Hello." Trey kept his voice flat, devoid of all expectations, since this probably wasn't a friendly "Happy Independence Day" kind of call.

The Colonel got right to the point. "Talk to your mother lately?"

A rush of guilt washed over Trey. He'd let all Mom's calls go to voice mail for the last three days. "No, why? Did something happen? Is she okay?"

"Of course she's okay. That woman's got titanium balls."

"Let's hope so, 'cause you've been kickin' her in the babymaker for years."

Dad's voice turned hard enough to crack a diamond. "Don't pretend to know the first thing about my marriage. One of these days, you're gonna push too hard and find out a few things—" he cut off and inhaled loudly through his nose. "Christ. Just mind your own damn business."

"What do you want, Colonel?"

The sarcastic use of the other man's title didn't appear to faze him. "I need you to talk some sense into her. She's being unreasonable."

"Hmm." Trey pretended to consider this request. "I think I'll follow your first order and mind my own damn business." Before his father had a chance to beat him to it, Trey disconnected.

He chugged the rest of his beer and tossed the empty can into his truck bed, then opened his cooler and downed two more. After retrieving the straw cowboy hat Bobbi loved so much, he pulled it low over his eyes and set out to meet the two women waiting for him: one he didn't want, and one he couldn't have.

———

Sarah Divine-Darling—yes, that was her real name, Bobbi checked the birth records—was so disgustingly perfect that Bobbi wondered if cartoon mice dressed the perky dance instructor each morning before transforming into stallions to tow her pumpkin-festooned carriage. Smelling of freshly plucked lavender, Sarah blinked lush, lash-fringed eyes even bluer than Trey's, if such a thing were possible, and at five feet eight inches tall, not an ounce of visible fat existed on her lithe body. She had the thinnest thighs Bobbi had ever seen, and when she glanced at Sarah's delicate feet, she half expected to see them encased in glass slippers. Wouldn't you know it—nude Manolo Blahnik sling-backs paired fabulously with a vintage skirt. Add "great taste in shoes" to Miss Darling's list of virtues.

Despite the acid burning a trail into her throat, Bobbi couldn't hate the girl—she was too freaking nice. Kindergarten teacher nice. Like she spent her free time delivering Meals on Wheels to oozing lepers.

This would be the recipient of Trey's kiss. His hot-enough-to-melt-the-camera kiss. The moment their lips met, an invisible symphony of violins would surely erupt into a romantic chorus as butterflies flittered about their heads to sanction the union for time and all eternity.

Bobbi almost threw up in her mouth.

"Are you okay, Miss Gallagher?" Sarah touched Bobbi's forearm with French-manicured fingers. "You're practically green."

No shit. Green with envy. "Oh, I'm fine. Just need to drink more." Tequila—a double shot. "This heat's brutal."

"I know." Sarah stroked her smooth, blond ponytail. "When the humidity's this bad, I can't do a thing with my hair."

How tragic. "Don't worry, you look great." Unable to take another moment of gilded small talk, Bobbi got down to business. "Now listen, I'm not trying to pressure you, but if the moment's right, feel free to…" she swallowed the bitter lump in her throat, "…k-kiss Trey. Don't wait for him to make the first move." See? There, that wasn't so bad. She could totally survive this.

Sarah smiled, revealing pearly whites that would make an orthodontist jizz in his pants. "My pleasure."

Oh god. Maybe she couldn't survive this. "Um, on second thought—"

"Hey, Sarah." Speak of the devil, Trey strode forward and extended a handful of vibrant daisies to his date. Bobbi sank a few inches. She loved daisies. Sarah brought the bouquet to her nose while Trey tipped back his hat with one finger and grinned at her reaction, flashing his deep dimples.

Bobbi didn't know how he'd managed it, but he looked even sexier now than he had fifteen minutes ago. The sun had stained the apples of his cheeks, giving him a rugged edge, especially when combined with that weathered cowboy hat. A few sweaty, blond tendrils of hair clung to his temples, and his black T-shirt hugged every blessed contour along his muscled torso, leading Bobbi's eyes to his long, lean thighs showcased beneath slightly dusty jeans. Just then, she decided she *was* perfectly capable of hating Sarah. Because that was the kind of woman Trey belonged with, not some hot-ass mess from Inglewood with enough debt to sink a small country.

Bong hopped out of his van and slung his microphone pole over one shoulder. He glanced at Bobbi's face and furrowed his brow. "What's wrong, boss?"

The Golden Couple tore their gazes away from each other to study Bobbi. Sarah rested one hand over her chest in a *bless her heart* motion and cooed, "I think she's overheated."

That was one way of putting it. "No biggie. I'm about to go grab a beer."

Her innocent words drew the attention of Weezus and Colton, who'd just approached from behind. "Drinking on the job?" Weezus asked, peering around the camera atop his shoulder. "That's a first."

"Ah, hell," Colton drawled, winking at her, "everyone knows beer doesn't count as drinkin'. It's nothin' but liquid bread." Still in uniform, he leaned back against the van and adjusted his utility belt. "Let's go get a drink together, honey. A good, strong one. My date bailed on me, and I need a shoulder to cry on."

Trey stiffened and cleared his throat, shooting daggers at his friend.

"She stood you up?" Bobbi asked, narrowing one skeptical eye. "Or you already nailed her and didn't call the next day?"

After a few low chuckles, Colt admitted, "Both." He pushed off the van and ambled over to her, then slung an arm around her shoulders. "I could sure use a stiff one. How 'bout it?"

With Colton, *stiff one* didn't necessarily refer to booze, but Bobbi knew how to handle him, and she needed a distraction from the impending Kissapalooza. It wasn't five o'clock yet, but what the hell. A margarita on the rocks couldn't tell time. "Fine." She raised her cell phone at Bong and Weezus. "Call if you need me."

"Hold on." Trey settled his hand on Sarah's lower back in a protective gesture, and Bobbi's stomach dropped to the asphalt. He seemed to have warmed up to her pretty damned quickly. "This is exactly the kind of stuff Luke asked me to watch out—"

"What're you afraid of, Lewis?" Colton smirked, clearly baiting Trey. "I'll take real good care of our girl since you're otherwise occupied."

Through a clenched jaw, Trey reminded Colt, "It's a dry county. There's no place to get booze around here."

"Well, now, you're absolutely right." Colt nodded, a grin practically splitting his face. "We'll have to go to my place."

"The answer's no."

"Enough." Bobbi rolled her eyes. She half expected them to free their tallywackers and hold a pissing contest right there in the parking lot. "Go film this date and—" *get it over with*. She darted a glance to the sky, where gunmetal clouds had begun to roll in. "And work in some shots of the parade before the storm shuts us down." Trey's prophetic leg had been right about the pressure change. "Guess this means no fireworks."

Taking her hand, Colton towed her away from the group. "C'mon, honey. We'll make our own."

"Goddamn it, Colt, I'm not playin'." Pure rage flashed in Trey's eyes, his tensed body twitching as if poised to spring on the deputy. Judas Priest, he was worse than Luke.

"Chill, Golden Boy." Unable to bear the sight of him at Sarah's side, Bobbi turned away. "I can handle myself. Just remember what I told you." She hoped Trey and the crew hadn't noticed the tremor in her voice, proof that she wanted that kiss to happen as much as she wanted a full bikini wax from Jack the Ripper.

"Where're you going?" Trey demanded.

Though still facing the other direction, she was aware of his eyes on her, a hot, electrical charge tingling along the back of her neck and spreading like warm honey over her shoulder blades. She heaved a sigh, desperately trying to rein in her emotions and act like a professional.

She could justify one drink in the middle of the day, but not driving into the next county when the crew might need her. And no way in hell was she setting foot inside Colton's skeevy palace of porn. "I guess I'll settle for an iced coffee."

Before Trey had a chance to object any further, she set off, briskly leading the way to Blessed Brew. Five minutes later, she and Colton had barely made it inside before the sky opened up and put a soggy end to the Independence Day festivities.

Bobbi sagged into a booth at the back of the café and faced the wall while Colton ordered their drinks. She didn't want to people-watch, only to drown her jealousy in sugar, cream, and caffeinated goodness.

When Colton rejoined her, it was with an iced mocha latte—extra whipped cream—and a consoling pat on the shoulder. "Here ya go, hon." He set it gingerly on the glossy Formica tabletop and took the seat across from her. "If that doesn't do the trick, you let me know, and we'll head to my place for somethin' stronger."

"I'll be fine, thanks."

Something, or more accurately some*one*, from behind caught Colton's attention, and he offered some lucky lady a wink and some filthy eye-sexing before returning his gaze to Bobbi. "You're not foolin' me, sugar. Neither is Lewis. Even a blind virgin could see you two're hot for each other. I never stood a chance."

She shifted on her seat, the vinyl clinging painfully to the backs of her bare thighs. "He's my subject. Getting involved with him is out of the question."

"And let me guess, playing matchmaker's eating a hole in your gut?"

"Yeah." She brought the iced mocha to her lips and sighed into the plastic cup. "I practically ordered him to get to first base tonight."

"Want me to kiss you?" Blue-green eyes twinkling with mischief contrasted against his russet skin, and Bobbi understood why half the women in Sultry Springs were sprung for the man. "This mouth," he said as he pointed to his own lips, "is guaranteed to ruin you for all other guys."

"Think I'll pass." She took a sip of sugared coffee and smiled. "No telling where your mouth has been."

A few smooth chuckles escaped said mouth. "Who am I to hide this gift from the world?"

"Maybe you haven't found the right woman to share it with." She decided to push for a few tidbits on Leah McMahon. "Or from what I heard, you did find her, and she got away."

With those words, his playful mood darkened—his eyes narrowed, jaw set, shoulders clenched halfway to his ears. Oh yeah, she'd hit a nerve.

"Trey told me about the pastor's daughter," she said casually, trying to keep him from shutting down. "Sounds like she really screwed you over. What happened?"

"Get this straight." Colt's typically seductive voice went sharper than a sword's edge. "She didn't do anything wrong. It was all me." He tipped his head, delivering a pointed gaze that warned her to back off. "It's bad enough that I have to live with what I did. I'm not talkin' about it with you. Leave her outta this."

They both fell silent, letting the squeak of wet shoes against tile replace their charged conversation until Bobbi peeked through her lashes and asked, "What if I could find her?"

His wide-eyed reaction was instantaneous—one of pure, unadulterated hope—but just as quickly, he bottled up those emotions and stuffed them down. She'd done it enough times to know. "Don't waste your time."

"Why? Because you think she won't forgive—"

She was interrupted by a pair of large, wet, male hands slamming against the Formica—hands she'd know anywhere because they'd made her body tremble on more than one occasion. She turned to find Trey braced against the table, his drenched black T-shirt molded to him like a second skin as turrets of raindrops streamed down his face and fell from his angular jaw. His straw cowboy hat cast a dangerous shadow over his stormy, blue eyes, which seemed to devour her where she sat. A thousand butterflies took flight, pirouetting inside Bobbi's stomach as her mouth went drier than Death Valley at noon.

"We need to talk," was all he said before turning on his booted heel and stalking into the hallway that led to the bathrooms and two defunct pay phones in the back.

Bobbi glanced over her shoulder, scanning the booths and tables, with no sign of Sarah or the crew. What on earth had happened out there?

"You'd better go on," Colton said, seeming to recover a fraction of his good spirits, "before he hauls you over his shoulder and smacks your ass again." He snorted a dry laugh. "Unless that's what you're after."

"I'll just be a minute." She scooted along the cushioned vinyl and pushed to standing.

"Take your time, honey. I need to get back on duty." He removed his Stetson just long enough to rake a hand through his long, raven hair. "But you know where to find me if you wanna take me up on that offer."

Her foggy brain couldn't summon a witty comeback, so she breathed, "Sure," and began on shaky knees toward the back hallway. Her limbs moved as if underwater, her pulse racing, though she couldn't identify why. Something about the furious heat in Trey's glare had made her equal parts eager and terrified of being alone with him. Her destination seemed farther away with each step.

When she finally reached him, he faced the emergency exit, one shoulder propped against the wall, arms folded in a combative stance. The faint glow from the exit sign overhead bathed him in red, serving to heighten the sense of foreboding in the dim space.

"What's going on?" she asked softly. When he didn't respond, she moved closer, resting her palm against the planes of his strong back. "Where's the crew? And Sarah?"

Slowly, he turned to face her, then stared her down for several long seconds. He advanced one inch at a time until he'd trapped her body between two walls—one of wood paneling, the other of muscled flesh. Bracing his palms on either side of her head, he murmured, "I sent them all home."

His simmering gaze swept her face and settled low on her mouth. Electric heat rolled off his body in waves, along with the scents of summer rain and pure male desire. She swallowed hard before managing to ask why.

"Because," he explained, eliminating all but an inch of space between them, "I couldn't stand being around her another second."

The predatory stance of his body, his closeness and fever, sent Bobbi's pulse into overdrive as tension coiled low in her stomach. "B-but she's perfect."

Trey shook his head, lowering it until they were eye-level. "Turns out she's got a pretty big personality flaw. A total deal-breaker."

Bobbi didn't understand—Sarah had it all: looks, brains, charisma, the whole package. "What could that possibly be?"

Moving his lips to her ear, he whispered, "She's not you."

His words tore a gasp from her lungs, or maybe it was his hot breath nuzzling the helix of her ear. Responding without conscious thought, she arched her back until her breasts conformed to his damp chest. He sucked in a breath, muscles tense. "Does this mean I can touch you now?"

God help her, he felt so good, like the first day of spring after an eternal, dark winter, and she didn't hesitate to say, "Yes." She craved his touch like a drug, wanted to feel it over every inch of her skin more than she wanted to breathe.

He wasted no time lowering his face to hers. With the rough hands she'd grown to love, he took her cheeks between his palms and kissed her so slowly it made her throat close, his wet mouth sliding over hers in one soft, simple motion that somehow managed to feel mind-blowingly erotic and tender at the same time. At once, she opened to him, sighing against his lower lip and inviting him to take more—and he did, tilting her head back to deepen the kiss and exploring her mouth with the tip of his soft tongue.

He tasted so deliciously sweet and sensual that she couldn't stop the moan from escaping her chest. She wrapped both arms around the thick pillar of his neck in a compulsion to pull him closer as their tongues twined and circled in their seductive dance. She needed to feel his weight crushing her, and he seemed to understand, pinning her to the wall with his hips, pressing every strong, solid contour of his body against her. In that moment, she felt whole, as if this man's warmth had been the one thing missing from her life all these years. Tangling one hand in her hair, he released a jagged breath before claiming her mouth again, harder, sucking and nipping at her lips in a clear show of possession that thrilled her to the soles of her feet.

She'd experienced plenty of kisses in her life, some hot in their own right, but never anything like this. Never a kiss that burned her up from the inside out, branded her, made her feel so utterly adored. Trey slowed down, brushed his soft lips against hers, and brought her palm to rest atop his chest, where his heart pounded a furious staccato for her. She glowed with the knowledge that right now he wanted only her—no other woman in the world.

He touched his forehead to hers, whispering, "Come home with me." His thumb stroked her lower lip, blazed a trail over her jaw and down the side of her throat. "Stay with me tonight."

Still drunk with his kisses, she let her eyes flutter open and tried to think straight. "I thought you didn't like girls spending the night."

"I don't." He licked his upper lip, then bent to kiss her again, pausing at the corner of her mouth. "But I know once won't be enough for either of us." When she shuddered against him in clear desire, he gripped her thigh, pulling it around his hips as he ground his erection against her aroused flesh in a slow rotation. "I want to make love to you, Bobbi. Then I want to wrap you in my arms and fall asleep while I'm still inside you. I want to bury my face in the curve of your neck and breathe you all night long."

Letting her head tip to the side, she groaned loudly, beyond caring about the dozens of patrons a stone's throw away.

"Say yes," he murmured with another lazy thrust that undid her.

"Yes." She couldn't have said no if she wanted to. This was more than animal lust. She needed this man inside her, filling and completing her on a primal level, consequences be damned. In that moment, she'd sacrifice anything—even her career—to join her body with his, to spend the night in his powerful embrace, and she couldn't wait another excruciating second to make it happen.

"Yes," she repeated with all the certainty and passion in her heart. "Take me home."

Chapter 11

TREY SHIFTED HIS CHEVY INTO THIRD GEAR AS HE navigated Main Street, then shifted his erection away from his zipper before he busted through the copper teeth. He'd never been so hard in his life. It was like his johnson knew it was about to enter the promised land and had already stowed its tray in the upright position. What it failed to understand was the copilot was still two car lengths behind, observing the speed limit and coming to a complete stop at each friggin' intersection. *Please, sweet baby Jesus, don't let Bobbi change her mind before I can get her home.*

He wished Bobbi hadn't insisted on driving separately. He'd hoped to pull her close and put his free hand to good use during the short trip to his place. But she'd had a valid point—everyone in Sultry Springs knew that purple hatchback, and it would get back to Luke in a flash if she left Bruiser on the curb all night. Better to hide it inside his garage.

Trey didn't know how they were going to explain Bobbi's absence to Luke, and a faint twinge of guilt pricked at his stomach. There wasn't enough blood left in his head—not the one on his shoulders, anyway—for a full-on attack of conscience, but he knew he'd feel like shit in the morning when he had to face his best friend on the job site. Especially with the night's debauchery fresh in his mind. And he would debauch Bobbi, make no mistake. He wasn't even sure if they'd make it to the bedroom for round one. Maybe he'd peel off her shorty-shorts, lift her onto the kitchen counter, and spend the first twenty minutes with his face between her thighs. The mental image made his pants even tighter, and he punched the accelerator, hoping the owner of those thighs got the message and quit lollygagging.

When he reached his driveway—after the longest five-minute ride of his life—he hit the garage door opener and pulled inside, making sure to leave plenty of room for her car. He was already out of his truck and almost twitching with need when Bobbi pulled in beside him. Would it be wrong to lay her across the hood of her hatchback and do her right there? Yeah, probably. Besides, he'd waited so long, dreamt about her night and day since she'd come to town, and he wanted to do this right—take his time and savor every smooth inch, binge on her sweetness…and hopefully get her out of his system.

He opened her car door and she peered up at him tentatively, as if equally afraid he'd changed his mind. Bending across her lap, he unfastened her seat belt and gave her a kiss that left no doubt about his intentions. Her mouth was hot and responsive, her tongue eager to please, and he tugged her to standing before nudging the door shut with his hip.

"I need you," she sighed against his mouth, wrapping one leg around his waist, "inside me, right now." Then she started grinding against his hard-on.

He moaned loud enough to wake the dead. "You keep doing that, and our first time won't last very long." Pulling her other leg around his waist, he hoisted her up and held her by the ass as he stumbled toward the door to the kitchen. After nearly tripping over an old paint can, he reached the entrance to the house, managed to get the door open, and rushed inside, hoping the place wasn't too messy. He was pretty sure he'd picked up all his dirty underwear and returned the girly mags to their rightful place beneath the bed.

Just as he crossed the threshold, Bobbi licked his earlobe, and he knew it was no use trying to get her to the bedroom. Setting her gently on the kitchen island, he began sucking and nibbling his way down her neck while reaching beneath her shirt to massage her firm breasts. They filled each of his palms to perfection, taunting him beneath a layer of lace. He lifted one breast to his mouth and softly bit Bobbi's nipple through her bra. She fisted his hair, groaning a litany of sensual curses and reaching down to stroke him with her fingertips.

He stilled her hand, in serious danger of finishing before they officially started. "Darlin', I wasn't joking when I said—"

All of a sudden, a new sensation pierced Trey's fog of lust and froze him in place. An overwhelming scent, warm and chocolaty, filled his nostrils, so thick it must've saturated the entire house. It smelled amazing in here, which didn't make sense. When he'd left several hours ago, the slightly acrid odor of Tex-Mex chili from last night's dinner had clung to the kitchen walls. Wrinkling his forehead, he glanced at the oven, noting the digital display that read *350 bake*. Bake? Had he left the oven on all day? He barely used the thing—didn't even know how to bake since his mother had never taught him.

Wait a minute.

He sniffed the air a few times, stomach lurching against his ribs as the puzzle pieces clicked into place.

"Oh, no. No, no, no." He recognized that smell. It was his mother's legendary double-fudge brownies, and since he doubted a burglar had broken in to whip up a tasty treat, that meant Mom was in here somewhere.

"Hey." Bobbi took his face between her hands, turning his gaze to her heavy-lidded, green eyes. "Where'd you go?"

Into his worst nightmare, that's where. "Let's get outta here."

"What?" She squinted in confusion. "But we just got—"

A shrill voice from the other side of the room yelled, "Great Caesar's ghost, Trey!"

Bobbi brought both hands to her chest and screamed, while Trey hung his head and fought the urge to bang his skull against the countertop. Why, God, why? What had he done to deserve this level of cosmic cockblockery?

Mom clutched the silk fabric over her heart, mouth agape as she took in the scene: a drenched, barely clothed Bobbi perched on the counter with her legs still wrapped around Trey's waist, his hand paused mid-grope beneath the front of her shirt.

Bobbi worked her way free from Trey's grasp and hopped down, clutching his bicep as she moved to hide behind him. Realizing Mom hadn't seen him with a boner since he was three, Trey repositioned himself strategically behind the island and asked, "What the holy hell are you doing here?"

After stammering for a few seconds, she smoothed her blouse. "Visiting you, obviously."

"You couldn't have called first?" The instant the words left his lips, Trey cringed inwardly, remembering he hadn't picked up in days. He should've known there was no escaping her. Damn it, why had he given her a key all those years ago?

"I did call! And left plenty of messages, which you clearly ignored." She bitched at him with the same voice she'd used since he'd worn Batman Underoos, making him feel four feet tall. One hand gripping her hip, she scoured Bobbi with that cold, signature Lewis family glare. "Now I know what's been keeping you so busy. Or rather, *whom*." In a tone that oozed disappointment, she prodded, "Aren't you going to introduce me to your…little friend?"

His "little friend" beat him to it. "Hi, Mrs. Lewis. I'm Bobbi. It's nice to meet you, though I'm a little embarrassed by the circumstances." She released a nervous laugh, pinching him hard on the back in retribution.

"I see." Mom did that thing where she lifted her face, so she could look down her nose at everyone. Trey knew it was born from insecurity and she didn't mean anything by it, but Bo wouldn't understand. He shot his mother a warning glance, which she coolly ignored. "Do you have a last name, Bobbi?"

Uh-oh. Warning bells chimed inside Trey's muddled brain, but he couldn't summon a believable cover-up before Bobbi announced, "Gallagher."

That did it. Mom associated the name Gallagher with all things evil, similar to the way Trey felt about the St. Louis Cardinals. Her eyes wrenched to his, widening just enough to warn him a shit storm was brewing.

"Turns out Luke has a sister," Trey said slowly,

sending Mom a clear message to tone it down. "She's spending the summer in town filming a...documentary." No way was he fessing up to his role in *Sex in the Sticks*. Mom would have a conniption duck fit.

"Is that so?" His mom gave Bobbi a hesitant once-over, as if reserving further judgment for now. "On what topic?"

"Uh..." Bobbi clearly understood—she'd made her feelings for this project clear and wouldn't advertise her involvement on a regular day, let alone when meeting Trey's mother for the first time. "It's...um...well, you could say it's about interpersonal relationships within the rural community."

Nice one.

"And," Bobbi continued, "Trey's helping me out."

"Oh, I can see that." Wrinkling her nose in distaste, Mom strode into the kitchen, making a *shoo-fly* motion at them with one hand. "My brownies are almost done."

It was clear Mom wasn't leaving any time soon, and as much as Trey wanted to, he couldn't hoist Bobbi over his shoulder and carry her into the bedroom to pick up where they left off. Wrapping an arm around Bobbi's shoulders, he pulled her to the end of the island, whispering, "This isn't over. I'll tell her I'm driving you home, then we'll get a room somewhere."

She nodded in agreement. "Let me use your restroom first."

"Sure." He pointed to the hallway. "First door on your left."

As soon as Bobbi was out of earshot, Mom shook her head and chided, "Really, Trey."

"Don't start."

She began rifling through the kitchen cabinets and drawers. "Where're your oven mitts?"

"Drawer to the left of the stove." He scrubbed his face with one hand, trying to will the blood flow away from his crotch.

"Another Gallagher," Mom continued without missing a beat. "Why am I not surprised? You're drawn to those people like a dog to garbage. How many *are* there, anyway?" From the inflection in her icy voice, you'd think she was discussing vermin with an exterminator.

"Just the two of 'em." Or at least, that's what he assumed. "And be nice. I like Bobbi."

"Well, of course you do." Quilted mitt in place, she opened the oven and bent to retrieve the square Pyrex brownie pan, filling the kitchen with dry warmth. "You're just like your father, a magnet for easy women."

Trey's spine stiffened. He didn't know which was worse, being compared to his father, or the implication that Bobbi was a slut. "Don't go there, Mom—"

"Why can't you find a nice girl for once? Like Mindy?"

"Sure, that's just what I need. Someone to sleep around behind my back and dump me."

Mom pressed two quick fingers against her dessert, seemingly satisfied with the results. "I'm sure it wasn't like that."

It was exactly like that, but Mom wouldn't listen. Mindy had been Trey's high school girlfriend, and more importantly, she hailed from one of Chicago's wealthiest families, which made her star wife material in Mom's eyes.

He tried changing the subject. "How long are you in town?"

Mom brushed a strand of silver hair away from her face, shoulders drooping as if offended by his question. "As long as you can stand having your mother around. I'm lucky if I get to see you twice a year." Great, she'd embarked on another of her intercontinental guilt trips. "You know, one of these days when you have children of your own, you're going to understand—"

"I didn't mean anything by it, Mom."

"Sure you didn't." Tossing the hot pad onto the counter, Mom huffed a sigh. "Just do me a favor, and listen for once."

He gave a mental eye roll. "I'm listening."

"Life doesn't usually give second chances, but you've got one—to clear your name and start from scratch. Don't let another Gallagher ruin your future. Don't be like your father and give up everything that matters for a few quick rolls in the hay." Her voice thickened and her eyes welled with tears she wouldn't allow to fall. She never did. "I promise she's not worth it. They rarely are."

Under any other circumstances, Trey would have shown her the door for her flagrant criticism of Bobbi, but he couldn't kick Mom when she was already down. "She's not like that. And besides, you've got nothin' to worry about. I'm not changing my mind about Dubai."

"Promise me."

"I promise."

A minute later, Bobbi padded into the room without meeting his gaze. She raised one hand in an awkward good-bye to his mother. "Nice meeting you."

"Mmm-hmm," Mom said, facing away. "Tell your brother hello. You remind me a lot of him." She turned, flashing a smile that didn't reach beyond her lips. "It's the eyes, I think. Such a lovely green."

The backhanded compliment wasn't lost on Trey, but fortunately, Bobbi didn't seem to catch on.

"Thanks." Hooking one thumb toward the door, Bobbi told him, "I'm gonna go. I'll have…um, Nathan… call you tomorrow."

"Who's Nathan?" he asked, following her into the garage. "And I want to see you home." He'd said the last part extra loud for Mom's benefit. What he really wanted to do was find a dark, private place to make love to Bobbi like the world was ending.

Once they'd stepped outside the kitchen, she whispered, "That's Bong's real name." Then, shaking her head, added, "Just stay. I'll be fine."

"Stay?" He walked Bobbi to the driver's side door, but when he leaned in to kiss her, she turned her face to the side, pressing one firm hand against his chest.

Trey stroked her hair, noticing the barest sliver of blond beginning to grow along her part line. It was the first time he realized she wasn't a natural redhead.

From out of nowhere, it occurred to him that if they had a son, he would likely be blond—a towheaded little boy with blue-green eyes and a gap-toothed smile. Trey's lips twitched into a grin against his will, but he banished the image. The last thing he needed in his tumultuous life was a baby. He didn't even like kids.

"C'mon." He leaned in to nip Bobbi's earlobe. "We'll stop someplace along the way."

"No." Ducking from the circle of his arms, she nudged him aside and pulled open the car door. "Stay with your mom. She's hurting. That's why she came. Go be a good son."

"I'd rather be bad…with you."

"Your mom needs you." Plunking into her seat behind the wheel, Bobbi delivered an abrupt, painful blow before slamming the door shut. "I don't."

While Trey stood there slack-jawed, Bobbi started the car and pulled out without so much as a glance in his direction. He watched the purple hatchback turn onto Main Street and fade away, wondering what the hell had just happened.

Bobbi gripped the steering wheel so hard the tendons in her wrists threatened to snap. The dark road ahead began to blur through a thick filter of tears, streetlights and yellow lines swirling together like abstract art, so she pulled onto the shoulder and threw the car in park, letting the engine idle and sputter as raindrops pelted the windshield.

Her breath hitched, sending one plump tear rolling down her cheek. *I promise she's not worth it.* For the life of her, Bobbi couldn't understand why those six little words had affected her so deeply, like a roundhouse kick to the gut. It wasn't as if she really cared about Trey— she didn't love him—so why did she give a damn what his uppity prune of a mother thought?

She shouldn't have eavesdropped, because she hadn't needed further proof that Trey's mom hated her—the woman's hostile glares had said it all. With a frosty sneer, Mrs. Lewis had raked her gaze over Bobbi's fat thighs, shaking her head pitifully as if to say, *Oh, honey, you should cover up those sausages.*

"Garbage," Bobbi whispered to herself, wiping away another tear. That's how Mrs. Lewis had described her, and it hadn't helped that she'd looked the part. Instead of her polished designer wardrobe, she'd stumbled into Trey's kitchen clad in Daisy Dukes and an old T-shirt, her shoes dripping wet, hair snarled, mascara oozing down her face. Not to mention wrapped around Trey and moaning like a porn star. What mother wanted to see her son with a woman like that?

Bobbi's insides felt raw, like she'd skinned her soul instead of her knees or elbows. She hadn't felt this exposed since the seventh grade, when she'd experienced her very first kiss. One of the popular boys, a cute soccer player named Ian Price, had asked her to walk with him behind the gym. Holding her hand, he'd kissed her so sweetly it had made the backs of her eyes sting with unshed tears—because *finally*, someone had seen beyond the grubby clothes and the unkempt hair to the girl underneath. But he'd walked her back to class without another word and ignored her each day afterward. A week later, she'd overheard two girls talking in the restroom and learned Ian had only kissed her to win a triple-dog-dare. She'd hidden inside her toilet stall, hugged her knees to her chest, and sobbed in silence for what felt like hours, while half the school laughed behind her back.

Now she understood the connection—why Mrs. Lewis's words had scraped her so bare. It was Trey. Bobbi'd opened herself to him, just like she'd done with Ian. The judgmental barbs that ordinarily wouldn't have fazed her had penetrated her heart because she'd made it vulnerable. She'd left it unguarded.

God, she was an idiot. Had she really been willing to sacrifice everything for one night with Trey?

"Why?" she demanded of herself, right before letting her forehead thunk against the steering wheel. "Why can't you just stay away from him?"

Enough, she decided. No more brooding. It was time to get her shit together and return home, where she could lose it again in the privacy of her guest bedroom.

Closing her eyes, she leaned back against the headrest and practiced the mental exercise her child psychologist had taught her more than a decade ago, after her third suspension for fighting. Focusing on her negative emotions, she imagined piling them like stones into a bulletproof box and locking them down tight.

At first, this was no different from all the other times, but when she imagined slamming the lid down, it wouldn't latch. All those horrible feelings started bucking inside, rattling the hinges like a deranged convict demanding freedom. Balling her fists with extra effort, she was eventually able to close and lock the box, but she didn't know how much longer the lock would hold. She didn't want to know what would happen if nearly two dozen years of sick memories and neglected emotions escaped their prison. For good measure, she imagined locking her box inside a larger one, then wrapping it in chains and dumping it into the ocean. Not even Houdini could escape that.

She sucked a deep breath in through her nose and released it in a loud puff. There, that was better. Satisfied that she could drive safely, she checked over her shoulder for oncoming traffic—what little of it existed in this town—before pulling onto the road and heading for Luke's.

Fifteen minutes later, she turned onto his gravel driveway and parked beside June's new car, a glossy Accord the color of grape cough syrup. June really had a thing for purple.

Tucking her leather handbag beneath her shirt to protect it from the rain, Bobbi jogged across the lawn and up the steps to the front porch. She'd just begun fishing for her house key when a sudden movement to her right tore a gasp from her throat.

"Sorry," said June's voice from the darkness. "Didn't mean to scare you."

Bobbi bent a few inches and squinted, barely making out her brother and sister-in-law, who sat cuddled on the porch swing, wineglasses in hand.

Luke checked his watch. "It's a holiday. Shouldn't you be out partying? Only boring married couples come home this early."

Boring or not, Bobbi couldn't think of a better way to spend a stormy night than snuggled up with a man who loved her, sipping wine and watching the rain from the warmth and safety of his embrace. Feigning indifference, she shrugged one shoulder. "I'm tired."

Even in the darkness she noticed Luke's posture change, hardening in alarm. He handed his wineglass to June. "Something's wrong. What happened?"

"Nothing," she lied, following up with a trifling laugh. "I was up with the sun this morning, and I'm just—"

"Have you been crying?" he demanded.

How on earth could he know that? He couldn't possibly see her puffy eyes from all the way over there.

"Your voice is all scratchy," he explained, "and you sound like someone ran over your dog." With the greatest of care, he took June's shoulders and pushed her forward so he could stand. "Just tell me who I need to kill."

"Don't be ridiculous. And by the way, I'm allergic to dogs." Changing the subject didn't deter him.

Muscled arms folded over his chest, he stalked closer. "This is what big brothers are for, to kick the teeth outta guys who screw with their kin." When he stepped near enough to study her face in the moonlight's faded glow, his brows lowered, forming a slash over his dark eyes. "You *have* been crying. Damn it, Bo, what happened? Did someone hurt you? Where was Trey? He's supposed to be handling stuff like this for me."

Bobbi's face heated. Her insides were still too raw, and for some backward reason, Luke's brotherly concern only served to provoke her anger. *Now* he wanted to protect her? Where was he a dozen years ago, when she really needed him? Where was Luke when Ian Price told the whole soccer team Bobbi was a lousy kisser who tasted like welfare cheese? Or when she'd started ninth grade at a new school and felt terrified the other teens would see through her designer clothes and trendy haircut to the poseur underneath? She could have used a big brother then. Where was Luke when Bobbi'd found their mother dead, slumped over the toilet like Elvis? Here in Mayberry, that's where, with June and Pru and a whole community of people who loved and supported him. He was going to church, feasting on fried chicken and buttered grits, getting everything out of life she'd been denied.

"I don't need Trey or anyone else watching out for me," she snapped. "While you were fishing and skinny-dipping and shit, I was learning how to throw a right hook."

With a deep, slow sigh, he patted her arm in a condescending gesture. "I know, hon."

"Don't do that!" She shoved his hand away. "Don't pretend to know what it was like for me. Not when you were living on some redneck version of Easy Street!"

"What?" Luke gripped his hips. "Is that what you think? That I had some *Leave it to Beaver* experience here when Mama left?"

"That's exactly what I think."

"Then you're delusional!"

June set both glasses on the wooden porch and hurried to her husband's side. Linking their arms, she began stroking his chest, almost petting him. He responded to her gentle touch immediately, shoulders sinking as his muscles unclenched.

"Let's not do this," June said softly. "It's not a contest. There's no prize for whoever had the worst childhood. We all had a rough time growing up, but we're together now, and we're happy. That's what matters, right?"

We're happy? Speak for yourself.

Damn it, Bobbi was brooding again, and she didn't want to turn into *that* girl—the bitter buzz kill who wound up living with a dozen cats. She silently counted to ten and tried to rein in her misplaced anger. "Yeah." None of her problems were Luke's fault. He'd provided free room and board—even a vehicle for the summer—without asking for anything in return, and she had no right to tear him down. "I'm sorry."

She opened the screen door, staring into the foyer, grappling with the right words to complete her apology, but nothing came. Instead of loitering in the dark, she decided to reorganize the kitchen pantry. Maybe the coat closet after that. And if that didn't make her feel better, there was always the toolshed.

Chapter 12

BOBBI WAS BEGINNING TO THINK SHE'D MISSED HER calling in life, because hot diggety damn, she stocked a mean grocery shelf. Using a damp dishrag, she wiped down a can of peas, removing the sticky residue from the sugar Luke had spilled inside the pantry last week, then lovingly placed the peas alphabetically in front of the pears and peppers. She rotated it ten degrees to the left so the label faced outward in perfect alignment with the others, then sat back to admire her work. Using the food pyramid as inspiration, she'd filled the top shelf with oils, sugars, and baking goods, followed by proteins like canned tuna and legumes, then fruits and vegetables on the shelf below, and ending with grains at the very bottom—bread, pretzels, crackers, and pasta noodles. The flawless symmetry with which she'd arranged these products gave Bobbi a soothing sense of accomplishment. She sighed in relief.

Funny, she hadn't thought of it in years, but this was exactly what she'd done her first night living with Papa and Daddy. Her dads had tucked her into bed, blissfully unaware of her scheme to whip the place into shape, and they'd awoken the next morning to a gleaming, meticulously reorganized kitchen. They'd vowed right then and there to make her "lighten up and enjoy life's little messes." Bobbi snickered. They'd failed miserably. She didn't *do* messy.

Standing, she brushed her hands together and grabbed a bag of M&Ms from the top shelf, figuring she'd earned a break. She sat at the kitchen table, sprinkled a few dozen candies onto the polished oak, and sorted them according to color. Then she proceeded to eat them one at a time in order from darkest to lightest. The sweet, crunchy chocolates lifted her spirits for an instant, until the scent reminded her of Mrs. Lewis's brownies.

Leave it to Trey's mom to taint a smell as comforting at cocoa.

"Hey," June said, taking the seat across from Bobbi at the table, "I eat mine like that too. Except I put them in seasonal color combinations first, like red and green for Christmas, and orange and brown for fall."

Bobbi shook another pile of M&Ms onto the oak and pushed them in June's direction. "Glad to hear I'm not the only one with OCD candy habits. I do it with Smarties too."

"Oh, I love Smarties." June pursed her lips a moment. "I wonder if anyone's invented a Smartie-flavored martini yet."

"If they have, I'll bet you can do it better."

"Aw, thanks." Flushing beneath ivory skin, June averted her gaze, clearly uncomfortable with accepting a compliment. Bobbi understood—she'd always had the same problem. "You're sweet."

Propping her elbow on the table, Bobbi rested her chin in the palm of her hand. "That's not the word most people would use to describe me." Tenacious? Sure. Assertive? You bet. Ballbuster? Sometimes. But sweet? No, that adjective was reserved for soft-spoken, natural caregivers like June.

"Luckily, I know you better than most people." June pointed a yellow candy shell at her. "And I say you're sweet." She tried using a forceful tone, but it was instantly neutralized by her wide, brown eyes and Shirley Temple ringlets.

"Not even my brother would agree with you. Where is he, by the way?"

"In the toolshed." June lined up her M&Ms and began flipping them right-side up. "Tinkering. It's how he deals, kind of like his version of alphabetizing the spice rack." Darting a glance at the open pantry, June wrinkled her forehead and nodded at the shelves. "No offense, but that creeps me out. It reminds me of the scene in *Sleeping with the Enemy* where Julia Roberts comes home and finds all the cans in her cupboard lined up and facing the same way."

"Oh, yeah, and then she runs in the bathroom and notices the towels are hanging just right."

"And that's how she knows her psycho husband's been in the house." June shivered.

"Sorry." Bobbi tossed a handful of candies into her mouth and spoke with one cheek full. "You can mess it up if you want. It's not the finished product that makes me feel better; it's the act itself."

While June absently rotated each M&M, she bit her lip and stared at the table in a way that warned Bobbi a change was coming in their small talk. "I can tell it's hard for you and Luke being together like this." Peeking through her lashes, she added, "Because you're both jealous of what the other one had."

"Luke? Jealous of *me*?" Bobbi felt her brows pinch together. "What did I have that he could possibly want?"

June replied without hesitation, as if the answer should be obvious. "A mother."

"Psssh," Bobbi scoffed. "She wasn't much of a mother. He didn't miss out on anything after she left."

"I know. I remember a little about her, and to be honest, he wasn't missing out on much while she was still here."

"Exactly. Mama was there in body, but not in mind or spirit. I don't know why she didn't leave us both behind, since she barely acknowledged my existence anyway." God only knows how she would've turned out if it hadn't been for her dads.

"That's the thing," June said, leaning forward. "I think it would've been easier for Luke if your mom had left both of you, but she didn't. Instead, she chose *you* and abandoned *him*. Like playing favorites, but on a bigger scale. Can you imagine how that would feel for a twelve-year-old boy who'd already lost his father?"

Bobbi nodded, the corners of her mouth drooping in a frown. "The ultimate rejection."

"Right, because nobody's supposed to love you more than your own mother. And by taking you to California with her, she basically told Luke you were worth keeping, but he wasn't. It really messed him up, and I'd know—he came to live with us after that. He was angry at first, breaking things and acting out, and even after he calmed down, he was really guarded."

Bobbi absently pushed her M&Ms across the table. "Poor kid." She could picture him, tall and lanky like Carlo with a cap of reddish-brown hair, desperately trying to act like a little man while bleeding on the inside. She wanted to wrap her arms around twelve-year-old

Luke and hug away his pain. "I wish he could've known how lucky he was, staying with you and your grandma."

June shrugged. "He sees that now, but it wasn't so easy back then. For the longest time, he had serious trust issues. The first time I told Luke I loved him, he lost his shit—oops, I mean sugar—and we didn't talk for almost ten years after that."

"When you moved away?"

"Yep. After we got married, he told me *I love you* were the last words his mom said to him before she left. So all those years, he assumed people didn't mean it. That's why he'd reacted so harshly with me, because deep down, he didn't think he was worth loving. It broke my heart to hear him say that." June lowered her voice, glancing from side to side as if someone might be listening. "But don't tell him I told you. He doesn't like people knowing. I think on some level, he's still ashamed that his own mama didn't want him, and that's why he never told Trey about you."

"That's awful."

"When I came back to town, I basically had to teach him how to love. It wasn't easy." She got a far-off look in her eyes and smiled sadly. "He fought me almost to the death, but I eventually got through to him."

"I'm glad." Bobbi reached out and patted June's hand. "I guess I should thank you for that."

Smiling, June gave Bobbi's fingers a squeeze. "You two are more alike than you think. I hope you can let go of what you missed out on, and focus on what you have. You've already lost so much time."

Bobbi took a few minutes to digest what June had just shared with her. Looking back, Mama'd had a dysfunctional relationship with members of the male sex, disdainful but codependent. She'd clearly despised men, but Bobbi couldn't remember a time when Mama hadn't had a boyfriend, or at the very least, a steady booty call. Maybe that'd been the motivating factor in her mother's decision to abandon Luke. At twelve years old, he'd just started to become a man—the embodiment of everything their mother had hated.

Bobbi cringed, remembering her own words. *Don't pretend to know what it was like for me. Not when you were living on some redneck version of Easy Street!* She'd had no idea how deeply Mama had cut Luke, nor how long his wounds had taken to heal. How arrogant of her to assume she'd been the only one to suffer.

"Think I'll go talk to him," Bobbi decided. "If I don't make it back in half an hour, come make sure we haven't killed each other."

June giggled. "Just do me a favor and don't hit him below the belt. I'm ovulating soon, so I need him fully operational tonight."

Bobbi did *not* need to know that. "I didn't realize you two were trying for a baby." As often as Luke plowed that field, June should've sprouted a seedling by now. It looked like Bobbi would be sleeping with her earbuds in.

"We're not. At least not officially." June bit her lip while a rosy flush mottled her cheeks. "He needs a little more convincing, but I think I can sway him."

What was Bobbi supposed to say to that? Break a leg? Or break an egg? "I'd better go," she muttered clumsily, "before I lose my nerve." She pushed to standing and scurried toward the exit, desperately trying not to picture the conception of her future niece or nephew.

"Hey," June called, "send him in when you're done. The wine's making me sleepy."

"You got it." *Note to self: never bunk with newlyweds again, no matter how broke.*

Bobbi stepped out the back door and shuffled down the porch steps, immediately stopping short at the eerie change in the weather. A thick, rolling fog had uncurled over the lawn, creeping lazily toward nowhere in particular. The rain had stopped, and a full moon hung low and heavy in the sky like an overripe melon, illuminating the dense night air. Sudden movement from within the tall cornstalks bordering Luke's property caused Bobbi's breath to catch. Images of knife-wielding, white-haired children of the corn flashed in her mind, and she broke into a run, bolting toward the shed's glow. It was probably just a raccoon scurrying through the field, but try telling that to her overactive imagination.

Without knocking, she threw open the wooden door and rushed inside the shed.

Eyes flying wide, Luke clapped a palm over his chest. "Jesus Christ, Bo! You scared the ever-loving shit outta me!"

She slammed the door and leaned back against the rough pine, trying to steady her breathing as the scents of wood glue and sawdust filled her nostrils. "Sorry," she panted. "Too many horror movies. Everyone gets whacked in the cornfield, usually with a scythe." When Luke quirked a questioning brow, she clarified, "There's something alive out there."

He shook his head, rolling his eyes as if to say, *You're such a girl.* "Of course there's something alive out there. About three dozen deer, on any given night. The only thing getting butchered in that field is the corn." He returned his attention to a round, white contraption about a foot in diameter that sat belly-up on his workbench. Sorting through multicolored wires, he squinted at the machine's innards, and Bobbi half expected him to request a scalpel.

"What're you doing?" she asked, shoving her hands into her back pockets. Glancing around the oddly tidy space, she observed this was more of a workshop than a shed, and unlike Luke's office, he kept his tools in pristine order, shovels and rakes neatly lining the walls, each wrench and screwdriver in its designated, labeled drawer. He'd even built a pegboard to hold larger instruments, like hammers and awls.

Luke made a guttural sound of frustration from the back of his throat. "June picked up this old Roomba at a yard sale, and she wants me to get it working again."

"What's a Roomba?" She stepped closer, observing two rubber wheels and a white plastic shell Luke had set to the side.

"A robotic vacuum. June's got it in her head that this thing'll clean the house while we're at Shooters." He snorted a laugh. "Gonna scare the piss outta the cat, though, so we'll have a mess to deal with either way."

Bobbi had caught a few glimpses of Lucky, June's half-crippled, black and white cat, but the timid animal had taken to hiding behind the furniture since Bobbi'd come to town. "How'd you wind up with a three-legged cat, anyway? I thought you were more of a dog person."

"I am." Luke pulled two oak barstools from the wall, offering one to her. "June rescued Lucky from a shelter years ago. Some animal attacked him, and they were gonna put him down. She paid for his surgery with her grocery money, and ate ramen noodles for the next six months."

Smiling, Bobbi dragged her stool opposite Luke at the workstation and perched atop the seat. "That sounds like something June would do. She's got a big heart."

"Mmm," he hummed in agreement. "Always has, even when we were kids. I was a real butthole to her back then, but she never quit sticking up for me."

"You know," Bobbi said, brushing a bit of sawdust from the tabletop onto the floor, "as much as I wish we could've grown up together, I'm glad you had June. She was kind of like the sister I couldn't be for you." She caught herself scratching her nose and tucked her hands beneath her thighs.

Bobbi didn't feel comfortable meeting Luke's gaze, but she sensed him watching her. "Well, I'm glad she was in my life, but I never thought of June as my sister." He cleared his throat. "I already had one of those, and I wouldn't let anyone take her place." After a few seconds of charged silence, he said, "I never forgot about you, Bo. I'm sorry I didn't find you sooner."

Now she glanced into his eyes, warm and green and overflowing with guilt. Guilt she'd dumped on him during her childish tirade earlier. "Don't do that to yourself. You didn't have to look for me at all." Honestly, by the time Bobbi'd graduated from high school, she'd forgotten she even had a brother. What little she'd remembered of Luke had been blocked out by her defensive subconscious years before.

"But if I hadn't waited so long—"

"What?" she demanded, softly. "You'd have taken over raising me when you were still a kid yourself?" She shook her head, then reached across the wood tabletop to nudge his hairy forearm. "I'm not the kind of person who thinks everything happens for a reason, but by the time you were old enough to get custody of me, I was already with my dads. If the courts had given me to you, I would've missed out on being a part of their family." She rested her hand atop his for one brief second. "This way, I get to have it all—you and them. Everything worked out the way it was supposed to."

"Still, I wish I could've been there for you."

She did too, so much that she ached for it. "There's no point wishing we could change the past." Bobbi remembered June's advice not to waste another minute. "You're here for me now, right?"

Luke nodded firmly. "Goddamn right I am. If you still need me."

Pushing off her stool, Bobbi skirted around the table. "What if I do?"

He didn't hesitate to rush to her side. He threw his arms around her and squeezed, giving her a bear hug that nearly cracked half her ribs but left no doubt about how much he cared. Despite their argument, despite all those years apart, he was still her brother, and he'd love her always.

Gripping her shoulders, he stepped back. "So are you gonna tell me who I need to pummel into the ground?" A lock of auburn hair fell over one eye, making him appear less like an avenging angel and more like a little boy. It brought a smile to her lips. "Who made you cry tonight?"

Bobbi decided to tell him the truth, but not the whole

truth. "I had the...um...unique pleasure of meeting Trey's mother."

"Awwww, shit." Luke stepped back and rubbed his stubbly jaw with one hand. "I didn't know she was in town."

"Neither did Trey." Not that it was any consolation, but Trey'd seemed less happy to see his mother than Bobbi had been. "Mrs. Lewis said all the right things, but she still made me feel like—"

"Trash," Luke finished with a knowing nod. "She's real good at that."

"Once she heard my name was Gallagher, it was over."

"I'm sorry, Bo." His nostrils flared as he pulled in a deep breath and released it in a huff. "It's not you she hates, it's me."

"I know. Trey told me."

"Yeah?" Mahogany brows arched in a stern V as he jutted out his chin. "What did he do about Mommy Dearest?"

"Down, boy," she teased, standing on tiptoe to pat his head. "He tried keeping her in check, but it didn't work. For what it's worth, she's going through a rough time right now, so I told him to stay with her and be a good son."

"What kind of rough time?"

"Ask Trey. It's his story to tell, not mine."

Luke crossed his arms over his chest and rose to full height, reminding Bobbi of the old *Monty Python* Spanish Inquisition spoofs. "So you know more about my best friend's private life than I do? Just how close *are* you two?"

"We're friends, that's all."

Shrewd eyes appraised her face, staring her down as if waiting for a confession. "I hope you're not bullshitting me. Trey's like a brother, but he's not the kinda guy I'd want to see you get mixed up with."

She didn't know why, but his words burned. A sudden urge to defend Trey hijacked Bobbi's vocal chords. "Why not?" When Luke's eyes widened, she stammered, "I mean, I'm not interested in him, but he seems nice enough. A total gentleman when I set him up on dates." *But not so gentlemanly when he's got me on the countertop with his teeth around my nipple.*

"He *is* nice enough, but he's too much like me—well, how I used to be. He's a player, and there's nothin' wrong with that, so long as he's not playin' with my little sister." He tugged a lock of her hair. "Know what I mean, jelly bean?"

"Yeah." A player? Bobbi tried to keep a straight face, hiding how deeply her brother's words had disappointed her, but it wasn't easy. "I almost forgot," she murmured absently. "I'm supposed to tell you to come inside. June's waiting for you to…uh…fulfill your manly duties or whatever."

He didn't seem pleased by the news. Reaching back to scratch his neck, he darted a glance around the shed until it landed on the disemboweled Roomba. "Tell her I'll be here awhile longer. I want to wrap up this project tonight."

Bobbi looked from the robot to her brother and back again. The only way he'd finish repairing that thing tonight is if God decided to add another five hundred hours to the day. "Let me make sure I understand. Your wife—the one you can't keep your hands off of—is inside waiting to do bad things to you, and you're choosing to stay here and tinker with a broken vacuum?"

"She's the one who asked me to fix it," he said defensively.

Bobbi held both palms out. "Okay, okay. None of my business." Maybe Luke wasn't as close to "swaying" as June thought. And who could blame him? Babies were an epic pain in the ass, and Bobbi didn't understand why anyone would bring one into the world when plenty of children were already waiting for good homes. "I'll see you in the morning then."

"'Night."

With a wave, she poked her head out the door. Glancing at the cornfield for movement, she ventured cautiously into the backyard and managed to make it to the porch without breaking into a sprint. Once inside, she tiptoed to the kitchen, afraid of waking June if she'd already fallen asleep, and poured herself a generous glass of Pinot Noir. Then she grabbed her bag of M&Ms and padded to the front porch to settle in one of the oversized, white rocking chairs.

As Bobbi sipped her wine, she couldn't help mulling over what Luke had said about Trey, that he was a playboy and not the kind of man she should tangle with. Surely as Trey's best friend, Luke knew him best, but she'd never seen any behavior on Trey's part to make her think of him as a love-'em-and-leave-'em kind of guy. If anything, he'd been *too* respectful of the girls she'd thrown into his path. Unlike Colton, Trey had foregone one-night stands, barely even sparing a glance for the eligible females of Sultry County. Heck, the only woman he had eyes for these days was…

Her.

Bobbi closed her fist, crushing the M&Ms to bits. Right before Trey had taken her face between his gritty palms and kissed her, he'd said he couldn't stand Sarah's company because of one deal-breaking character flaw: she wasn't Bobbi. Then he'd dizzied her mind with his kisses and made it impossible to think, but now—with a clear head—Bobbi could see Trey's feelings for her went beyond simple lust. Way beyond. Maybe it wasn't love, but he'd grown to care for her so deeply it had affected his ability to hook up with anyone else.

This realization both thrilled and terrified her in equal measure. Her pulse responded in turn, galloping though her veins with wild abandon.

There was no point denying she cared for Trey too. Sure, there was plenty of lust in the mix, but she wanted more than just a quick tumble between his sheets—she wanted…well, just *more*. How much more, she didn't know.

But that didn't mean getting involved with him was wise. Just look what had happened tonight. She'd opened herself to him, in more ways than one, and had wound up sobbing in her car, struggling with old Jedi mind tricks to maintain her sanity. Besides, there was the whole issue of her journalistic credibility and the success of *Sex in the Sticks*.

No, she simply couldn't get involved with Trey, no matter how tempting. She'd be risking too much—both emotionally and professionally. No man was worth it.

Bobbi knew she should run to Luke, confess everything, and replace Trey with another subject, but instead, she stayed put, resting her heels against the wood planks and sipping wine as she brainstormed another solution. Because what she *should* do and what she *wanted* to do were two different things.

If she took Trey off the project for personal reasons, Luke would probably understand, but would that solve her problem? Just look at her past behavior. She'd proven she couldn't stay away from Trey even if he wrapped himself in barbed wire and bathed in acid. What she needed was a way to make Trey unavailable to her, but how could she do that when he wanted her too? She'd already tried pairing him with the perfect woman, and that hadn't—

Bobbi gasped, the answer suddenly clear. An idea took root inside her mind, spreading faster than ivy, and she couldn't believe she hadn't thought of it before. She knew the perfect way to make Trey unavailable and help *Sex in the Sticks* become a success, all at the same time. Trey might not like it, but then again, it could change his life for the better. Maybe he'd thank her one day.

Bobbi finished her wine and took a deep breath, trying to steel herself for what lay ahead. All she needed now was the will to carry out her plan, because one thing was certain—it would break her heart.

Chapter 13

LIKE RAPPER B-REAL OF CYPRESS HILL, TREY WAS going insane in the membrane.

Why, you ask? Just take your pick. For starters, a week had passed since his mom's brownie ambush, and she'd been so far up his ass the whole time that Trey could stunt double for the Asian guy in *Human Centipede*. It hadn't taken long for Mom to find out about *Sex in the Sticks*, and the nag-a-thon he'd endured over the past several days had left him with the overpowering urge to drive a butter knife through his temple. But every time he'd dropped hints about Mom returning home, she'd go all wide-eyed and sniffle and start bitching about his dad.

If that weren't enough to drive him to drink—well, drink *more*—the new building inspector wanted his palm greased, and one of the yahoos on the crew had accidentally cut the power line while planting a cedar tree behind the community center. It was a miracle the idiot hadn't electrocuted himself. Sultry Electric posted those "call before you dig" signs for a reason.

But those annoyances seemed like trifling mosquito bites compared to the real problem eating him up inside, and that was Bobbi. Or rather, the absence of Bobbi. According to that giant, blue-haired dude, Weezer or something like that, she'd left town to meet with her boss and "call in some favors." And while she'd been in constant contact with her crew over the last six days, she hadn't responded to any of Trey's calls or texts.

And that shit made him crazy.

"Hey, man." Luke pointed to the breakfast burrito in Trey's fist. "You gonna eat that?"

Trey glanced at the tortilla, bursting with scrambled eggs, green peppers, and sausage. Heaving a sigh, he passed it to his buddy. It smelled heavenly, but the thing would taste like cardboard. All his food did now. "Mom made it," he warned Luke, knowing the hatred between those two was mutual.

"S'okay." Luke shoved half the burrito in his mouth and spoke around a cheek full of eggs. "If she made it for you, she probably left out the rat poison."

Kicking aside a discarded shingle, Trey leaned a shoulder against one of the newly erected pillars that flanked the community center's main entrance. He folded his arms to fight off a shiver, squinting against the low, morning sun and wishing the weather would make up its mind already. Each day since Bobbi left had been colder and darker than the last, as if Old Man Winter had dementia and didn't realize it wasn't his turn to come poking around yet.

"You okay?" Luke asked, just before devouring the second half of Trey's breakfast.

No, Trey most certainly wasn't okay, but he couldn't tell his friend why. *I came this close to making sweet, sweet love to your little sister, and now she won't talk to me*. Luke would kill him, give him CPR, then kill him again.

"Just tired," Trey lied, "and ready to have the house to myself again. My mom snores."

After wiping his greasy palms against his jeans, Luke clapped Trey on the back. "Sucks, man, but what're you gonna do? Send her packin' at a time like this?" He knew about the divorce. Trey had told him last week. "Not even I would do that to her, and I can't stand the bit—uh, the woman."

Trey slid a heated gaze at his buddy, miffed at the near slip. Ice Queen or not, you didn't bad-mouth a guy's mama. "No shit. Why'd you think I haven't hog-tied her and put her on the red-eye to Chicago?" Yet.

"Just sayin'…" Luke held out a defensive hand, but before he finished his thought, Stevie Ray Vaughn's *Pride and Joy* rang out from the cell phone in his pocket. It was June's ringtone; she loved that song. But instead of glowing like a sixty-watt bulb at the contact, Luke grimaced. "Dammit." He pulled out the phone and silenced it, sending the call to voice mail.

Uh-oh. Trey sensed trouble in paradise. "What's up with that?" he asked, nodding at the cell.

"I already know what she wants."

"Which is…?"

"To meet me at home for lunch."

Trey shrugged, shaking his head in confusion. He didn't see the problem.

"For sex," Luke clarified.

"Dude, I'm still not seeing the problem."

"Sex with a purpose." Dipping his head, Luke delivered a dark, pointed look and sank to the concrete steps, where he slumped over, hugging his knees like a kid waking from a nightmare. "She's got baby fever."

"Oh, snap." Well, hell. That'd take the jingle out of any man's junk. "Too bad there's no Tylenol for that."

But then something occurred to Trey. "Wait, I thought you wanted kids." Luke and June had been married for two years. Wasn't that about the time most couples started trying for a stinky little bundle of joy?

"I do."

"So what's holdin' you back?"

Luke darted a gaze around the property, noting the location of each worker as if afraid they'd overhear. Then he stared at his folded hands, licking his lips, hesitating to speak. This came as no surprise. Luke had always been an overly private man—which explained why he'd never mentioned Bobbi before she'd come to town.

"Out with it," Trey pressed.

"It'll sound stupid."

"I'd expect no less from you."

A soft snort of laughter shook Luke's chest, breaking the ice just enough for him to admit, "I don't wanna share her." Taking a slow, deep breath, he twisted the wedding band around his left ring finger. "How am I supposed to explain that to her without sounding like a selfish prick?"

"I've seen the way *Jooonbug* looks at you. No baby's gonna change that."

"I know." Luke shrugged, still fidgeting with his gold band. "But I wish we could've had more time, just the two of us. I wish I'd married her ten years ago."

"Buddy, you weren't ready ten years ago."

Luke gave a sad nod of agreement. "I know that. But every minute I wasn't with June feels like wasted time now. Time I'll never get back. I like having her all to myself, and I'm not ready to give that up yet."

"Then tell her." Anyone with eyes could see that June thought her husband hung the moon and lit the stars. No woman had ever looked at Trey like that. "She'll understand. Worst case scenario, you compromise."

"Compromise what? You can't have half a baby."

"Well, no, wiseass, but if she wants a kid now, and you wanna wait four years, you settle on two—" Trey bit short his reply as his head whipped toward the parking lot of its own volition.

All thoughts of Luke and June's hypothetical babies instantly ceased when Bong's white van pulled into the nearest parking space. Trey's pulse did the fifty-yard dash though his veins in anticipation of seeing Bobbi.

She's back!

Trey pushed off the pillar, finger-combed his hair, and stood ramrod straight, then realizing he'd appear too stiff that way, relaxed his posture, tucking both hands in his pockets so as not to seem too eager. But in truth, his eyes ached to take in the graceful curve of Bo's face, the way her green irises warmed when locked with his, her lush, pink lips parted in a smile just for him. Christ, he'd missed her. Hard.

He even had a present to give her once Luke took a hike. It wasn't anything fancy—just a handheld Tetris game he'd spotted while picking up a few things at the General Store. He'd thought of Bobbi at once, imagining how good it would make her feel to put all those little squares in order. Maybe she could keep it in her purse and whip it out whenever the compulsion to organize Luke's CD collection took over.

"What the hell?" Luke demanded. "You look more nervous than a nun in a Hustler shop."

Feigning indifference, Trey dipped his chin and joined Luke on the concrete steps. "They just surprised me is all."

With narrowed eyes, Luke's gaze moved over Trey's face as if trying to see the hidden image in one of those three-dimensional puzzle posters. He grit his teeth, grinding out, "She's not with 'em."

Bobbi wasn't back? Trey's heart froze and sank into the general vicinity of his lower intestine. "Who?" he asked, summoning an ignorant mask.

"My sister, that's who."

"I know that," Trey scoffed. He used his peripheral vision to watch the camera and sound guy cross the lot, noting Bobbi's absence. "She's in California."

"Uh-huh." Clearly, Luke wasn't fooled. "Don't pretend you—"

"Hey, boss." Carlo loped into view, saving Trey from yet another lecture on keeping his snake in its cage.

"Gopher," Trey greeted with a nod. He scanned the kid, noticing he'd finally started to fill out, the bones in his sternum no longer visible beneath his thin T-shirt. And damn, if he hadn't sprouted another inch in the past week. He was starting to look like a man, sort of. This young apprentice had come a long way since he'd joined the crew. A needling of regret tingled inside Trey's chest when he imagined leaving his little buddy behind at summer's end.

Carlo hooked a thumb over his shoulder. "I finished mulching out back. Whadaya want me to do now?"

"Done already?" Trey elbowed Luke. "Didn't I tell you Gopher's the best guy on my crew?"

While Luke nodded, Carlo ducked his head and

beamed brighter than a new penny. When the camera crew approached with their equipment, Carlo stepped back a few paces, staying out of the shot since his parents hadn't signed the consent form.

"Go find my cooler," Trey told the boy. "I've got an extra breakfast burrito in there. Then head inside and we'll get the walls primed."

"'Kay." Not one to mince words when food was involved, Gopher darted off in search of his meal.

"Kid thinks a lot of you," Luke observed quietly. "What's gonna happen when you leave?"

Trey didn't need reminding. His guilty conscience had been working overtime. "Been meaning to talk to you about that. His hours are almost up, but I want him to stay on with you while I'm overseas." Trey stood and brushed off his backside. "He's a quick learner, but you gotta keep an eye on him. Not much support at home, and I don't want him getting into trouble again. I don't think they feed him enough either. And you might have to buy him some clothes now and then—I'll mail you some cash—just be careful how you give it to him. Say you were going through your old things—get creative. He doesn't like taking charity. No man does." He glanced down at his friend, hoping he'd agree. Teens could be a pain in the keister, and Trey knew he was asking a lot.

Luke said nothing, just grinned at Trey with an expression that reminded him of Bobbi's face the first time she'd visited the job site—disbelief mingled with approval.

"What?" Trey asked, hands on his hips.

"You know, you just might make a halfway decent dad someday."

"Jesus, bite your tongue." Trey crossed himself; never mind that he wasn't Catholic. The last thing he wanted was fruit springing from his loins. "Don't jinx me like that."

Luke barked a laugh, then pushed to standing. "Sorry, man, I take it back." Wiggling his fingers in the air as if casting a spell, he crooned, "May you *aaaaaalways* shoot blanks."

"Jackass," Trey muttered with a chuckle. Just as he geared up for a playful slug to Luke's bicep, the cell phone vibrated inside his back pocket. When he retrieved it and glimpsed the sender's name, his heart bounced back and forth against his tonsils like a paddle-ball. Finally, a text from Bobbi!

Meet me @ Shooters tonight, 9pm. I have a surprise 4 u!

Trey's lungs inflated with pure heat and expanded inside his chest. Bobbi was back, and she had a surprise for him. He hoped it involved her naked thighs and a can of Reddi-wip, but no matter what, at least he'd get to see her again—fill his nostrils with her scent of sweet cinnamon and watch her rub that little button nose when he made her nervous. Which he would, with pleasure.

Trey's fingers trembled as he turned from Luke's line of vision and typed a response.

Can't wait 2 c-u, Bo Peep :)

After tucking his phone into his pocket, Trey wiped his sweaty palms on his jeans, marveling at the butter-flies slam-dancing against his stomach lining. He hadn't felt this anxious over a girl since eleventh grade, when he'd asked Mindy Roberts to junior prom in front of all of her snooty friends. Damn, it was gonna be a long day.

With a grin splitting his face in two, Trey checked his watch. Twelve hours and counting.

———∿∿∿———

At precisely eight forty-five that evening, Trey sat in his truck cab and scrutinized his appearance in the rear-view mirror, running one palm over the smooth edge of his freshly shaven jaw and tilting his face from side to side for any spots he might've missed. As keyed up as he'd been while getting ready, it was a wonder he hadn't cut himself to ribbons. He straightened the collar of his short-sleeved, button-down shirt—the one Bobbi'd complimented the night of the church barbeque—and raked his fingers though his hair, still slightly damp from the shower and smelling of Suave shampoo. He looked pretty damned good, if he did say so himself.

Trey checked the dashboard's digital clock—eight forty-six—and scanned the Shooter's parking lot for Bobbi's purple car, spotting only the crew's van. Maybe she'd ridden with Bong or parked around back with June and Luke. Or maybe she wasn't here yet. Either way, Trey decided a seat on his bar stool and a cold Bud in his hand easily trumped loitering in his Chevy. He made his way inside, taking a deep breath to steady his churning guts.

Striding blindly to his designated place at the bar, Trey pulled in the comforting scents of hops and crushed peanut shells as his eyes adjusted to the darkness.

"Bud draft," he told the bartender, the same red-headed kid who'd served him the day Bobbi had come to town. June was probably in the back office with Luke, where she usually stayed until things got busy. Tossing a couple of bucks tip onto the gleaming oak, Trey climbed onto his stool, then swiveled around to check out the place. Hard as he tried to maintain a cool facade, his frenzied gaze swept over each tableful of bodies with one mission: to spot Bobbi, the neurotic little neat freak who'd turned his brain into banana pudding. He released the breath he'd been holding. She wasn't here yet.

He found the crew though, already set up at the pool tables in the back and filming Colton as he melded his body against a busty blond, showing her how to break a shot. Trey squinted, leaning forward to get a better look at Colt's woman of the hour. She looked familiar, something about her body...*oh shit*.

He recognized those double-Ds, and more importantly, the psycho attached to them. Trey couldn't remember her name, but she'd come on to him a few months ago at a bar over in Hallover County. He'd shot her down instantly—she'd put off a loony vibe thicker than skunk musk—and it'd taken two hours to shake her. A stage-four clinger, that one. He should let Colt know, discreetly, of course, so as not to get his tires slashed. As soon as Colt glanced up, Trey waved him over.

Colton left his lady friend, but not before pulling her into a long kiss for the camera. Poor bastard didn't know what he'd just done. Now the cling-on would be harder to remove than a tick off a honey badger. Trey shook his head, laughing as his buddy approached.

"Make it quick, Lewis," Colton said, tipping back his Stetson to scratch his forehead. He gestured toward the blond. "She's hot to trot."

"Do yourself a favor, and throw that one back," Trey advised. "I've met her before. She's got crazy eyes."

"She's got eyes?" Colt cupped both hands in front of his chest as if juggling watermelons. "I was too distracted by those tig ol' bitties to notice." Without asking, Colt reached over and took a swig of Trey's beer. Man, that shit just wasn't cool. "Not to worry, my friend. It's not her eyes I'm after tonight."

"Suit yourself." Let the smug moron learn the hard way. "And take the Bud. I'm not drinking after you. No tellin' where your mouth's been."

With a cocky grin, Colt drawled, "That's exactly what the Bodacious Gallagher said last week." After another deep pull of beer, he clarified, "When I offered to kiss her."

Trey slid from his bar stool, ready to close his fist around Colton's throat when the jerk danced away, pointing at the front door. "Speak of the devil."

All thoughts of violence vanished as Trey whirled toward the entrance with his stomach in his throat. It was Bobbi, and sweet mother of Sammy Sosa, she looked more stunning than he'd ever seen her, and that was saying a lot. Smoothing her already meticulously styled red hair, she spoke to someone still in the parking lot and brushed lint from the swell of her breasts, showcased beneath a skintight, black, one-shouldered minidress. Trey let his gaze follow the curves of her long, tanned legs, ending with her slender ankles and strappy, hot pink high heels. Goddamn, he wanted her even more now than the last time he'd had her in his arms, and he hadn't thought that was possible.

He didn't spend another second watching from afar. In record time—image be damned—he crossed the bar and met Bobbi's gaze, smiling with all the exuberance in his thumping heart. Her eyes widened, mouth dropping into a pretty oval, and all the color drained from her face as if he'd scared the life out of her. She recovered almost instantly, plastering on the kind of cold, stiff grin he'd come to expect from DMV workers. Seemed he'd have to warm her up again.

"Hey, Bo Peep." He pulled her in for a hug, but her typically responsive body stiffened, and she returned his embrace with a detached pat on the back before pushing away. "What's wrong?" he asked.

"Nothing." She scratched her nose and then quickly dropped her hand. "Nothing at all. In fact, I've—"

"Hold up." Trey reached into his back pocket and handed Bobbi the Tetris game he'd bought for her. "When I saw this, I knew you had to have it." With tentative fingers, she accepted his gift and turned it over, smoothing her thumb over the glossy, gray screen. "Now," he said with a gentle nudge, "you can leave Luke's junk drawer in peace."

"You bought me Tetris?" It didn't make sense, but she looked hurt, biting her bottom lip and going glassy-eyed, chin quivering. Well, damn. Had he done something wrong? With women, he never knew.

"It's just a game, darlin'," he reassured her. "I thought you'd like it."

"Right." She gave a tight nod as she locked eyes with someone behind him and waved. A quick glance over his shoulder showed the crew making a sudden beeline for him. "Thanks for thinking of me," she said, tucking the gadget inside her purse.

"Sure." Trey took a chance, leaning in to kiss her cheek, but she took a step back. "Let's get outta here. Go somewhere quiet, maybe the springs." As cool as the temperature had been lately, they could skinny-dip in nature's hot tub. He couldn't wait to feel the cushion of Bobbi's thighs wrapped around his waist. "I missed you while—"

"Ready for your surprise?" She cut him off, smiling wide and making a *let's roll* motion to her crew, who'd just positioned themselves around him. Alarms went off inside Trey's mushy brain. Something was wrong here.

She opened the front door and whispered, "Come on," to a person on the other side. Before Trey could tell Bobbi the only thing he wanted was a moment alone with her, a ghost from his past stepped inside—a very lovely ghost, linked hand-in-hand with his mother. All the air inside Trey's lungs left in a whoosh, creating a vacuum that made it impossible to breathe.

A petite brunette in jeans and a simple, black T-shirt stood before him, mahogany curls framing a heart-shaped face, and hazel eyes smiling back beneath thick lashes.

Trey blinked a few times to make sure he wasn't hallucinating. He wasn't. God Almighty, he hadn't laid eyes on this girl in ten years, and aside from the slightest added fullness in her blushing cheeks, she hadn't changed a bit. Heck, she even wore her hair the same way as the last time he'd seen her, the day she'd sent him off to basic training with a kiss and a promise to wait forever. Turned out "forever" had meant six weeks.

Trey managed to fill his chest with enough air to stammer, "Mindy?"

Chapter 14

HATE WAS A STRONG WORD—BOBBI'S DADS HAD always said so. But no matter how powerful, it didn't capture the depth of Bobbi's loathing for Mindy Roberts, the ex-girlfriend who'd broken Trey's heart, and now wanted another chance with "the one that got away," as she'd described him in their preliminary phone interview last week.

Bobbi didn't believe in second chances for the unfaithful—once a cheater, always a cheater—but this wasn't about her. Mindy had promised to focus her wandering eye and treat Trey right this time. If they'd kept the spark alive all these years, then Bobbi wanted Trey to be happy with the kind of girl his mother could approve of. And judging by the unholy light glowing in Mrs. Lewis's eyes, she was ready to drag the pair to the altar by their throats and perform the ceremony at knifepoint.

"Hi, Pooh Bear," Mindy said to Trey in a puke-worthy, breathy voice. Who would nickname a guy like Trey *Pooh Bear*? Someone who didn't deserve him, that's who. "You look amazing."

He really did—as "amazing" as Bobbi had ever seen him. He'd worn the shirt she loved, the one that matched his sea-blue eyes and hugged the hard contours of his broad shoulders, paired with worn, faded jeans, somehow more flattering on his lean hips than any designer denim she'd ever seen. When he'd approached her seconds ago, he'd stolen her breath with his thousand-watt smile, and the temptation to send his visitors packing had nearly won.

"You too." Trey held out his arms, giving his ex a welcoming hug that made Bobbi's vision go spotty. The pair held each other for a few beats too long, forcing Bobbi to drop her gaze until they parted. After stepping back, Trey glanced at each woman. "But what're you doing here?"

"Miss Gallagher called me," Mindy said, cupping Trey's cheek with one hand and using the other to smooth the fabric over his chest. A touchy-feely little thing, wasn't she? "She told me about the show and—"

"That's the surprise," Bobbi interrupted in a syrupy tone, smiling at the camera. "I thought it'd be fun to do a first love reunion episode. You know, catch up with an old flame. Reminisce," she added in a voice louder than she'd intended, "about the good old days."

"A what?" Colton asked, unceremoniously shoving Bong aside as he stepped closer. He shook off the buxom blond suction-cupped to his side and darted a glance at the front door, his brows raised expectantly. Swallowing hard enough to shift his Adam's apple, he turned to Bobbi with pure anticipation illuminating his face.

"Oh, Colt." Bobbi brought a hand to her mouth. She didn't mean for Colton to think his first love was out there too. Until now, she hadn't realized just how deeply he cared for the preacher's daughter, and she felt awful for getting his hopes up this way. Linking their arms, she led him away from the group.

They wove between scattered stools and tables until

they reached a quiet spot by the side wall. "I'm sorry, but I couldn't find Leah. I really tried." She squeezed his bicep and added, "Listen, for what it's worth, my boss did everything short of violating privacy laws to track her down. Someone who's buried herself that deeply doesn't want to be found."

He lifted his face and gazed blankly at the pool tables in the distance, hands on his hips, clearly crushed and trying his best not to let it show.

"Maybe it's time to let her go," Bobbi said gently, as if lowering her voice could soften the disappointment.

Colt whipped his head around, narrowed eyes burning into hers. "I already did." He tore off his Stetson, ran a trembling hand through his black hair, and replaced it, pulling the brim low over his forehead. "I'm glad you didn't find her. You got no business dumpin' a can of worms like that into someone's life." Then, gesturing to Trey and Mindy still conversing at the front entrance, he scolded, "You didn't do Lewis any favors with that one. What's wrong with you?"

"Me?" she asked, resting a hand over her heart. "I thought it would make a great show."

Colt inclined his head, a smirk tugging one corner of his mouth. "You can't bullshit the bull, honey."

"I don't know what you're talking about," she lied, interlacing her fingers to keep from scratching her nose.

"You're crazy about him, and you're sabotaging yourself." When she opened her mouth to object, Colt cut her off with a shake of his head. "I've done it enough times to know it when I see it. So what's got you so scared that you'd rather see Lewis with another woman than with you?"

"I can't have him," she blurted before thinking better of it.

"That's a cop out."

"No, it's not. I can name half a dozen reasons—"

"Lame."

"He's leaving—"

"Weak."

"We're both—"

"Excuses."

"Dammit, Colt, it's none of your business!"

"Listen up, Gallagher. I'm gonna tell you something I wish I'd'a known years ago." Colt bent low, bringing his mouth to her ear. "Love's not for pansies. If you don't have the *cajones* to take what you want, then you don't deserve it."

"Wha—" Before she had a chance to tell him where to shove his *cajones*—because she wasn't in love!— Colton spun on his booted heel and stalked away, snagging his blonde, who'd been waiting patiently by the bar this whole time. After declaring, "No cameras!" he towed his date out the door and disappeared into the parking lot.

Well, that could've gone better.

"Same goes for me," Trey said to Weezus, holding one palm forward. When the crew tried cajoling him into changing his mind, he insisted, "This is private," and he led his mother and Mindy out the door without saying good-bye.

Bobbi's lips parted in shock. She couldn't believe he'd taken his prize and left so quickly.

He really did it. He's really taking her home. Bobbi struggled to catch her breath. She perched on the nearest stool and immediately berated herself. Of course he'd taken Mindy home. What had she expected—that he'd denounce the curly-haired beauty in front of an audience of millions and send her back to her penthouse in Chicago? No, not when they shared such an intimate history, not when she'd occupied such a special place in his heart. It was only natural for Trey to take his first love home and spend the night playing "remember when?" and laughing and touching and…whatever else happened afterward. Bobbi couldn't think too hard about that "whatever else" and maintain what was left of her sanity.

Damn it to hell, Bobbi had gotten exactly what she'd wanted. Or at least what was best for her—no use pretending that Trey and Mindy's reunion was what she wanted.

Bong collapsed his microphone pole and joined her. "You okay?" he asked, smoothing the frayed ends of his blond soul patch. Weezus loped over and closed the distance in four of his oversized strides. Setting his camera on the bar, he repeated the same question.

"Of course," she lied for what seemed like the hundredth time that day. "I just wish the Golden Boy would've let us film the good stuff." Oh god. Just thinking about the "good stuff" Trey and Mindy would do later made bile rise in her throat. "That's what people want to see."

"Sex sells," agreed Weezus, shaking back his blue dreadlocks. "But look on the bright side."

"Which is?" She leaned in and sniffed the air a few times. Something smelled good, and she thought it was the crew. That couldn't be right.

"We've got the night off." He lifted his indigo brows, dyed to match his hair. "Are you smelling me?"

She recognized that scent. "You're wearing real deodorant." Store-bought, with chemicals and everything. "And cologne!" It came out like an accusation, and she quickly checked her tone. "Not that I'm complaining." She'd been rallying for this a long time and didn't want to scare them off modern hygiene.

"Ladies around here don't appreciate a man's natural scent," Bong explained.

"The way a man *should* smell," Weezus elaborated.

Bobbi pointed to herself. "This lady's never appreciated it."

"Yeah, but you don't count." Weezus patted her on the head.

"Good to know." Shoving his giant hand aside, Bobbi nodded toward the pool tables. "You two up for a game?"

"How about a rain check, boss?" said Bong. "There's something going down at the hot springs tonight." A flicker of light dawned in his eyes, as if he realized he'd said too much. He muttered a quick, "Um…you can come too…if you want."

Clearly, the guys wanted to be alone with whomever had enticed them into abandoning crystal deodorant, and Bobbi didn't want to be the fifth wheel. She wasn't *that* big a loser. Yet. "Thanks, but I think I'll head home."

Within five minutes, they'd packed up the equipment and left her in the dust.

To add insult to injury, a slow, twangy country song played from the jukebox, and big-bellied farmers left their seats, partnering with willing females to dance between tables, not one of them asking Bobbi to two-step. Okay, so maybe she didn't know the two-step, but she could learn, couldn't she?

It seemed everyone had paired up, both inside the bar and out—Trey and Mindy, June and Luke, Judge Bea and Pru, even her hippy-dippy crew had found *amour* in this Podunk town.

"And as usual," Bobbi grumbled to herself, "the cheese stands alone."

Well, not completely alone. She reached into her bag and retrieved the Tetris game Trey had given her. "Hey, small, dark, and handsome," she said to her date for the night. "Want to come back to my place and play?"

"You talkin' to me?" wheezed an old guy beside her at the bar. Tossing a peanut into his mouth, he gave her an approving once-over before shaking his head. "'Cause I'm hitched, sweetheart."

Nice. She couldn't even score with the Crypt Keeper. "Oh, well." She snapped her fingers and smiled sweetly. "My loss."

Two hours later, Bobbi swayed on the front porch swing, barefoot and wrapped in a Texas Rangers Snuggie with her backlit boyfriend curled between both palms. The typically humid night air was crisp with a frosty edge that stung her nose, but she couldn't hole up inside Luke's house another minute.

As she topped her own high score for the fourth time, she reflected that while Tetris wasn't the most expensive gift she'd ever received, it was—hands down—the most thoughtful, because it showed that Trey knew her. He'd seen this game displayed by a cash register and had thought of her, and that was the real reward. This wasn't some token present from the jewelry store like the hastily purchased white gold earrings her ex had given her for Christmas a couple of years ago. Lovely hoops, to be sure, but Bobbi must've mentioned half a dozen times that she was allergic to white gold. She would've rather received a handwritten love note than a lavish gift with no sentiment behind it.

"Level eight!" she bragged to the crickets, who ignored her and continued their mating calls. Even the bugs were getting lucky tonight. With a sigh, she hit the pause button and reached down to grab her glass of sangria. That's when she noticed the distant sound of gravel crunching beneath tires.

The noise grew louder by the second, giving her the impression that someone was hauling ass down the narrow lane leading to Luke's property. Bobbi's first instinct—courtesy of growing up in the inner city—was to run inside and lock the door. Reminding herself this was Sultry Springs, not Los Angeles, she took a sip of her sweet wine and tried to relax, but she couldn't help recalling that *Texas Chainsaw Massacre* was based on a true story.

Soon an oversized vehicle fishtailed into view, causing Bobbi to shield her eyes against blinding headlights. The truck skidded to a halt, spitting rocks against the porch steps. Just when Bobbi'd gathered her Snuggie and bolted for the house, the driver cut the lights and Bobbi exhaled in relief. The heavy moon illuminated a Chevy she knew well, not to mention its driver, who'd just kicked open his door, jumped down, and slammed it hard enough to shake the whole front end.

It was Trey, and he looked *madder than a mosquito on a mannequin*, as Pru had said a couple of weeks ago.

Bobbi squinted at the passenger seat, finding it vacant of everything but a carry-on suitcase, then back to Trey's narrowed eyes as he stalked up the porch steps and paused. He curled one trembling hand around the wood railing, gripping the pine like he wanted to choke the sap out of it. His jaw clenched so hard she feared he'd break his own face, his broad chest heaving with each labored breath. Instinctively, Bobbi backed up a few paces.

"Where's Mindy?" she asked.

He didn't answer, just inhaled loudly through his nose and scorched her with the fury of his glare. The light streaming from the kitchen window cast his face in shadows, making him seem ghoulish—purely wicked and beyond reason. Bobbi knew he wouldn't hurt her, but for good measure, she kept retreating until her back-side met the door.

"Who the hell," he finally whispered, "do you think you are?"

Experience told her there was no right way to answer that question. Bobbi's palms grew clammy, and she reached beneath the blanket to wipe them on her dress, sweat stains be damned. Pulling the Snuggie tightly around her like armor, she cleared her throat and repeated, "Where's Mindy?"

"In my bedroom." He crept one step closer, floor-boards creaking beneath his weight. "Because my mother's in the goddamn spare." Another slow step. "Thanks to you, I've been run out of my own home." And another. "I wanna know why you did it."

"You left home?" That explained the suitcase. "But I thought—"

"Answer my question!" His shout silenced even the crickets.

She stalled, unable to admit the truth—that she'd needed to make him unavailable because she wasn't strong enough to keep her legs closed when he was around. "Which one?"

He opened his mouth to yell again but snapped it shut, along with his eyes. Gripping his hips, Trey hung his head and sucked in several deep breaths, obviously struggling to contain his anger. When he glanced up, the look on his face—blue eyes wide, lips pressed together—stung even worse than his rage. He was hurt.

Oh god, she'd hurt him. A dull ache pulsed inside her chest with each second he remained silent, wounded, and waiting. "Trey," she stammered, unsure of how to make this better, "I didn't mean to—"

"You had no right." When he folded his muscled arms across his chest, Bobbi noticed goose bumps puckering his tanned skin. She quickly pulled both arms out of her wearable blanket and handed it to him, an admittedly weak peace offering. He snatched the fabric and tossed it onto a nearby rocking chair. "No right to play God, and no right to lead Mindy on like that."

"I thought if you could be friends, then maybe—"

"I've got enough friends," he interrupted. "Besides, you and I both know that's not what Mindy wants, and it was cruel of you to let her think she had a chance. You should've seen the look in her eyes when I shut her down." He squeezed his temples between two fingers as if to expel the memory. "If you'd've just talked to me, I would've told you I don't want her in my life. There's a reason I haven't kept in touch with her."

"I'm really sorry," Bobbi whispered, meaning every word. "I thought you might still love her."

"Why?"

"Because she was your first, and it's really hard to get over—"

"No." He closed the distance between them, moving so close she could make out the faint, golden stubble along his jaw, his white-blond lower lashes contrasted against eyes so blue they didn't seem real. Bracing both palms against the door, he trapped her between two walls, much like he'd done the first time he'd kissed her. "Why'd you do it?"

The warmth from his body, his delicious scent of sandalwood, overwhelmed her senses and made it impossible to think. She wanted to save herself, but she didn't know how. From deep within, her lockbox of emotions began to rise from the ocean floor where she'd buried it. She closed her eyes, struggling to imagine its chains secured to a ten-ton anchor.

"Hey." Trey sighed, stirring the hair at her temple. She sensed him hesitate, then he brought his hand to her face and brushed one rough thumb over her cheek. "Don't cry; just talk to me."

Bobbi opened her eyes. "I'm not crying." But one glance at the glistening bead of moisture on his thumb made her a liar. Using her own fingers, she dabbed at her face, finding it wet with leaking tears.

"Look at me." He cupped her chin, tilting her face until their eyes met. "Why?"

Though still smoldering, his gaze moved over her face with tender care, the touch of his hand a reassuring promise to protect her from anything—even herself. It gave her the strength to confess what she'd done.

"Because," she whispered, then paused to swallow her fear. "I can't stay away from you."

He didn't respond at first. Tipping their foreheads together, he cradled her face between his rugged palms and breathed long and deep. Eventually, she matched her breaths to his, and the lockbox sank slowly until it came to rest again on the ocean's sandy floor.

"That was selfish," he said, still not looking at her. "And stupid."

"I know." She tried to nod, but his grasp kept her immobile. "I'm sorry."

"Bobbi," he spoke into her hair, "you don't have to go digging up my old girlfriends. I'll find a way to leave you alone if that's what you want." Caressing her cheeks, he moved his mouth to her ear, where he whispered, "It won't be easy, but I'll do it for you." He placed one gentle kiss on the side of her neck before nuzzling her with his nose. "Is that what you want?"

A soft whimper bubbled up from Bobbi's throat. She tilted her head to give him free rein, using one hand to pull his face harder against her neck, and when he sank his teeth into the erogenous patch of skin at the base of her shoulder, her soft whimper turned into a groan.

"What do you want?" he whispered in her ear, coaxing chills to the surface of her skin.

"You," she replied without another moment's hesitation. "I want *you*." She wrapped both arms around his strong back and tugged him forward, eliminating the sliver of air between them.

Keeping her face within his grasp, Trey pulled back just enough to bring them eye-level. "You're sure?"

"Yes."

He darted a glance through the kitchen window. "When's your brother coming home?"

"Around three." Luke and June were scheduled to close Shooters together. "But if—"

Before Bobbi had a chance to offer an alternative, Trey bent low, leaned into her midsection, and tossed her over one shoulder, exactly like the day they'd met. He threw open the front door and carried her into the house and up the stairs like the caveman she'd once mistaken him for...only this time, she didn't fight back.

This time, she was his.

Chapter 15

TREY WASN'T GENTLE WHEN HE UNDRESSED HER, AND that suited Bobbi just fine. A thrill tingled along her spine as he unzipped her dress and forced the rayon fabric to the floor in one rough motion that stung the skin on the outsides of her hips. Just as quickly, he reached behind her back, easily unlatched her strapless bra, and tossed it aside before turning his attention to her black satin panties. It was then that he slowed things down, kneeling at her bare feet and pressing her back against her cool bedroom wall. He smoothed his palms up and down the length of her legs, gazing at them in worship and murmuring, "Christ, I've waited a long time for this."

Nudging her apart, he curled his fingers around the backs of her thighs, kneading deeply while he kissed a trail up the inside of each one. The hallway light sliced through the open door, illuminating the darkness. Bobbi wished she'd had a chance to turn it off. She hated that Trey had an up-close and personal view of the fattest part of her body. Everyone was thin and perfect in the dark.

"Let me get the light," she breathed, squirming as he nibbled the skin just beneath the crotch of her undies.

"Good idea." He rose high enough to flip on the bedroom switch, flooding her eyes with brightness. She squinted and quickly shut it off again.

He glanced up in confusion. "What'd you do that for?"

"I meant the hall light."

Lowering one brow, he considered a moment. "But then I won't be able to see you."

"That's kind of the point." She tried blocking his view with her hands, but she couldn't hide fifteen pounds of flab with ten bony fingers. The hip-hugging shorts and high heels she usually wore had elongated her legs, making her seem slender, but now there wasn't a scrap of fabric concealing her flesh. Damn it, why couldn't he fixate on her boobs instead? She had great boobs.

"Listen to me." He pushed her hands away and resumed kneading with those strong, rough hands. "You've got the most gorgeous thighs I've ever seen in my life."

Bobbi shook her head, feeling the heat rise in her cheeks.

"Yes, you do," he insisted. "It was the first thing I noticed the day you walked into Shooters in those hot-ass shorty-shorts, and I've been dreaming about you ever since."

"Are you serious?"

"Don't believe me?" He pulled her down to the floor until she knelt beside him, then he pressed her hand against the enormous bulge straining the front of his Levis. "Think I'd be this hard if I wasn't turned on by your body?"

"Maybe?"

"No." He moved her hand to his mouth and kissed her open palm. "Have I ever lied to you?"

While chewing her bottom lip, Bobbi replayed the last several weeks, realizing that while she'd hidden like a thief from Trey, refusing to trust him with her feelings or the details of her past, he'd never once misled her or kept secrets. It was disbelief that had her shaking her head.

"Then believe me when I say you're perfect. Let me look at you."

She met his gentle blue gaze. "Just the hall light, okay? The other one's too bright."

"Deal." He trailed one fingertip down her cheek. "Now come here."

She straddled his lap, unbuttoning his shirt as Trey tangled his fingers in her hair and pulled her in for a slow, sweet kiss, just a brush of lips and a taste of warmth that turned carnal when their tongues found each other. Each moist sweep, each deep probe sent blood pulsing between Bobbi's legs. She fitted herself to Trey's hips and rocked against his steely length while sliding his shirt over his shoulders. A deep groan rumbled his chest, and she felt the vibration through their fused skin. She ran both hands over his back—God, he had the strongest back of any man she'd ever seen, let alone had the privilege to touch. A rush of desire overtook her, and she couldn't wait for Trey's weight to anchor her to the wood floor, to feel those powerful muscles flex beneath her fingers as he pumped in and out of her aching center. Now. She wanted him right now.

Reaching a hand between them, she tore at the button of his jeans, whispering, "Hurry."

"No." He stilled her hand, then swept his gaze over her breasts before taking one in his hot palm. "I'm in no rush tonight." He brushed his knuckles over her nipple, puckering it with pleasure and bringing a sigh to her lips. "We've got hours, and I'm gonna need each one for what I've got in mind."

"What's that?"

He glanced around the room for a moment, his eyes eventually settling on something over her shoulder. "Do you trust me?"

"Yes." The word escaped without conscious thought. She trusted this man completely.

Pushing her off his lap, he ordered, "Then go lie down on the bed."

She obeyed, standing first and hooking her thumbs around the waistband of her panties.

"Don't," he said in a husky voice. "I wanna take those off myself."

His fevered gaze sent Bobbi's heart stumbling over its own beats. She walked to the bed on shaky knees, threw back the comforter, and positioned herself on the center of the mattress, eagerly awaiting the heat from his broad chest against her skin. She reclined, flat on her back, fisting the starched, white sheets to keep from trembling in anticipation.

"That's good." When she looked up, Trey was kicking off his boots. He held her black silk scarf—the one she'd left on the dresser a few days ago. Nodding at the headboard, he commanded, "Now grab that bedpost with both hands."

Wait, wait, wait. He wanted to tie her up? Bobbi had never experimented with bondage—hated the idea of being helpless. Besides, she wanted to use her hands, feel his burning, sun-kissed skin. She wasn't so sure she could do this.

"I won't hurt you." He sat on the edge of the bed, shaking the mattress with his added weight. "If I do something you don't like, just tell me to stop." Trailing his index finger from her throat to her navel, he added, "But I don't think you will, darlin'."

His seductive promise gave her the courage to lift both trembling arms above her head, where Trey secured them to the headboard at the wrists, snugly, but not tight enough to cause her any pain. Face-up in the vulnerable position, she'd never felt so exposed, and she needed him to cover her with his body.

"Trey…" she pleaded.

He seemed to understand, moving over her and supporting his weight on his elbows. Starting at her temple, he kissed his way down the side of her face to her ear, where he grazed her tender lobe with his teeth. All the while, his left hand explored her curves, grasping her bottom, massaging over her panties, while his warm breath panted in her ear.

With jean-clad legs, he parted her, holding his hips barely out of reach. Bobbi dug her heels into the mattress and arched against him. Her reward was light friction where she needed it most, just a feather graze that served to multiply her hunger instead of sate it.

"More," she whispered, straining harder against him.

He indulged her—grinding in small circles, the taut muscles of his abdomen bunching against her flesh, his hard length stroking her into a luscious stupor—but instead of taking her all the way, he abruptly withdrew, rising to his knees and leaving her writhing on the bed and gasping, "No, don't stop."

"Be still," he murmured, pinning her hips to the bed with his firm grip. "Calm down a little first." Once she'd pulled a few deep breaths through her nose, he released her, turning his attention to her breasts.

Leaning over her on all fours, he dipped his head and flicked his tongue over her nipple, then teased, circling the hardened tip again and again, until she bowed her back, willing him to take more. When he cupped one breast and drew her into his blazing, wet mouth, her lips parted in a silent scream, her hips vainly seeking the solid ridge of his erection, which he'd held far beyond her reach. He moved to the other breast, suckling greedily, and she felt each deep pull right between her legs, where she'd grown wet and aching and unfulfilled.

A desperate noise, half whine, half moan, escaped her throat, and it was then that he sat back on his heels and gave her momentary relief, rubbing his hand over the dampened fabric of her panties just long enough to silence her.

"I think these can go now." He slipped his fingers beneath the satin and peeled the garment down over her thighs, past her knees and ankles, eventually tossing them over his shoulder. "And if I remember correctly," he said, scooting toward the foot of the bed, "I made some lofty promises."

"Yes," she breathed, shamelessly spreading her legs and tensing for the touch of his mouth, needing his tongue to extinguish the flames he'd stoked inside her.

Of course he took his sweet time, toying with her, blowing cool air over her swollen folds before placing a chaste kiss there. But then he began in earnest, and oh god, that first lazy lick tore an almost painful gasp from her lungs. He followed with another, harder stroke of his tongue, lapping at her vulnerably parted flesh like a child with an ice cream cone, moaning with enjoyment, savoring her taste. The vibration from his lips melted her bones, and when he isolated her most sensitive spot and drew it into his mouth with firm suction, her legs trembled with pleasure. White spots danced before her eyes, obscuring her vision, and she realized with disbelief that he'd made good on one of his claims: *I can make you see stars*.

Propping both hands beneath her bottom, he angled her toward his face and deepened his erotic kiss, delving deep inside with quick thrusts of his tongue, driving her half mad with need. She moved with him, so close to climax that her inner muscles coiled, preparing to spring in tantalizing release. Trey seemed to sense the change in her, because he withdrew, once again leaving her crying out and pleading for more.

"Don't stop," she growled, lifting her hips and clawing at the bedpost. "Damn it, don't stop!"

"Shhh." Forcing her legs together, he straddled the outsides of her thighs and held her immobile, then bent low to rain kisses on her eyelids, nose, cheeks. "It's too soon."

"Just let me come," she begged. "Then we can keep going."

"Not yet." He skimmed both palms over her nipples, forcing her to bite her lip to contain another sharp cry. "Be still, and let me take you further."

She couldn't lie still, not even within the confines of his powerful legs. She tugged at her restraints, convinced the only reason he'd tied her to the bed was so he could tease her into insanity.

"Trust me," he said, and she opened her eyes to his heavy-lidded gaze, so filled with concern that she couldn't doubt his intentions. His face shone with beauty and lust, wheat-colored strands falling over his forehead as he fought for oxygen, clearly every bit as aroused as she was. "Let me make you forget how to breathe."

Licking her lips, she took a cleansing breath, trying to steady her pounding heart. When she'd found her voice again, she whispered, "Kiss me."

He didn't object, and he didn't hold back. Claiming her mouth, he gave her a kiss so passionate it made her heart swell. He cradled her face as if she were crafted from the frailest, hand-spun glass, his mouth urgent and possessive, his tongue sliding again and again between her bruised lips to mate with hers. He used his body to cherish her, to claim her, making her feel like the only woman alive.

Over the next hour, he used his fingers and tongue to drive her nearly to the brink before bringing her down again, an endless cycle of titillation that had her shaking with desire and pleading for release. Each time he denied her, she felt her control crack, her long-buried emotions bubbling to the surface as unbidden moisture leaked from the corners of her eyes. It was too much—her body could no longer handle the sensations; her mind couldn't focus beyond her most basic, carnal needs. Her nerve endings were on fire, the flames relentlessly licking the throbbing apex between her thighs. She was so engorged she feared she'd burst. Thrashing her head from side to side, she openly begged without shame.

"Please," she groaned, "please, I can't take any more."

Trey's warm breath shuddered against her throat, his chest heaving, body trembling with his own desire. "Now," he promised. "I have to be inside you right now."

Relief flooded through her until she wanted to cry from it. Beneath lids so heavy she could barely see, she watched him sink back on his heels and lower his zipper. He forced his jeans and briefs past his thighs, freeing his jutting erection, long and thick and so huge it would have worried her had she been capable of coherent thought. Without bothering to undress any further, he tugged her into his lap, stretching her arms taut above her head, wrists straining against their silk binding. Letting her lids close, she held her breath and spread herself wide for him.

"Open your eyes," he murmured, thumbing slow circles around her aching, swollen flesh. "Watch with me."

She did, gazing through her lashes at his plump velvet tip, which glistened with a bead of moisture in the dim light. He gripped her thighs and rocked forward, easing inside so slowly her knees trembled. Struggling to focus, she watched as he pulled back and dipped in farther, stretching her inner walls, impaling her with a tiny stitch of pain that only served to heighten the pleasure.

They each released a moan, their eyes meeting for one hot second before they glanced at his wet shaft sinking deeper, pulling back, and sinking deeper still. Her body sang with each pumping caress, each slippery stroke. The air was thick with heat and sex and the sound of her own wetness as he slid in and out.

"Wrap your legs around me," he ordered in a voice so rough she barely made out the words. "I want to be deep inside you."

She obeyed, locking her ankles behind his waist and letting her knees fall open to accommodate more of him. Releasing her hips, he stretched out and lowered onto her body, tucking both hands beneath her bottom to angle her for deeper penetration. Crushed beneath his weight, she delighted in the feeling of safety and warmth, surrounded in his skin and scent.

With one hard thrust, he buried himself completely as she cried out with pleasure. She was so deliciously full, so inconceivably *full* for the first time in her life, and her only wish was to use her hands to grip his iron buttocks and trap him there forever. Holding still, he lifted his face, his eyes sweeping over her features with pure desire burning from within. He moved his hands to cup her cheek, sliding his mouth over hers as he resumed a hypnotic tempo with his hips.

Her moans grew hysterical as he repeatedly drew back and plunged deep, every stroke more decadent than the last. Arching her lower back, she matched each thrust, rocking hard against him as he rode her faster and faster, panting for air. Her body tensed like a bowstring ready to snap, mind reeling with emotions she didn't know existed. He drove her higher and higher toward the peak, her secret muscles tightening around his pumping shaft.

"That's it," he whispered against her mouth. "Come for me."

The first pulsing wave of release shattered her into a million pieces, the pleasure intolerable in its intensity. Her lips parted, but she couldn't make a sound. Pure ecstasy filled her lungs, smothering her beneath an orgasm so fierce it could not be described. She couldn't draw air. He'd done it—he'd made her forget how to breathe. Several eternal seconds later, she gulped her first breath, but the wild spasms wouldn't stop. One triggered another and another and another, until she didn't think she could survive the jagged bliss.

"Bobbi," Trey gasped, resting his sweaty forehead against hers, "I can't—oh god." He bucked against her, and again, even harder, slamming into her and filling the room with the rhythmic staccato of skin slapping skin. Seconds later, he stiffened with a low, rumbling groan that announced his own climax. She continued to pulse and shudder around him for several beats before her muscles finally relented, sated after the longest, most ravaging release of her life.

Then something happened that caught her completely off guard. Her lockbox, once chained deep beneath the ocean of her subconscious, burst open, spewing a decade of repressed feelings and disappointments that she wasn't equipped to handle, now or then. Like a tidal wave, they surged inside her, and Bobbi let out a great, heaving sob. Another followed, and another, much like her climax, and before she knew it, she was in the throes of the ugliest cry of her life.

"Bobbi?" Snapping to attention, Trey cradled her cheeks between his palms. "Did I hurt you?"

She couldn't speak, so she shook her head.

"Baby, what's wrong?" He scrambled to untie her wrists, still bound to the headboard. Swearing quietly to himself, he tugged at the knot, struggling in his panicked state. After what seemed like an eternity, he freed her. She wasted no time in wrapping her arms around his neck and burying her wet face in the crook of his shoulder.

"You're scarin' me, darlin'." Carefully, he pulled out of her and rolled to the side, bringing her body with him and brushing the hair away from her face. "Did I do something wrong?"

"N-n-n-n-n—" Damn it, she couldn't even get one word out. Massive sobs wracked her chest, hot tears plunking onto the sheet below. Memories she hadn't revisited in ages came flying out of nowhere—the first time she'd fought a bully in the school parking lot and lost; a cold slap on the face when Bobbi had stood between Mama and her syringe; watching white-uniformed paramedics haul Mama away in a zippered vinyl bag; her first night in temporary foster care, and her adoption hearing, where she'd changed hands from one mother to two fathers.

On and on it went, but Trey never faltered. He held her tightly within his arms, rocking her and kissing the top of her head. After at least fifteen minutes of solid, manic crying, the tears began to slow, and then the reality of what she'd done—bawling like a lunatic after they'd just made love—hit her like a shovel to the gut, heating her face with embarrassment. Her breath hitched, but she was finally able to fill her lungs with enough air to whisper, "Sorry."

Trey tucked a strand of hair behind her ear. "Tell the truth—did I hurt you? I know I wasn't too gentle there at the end."

"No. It's n-n-not you."

"Then what, hon?"

"I…I'm n-n-not s-s-sure."

Gathering her wrists, he massaged the inside of each one with his thumb. "Is it because I tied you down? Did that trigger something bad that happened when you were little?"

She shook her head.

"Bobbi, you gotta talk to me."

"You'll think I'm crazy," she whispered.

"No, I won't." He placed a reassuring kiss on the tip of her nose. "In case you haven't noticed, I think you're amazing. I'd never call you crazy." He linked their fingers, swept his lips back and forth over her knuckles. "I'm asking you to trust me again."

Somehow, he must've known that talking would be easier for her without making eye contact, because he moved onto his back, pulling her snugly against him to rest her cheek on the solid contours of his bare chest. Steely arms closed around her, enveloping her in safety and affection, and she couldn't say no when he'd made her feel so secure.

So she told him about the box, beginning her story at age twelve, when a well-meaning psychologist had taught her how to manage her overwhelming feelings instead of acting out at school. Parceling away her emotions had proved easier than dealing with them, so she'd never quit the practice like she was supposed to.

"It's been harder to control since I came to town," she said, "and then everything just blew to hell. I'm sorry you had to see that. I feel so stupid."

"Honey, that cry was long overdue." Stroking her bare arm with his thumb, he told her what she'd just learned the hard way. "You can't box that shit up. It keeps growing, and it always finds a way out."

"I know."

"Well, don't feel sorry. I'm glad I was here when it happened."

"Me too."

"I just wish I could stay with you tonight. I hate leaving you like this."

Bobbi perched her chin atop his chest and peered at Trey's stubbly jaw. "I'll be fine. It's weird, but I feel better than I have in years." It was like she'd lost twenty pounds, all from her chest. The weight from that heavy lockbox had dragged her down with it, and now she was free.

"That's not weird. You just purged your system of some awful stuff."

"Thanks," she said softly, "for being so great about all this. And for the other thing too."

"What other thing?"

"You really did make me forget how to breathe."

His face beamed with pride, his mouth curving into a smile that tugged his deep dimples into view. She lifted a finger to trace one, but just as she touched his cheek, his smile faltered, dimples vanishing.

"Oh," he said, "I meant to apologize about before, when we…uh…" He seemed to struggle with what to say next. "I should've asked if you're on the Pill. I'm usually careful, but I was out of my mind, and I couldn't wait another second…" Shifting his head on the pillow, he met her gaze. "You're taking something, right?"

Bobbi's lips parted—she hadn't thought about it either. Like Trey, she'd been so filled with need that safety hadn't crossed her mind. "No." She'd lost her health insurance and couldn't afford out-of-pocket birth control. Besides, it had been so long since she'd had sex, she'd figured she didn't need to fill her prescription.

"*What?*" Every muscle in Trey's body clenched as he lifted his shoulders off the bed.

"Wait, let me think a minute." When was her last period? Not too long ago. Once she remembered the date, she began doing the math, calculating her most fertile window. "I think we're okay." She exhaled a shaky sigh of relief. "If there's ever a good time to slip up, it's right now."

"Jesus, Bo, I'm sorry." He lay back against the pillow. "I had a condom in my wallet. I was just too stupid to use it."

"It's all right." She patted his chest. "We'll be more careful next time."

"Damn right, we will." Pushing onto one elbow, he glanced at the clock on her bedside table. "And speaking of careful, I shouldn't stay too much longer."

Bobbi groaned, clinging to his warmth.

"I know." He squeezed her tightly. "Once I get rid of my *guests*, we'll think of an excuse for you to spend the night." Nuzzling her ear, he reminded her, "I still wanna fall asleep inside you."

"Mmm, I want that too." She burrowed deeper into his chest, determined to enjoy every moment she had left with this man. "Don't worry," she said. "We've got plenty of time."

Chapter 16

"WHAT'RE YOU SO DAMN HAPPY ABOUT?" LUKE scowled at Trey, crinkling a thick smudge of plaster that had dried on his forehead. The motion sent white flakes drifting onto his eyebrows until he resembled a cranky Groucho Marx. "We just got our asses rammed." Shielding his eyes from the afternoon sun, Luke turned his glare to the Sultry County Courthouse, where they'd spent the last twenty minutes arguing with a crooked building inspector.

Trey glanced at the bleached, stone steps, unable to look at his friend. *Why am I so damn happy? Because your sister came to my place for lunch. I laid her down on my kitchen table and ate something a whole lot better than a sandwich.* He hadn't been able to stop grinning ever since, despite the guilt weighting his stomach. "Drove my mom to the airport last night," he said instead. "Feels good to have the house to myself again." With an innocent smile in place, he glanced back up.

Luke scrutinized Trey before nodding in agreement. "Yeah. I know what you mean. Bo's going out of town. First time in months me and June have had the place to ourselves."

"You sound happy about that. Did you settle the whole baby issue?"

"Yeah. We agreed to wait another year."

"See? Told you she'd understand." Trey clapped Luke on the arm. "Enjoy the empty house while you can."

Thank God Luke had plans—that he hadn't asked to watch a game together or grab a beer. Because Bobbi wasn't leaving town. In truth, she was coming over for an X-rated slumber party, to spend the whole night in Trey's bed and in his arms. Just thinking about the things she could do with that hot, wet mouth quickened his pulse and had him bouncing on his toes. He was more keyed up than a kid on the last day of school.

For the past few weeks, they'd been sneaking around like a couple of teenagers, stealing quickies in the back-seat of her car, which was definitely not designed for sexin'. But even though that damned middle seatbelt had left a permanent dent in his ass, he couldn't stop. Sex with Bobbi was a drug, and like a true addict, he'd do anything for a fix—betray his best friend, empty his bank account, sell all the shit inside his house. Hell, he'd sell the house itself to keep making love to her.

They'd agreed to a no-strings-attached summer fling, and he wanted as much of Bobbi as he could get before they burned out on each other. Which they would. Nothing this hot was meant to last.

"So what're we gonna do?" Luke asked.

"About what?"

Luke screwed up his face. "About that thieving dick-head! What kind of man asks for bribes from a charity?"

"Nonprofit," Trey reminded him, forcing his thoughts away from Bobbi's gifted tongue. "But yeah, I'm with you. I've been dealing with the little weasel all summer. He's not gonna budge."

"I hate going to Bea without evidence."

"So don't make any accusations. Just drop in for a friendly chat and mention we're butting heads with the new inspector. Ask if he'll talk to the guy." Maybe the pecker would toe the line if he knew the county judge was watching.

Scratching the back of his neck, Luke stared at the courthouse doors in obvious reluctance. "Guess I could do that." He lifted one dusty brow and nodded at Trey. "You comin'?"

"No, you go on. I'm gonna run to the sheriff's office and return Colton's house key." He'd never expected Mom and Mindy to stay so long. Now that they'd abandoned their matchmaking schemes and gone home, he could quit couch-surfing and do the same.

A low chuckle escaped Luke's chest. "Miracle you didn't catch an STD from his sofa."

"Nah. He never brings the ladies home. I think I'm safe." Worst part had been fielding interference for the big-boobed psycho Colt had picked up at Shooters last month. Trey'd warned Colt about her crazy eyes, but had the horny bastard listened? Nope. Now the stalker was popping up everywhere like a cheesy porno ad.

"Well, I'll meet you back at the site." Luke jogged up a few steps and stopped short. Turning back to Trey, he called, "Oh, yeah. I'm supposed to remind you to—"

"—call my dad. I know." He hadn't forgotten. Right before Mom had left, she'd confessed the real reason behind her extended stay. It seemed the Colonel had grown tired of playing nice, so he'd threatened to air their dirty laundry—which probably entailed Dad's skirt-chasing—if Mom didn't quit fighting the divorce. Her parting words had been a hysterical, "I'll never be able to show my face in Chicago again! Maybe I'll move here to be closer to you."

And if that shit wasn't motivation for Trey to get his old man to back off, he didn't know what was. He waved a quick good-bye to Luke, then marched down the steps to stand in the shade of a tall cedar while he made the call. Tapping the numbers slowly, he held his breath and prayed the call would go to voice mail. Six rings later, his prayers were answered.

"Hey," *you whoring jackass*, "it's me. Mom's upset because she thinks you're gonna ruin her reputation. I convinced her to let the lawyers handle everything and give you a divorce, so you can leave her alone now." Before hanging up, he couldn't resist adding, "Unless you get off on hurting the woman who gave you a family. In which case, I hope you rot in hell."

Christ, he hated that man. Even the slightest connection with the jerk—a voice mail message from a thousand miles away—had made his eye twitch. Trey hoped assholery wasn't inherited, or at least that it skipped a generation, since he wasn't having kids. He'd rather hurl himself off a cliff than turn out like his old man.

Closing his eyes, he took a deep breath of warm, summer air. The smoky aroma of grilling meat from the diner on Main Street drove out thoughts of his father and issued an important reminder. He needed to make a special supper tonight. It probably wasn't gentlemanly to ravish Bobbi for twelve hours without feeding her first. Though most of Trey's talents lay in the bedroom, not in the kitchen, he could manage something decent. But what?

While crossing to the sheriff's building, he replayed

every conversation he'd had with Bobbi to determine what she'd like. By the time he pushed open the front door and stepped into the air-conditioned lobby, he'd decided on vegetarian pasta. Bobbi had too many allergies, and he didn't want to risk shellfish or meat.

"Hey, gorgeous," Trey said, winking at Mrs. Bellabee, the gray-haired receptionist.

Beaming, she waggled her fingers and pushed her horn-rimmed glasses up the length of her nose. "Hiya, hon." As was their routine, she plucked a framed photo from her desk and thrust it at Trey's face while he pretended to admire the young woman inside, Amy Bellabee. "My granddaughter's comin' to visit next month. She's still single…" her voice trailed off, thick with implication.

Trey didn't need to study the picture. He knew Amy'd been crowned Miss Sultry Springs before she'd graduated and left for college. Mrs. Bellabee wouldn't let him forget. But lovely as Amy was, she didn't impress him.

She didn't have a razor wit and soft thighs. She hadn't dedicated her life to defending the underdogs of the world. She didn't smell like candied cinnamon. She didn't rearrange his tools so they lined up in order from largest to smallest, which made no sense but made him smile anyway. She wasn't Bobbi.

"Sorry, ma'am," Trey said. *I'm taken.* "I'm leaving town in a couple weeks."

"I'd heard that." Puckering her mouth in disappointment, she set the frame back in line with a dozen others. "Any chance you'll change your mind?"

"No, ma'am."

"Well, we're all gonna miss you."

"Thanks, that means a lot." He'd miss this town too, but he didn't want to dwell on it. Not now. Nodding toward the hallway, he asked, "Colton around?"

"Yeah, honey, go on back."

He gave her shoulder a playful squeeze and strolled around the reception desk, his rubber-soled work boots squeaking against the waxed floor tiles. Making his way down the hall, he peered at the flyers peppering the wall—an odd combination of FBI Most Wanted posters and vehicles for sale by owner. He passed the restrooms and continued to the open room in the back where half the deputies of Sultry County hunched over their desks, dutifully completing paperwork…except one.

Colton had kicked back, boots resting on the corner of his desk as he squinted at a widescreen computer monitor. At the sound of Trey's noisy footsteps, he glanced up and waved, then immediately minimized his browser. There was only one reason a guy did that.

"Watchin' skin flicks on the job?" Trey asked. If Colt was using one of those free sites, his laptop probably had more viruses than a hooker's toilet seat. Not that Trey would know or anything. "As a taxpayer, I'm outraged."

Colton chuckled to himself. "Unclench, Lewis. This is actually law-related."

"Uh-huh." Trey tossed his friend's house key onto the desk. "Hot, naked cops?"

"I wish." After leaning to the side to verify the sheriff's office door was closed, Colton showed Trey what he'd been hiding. And it sure wasn't porn. Hell, what Trey saw made his wang shrink back in fear.

"Crazy-eyes," Trey breathed. Or, according to her record, Barbara Lee. And her mug shot was scary as balls. Crimped, snarled tufts of blond hair framed one side of her dirt-streaked face as if she'd skidded, head first, into home plate right before getting arrested. Her wide, bloodshot eyes smiled maniacally, right along with her fuchsia lips, and her nostrils flared like she'd smelled Trey's fear—and liked it. Goddamn. "What'd you get yourself into?"

"A clusterfuck, that's what."

Trey hated to say I told you so, but…"Told you she was nuts."

"Thanks. That's real helpful." A frown tugged at Colton's mouth. He slid a glare at Trey. "Maybe next time she comes around, I'll give her your number. Since you've got all the answers and all."

Actually, Trey did have the answer. He couldn't believe Colton hadn't thought of it first. "If my granddaddy were the county judge, I'd ask him to sign off on one of those restraining orders." He leaned in to peer at the screen. "What's on her rap sheet?"

"Shh!" Colt whipped a glance over both shoulders. "Back up, man. I'm not supposed to show you this."

Trey held up both palms. "She got a history of stalking?"

"A few charges, but nothing stuck." With a groan, he dropped both feet to the ground. "Maybe if I keep ignoring her, she'll go away."

Right on cue, Colt's cell phone chirped, alerting him to a new text message. Trey leaned over his buddy's shoulder to snoop.

From Boobalicious Barb: Hey, big daddy! Hit me up.

"Yeah," Trey said, "I don't think she's goin' anywhere."

"Maybe if I—"

Chirp! From Boobalicious Barb: Why haven't you called?

"Or, I could—"

Chirp! From Boobalicious Barb: QUIT IGNORING ME, ASSHOLE!

"I'm gonna have to—"

Chirp! From Boobalicious Barb: I'm sorry, baby. Didn't mean to yell. Luv u!

"Try blocking her number," Trey said.

Colton took his advice, and precisely five seconds later, his desk phone chimed out, startling them both. They exchanged a wide-eyed glance, clearly sharing the same assumption. There was no escaping this whacko.

"You answer it," Colt pleaded. "Say you're Deputy Horace."

At the sound of his name, the real Horace turned his head and arched a questioning brow. Like that horror movie, *Scream*, the shrill clangor added to the tension, making Trey's arm hair stand on end. Someone had to answer, or she'd just keep calling. After the fifth ring, Trey shrugged and picked up the phone, hoping this didn't count as impersonating an officer.

"Sultry County Sheriff's office," he said, adding a little twang to his voice. "Deputy Sheriff Horace speakin'."

Silence.

"Hello?" he pressed. "Anyone there?" If he listened closely, he could just make out light breathing on the other end of the line.

Trey was about to hang up when a woman's voice whispered, "I know he's there. I can sense him." Before he had a chance to respond, she disconnected.

Oh, man. Colt was *so* screwed. "It was her, all right." He set the receiver back in its cradle and gave his friend a consoling pat on the arm.

"Damn." Colt raked a hand through his hair. "Maybe you're ri—"

He was interrupted by a soft *ping!* from his laptop. They huddled around the screen, where an instant message had popped up.

From Barbie91: Playing hard to get, big daddy?

"Oh my god." Colton pinched the bridge of his nose. "I didn't even know I had an IM account."

Ping! From Barbie91: That's okay, sweet cheeks. I love the chase.

"You'd better call your grandpa," Trey said. "Sweet cheeks."

Ping! From Barbie91: Bad boys get punished. How do you want to be punished?

In one swift motion, Colt closed his laptop and shot to his feet. "Enough of this shit." As Colt tugged on his Stetson, Trey heard him mumbling, "She wasn't even that good."

Trey watched his friend charge out the back door, realizing this was what his late grandma used to call a natural consequence. Like touching a hot stove. Sure, it burned like a bitch, but you'd only make that mistake once. Best way to learn lessons in life.

Though Trey felt awful for Colton, the gigolo was long overdue for a little maturity. Actually, a lot overdue. He wished his friend the best of luck and headed to the community center. The sooner he finished installing the track lighting, the sooner he could head home and start dinner for Bobbi. He should probably vacuum too—spruce up the place. Maybe buy some flowers.

A wide grin stretched his cheeks as he strode, lighter than air, back the way he'd come.

———m———

Bobbi circled downtown Sultry Springs to lose the sedan that'd been tailing her for the last half mile. When its driver pulled into the Sack-n-Pay parking lot, she exhaled with relief and turned off Main Street toward Trey's house.

After checking the rearview mirror to ensure she hadn't been followed, Bobbi barreled into Trey's open garage at twenty miles an hour. Slamming on the brakes, she screeched to a halt beside his Chevy and immediately punched the spare garage door opener he'd leant her. The metal door closed behind her one slow inch at a time, and her gaze followed, scanning for traffic or passersby who might identify Bruiser, her notorious purple clunker.

The cloak and dagger act brought a nervous snicker to her lips. She was more paranoid than Bong after a blunt run, but it only took one nosy neighbor to tattle to her brother. When she returned to California, she intended to leave Luke and Trey's friendship intact.

She stretched up to check her reflection in the mirror, smoothing an errant lock of hair she must've missed with the flatiron. Half an inch of blond roots had grown along her part, contrasting with the artificial red, but with any luck, Trey would be too distracted by the plunging neckline of her skintight blouse to notice. Heart racing, she wiped her clammy palms on a discarded McDonald's napkin from lunch. She hadn't felt this nervous since her first date at age fifteen. It'd been like this all day too. Her fingers had trembled so badly, she'd barely been able to zip her skirt.

It wasn't only eagerness to see Trey that had her in knots. Bobbi was 99 percent sure she was pregnant.

Before she could obsess for the thousandth time about how to break the news to Trey—or more importantly, what the hell they were going to do—he stepped into the garage and stole her breath.

Electric-blue eyes shone at her above a wide smile and dimpled cheeks. He must've just stepped out of the shower, because his damp, sandy hair had dripped onto the broad shoulders of his white T-shirt, rendering the fabric nearly transparent and revealing the tanned skin underneath. In his faded jeans and bare feet, he was infinitely sexier than the polished metrosexuals she'd once admired in LA. Now she wondered what she'd ever seen in those men. Trey waved her inside, probably wondering why she was still lingering inside her car.

If they'd made a baby, she hoped the little guy was the spitting image of his father.

Wait, no. She mentally slapped herself.

She shouldn't be thinking like that—assigning the fetus a gender or imagining its pudgy, dimpled face. Having a child right now would mean disaster. What about her career, and Trey's impending deployment? What would Luke say? And Trey's mother? She'd probably claim Bobbi had gotten knocked up on purpose. This cloud didn't have a silver lining.

Taking a fortifying gulp of air, she stepped out of the car and clicked across the cement floor on her high-heeled sandals, grappling for the right words to break the news. Trey met her halfway and scooped her into his muscled arms, twirling her in place as if they'd just reunited after a decade apart. He was warm and solid and smelled of sweet apples and spicy marinara sauce. He smelled like home. Wrapping herself around him, she buried her nose at the base of his throat and pulled in his scent.

"I'm glad you're here," he said. "Been a hell of a day." After lowering her feet to the floor, he took her face between his palms and kissed her, a light brush of lips that flushed her skin and had her raising onto her toes for more. He smiled against her mouth, then pulled away. Linking their fingers, he towed her through the doorway and into the kitchen, where the rich scents of tomatoes and garlic hung heavily in the air.

"Mmm," she said. "Smells like heaven in here." The tiny, two-seater kitchen table was already set with salad, bowls of steaming pasta, and a bottle of Merlot. Oh, no. Could she have wine?

"I hope you're hungry." Trey brought their linked fingers to his mouth and kissed her hand. "I figured spaghetti was safe. Is that okay?"

"Safe?"

"With all your allergies," he explained.

Bobbi's heart puffed inside her chest like a toasted

soufflé. She'd only mentioned her food aversions once, over a month ago. He'd listened and remembered. He'd put real thought and extra care behind this simple meal. Just when she didn't think she could adore Trey any more, he outdid himself.

"I love spaghetti," she said. But instead of following him to the table, she freed her hand, then proceeded to scratch her nose. She had to tell him about the baby before she went insane or lost her nerve. Or both. "But let's talk first."

His perpetual grin faltered, likely because nothing good ever followed those words. "Sure." He leaned one hip against the counter and folded his arms protectively. "What's up?"

Bobbi swallowed hard. "I'm late."

His eyes darted to the stove's digital clock. "No, you're not. You're right on ti—" His breath caught, the blood drained from his face like water through a sieve, until his typically tanned cheeks turned to wax. Returning his gaze to hers, he asked, "*Late*, late?"

She nodded.

"How late?"

"About a week." Which might not worry the average woman, but Bobbi's meticulous, twenty-six-day cycle had never faltered. She'd never, ever been late before. "And my boobs are sore." She cupped them gently, glancing at the cleavage spilling from her scoop-neck top. "And bigger, don't you think?"

Though his eyes had gone glassy, Trey gave her breasts a thorough appraisal. He held both hands out as if fondling her from a distance. "I guess so. Did you take a test?"

"No." But she'd wanted to. "Everyone knows my face. I was afraid it'd get back to Luke if someone saw me buying a pregnancy test."

"You're probably right. It's a small town, and folks love to gossip." He inhaled deeply, his wide chest stretching the seams of his T-shirt. After considering a moment, he gave a decided nod. "I'll do it."

"Buy the test?"

"If there's gonna be talk, I'd rather it be about me than you."

Bobbi brought a hand over her heart. To hell with opening doors and pulling out chairs—this was the most chivalrous thing any man had ever done for her. "Thank you."

His gaze danced back and forth between Bobbi and the supper beginning to cool on the table. Eventually, he decided, "I'd better go now. Before we worry ourselves sick."

"Good idea." Maybe she should drink some water while he was gone. How much urine would she need for one of those tests? She had no clue.

His eyes searched her face as he stepped forward and wrapped an arm around her shoulder. "You feel all right?"

"I'm fine."

Ignoring her reply, he ushered her into the living room, where he insisted she take a seat on the leather sofa. "Here," he said, grabbing a couple of throw pillows, "put your feet up."

"I don't think that's—"

At her protest, he took matters into his own hands, grabbing her ankles and swiveling her into a reclining position with her heels resting on the pillows. Then he began unfastening her sandals.

"You need anything before I go?" he asked. "Crackers, or...uh...ice cream, or Alka Seltzer, or something?" After tossing her shoes to the carpeted floor, he knelt by her side and pressed one palm against her forehead as if checking for fever.

She couldn't help giggling at his reaction. "I'm fine."

"Right, right." He rubbed his hands together, practically vibrating with nervous energy. "I'm gonna go." Hitching a thumb toward the door, he assured her, "It's only five minutes to the Sack-n-Pay, but I've got my cell phone if you need me."

"Okay."

"You sure you don't need any—"

"*Trey!*"

"I'm goin', I'm goin'!" Without further ado, he scurried out of the house to his truck. Bobbi heard the Chevy start, then the garage door opening and closing, followed by the squeal of tires as he peeled down the street.

Eight minutes and thirty-seven seconds later, he came tearing back inside, plastic bag in hand. "I got the digital kind," he announced, reaching inside and producing said item. "Says it's just as accurate as a doctor's test." He tapped the box with his index finger. "No lines, or plusses, or minuses. It'll tell you 'pregnant' or 'not pregnant.'" Then he felt the need to clarify, "I mean, it won't actually *tell* you out loud, but the words—"

"I know. I've seen the commercials." The poor guy was even more frantic than she was. Wrenching the box from his grip, she stood from the sofa and walked on wobbly knees to the hall bathroom. But just before she closed the door, Trey stopped her.

"Wait." He followed her inside. "Before you take the test, I need you to know something."

Bobbi's stomach dropped. She couldn't handle any more emotional turmoil today. She hoped Trey wasn't about to confess a secret girlfriend, or a few secret kids, or worse—a secret wife.

"What's that?" she asked.

Using one finger, he tipped her chin until their eyes met. "No matter what happens," he said firmly, "no matter what that test says, we're gonna be okay." He bent at the knees, lowering to her height. "I'm gonna take good care of you, Bobbi, and I want you to know that." His thumb stroked her cheek. "Do you believe me?"

Bobbi's throat closed. She could only nod. When would she trust him and stop expecting the worst? She wanted to tell Trey he'd make a phenomenal father, but words still wouldn't pass through her thickened airway. Instead, she kissed the tip of his nose and gently pushed against his chest until he backed out into the hall. Then she closed the door and tore open the package.

The process was easier than she'd expected. Before long, she'd gingerly placed the used test stick atop a tissue on the counter. She never took her eyes off the results window while washing her hands. As the seconds ticked by far too slowly, her heart pounded so hard she feared she'd break a rib. It was pure torture waiting for this miniature Magic 8 Ball to determine her future. From beyond the door, the wood floor creaked beneath Trey's pacing footsteps. He had to be dying too.

Oh god! Something was happening in the test window!

Words were forming, beginning to darken! Bobbi held her breath, bit her lip, and leaned closer, gripping the countertop for support so she didn't pass out.

Not pregnant.

Not pregnant? She straightened, furrowing her brow. That couldn't be right. The glare from the old fluorescent lights above the mirror had probably played tricks on her eyes. Bobbi placed a cap over the absorbent tip and held the test at an angle, away from the flickering glow.

Not pregnant.

Her heart sank. Maybe she'd done something wrong—used too much urine or not enough. Wasn't she supposed to replace the cap before setting the test on a flat surface? Perhaps that had skewed the results. She shook the stick like a thermometer for a few seconds, then checked the reading again.

Not pregnant. There it was, in black and white, refusing to change.

She slumped down onto the toilet lid, still staring at the test in disbelief. The backs of her eyes stung. Her lungs compressed and felt heavy, bowing her over with their leaden weight. A wet sob worked its way up from her throat, and as the first plump tear spilled onto her cheek, Bobbi realized with shock that these weren't tears of relief. They were of disappointment.

She'd wanted that baby. Trey's sweet, dimpled, blue-eyed baby. She'd never planned to have children, much less now, at age twenty-three, with her career in shambles, neck-deep in debt, swept up in an affair with her brother's best friend. She should be bouncing with joy, not crying.

Oh god, what was wrong with her?

Trey pressed an ear to the bathroom door and listened as Bobbi sniffled on the other side. Crying could only mean one thing: she was pregnant.

Holy shit, he was going to be a daddy.

His head spun, and he clutched the wall to keep from falling. But a surprise grin lifted the corners of his mouth. He was going to be a daddy!

Okay, so the timing sucked, but when he thought about it, there was no reason why things couldn't work. He was crazy about Bobbi, and she seemed to like him too. The thought of marrying her and starting a family made his chest light and tingly, like he'd spilled warm champagne down the front of his shirt. Bobbi would be all his. He'd get to come home to her at the end of a long day and spend the night in the haven of her arms. And though Luke would be furious at first, he'd come around. Hell, they'd be brothers!

As for Trey's defense contract, he'd break it. He'd have to repay the signing bonus, and his military record would remain unclear, but who cared? Right now, an other-than-honorable discharge seemed trivial compared to bringing a child into the world.

He could already picture the three of them—the Lewis family—cuddled beneath an evergreen tree for their first Christmas. How old would the baby be next December? Trey took a moment to crunch some numbers. About eight months old. He glanced into the living room where he typically assembled his artificial tree. He could almost see his tiny, towheaded son crawling toward a shiny ornament hung too low on the branches.

Trey's fingers twitched to hold his baby boy. They could really do this—be happy together.

Just as he drew a hopeful breath, Bobbi opened the bathroom door. He spun around to find her red-eyed, but smiling.

"It's negative," she said, holding up the pee stick as evidence.

"What?" He must not have heard her right.

She pointed to a small oval window. "Not pregnant." Squinting, he brought the words into focus.

When Trey was a freshman in high school, one of the seniors had played a prank on him in the lunchroom, pulling his chair out from under him just before he'd sat down. He'd hit the tile floor so hard it'd knocked the wind out of his lungs. He felt that way now.

"Oh." He blinked away moisture welling in his eyes. "I heard you crying, and I assumed—"

"I was just so relieved," she explained, shrugging. She leaned into the bathroom and tossed the test into the wastebasket. "Good news, huh?"

"Of course." And it *was* good news, logically. So why did he feel sucker-punched? Why did it seem like he'd lost a family that had never even existed?

"Now we can eat." She pressed a hand against her tummy—her now vacant tummy. "I'm starved."

"Sure. Me too."

Trey collected himself long enough to fake a smile and reheat dinner, but something shifted inside him. For the first time, he realized he wanted something more from his life. More from Bobbi.

When he took her to bed that night, it wasn't for down-and-dirty sex. He made love to her slowly. Softly.

Sharing the same shuddering breaths and gazing into her warm, green eyes as if to brand her. He made her come half a dozen times, but he denied his own release for hours, because he needed the closeness. Needed to recoup what he'd lost. But when he drove himself inside her wet heat and finally climaxed, he could've sworn he'd lost half his soul to her in the process.

He rolled them both to the side, and as he fell asleep, still buried deep within Bobbi, their limbs entwined, surrounded in their mingled scent, he feared letting her go might actually kill him.

What the hell was he going to do?

Chapter 17

"GOING OUT OF TOWN *AGAIN*?" BONG SCRATCHED HIS blond, bean-sprouted chin while aiming an incredulous stare at Bobbi from the other side of the bed. He nudged her outstretched, jean-clad leg with the tip of his sneaker. "That's three times in the last two weeks."

"Four," corrected Weezus, who sat cross-legged on the opposite bed, uploading last night's footage of Trey and Colton riding the mechanical bull at Shooters. Neither man had lasted longer than three seconds. She, on the other hand, had held on a full two minutes. And she had the throbbing nether region to prove it. "Where're you going this time?"

Bobbi turned onto her back, tracing the swirling patterns of the hotel room ceiling with her gaze. "Not far. Just a few counties away to interview a subject. I'll be back first thing in the morning."

"Mmm-hmm." Bong's eyes moved over her face skeptically. He wasn't buying it. "How come we've never met any of these subjects?"

"They weren't right for the project."

"Liar, liar, pants on fire—" Weezus chimed.

"—nose as long as a piano wire," Bong finished incorrectly.

Bobbi grabbed the pillow beneath her head and used it to whack Bong in the stomach. "It's telephone wire, you stone hound."

Clutching his gut in mock agony, he warned, "I'm calling my union rep in the morning!" When she glared at him, he added, "But I accept the apology in your eyes."

"Dork."

"So," Weezus said, shutting down his computer, "when are you meeting your lov-*ah*?"

"I don't have a lover," Bobbi lied, "and I'm leaving after tonight's shoot." She propped up on her elbows and turned the subject away from her personal affairs, no pun intended. "Hey, has anyone else been getting calls from that psycho who's stalking Colton?"

"Uhn-uh." Weezus shook his big, blue head.

"Nope," Bong said. "Why? She bothering you?"

"Not really." Bobbi reclined again, folding both hands behind her head and crossing her legs at the ankles. "Just one strangely polite voice mail." But Barbara's creeptastic, *Please stop tempting my Big Daddy with other women. He belongs to me. Have a blessed day!* had chilled her blood worse than a thousand angry swears.

"Colt's got a restraining order, right?" Bong asked.

"Yeah," Bobbi said. "But she's not violating it by contacting me."

"Hmm." Bong didn't appear to like that. "Well, watch yourself. At least for the next week—then we're outta here."

If Bobbi hadn't been lying flat on her back, she would've slumped to the floor like a puddle of goo. One week. That was all the time she had left with Trey. In fact, tonight was his big farewell party at the church fellowship hall. She could return to visit Luke and June, but not the Golden Boy she'd grown to...*grown to what?* Love? She wasn't sure, but she'd miss him. A lot. The idea of leaving him behind made her stomach heave and her body ache all over like the flu.

Every day was precious now. She was watching the sand in her hourglass run out, willing each fleeting grain to slow down and plug the channel, but it never did. So she'd determined to enjoy her final moments with Trey and worry about the consequences—and the withdrawal—later.

Weezus stood from his bed, nearly clocking his forehead on a fire sprinkler attached to the ceiling. "Want to get some lunch?" he asked her. "There's a farmer's market a few minutes from here."

"No, thanks. I've got plans."

Bong poked her in the ribs. "With Trey *Leeeeeeewis*?"

She nearly gave herself whiplash turning to face him. "No!"

Laughing, Weezus pointed to her nose, which she'd unconsciously started rubbing. "You're the worst liar I've ever met. Anyone with eyes could tell you're into him."

"And vice versa," Bong said. "You should've seen his face last night when that redhead behind the bar asked for your number. I thought Trey was gonna bust a brain vessel."

"Don't worry, boss." Weezus tugged her sandal playfully. "Your secret's safe with us."

If her feelings were that transparent, thank goodness Luke had been too busy operating the mechanical bull to notice. She pushed off the mattress and feigned ignorance. "You're seeing things that aren't there. Can smoking too much reefer make you hallucinate?"

"No," they both said, smiling.

And they called *her* a liar. "Whatever. I'll catch you

at the church. Six-thirty, so we can set up before the guest of honor arrives."

"Right. Your lov-*ah*." Weezus dodged two pounds of feathers when Bobbi threw her pillow at him. Well, technically, *his* pillow since this was the crew's room. And as it appeared she'd worn out her welcome, she joined them near the door.

As she stepped outside into the parking lot, Weezus said something that made her think. "There's a lid for every pot. No shame in using the stove once you've found your match."

Her match? Bobbi wrinkled her brow while climbing into her car, and by the time she arrived at the community center, she'd worried a crease into her forehead not even Botox could remove.

She didn't like her cameraman's words. They implied she had only one true companion on this vast earth, one fit, and she didn't believe in soul mates. Each man and woman had thousands of potentially compatible partners out there. It was just a matter of crossing paths with one of them at the right time. Sure, Trey might be one of those people—or not—but either way, the timing was all wrong. That didn't mean she'd never find love with another man. Someone who'd make her forget Trey's dimpled smile and his sapphire eyes.

But when Bobbi pulled into the parking lot beside his Chevy and caught a glimpse of him from afar, her heart catapulted out of her chest. Oh hell, who was she kidding? No man could ever make her forget Trey Lewis. Still, there was another lid to her pot somewhere out there, and she'd find him when the time was right. She had to believe that.

Turning off the ignition, she studied Trey as he sat on the front steps, shoulder-to-shoulder with Carlo, his young apprentice. Neither male noticed her as they consumed their sandwiches with gusto, their postures a mirror image—elbows resting on knees, hands curled around identical six-inch subs. They even had matching mayonnaise moustaches. Seeing them together made her smile.

Bobbi reached into the backseat to retrieve her camcorder, then silently rolled down her window to capture a few minutes of Trey and mini-Trey on video. The boy's parents had refused to sign a waiver, but this wasn't for *Sex in the Sticks*. This was just for her, to replay on cold, dark days when the summer's memory had begun to fade.

Carlo grabbed a handful of Bugles from the open bag near his feet. After pushing a corn chip cone onto the tips of each finger, he used his "claws" to scare Trey, who chuckled and dug into the bag to do the same. When they'd grown tired of the charade, they brought each finger to their mouths and munched them clean.

Camera in hand, Bobbi stepped out of her car and continued filming as she approached them. Her subjects glanced up, each displaying a very different reaction to her presence. Trey's eyes flashed with uninhibited joy. He smiled around a bite of sandwich while wiping his mouth on a paper napkin. Carlo, on the other hand, jutted out his bottom lip and slouched, clearly resentful of the disruption. It seemed quality time with Trey was in high demand these days.

"Hey," she said, pointing to Carlo's new buzz cut, "I like your hair. I can actually see your eyes now."

He responded with something that sounded like "Mmrrmph." After an elbow in the ribs from Trey, Carlo muttered a reluctant, "Thanks." He pointed at his mentor. "He made me do it."

Trey grazed the boy's shorn scalp with his palm. "Damn straight. He looks like a man now, don't you think?" A quick wink from Trey told her to play along.

"Oh, yeah." Bobbi gave a thumbs up. "You look five years older. Real handsome."

Carlo gave a flippant shrug, but he couldn't hide a small, lopsided smile. In truth, the kid did look older than the first time she'd seen him. He'd gained a couple of inches and at least ten much-needed pounds. Amazing what some old-fashioned TLC could do for a child.

An idea came to mind to follow Carlo's progress over the years—document his transformation from troubled teen to stable adult. If his family remained local, which, for Carlo's sake, she hoped they did, she could interview him when she flew back to visit Luke. And Trey would probably like to receive updates on his little buddy.

"You going to keep working with my brother when your hours are served?" she asked Carlo.

"Uh-huh." Carlo took a few loud slurps from his iced tea. "Till Mr. Lewis comes back. Then I'm gonna work for him."

A bittersweet grin played on Trey's lips.

"You coming to Mr. Lewis's party tonight?" she asked Carlo. "I can pick you up if you need a ride."

"I got one."

Trey elbowed him again.

"I mean," Carlo corrected, "thanks, but I already got one."

"I'm taking him." Trey crumpled his napkin and tossed it into his empty lunch cooler. "And we've got a lot of work to finish before then. That back path isn't gonna pave itself."

The young man took the hint, finishing his tea and offering a quick wave good-bye before jogging out of sight.

Trey glanced around the property to make sure no one was watching, then picked up a long stick and used it to brush the outside swell of her hip. "Can't use that footage of him, you know."

"I know." She zoomed in on Trey's face, capturing a wicked smile that gave her dirty thoughts. Dirty thoughts she intended to turn into dirtier actions. "Can we go somewhere private? I need an interview."

"You can't do it here?"

Biting her lip, she peered at him from above the camera. "That's not the kind of exposé I had in mind."

Understanding dawned in his eyes, and his sinful smile turned downright torrid. "Why, Miss Gallagher, I'm scandalized."

"Do any of those inside rooms lock?"

He nodded slowly, his mischievous gaze heating her face all the way from cheeks to hairline.

"Then lead the way, Mr. Lewis."

He obeyed, and she followed, making sure to catch plenty of footage of his incredibly strong back and the hard curve of his backside. *Mmm*. Whoever said a picture was worth a measly thousand words had never seen Trey's ass.

They passed the kitchen, now complete with gleaming, stainless steel appliances, and continued to the boardroom at the far end of the building. The space was dim, smelling of fresh paint, vacant with the exception of a long, mahogany table by the wall. As Trey closed and locked the door, Bobbi adjusted her camera's aperture to adjust for the change in lighting.

She backed up and leaned against the table. "You know, I think you'd feel a lot more comfortable without that heavy shirt on."

He pinched the lightweight cotton between two fingers. "This?"

"Mmm-hmm. Take it off, Golden Boy."

"I didn't hear the magic word."

"How's this for a magic word? *Reciprocity*." She worked the buttons of her blouse with her free hand.

"Best word ever!" Without further argument, he grabbed his T-shirt hem in one hand and inched it up, revealing his tight, flat belly. "This what you want?" Playfully, he rolled his body like a Chippendale dancer, rippling and flexing his abdominal muscles beneath smooth, tanned skin.

"If only I had some dollar bills…" She shimmied out of one sleeve, changed hands with the camera, and let her blouse fall to the newly waxed tile floor.

"For you, I'll dance free of charge." Slowly, while undulating his lean torso, he peeled his T-shirt over his head, whirled it in the air a few times, and let it fly across the room. Though they both laughed at the mock striptease, the sight of his bunching shoulders and contoured chest made Bobbi's blood heat and pool right between her thighs.

After a few tries, she gave up on unclasping her bra. "I can't get this off." She shook her hair back. "If only I had a big, strong man to help me."

"Lucky for you, I never leave a damsel in distress." Instead of blocking the lens, he circled behind her. His warm, rough fingers unfastened her bra while his teeth grazed the sensitive flesh at the base of her neck. He pushed the straps down her shoulders, then cupped her heavy breasts in both hands, massaging lightly and bringing a groan to her lips.

She closed her eyes and leaned into his chest, dropping her arm to her side, camera be damned. He thumbed her nipples in slow circles and bit her shoulder, making her ache with wanting him. There was just one problem, and she told him when he trailed a hand beneath the waistband of her jeans. "I'm sore from last night." What had possessed her to ride that stupid bull, anyway?

"Want me to kiss it," he whispered in her ear, "and make it better?"

Goose bumps prickled her skin. That sounded awfully tempting. She turned to face him, setting her camera on the tabletop. "Only if you let me reciprocate."

His crooked smile tugged one dimple into view. "Well, it *is* the magic word."

"Okay, then."

"Can you stay quiet?" He unbuttoned her jeans, then lowered the zipper.

"I think so."

Kneeling at her feet, he pushed her pants down to her ankles. Nodding at the table behind them, he ordered, "Sit down, and put your heels on my shoulders."

She did as he commanded, hooking her jean-trapped ankles behind his head. In all her life, she'd never felt so exposed. Her muscles stiffened, but he relaxed them again, stroking her skin reassuringly.

He glanced at the lens. "That still on?"

A sudden boldness overtook her. She nodded and tested his reaction by angling the camera to record their intimate act.

He didn't object, only flashed one final, devilish grin before dipping between her thighs, where he licked her into silent ecstasy.

―∽∞∽―

Hours later, she attached that same camera to her tripod and set up in the corner of the Holy Baptism by Hellfire fellowship hall, hoping God wouldn't strike her dead.

She took a moment to scan the open room, smiling appreciatively at the fruits of Pru's labor. Two linen-draped, cafeteria-style folding tables against the side wall offered lime punch, finger sandwiches, cookies, and an assortment of Crock-Pots bearing Swedish meatballs and miniature sausages. The scent of barbeque sauce made Bobbi's mouth water. Or maybe it was the oversized photos of Trey plastering the walls. Either way, this party proved Trey was well loved here.

"Message station?" Bong asked, assembling his long microphone.

"Yep." Bobbi pulled a folding chair opposite the lens, so Trey's friends could stop in throughout the evening to record farewells. "I'll splice them together and mail it to him on disc." *Maybe along with the amateur porno we shot.* She tapped the LCD screen to make sure she'd deleted that afternoon's raw footage when she'd uploaded it to her laptop. She didn't want anyone getting an erotic eyeful if they tinkered with the controls behind her back. "Might cheer him up if he's feeling homesick."

"Huh. You really do like this guy."

"Yes. As a friend."

Bong rolled his slightly bloodshot eyes. "You're keeping in touch while he's gone? I thought it was just a summer fling."

"There's nothing going on." But her nosy sound boom guy was right—she and Trey had promised not to get attached. They hadn't discussed keeping in touch. Was Trey okay with exchanging emails and sharing a few phone calls?

"You gonna do the long distance thing?" Bong tucked his hair behind both ears. "None of my business, but two years is a long time."

"We're just friends." With benefits. Heart-pounding, toe-curling benefits.

"Whatever." He huffed and ground his teeth, the closest he ever came to losing his temper. "You know, we've worked together for years. It kind of hurts when you freeze me out like this."

"What?" Bobbi's hand slipped off the tripod leg.

"You don't trust folks easily. But after Weeze and I stuck with you through all that crazy Smyth stuff, I figured you'd realize we're not the enemy."

"I don't think of you that way!" So she was an ice queen now, just because she wanted to keep her love life private? "It's not like—"

But he was done listening. With stiff shoulders, Bong marched across the streamer-festooned room to join his partner at the front doors. Just as Bobbi began to follow him, Pastor McMahon cleared his throat from behind.

"Can I record my message now?" he asked in a thick drawl, rubbing his distended belly. When the pastor smiled, his gentle spirit shone through hazel eyes as warm as chai tea, and she couldn't say no.

"Of course." She indicated for him to sit.

McMahon lowered onto the folding chair, which groaned beneath his weight. He combed the few strands of hair still remaining atop his balding head. Which didn't amount to much.

"Whenever you're ready," she prompted. When he nodded, she tapped the record button.

"Trey," he began, widening his grin, "I'll never forget the first time we met. You'd just rolled into town—hadn't even checked in at the motel yet—and you stopped by the side of the road to change my busted tire. When I shook your hand, I knew Sultry Springs had gained someone special. I'm gonna miss you, son. Stay safe, and come back to us soon."

Bobbi paused the recording and thanked the pastor for his contribution. As he waddled toward the dessert table, she pondered his last words. *Stay safe.*

She'd never considered Trey's assignment a dangerous one, but now that she thought of it, security detail in a foreign country carried its share of risks. Her heart turned cold and quivered at the mental image of Trey's smooth chest—where she rested her cheek at night—bloodied and marred by a bullet. Would the contractors issue him a Kevlar vest?

"Hey, what's wrong?" Luke plopped into the seat the pastor had just vacated. June wasn't far behind. She sat on her husband's knee and wrapped one arm around his neck.

"Just thinking."

"Ah," Luke said with an impish twinkle in his eye.

"That explains the smoke leaking out of your ears." June giggled at the lame joke while absently running her fingers through Luke's hair. Then they shared one of those looks again—so full of unadulterated worship it made Bobbi want to puke with envy.

Bobbi sighed. Despite the earsplitting sex keeping her awake all night and the nauseating exchanges the next morning, she'd miss her new family. Luke, her big brother, who'd openly volunteered to kick the teeth out of anyone who messed with her. And June, the sister she'd always wanted. Bobbi had come to adore their predawn gab sessions. Insomnia wasn't so bad when you added girl talk and a forkful of pecan pie.

"I'll go first," June said, straightening on Luke's lap. "Is it recording?"

Bobbi focused on June's cherubic cheeks. "It is now."

"Okay." Pressing her lips together, June took a deep breath as if fortifying herself. "Holy sugar, Trey, I hardly know where to begin." At once, her eyes welled with tears, and she took a moment to fan herself and blink them dry. "If it wasn't for your help, I don't know if Luke and I would be together. I think we both needed that little push, and you didn't hold back." While Luke's arms tightened around her waist, June added, "Speaking of 'push,' I'm sorry for knocking you off Mr. Jenkins's roof."

"Oh," Bobbi interjected from behind the camera, "I heard that story. If I remember correctly, you were trying to score a date with him before he fell."

Luke scowled, shooting daggers into the lens. "Do we have to talk about that?"

"Yes," Bobbi decided, "I think we do."

"Well, too bad." Crinkles formed around his narrowed eyes. "Because it's my turn."

Now she understood why siblings loved screwing with each other. This was fun. "I don't know, Luke. I think you owe Trey some gratitude for stepping aside so you could marry his woman."

"You're real fuckin' funny."

June gasped loud enough to draw the attention of everyone within a five-foot radius. "Language!" she hissed.

Nuzzling his wife's neck, Luke murmured, "I had *you* swearing like a fishwife last night."

"But not in a church!"

"Oh, gross." Bobbi couldn't take much more of this. Besides, a line had formed, four people deep. "Wrap it up, Casanova."

"Fine, fine." Luke peered around June's shoulder and spoke to the camera. "Listen, buddy, I'm not gonna get all mushy and lay a bunch of sappy shit on you—"

June smacked him on the thigh.

"Uh, I mean sappy *stuff*," Luke continued. "Aside from Junebug here, you're my oldest friend. You've had my back more times than I can count. I trust you with my life." With a teasing glance at Bobbi, he said, "Hell, I even trusted you with my pain-in-the-ass kid sister. I know that wasn't how you wanted to spend your summer, but thanks for keepin' her out of trouble." Good thing he couldn't see her face flaming behind the camera. Luke wouldn't feel so thankful if he knew about her pregnancy scare a couple of weeks ago. "Anyhoo, take care, and keep in touch. We'll keep your seat warm till you come home."

The pair left the message station and circulated

through the hall, which had quickly filled with at least a hundred supporters, all joined by their affection for Trey. If the people of Sultry Springs had opened their arms this widely for an outsider from Chicago, she wondered if they'd do the same for her. Could she fit in here—in a red state where the men were men and the sheep were scared?

Not that it mattered, because she couldn't stay.

Her life—every opportunity to reclaim a career she loved more than breathing—was in LA. Besides, Trey would settle here after his contract expired, and he wouldn't stay single long. He drew female attention like moths to a lightbulb, and Bobbi wasn't sure she could handle bumping into Trey and his next flame while browsing Main Street.

Between tapings, she watched Trey from afar as he shook hands, hugged necks, and even kissed a few cheeks. Her chest constricted when she imagined who'd share his bed next. Some wealthy vacationer in Dubai looking for a good time? A foreign dignitary's wife?

No, Trey wouldn't do that. Daughter, maybe. Sister, definitely. But honorable men didn't pursue other men's wives, and Trey was the most honorable man she'd ever met. She, on the other hand, had nothing special to offer. How long until he forgot her?

Trey must've sensed her staring at him, because he turned and locked eyes with her. His gaze softened, and that easy, dimpled grin she'd come to cherish curved his mouth. She wished they didn't have to keep their romance a secret. More than anything, she longed to cross the room and pull him into a long, possessive kiss. To show everyone he belonged to her.

Though he didn't.

She couldn't wait to go home with him tonight. She was still sore, but she needed him inside her—to claim and complete her—despite the pain it would cause. The vacancy in her soul ached a hundred times worse than her bruised flesh, and only Trey could make her whole. Her body seemed to recognize him as a missing half, which reminded her of Weezus's lid and pot comment. She began to doubt she'd find another—

"Hey, Missus Gallagher?" Carlo waved his fingers in front of her face, snapping her to attention. "Do I just stop talkin' now?"

Whoa, she'd missed his entire message. How long had she zoned out? "I'm sorry, hon. Yeah, you're all done."

As usual, the boy wasted no time in hightailing it to the nearest food source. Within seconds, he'd stuffed both cheeks full of meatballs like a carnivorous chipmunk.

One by one, the congregation filed through, offering words of thanks—for everything from lending a sympathetic ear after a divorce to building free tree houses with spare lumber. Their stories humbled Bobbi and made her understand how little she'd known about Trey. He was more than a charmer with a kind heart. He was *good*, all the way down, in an unusual way she'd rarely seen in human beings.

Hours later, Colton sidled up, dressed in his brown, short-sleeved deputy's shirt over jeans. He'd foregone his Stetson tonight and let his long, ebony hair hang loose against his shoulders. But nothing else hung loose on his tense body. His neck and shoulder muscles were so rigid, he'd probably given himself the equivalent of a full gym workout during the party. Odd, how subtle reminders of the preacher's daughter had the power to affect him after all these years.

"You ever consider therapy?" Bobbi asked him.

Leaning back in his chair, he folded both hands behind his head and grinned. "Sure, honey. Ever heard of sexual healin'?"

"Mm-hmm. Not to be confused with promiscuous, sexual dysfunction."

Colt shrugged casually, but he couldn't hide the sadness behind his blue-green eyes. "Haters gonna hate."

"You can't outrun the loss, you know. You have to deal with it." She'd discovered that the hard way. "Womanizing is a Band-Aid for you, and sooner or later, it's going to fall off. Then what?"

"Find a hot nurse to give me another one?"

"Whatever." One day he'd learn. Bobbi tapped her nails against one tripod leg. "Got something to say to the camera?" She glanced around the room, where only a handful of merrymakers remained. Pru and her friends had begun pulling down streamers and carrying empty trays to the kitchen. It seemed the party was over. "You're the last one."

"I've got somethin' to say to both of you."

"Both of who?"

"You and Lewis."

Her gaze automatically found Trey, who leaned against the front wall chatting animatedly with June and Luke. Carlo stood in rapt attention by his idol's side, a pink-frosted cupcake in each hand.

"Yeah," Colton drawled in a cocky voice. "You got it bad."

There was no use denying it, at least not with Colton. "I'll live."

"No, you won't." Leaning forward, he rested his forearms on his knees, expression transforming from dull to completely dark. "You'll survive, but you won't live. Trust me, there's a difference."

"Stop projecting." Bobbi shut him down, fast. Sure, getting over Trey would hurt like hell. It would take time. But she wouldn't shrivel up and die. She'd deal with the pain, heal, and move forward. Just like she always did. "There's more to life than sex and love. And I've got more than one lid, damn it!" Her raised voice drew the attention of Pastor McMahon, and she offered an apologetic wave.

"Lid?" Colt asked in confusion.

"We're done." Enough of this garbage. She switched off the camera and unscrewed it from her tripod.

"Looks like I struck a nerve."

"Now you're projecting *and* being egocentric." She snapped on the lens cap with a bit too much force. "It's been a long day, that's all."

"Uh-huh. Keep tellin' yourself that."

She refused to engage him further, but that didn't stop the persistent jerk from dropping comments like, *Denial's not just a river in Egypt, honey,* as she collapsed her titanium tripod and stuffed it into her shoulder bag.

After she helped stack the folding chairs, Pastor McMahon wrangled her, along with the other dozen-or-so stragglers, to the parking lot. He thanked them for coming and released them from clean-up detail.

A pair of floodlights affixed above the church doors outside drew half the bugs in Sultry County, forcing everyone across the asphalt into safer darkness. The humid night breeze stirred tendrils of loose hair around Bobbi's face. She reached to tuck one lock behind her ear, but a hand from behind beat her to it.

"I didn't get a chance to talk to you tonight," Trey whispered in her ear. He didn't let his touch linger, probably a wise move considering her brother was nearby.

Bobbi checked to be sure Luke was out of earshot. "I'll meet you at your place in thirty minutes." Which should give him plenty of time to drive Carlo home. "Then you can make it up to me."

"I can't wait." The heat behind his turquoise gaze promised a night she'd never forget. She couldn't wait either.

"G'night, boss," Bong called while striding to his white van. "Safe travels." His voice was thick with sarcasm, and he shared a snigger with Weezus, who made teasing kissy noises. At least they weren't angry with her. Of course, habitual weed consumption made that pretty much impossible.

She said goodnight to June and Luke, who didn't loiter. Not surprising considering they were newlyweds with a vacant house ten minutes away.

Fishing her keys from her purse, Bobbi crossed the parking lot to her hatchback and unlocked the driver's side door. Honestly, she didn't know why she bothered locking it. If anyone decided to steal this old clunker, the joke was on him.

Just as she'd rested her camera bag on the passenger seat, the high-pitched scream of spinning tires shattered the night air, followed closely by the stench of burnt rubber. Bobbi's heart jumped, and she glanced over her shoulder just in time to see a speeding sedan hurtling toward a cluster of partygoers who still lingered by the church entrance. She gasped while her stomach dropped to her toes.

Then everything happened in an instant.

Before a scream could even form on Bobbi's lips, Trey lurched forward and pulled Carlo out of the car's trajectory. The side-view mirror clipped the boy's elbow, spinning him like a top into Trey's body and sending them both to the pavement. Without slowing, the driver struck Colton head-on. He hit the windshield with an audible crack, then tumbled over the car's roof, bounced off the trunk, and rolled several times until his limp, broken body finally came to rest on the asphalt.

Tires still screeching, the driver accelerated, peeling out of the parking lot and onto the main road. Bobbi sprinted forward and squinted, memorizing the license plate before it disappeared from view.

Barbie91.

Chapter 18

I TANGLED WITH A FORD TAURUS, AND ALL I GOT WAS this lousy full-body cast.

Bobbi smiled at the words scrawled in black marker across Colton's chest. "Who wrote that?"

He didn't answer at first, only turned his empty gaze to the window, which offered a sunny, high-rise view of the parking lot. Not very scenic, but it didn't matter. These days, it seemed he looked, but didn't truly see. Wasted were the vibrant tulips and calla lilies, the leafy-green ferns, and plump, silver Mylar balloons that encouraged him to *Get Well Soon!* He stared blankly through them all. She couldn't blame him. If she were trapped from chest-to-ankle in itchy plaster while her jagged, fractured bones throbbed beneath lacerated flesh, she'd feel depressed too.

"Lewis," he eventually said with less enthusiasm than Eeyore.

That didn't surprise her. "Sounds like Trey." She moved an armload of teddy bears from Colt's bedside chair and shifted them to the floor so she could sit down. "He's coming to see you tonight. To say good-bye." The first leg of Trey's flight to Dubai would leave tomorrow morning. But she couldn't think about that right now.

"Mm-kay."

An errant lock of raven hair covered Colton's left eye, but he didn't care enough to move it. Before taking her seat, she leaned over his supine form and swept the strands aside, careful not to snag the stitches that closed the gash along his tawny forehead. He didn't thank her, didn't offer one of his signature, cheesy pickup lines. He didn't even glance down the front of her blouse to sneak a peek at her cleavage.

It was worse than she'd thought.

She'd wanted Colton to grow up and change, but not like this. If that psychopath, Barbara Lee, weren't already locked in a padded cell, Bobbi would throttle her for what she'd done to this once exuberant man.

"I saw your parents out there." She pointed toward the hall as she tugged her chair closer to the bed and lowered to the vinyl cushion. "Talking to some guy called Doc Benton." She picked up a stuffed bear and used its fuzzy ear to tickle the tips of Colt's fingers. "He looks twelve years old. You sure he's a real doctor?"

Colton didn't smile.

"I overheard him saying they got your internal bleeding under control," she continued. "That's good."

"Mm-hmm."

"And don't they say broken bones heal stronger?" When he didn't respond, she went on. "If that's true, you'll be the next Bionic Man."

Silence. Not even a glance in her direction.

"Hey, I brought something to cheer you up." She reached into her purse and pulled out the *Super Troopers* DVD she'd borrowed from Luke's collection. Though she'd found the film's humor a bit low-brow, she'd laughed at the impish, syrup-chugging cops. She'd identified a lot of the old Colton in their shenanigans. "Want me to put it on? I saw it last night, but I don't mind watching it again."

Colt focused on the case. The movie elicited a reaction in him, but it wasn't the one Bobbi'd expected. His countenance hardened, eyes flashed with anger.

"Put that away," he growled. "I don't wanna be reminded of that shit."

"What shit?" Had she missed something? "You mean law enforcement? The doctor said you'll be able to go back to work. After physical therapy, you'll be good as—"

"Not that." He closed his eyes. "Of what a reckless jackass I was." With his left arm, the only one he hadn't broken, he gestured at his mummified body. "This is my fault."

"No, it's—"

"I brought that crazy bitch into our lives. And I didn't just hurt myself, the kid got hurt too."

He meant Carlo, who'd been treated and released after the attack last week. "Just a fractured elbow. He's fine."

"Yeah. But it could've been worse. If Lewis hadn't been there, the kid'd be dead."

"But he's not." Bobbi tried holding Colt's hand, but he shook her off. "And this isn't your fault."

"I knew she was nuts." He swiveled his head just enough to meet her gaze. "But I didn't give a shit, 'cause she was an easy lay with big tits. Tell me I didn't get what I deserved."

"Not this." Bobbi shook her head. "You didn't deserve this."

Colt snorted dryly. "Whatever." He pointed at the DVD case. "Forget about the movie. The TV show too."

Bobbi's eyes automatically darted to the television mounted on the opposite wall. "What show?"

"*Sex in the Sticks*. I'm done. I'm revoking my participation waiver."

The blood in Bobbi's veins froze. "That's the morphine talking, right?" Without that waiver, she couldn't use a single minute of the footage the crew had shot of Colton. The entire summer would be wasted, the project tanked.

"I'm not screwing around, Gallagher."

"But, that means I can't—"

"I know what it means." His once playful gaze was hard as slate. Colder than she'd ever imagined possible. "I made an ass of myself, and I won't have it slapped on TV. I'm done embarrassing my family. I'm done. Understand?"

Bobbi's lips parted, but the lump in her throat blocked any sound from escaping. Colton had been her star playboy. His antics were crucial to the project. Without him, she had nothing. Her one chance to redeem herself and kick-start her ailing career would be gone.

"I don't wanna get a lawyer," he threatened, "but if you fight me on this, I will."

When she was finally able to speak, her voice sounded breathy and fragile. "I won't fight you." Even if she wanted to, the show wasn't worth Colton's soul.

"Good." He hitched one thumb toward the door. "You should probably go now."

"Just like that?"

"I wanna be alone." He closed his eyes again, shutting her out. "Tell my folks too."

She held on a few moments, hoping he'd change his mind, but he behaved as if she'd already left, returning his blank gaze to the window. After collecting her purse, she stood and shuffled to the door.

"Bye, Colton." Despite his frigid change of heart, she'd miss him. "I hope you feel like yourself again soon."

"I won't." He left her with five final words. "That fool's gone. Good riddance."

———∿∿∿———

That evening, Trey let her cry on his shoulder, even though it put a damper on their last night together. In turn, she listened as he detailed the latest drama between his parents, who were duking it out over whether or not Mrs. Lewis would keep her last name. It seemed Colonel Lewis's fiancée—yes, the cheating jerk had already proposed to his mistress—didn't want to share her name with an ex-wife. Trey'd left a scathing message for his father, but hadn't heard back yet. Bobbi felt awful for Trey, not to mention his mother, despite the woman's nasty judgment of her.

After dinner, she and Trey stretched out on the sofa and cuddled together like spoons, his strong arms wrapped around her from behind. A single, flickering candle illuminated the living room while Mumford & Sons sang softly from the stereo.

"I'm screwed," Bobbi said for the tenth time. "No offense, but you didn't give me much to work with. We pinned everything on Colton."

Trey kissed the top of her head. "It's a setback, but look at what happened to Colt. Doesn't that put things in perspective? At least we're all okay."

Snuggling closer against him, Bobbi grumbled in reluctant agreement. He was right. It was a miracle Barbara hadn't killed them all.

"And once this blows over," he continued, "you can

work on him some more. I'll bet he'll change his mind. Right now, he's mad at the world."

"No." Bobbi ran her fingernails through the blond hair on Trey's forearm. "He's mad at himself. That's worse."

"Either way, I don't wanna spend another minute talking about Colton." He tugged her shoulders, helping her rotate on the couch until she faced him. "I don't wanna spend another minute talking at all."

Curling one hand behind her neck, he pulled her mouth to his, nipped her lips gently before his tongue sought hers and curled in a seductive dance. Her body responded without conscious thought, softening and molding to his form, her lips parting to welcome him, to take more, always more.

While cherishing her mouth, he brushed his callused fingers over her face with unhurried precision, as if to commit each freckle and curve to memory. She did the same, caressing his gold-stubbled cheeks, the strong edge of his jaw, willing her hands to capture this moment and store it away forever. She hitched one leg around his waist to draw them together, compelled by her swollen heart to press as close to him as possible. But it wasn't enough. She needed all of him. She rocked against his swelling erection, sparking to life a thousand nerve endings between her thighs.

"I need you inside me," she whispered against his mouth.

"Soon," he promised, then kissed each of her eyelids. "Let's take our time tonight."

At her groan of protest, he sated her with a long thrust that sent a thrill of pleasure down the length of her legs and curled her toes.

"Let me love you," he said. "All of you, real slow."

"Yes." *Love me*. She wanted that—Trey's love.

Tangling her fingers in his hair, she claimed his mouth again, absorbed his sweet taste, massaged his probing tongue with hers. He fed tenderly from her lips, his kiss sensual and intoxicating, his hands adoring as they stroked her hair, temple, throat. He treasured her with every touch, and now, Bobbi truly understood the difference between sex and lovemaking. They were making love this time, and it was beautiful.

Trey broke the kiss, tipping their foreheads together. "God, Bobbi." He pulled her closer, crushing the soft curves of her breasts to his solid chest. "I don't wanna leave you."

She wrapped both arms around his neck and rolled him atop her, desperate to bear his weight. "I don't want you to go either."

He rose onto his elbows above her, cupping her cheek as his blue eyes searched her face for what felt like an eternity. Then he said something she hadn't expected. "Ask me to stay."

"What?"

"Ask me to stay, and I will." He brushed a thumb across her lower lip. "I want to be with you, Bo. I love you so hard it hurts."

At his words, her heart warmed, spreading tingly heat throughout every cell in her body. He loved her. The backs of her eyes prickled, her throat thickening until she could barely breathe. He gazed down at her as if nothing else existed, and she recognized that look—it was the one her brother gave June. The way she never thought a man would regard her.

"Ask me," he pressed.

"But what about your record?" Reputation meant everything to Trey. If he broke his contract, he couldn't clear the other-than-honorable discharge from his military file. And then what? A lifetime of employer rejection? He'd be trapped in a stagnant career, all because of her.

"I don't care anymore," he said. "Nothing matters but you."

Stay! Stay with me! The words crouched on her tongue, poised to leap, but then she heard Mrs. Lewis's voice echo inside her head, and she couldn't speak over it. *Life doesn't usually give second chances*, his mother had said. *Don't let another Gallagher ruin your future. Don't be like your father and give up everything that matters for a few quick rolls in the hay. I promise she's not worth it.*

"Baby," Trey kissed her lips and breathed, "please tell me to stay."

She had a better solution, though it involved delayed gratification. "Let's keep in touch while you're gone, then pick up where we left off."

"No." He didn't hesitate, shook his head firmly. "I tried that before. It doesn't work. I'm not going to risk losing you. Let's start our life right now."

He didn't believe she'd wait for him, probably because of that damned Mindy Roberts. "I'm not her," Bobbi promised. "We can make it work."

"No." The resolution in his voice said he'd made up his mind. "I'm not leaving you."

Tempted as she was, she couldn't do it. She couldn't be the one who stood between Trey and his second chance to start fresh. Not only would his mother hate her, but Trey would come to resent her for his decision, many years from now, when she'd saddled him with the responsibilities of marriage and children. That life would make it impossible for him to take advantage of the opportunity he was so willing to throw away right now. She refused to turn their love into regret.

So Bobbi did something that tore her soul in two. She met his desperate gaze and said, "I *like* you, Trey. We've had a lot of fun this summer, and I don't want it to end, but this is getting way too heavy for me." When his eyes widened in obvious pain, she struck again. "We promised no strings. Remember? I need you to keep your word."

Trey's lungs deflated into empty sacks. *You don't love me?* formed silently on his lips, as if his brain knew hearing it aloud would prove too much to bear.

"The sex is amazing," Bobbi went on, "but that doesn't mean we should start throwing around the L word."

Sex? That's all their affair had meant to her?

She grabbed his ass and started grinding against his hard-on like nothing had happened. Like she hadn't just ripped his heart from his open chest, thrown it to the ground, and stomped it with her strappy little high-heeled sandal. Then she said, "Let's not ruin our last time, okay?"

Too late.

He pushed off of her and retreated to the far end of the sofa.

"Hey." She sat up and rested her fingers on his back. "Don't be like that. I really do like you. I want us to stay friends."

He drew just enough air to tell her, "I don't need any more friends."

Did she really think they could pal around after this? That he could survive it? He knew what would happen. Each time he healed a little, he'd see her again, and she'd tear off the scab. It would keep happening until he bled to death, one excruciating drop at a time. This was why smart guys didn't hook up with their best friends' sisters. As long as Luke was in his life, Bobbi would be too. Trey was an idiot to let this happen.

"That's not gonna work for me," he said. "I need a clean break."

"Sure." Her tanned face blanched, but she straightened and gave a curt nod like they'd just closed a business deal. And to think Luke had thought his sister was damaged and vulnerable. "If that's what you want, then I won't—"

"Right now. It won't be any easier in the morning." He stood and walked to the front door numbly. As much as his body begged him to make love to Bobbi one last time, as desperately as he craved her touch, he couldn't do it. He couldn't give any more of himself to her, or he'd be left with nothing.

She took the hint and found her handbag. But just as Trey remembered she'd parked in the garage, not on the street, someone from outside pounded on the door, startling them both.

Trey squinted one eye and checked the peephole. It was Luke, and he looked madder than a cut snake. "Shit."

"I know she's in there!" Luke yelled from the front stoop, alerting half the neighborhood. "Open the damn door!"

Trey hung his head and sighed. What the hell, he might as well get it over with. At least this night couldn't get any worse. Opening the door, he faced his furious best friend. At once, Luke's eyes found Bobbi, who stood by Trey's side. She was clothed, but her rumpled blouse and frazzled hair showed what they'd been up to a few minutes earlier. As the saying went, the jig was up.

"Come out here," Luke said to Trey. "So I can kick your ass."

Bobbi pushed herself between them in a Hail Mary attempt to diffuse the situation. "Don't be an idiot! There's nothing going on between us. And even if there was, it'd be none of your—"

"*Nothing going on?*" Luke screamed, raking one hand through his hair and setting it on end. "Do you know what I just saw?" He scrubbed his face and shook his head as if desperate to clear it. "My computer crashed, so I borrowed your laptop—"

Bobbi interrupted him with a loud gasp. "Oh no!"

"Oh yes!" Luke held a pair of imaginary knives and made stabbing motions toward his own eyeballs. "Christ, Bo, I can't un-see that! I'll never be the same!"

Trey scrunched his forehead in confusion, but then understanding penetrated his foggy brain, and his stomach settled somewhere in the vicinity of his crotch. Bobbi hadn't deleted the dirty video they'd made. And, sweet Jesus, Luke had seen it?

Trey spun on her. "You put it on your laptop?" Why would she do that? "Please tell me it's not on the Internet!"

"Of course I didn't put it online! That was just for me!"

"Get your ass out here, Trey!" Luke backed up into the lawn and started flexing his fingers, gearing up for a fight. "Or I'll come in there and drag you out."

Damn it. Trey knew two things about his oldest friend—one, he didn't back down from a fight, and two, he had a left hook like a bazooka. But Trey would take the punishment. It was probably no less than he deserved.

"Fine." Trey jogged down the four front steps leading to his lawn. He pointed to his jaw and approached Luke. "I'm not gonna fight you, but I'll give you one free shot."

He'd expected Luke to balk and tell him that shit was for pansies, but instead, the man he'd considered a brother drew back and delivered a blow to Trey's cheek that had stars exploding behind his eyelids. He reeled backward, flailing to remain upright, while white-hot lightning bolts singed his nerves. Once he'd steadied himself, he worked his throbbing jaw back and forth, trying to determine whether it was broken. A persistent popping noise told him he'd at least dislocated it.

"Son of a bitch!" Luke cradled his fingers against his chest. "You broke my hand!"

"Well, I hope you're not looking for an apology, you jackass! I think you broke my face!"

One of Trey's neighbors, old Mrs. Denton across the street, stood on her front stoop, shaking her cordless telephone in the air. "I'm callin' the law!"

"That's not necessary, ma'am," Trey called out. "But thanks all the same."

"One thing!" Luke said, still protecting his hand. "I asked you for one thing—don't bang my sister—and you couldn't handle that."

"Hey!" Bobbi stormed outside, pointing her black handbag at her brother. "I'm a grown woman, and who I bang is none of your business. We didn't do anything wrong!"

With his good hand, Luke pointed to the house. "Just get your shit and go home. This is between me and him."

Bobbi made one of those furious girly noises, part growl, part squeal, and even in the moon's dim glow, Trey noticed an eerie redness creep from her neck to her hairline. "Get my shit and go home? Who the hell do you think you are?" Without giving her brother a chance to respond, she declared, "I will go home. To Inglewood. And it'll be a cold day in hell before I come back here." She bolted inside, and seconds later, the garage door opened, revealing her purple hatchback. She backed into the street and sped away without a backward glance.

This wasn't how he'd envisioned their last good-bye.

"Just great," Luke said. "Now look what you've done." He stomped across the yard to where he'd parked his black F-250, half on the curb, half in the grass. He lumbered into the cab, and moments later, he was gone too. Just like that.

Trey's jaw pulsed in time with his bruised heart. He sank onto the front steps, weighed down by the heavy ache in his chest—Bobbi's parting gift. He still couldn't believe it had ended this way. Just five minutes ago, he'd held her warm, responsive body in his arms, kissed her lush mouth...

"Stop," he told himself. He needed to quit wallowing and figure out what to do next. Not only had he lost Bobbi, but his best friend too—the reason he'd settled in Sultry Springs to begin with. What kind of life awaited him here two years in the future? An awkward acquaintance with Luke? A handful of excruciating encounters when Bobbi came to visit, which she surely would.

Screw it. If Sultry Springs didn't feel like home anymore, he'd settle elsewhere. Maybe if he called his realtor now, there'd be time to get the house listed before he left for Dubai in the morning.

An image of Carlo's face flashed in Trey's mind, and his already aching gut twisted with guilt. He'd told the boy he was coming back, but kids were resilient, right? In two years, Carlo would've forgotten Trey even existed. But still, maybe he could use some of his housing profits to add a teen room onto the community center. Start a small scholarship fund too. The money would help Carlo a hell of a lot more than Trey's presence. What did he know about kids, anyway?

The cell phone clipped to Trey's belt interrupted his pity party. He glanced at the incoming number and debated letting it go to voice mail. He was in no mood for his father's horseshit, but in the end, he answered the call. The night couldn't possibly get any worse, right?

"Colonel," Trey said flatly.

"I didn't want to do this." The old man sounded pissed, as usual. "But you just wouldn't leave it alone."

"Yeah," Trey said. "Talkin' to you isn't too high on my wish list either."

"You ever wonder why you're an only child?"

Trey drew back, surprised at the abrupt change in subject. "You achieved perfection on the first try?"

"No, wiseass. Because I'm sterile."

That was more information than he wanted to know about the old man's junk, but whatever. "Okay. When did that happen?" Probably radiation exposure, or some injury he sustained during one of his tours.

"It didn't happen. I was born like this."

The message sank in slowly, then, like floodwaters breaking a levy wall, the truth slammed him and swept him under. Trey's fingers went slack, and he nearly dropped his phone. If his father had always shot blanks, that meant...

"You're not my son." To give the Colonel credit, he didn't seem to take pleasure in dropping the bomb. His voice softened. "The year before you were born, I came home from a six-month deployment and found out your mother was four months pregnant."

Trey shook his head. Was he dreaming? Had this whole, awful day been a nightmare? He sure as hell hoped so, because this was too much.

"I agreed to raise you as mine," his dad said, "but as far as I was concerned, the marriage was over."

"This is insane."

"I wanted a kid," the old man explained. "I promised I'd never tell you, but I won't have you vilify me while you crusade for that woman like she's some kind of saint."

"So, who's my—" real father. Trey couldn't complete the sentence, still didn't believe it.

"From what I hear, it's a toss-up between a handful of MPs on post."

A handful? Of military police? *His* mother knocking boots with enlisted men? The same woman who refused to make eye contact with anyone making less than six figures a year? Her choice of bed partners came as a greater shock than his questionable paternity.

"For what it's worth," the Colonel said, "I don't regret my choice. But now, I've found someone who makes me happy, and I'm done playing house with that whore."

"Careful!" Whore or not, she was still his mother.

"Look, I laid some heavy shit on you. Take some time to let it sink in."

Sure, like that was gonna happen.

Before disconnecting, Trey's "father" left him with one final bit of advice. "Only a fool says no to a second chance. I've got mine. Now go get yours. Call me when you clear that record." Then the line went dead.

Trey stared into the darkness. Well, goddamn. In the last five minutes, he'd lost his best friend, the love of his life, and his father to boot. At least this day couldn't get any—

No, he'd better not think it. Shit could always get worse. He'd learned that lesson tonight.

Chapter 19

"SUCKS THAT WE CAN'T USE THIS," WEEZUS SAID, wrapping his index finger around one blue dreadlock. He used his free hand to gesture toward the forty-inch flat-screen monitor affixed to the Goldblatt studio wall, where Colton streaked the mayor's inauguration wearing nothing but a *Nacho Libre* mask.

Bong leaned forward in his rolling chair, studying Colt's bare bottom. "Is it just me, or does that look like a butterfly tattoo?"

"It's just you," Bobbi said from her chair beside him.

While Weezus paused the footage and zoomed in on the tattoo—a pair of angel wings, not a butterfly—Bobbi drummed her nails on the black, lacquered computer console and visited her happy place, envisioning life's obstacles as dozens of tiny Tetris shapes falling into perfect order. It calmed her frayed nerves, but reminded her of Trey, so she blocked the puzzle and focused on the nude subject in front of her. Nice ass. But not as nice as Trey's.

"Any chance he'll change his mind?" Bong asked.

"No." She'd tried for weeks, but Colton wouldn't budge. "He's not taking my calls anymore."

"Think your brother can soften him up?"

She shook her head. "Not for lack of trying." Luke had felt so badly about his reaction at Trey's house that final night, he'd pestered Colt each day on her behalf. But no dice. And if Colt had truly turned over a new leaf and wanted to start fresh, who was she to interfere with that? But now she needed to make Garry understand why the project he'd financed was a total loss.

"Then there's only one option," Weezus said.

Bobbi snorted. "Beg Garry not to break my kneecaps?"

"You're so negative," her cameraman chided. "It's blocking the universe from giving you what you want."

"You know I love you," she said, patting his forearm, "but you're such a hippie."

"He's right." Bong wheeled his chair closer until their armrests bumped. "You don't trust yourself, and that holds you back."

"Trust myself to do what?" she asked. "Slip a roofie in Colt's apple juice and force him to sign the waiver?"

"Check this out." Weezus tapped the electrical panel, skipping through the summer's footage until images from the church barbeque played on screen. "Look what you're missing."

Leaning back in her seat, Bobbi crossed her legs and regarded the big-screen monitor, where she stood shoulder-to-shoulder with Trey, watching Pru accept Judge Bea's proposal. She recognized this scene—her misogynistic freelancer had shot it—and she didn't like it any more now than she had then. The longing in her face was easier to read than a neon billboard.

She didn't see Weezus's point. "What am I missing? That I'm pathetic?"

"There you go with the negativity again," he scolded. "Look at this frame." He turned a dial to decrease the playback speed, so she and Trey turned to glance at each other in slow motion. Then Weezus froze the scene. "Right there!"

Bobbi's heavy heart sank an inch. She understood what Weezus had noticed—even the most blackened cynic couldn't deny the light in Trey's Technicolor-blue eyes when they met hers. He'd loved her even then, though he probably hadn't known it yet. These daily reminders of him—the humor in his deep voice, his winking dimples—were like paper cuts, a thousand shallow gashes that burned worse each day. Whoever said time healed all wounds had obviously never lost the lid to his pot.

"I know it's not what Garry wanted," Weezus said, "but there's a love story here."

Bobbi rotated her chair toward him, knocking Bong's armrest in the tight space. "You can't be serious." Switch the focus of the documentary from Colton to her and Trey? It was out of the question. Career suicide.

"Keep an open mind," Weezus advised.

"Yeah." Bong grabbed her seat back and swiveled her to face him. "There's more than enough footage of you and him together, and it's kind of cool to see your feelings change over the months."

"Dude," Weezus said, "it's not just cool. It's beautiful."

"True 'dat," Bong agreed, scratching his scruffy chin. His mouth curved into a dreamy smile. "Like a double rainbow."

"Oh my god." She rolled her eyes. "Hippies."

"Don't you love him?" Bong asked.

Her first instinct was to say no, to guard her feelings, but then she remembered his words at Trey's farewell party. *It kinda hurts when you freeze me out like this.*

Bong had said she didn't trust easily, and he was probably right. But she didn't want to be an emotional weakling anymore, so she met his bloodshot gaze, slowly gathering the courage to say, "Yes."

"And he's into you, right?"

"He *was*." Until she broke his heart. And, indirectly, his jaw. "But that doesn't matter. I'm not telling the whole world I had an affair with one of my subjects. Nobody'll take me seriously again."

"Who cares?" Bong demanded. "If you produce quality work, nobody's going to give a damn about your private life. Heck, being eccentric is a job requirement around here."

"I care, and I'm not eccentric. I'm a professional." She didn't want people gossiping about her, whispering behind their hands like children in the school yard. She'd had enough of that as a kid, and she wasn't that dirty, helpless, hot mess anymore.

Weezus posed a serious question. "Do you really think Goldblatt's going to give you a second chance?"

"*Third* chance," Bong clarified, "if you count the Smyth thing."

"Right," Weezus said. "Garry handed you a small fortune, and you're giving him nothing. At best, he'll fire you. At worst, he'll sue you." Weezus leaned forward, resting his long arms on his knees. "I get that you don't want to share something so personal with the world, but I don't see any other choice."

Bobbi chewed the tip of her tongue. The word "lawsuit" practically gave her hives, but so did the idea of airing her scandalous summer lovin' to an audience of millions. "I'll think of something."

"It better be good."

Bobbi checked her watch and wiggled her rolling chair backward from between the crew so she could stand. "I've got to run. Be back in an hour or so, and then we can keep brainstorming."

"Where're you going?" Bong asked over his shoulder.

"Lunch date." She rubbed her nose and hoped he didn't ask—

"With who?"

Damn it. "Uh…" Her gaze wandered around the small, boxy studio, settling on a hairline crack near the ceiling. Trey could fix that. No! Stop thinking about Trey! She squeezed her eyes shut, but his stunning face was still there, smiling teasingly as if to say, *Lighten up, Bo Peep.*

"Who're you meeting?" Weezus pressed.

She drew a breath. "Just an old friend."

Weezus narrowed his eyes. "Liar."

"Okay, okay." This trust and honesty business wasn't so easy. "It's Derek."

"Derek *Spaulding?*" Bong jumped out of his seat and cracked his head against a low-hanging speaker.

"Oh, hell no!" Weezus added, shaking his finger like a teenage girl with an attitude.

Bobbi held up one palm. "Chill. He's back from sabbatical, and he wants to apologize."

"That better be *all* he wants!" The rare anger in Bong's eyes warmed her heart. He must've known how deeply Derek had hurt her last year, though she'd tried not to show it.

"Hey," she told them sweetly, "I thought forgiveness was good for the soul." There. She'd appealed to their flower-power senses. They couldn't give her a hard time now.

"He's toxic," Weezus said. "And your soul's fine the way it is."

A giggle bubbled up from her throat, the first one in weeks. It felt good to laugh again. "I promise I won't let him suck me in. One free lunch and a quick act of forgiveness, and then I'm out of there."

"Order the most expensive thing on the menu," Bong demanded, folding his arms.

"It's a deal."

Twenty minutes and two bus transfers later, she stood outside one of LA's trendiest restaurants and smoothed the wrinkles from her zebra-print skirt, uncertain her churning stomach would hold down a meal. Her palms were sweaty, her heart racing. She hadn't seen Derek in almost a year, and she hated the power he still held over her.

But he didn't need to know that.

Time to find some courage. Raising her chin, she summoned an unaffected mask and pushed open the front door. A cool burst of air conditioning frosted her cheeks, and she inhaled deeply through her nose for a little extra fortification as she clicked briskly to the host station. The maître d', a middle-aged man with a gentle smile, stepped from behind the desk to greet her. His warm brown eyes reminded her of Pastor McMahon, and her tummy gave a little tug.

"Table for one?" he asked.

"No, I'm—"

"The lady's with me," said a familiar voice.

Bobbi spun around and locked eyes with Derek.

"Hey, beautiful," he said, shoving his hands into his pockets and curving his lips in a hesitant grin. He made no move to embrace her, only studied her face as if gauging her reaction before risking anything more.

A quick scan of his lanky form revealed he'd lost a few pounds, but otherwise he looked exactly the same—chestnut hair tousled in waves, straight, aristocratic nose, and hazel eyes fringed by thick, dark lashes any woman would kill for. Funny, the mere sight of him used to send her stomach into somersaults, but now she felt nothing. Not even a quiver.

With each passing second, his shoulders tensed, and when he began chewing his lower lip, Bobbi decided to put him out of his misery. After all, she'd come here to forgive him. She faked a wide smile and held out her arms for a hug.

He closed the distance between them and embraced her loosely, not the kind of hearty bear hugs she'd grown to appreciate in Sultry Springs. She pulled in his scent, which had once seemed so intoxicating. Instead of sandalwood, Derek smelled of fruity hair products and expensive cologne. He smelled like a girl. Dressed like one too, at least compared to the rough-and-tumble men she'd spent the summer filming. Derek's designer jeans were meticulously torn and frayed by their manufacturer, not by hard work, and though his black T-shirt epitomized simplicity, she knew it had cost him more than what most people made in a week.

"It's great to see you," he said, pulling back.

"You too," she lied. She nodded toward the dining room, eager to get this over with and return to the studio. "Ready?"

They strolled past the other diners and settled at a quiet table in the corner. The savory scent of gourmet pasta sauce watered her mouth, but only because she'd skipped breakfast. What she really craved was one of Pru's famous chicken biscuits.

When the waiter asked for their drink order, Bobbi replied without thinking, "Sangria," but instantly changed her mind. It wouldn't compare to June's recipe. "No. Make that a vodka tonic."

Derek leaned forward, whispering, "At noon?"

"Yep. Vodka can't tell time."

His already stiff smile faltered. "I'll have a raspberry-ginger iced tea, sweetened with honey. Lemon wedge on the side."

Oh brother. He even drank like a girl.

The waiter tipped his head and retreated to the bar, leaving Bobbi and Derek to face each other in awkward silence. She unfolded her linen napkin and placed it across her lap, waiting for him to apologize, but empty seconds continued to tick by. He fidgeted with his silverware, his gaze flicking up and down at her in clear discomfort.

Derek was a bit of a chickenshit, wasn't he? What had she ever seen in him?

"How was your sabbatical?" she finally asked.

He released a shaky breath. "Wonderful. Just what the doctor ordered."

"That's great." *Glad you enjoyed your vacation while I stayed behind to account for all your lies.* "Where'd you go?"

"Mykonos. My family has a house there."

"Oh, the Greek isles." She hoped he couldn't hear the jealousy in her voice. "Lovely."

Derek pulled his fingers through his hair and withdrew them quickly, probably afraid of mussing his meticulously styled waves. "Listen, Beebs, this isn't easy."

Beebs. She'd forgotten his nickname for her, and it sounded foreign to her ears now. "It's okay. You don't have to do this." And she'd told him so on the phone last night.

"I have to." Then he said something that revealed his true nature. "For me."

She nodded for him to continue. Weezus was right—the bastard really was toxic.

"I'm sorry for the...uh...Smyth misunderstanding. I want to make it up to you."

Misunderstanding her ass. Bobbi wanted to offer her full forgiveness, but he wasn't making it easy. "Well, unless you can turn back time..." she trailed off and bit her tongue.

In a bold move, especially for him, he reached across the table and took her hand. Bobbi gasped, shocked by the sensation of his baby-soft fingers curled around hers. She'd come to expect a man's hands to feel like the fine-grit side of a nail file. Derek's touch felt all wrong, as if she'd opened her mouth for a bite of apple, and received a chunk of onion instead.

She freed her hand and rested it in her lap. "What did you have in mind?"

He dipped his chin, giving her a pointed look. "The opportunity of a lifetime. A dream job." When she widened her eyes in surprise, he continued. "I convinced my dad to finance a documentary on the corruption and greed within military contracting. You know, paying crooks a hundred dollars an hour to drive supply trucks and billing the taxpayers for it."

Bobbi straightened. "There's a reason they're paid so much." She'd seen pictures of servicemen and women—both civilian and active duty—recovering in burn wards. They earned extra pay for navigating land mine-filled roads because nobody else wanted the task. And Trey. They hadn't discussed his salary, but she hoped he was being well-compensated for risking his life in Dubai.

"Yeah." Derek sniffed in that arrogant way of his. "Because Uncle Sam keeps feeding the fat cats."

Fat cats? Who actually said that anymore? She shook her head.

"Hear me out, Beebs. We'll co-shoot it, and I'll give you top billing. This'll put you back where you belong." With a casual but cautious shrug, he slid a flirtatious glance at her to test the waters, the kind that used to melt her insides. "And I've missed you. Imagine it: you and me in the Middle East, taking on The Man. We'd make a great team."

She could picture it, but the mental image left her cold. The thought of spending months in Derek's close company turned her stomach, and not in a good, somersault kind of way. But she couldn't dismiss this opportunity based on emotions. That was just as irresponsible as her previous mistake of trusting him blindly.

"I can't give you an answer right now," she said. "Let me think about it."

He wrinkled his nose like he'd smelled garbage. "What's to think about? I just gave your career back on a silver platter. If we do this right—and you know we will—we're talking award-winning material here. It's a no-brainer."

"It's not that simple. I can't just take off." She bit

her lip, then confessed, "I'm in a bind." Over the next few minutes, she explained her Garry Goldblatt predicament while Derek listened, nodding in businesslike understanding. "So," she finished, "I have to give him new episodes, or repay the advance. Maybe a penalt—"

Derek cut her off with a wave. "Not a problem. I'll have the old man bail you out."

Her arm froze in place, mid-reach for the ice water. "What?"

"It's the least I can do."

Bobbi managed to lower her arm, but she couldn't form an articulate response. Holy greenbacks. How much money did his family have? And if cash was no object, why the hell hadn't Derek offered to pay her attorney's fees, or help cover a portion of what the judge had awarded Smyth after the lawsuit?

"Beebs," he said, "let me do this for you. I spent the last year feeling like pond scum for what happened."

She couldn't think. Too many conflicting thoughts were pinging off the inner walls of her mind. "Give me a minute to process this."

He smiled and sat back in his chair, clearly pleased with himself. "Sure, babe."

The waiter arrived bearing drinks, and Bobbi's vodka tonic barely made contact with the table before she scooped it up and nursed it like an addict. As she sipped the tart libation, she listed the pros and cons of accepting Derek's offer.

While it would give her what she'd wanted most—career redemption—she wasn't sure she agreed with the message behind the project. Wouldn't that make her a hypocrite? Did that even matter? People committed far

worse atrocities to get ahead in life. If she really wanted
to succeed, maybe she should do whatever it took.

She swirled the frigid drink in her hand, listening to
the ice cubes tinkle and clink against the crystal. Her
mind told her to accept Derek's offer, but her spirit
begged her to reconsider. She glanced at him, still uncertain of what to say, when a baby wailed from a nearby
table and tore her attention away from business.

When she glanced over her shoulder toward the
clamor, her fingers went slack. She dropped her drink.
She heard Derek scramble to dab at the mess with his
napkin, but nothing, not even the icy liquid pooling
in her lap, could tear her gaze away from the dimpled
cheeks of the blond infant peering at her from above his
mother's shoulder.

It was her baby—the spitting image of the son she'd
envisioned during her brief pregnancy scare. In an
instant, all the emotions she'd battled in Trey's bathroom the night she'd lost that phantom child swelled
inside her until tears pressed against her eyelids.

The boy wailed again, and his mother bounced him
in a soothing rhythm that quieted his cries. The woman
sat opposite her husband, who handed a pacifier across
the table and murmured something that made his wife
laugh. They looked so happy together—one lid, one pot,
and the breathtaking life they'd created together.

Bobbi's chest burned with an envy she couldn't
quench, and it was then she knew what she truly wanted.
Not a stellar reputation or a shelf lined with Golden Calf
awards. She wanted her other half, and that was Trey.
No one else would fit. And someday, she wanted to bear
his towheaded son. She saw her future play out like

studio footage—Trey carrying her over the threshold of his home, their first Thanksgiving meal at his tiny kitchen table, his hand resting atop her rounded belly during their first ultrasound—the images so striking and poignant it sent one, plump tear trailing down her cheek.

"Hey." Derek tugged at her sleeve. "Where'd you go?"

Slowly, she returned to him and used her napkin to blot the tonic dripping down her legs. "Sorry, I was just thinking."

"Breeders." He nodded at the family and snorted disdainfully. "It's not enough that they ruin the planet with their giant eco footprint, they have to ruin our meals too? They shouldn't let kids in here."

Trey had been right, Derek really was a dick. But then she realized that if it weren't for Derek's lies and the Smyth catastrophe, she never would have agreed to film *Sex in the Sticks* to begin with. She never would have met Trey.

The translucent hair on her arms stood on end. Bobbi had never believed in fate, but now she saw her life's most devastating obstacles had served a greater purpose. They'd led her to Trey. To her one and only lid.

Smiling so widely she must have seemed insane, she told Derek, "No."

He searched her face a moment. "No, what?"

"I don't want the job." She grabbed her handbag and stood from the table, sending an errant ice cube to the floor. Forget lunch, she had a proposition for Garry Goldblatt, and it couldn't wait another minute. "I forgive you, so forgive yourself."

"Beebs," Derek asked, holding out one hand in concern, "are you okay?"

"Not yet." She wouldn't feel whole until she'd won back her Golden Boy. "But I will be." Before leaving him stunned and alone, she added, "Thanks, Derek. You changed my life."

Chapter 20

TREY FOAMED HIS CHEEKS WITH SHAVING GEL, CAREFUL to avoid the sensitive bruise along his jaw that had lightened to the shade of a ripe avocado. As quickly as he could manage without nicking himself, he tugged a razor over his thick stubble. His guesthouse roommates stirred outside the bathroom door, pressuring him to hurry. He hadn't shared a toilet or shower with anyone since his army days, and he missed having a big, quiet house to himself. He missed a lot of things.

With a sigh, he rubbed one hand over his buzz cut. The blunt edges of his fuzzy, shorn hair felt odd against his palm, another reminder of his time in the military, but hey, at least it didn't hang in his eyes anymore. He had to look at the bright side—take pleasure in the small, unexpected aspects of life now. Otherwise he'd throw himself into the path of a freaking bullet.

After he'd finished shaving, he shook some talcum powder onto his bare chest and dusted his belly, hoping to ward off any more chaffing. It seemed his friends, Kevlar and the fierce Dubai sun, had conspired to skin him alive, the hateful bastards. He tugged on his uniform: black T-shirt, black cargo pants, black beret, and black combat boots. Even his Jockeys were black. He looked like a damned mercenary.

As soon as he opened the bathroom door, one of his new buddies, a tank named Anders, rushed inside, bumping Trey's arm so hard he spun a half rotation like a clumsy ballerina.

"Sorry, man," Anders called while barreling to the john. "Gotta piss like a racehorse."

Trey rubbed his triceps. Five dudes and one bathroom. It was gonna be a long deployment.

He shuffled to his bunk, stepping over piles of dirty laundry, spare boots, discarded towels, and scattered magazines—both of the girlie and ammunition variety. Bunch of slobs, the lot of them. Trey's home may not have been a showplace, but he'd kept it tidy.

He opened the footlocker at the base of his bed and pulled out his cell phone to check messages. Once he went on duty, he'd have to stow it again. A quick glance at the screen told him he had no new voice mails but four unread texts. Scrolling through the inbox, he skimmed repeated apologies from his mother, along with requests to call home, but he wasn't ready for that. Despite what Mom had done, she deserved respect, and he wouldn't speak to her until he'd calmed down enough to control his tongue. Which might take until Christmas.

What he'd really wanted was a message from Bobbi, but after a month, maybe it was time to give up hope.

Just as he poised his thumb to swipe the power button, the phone chirped, alerting him to a new text. Like Pavlov's pooch expecting a treat, Trey's heart jumped, and he tapped the screen with his trembling index finger while searching for her name. His shoulders slumped. Not her. But it was the next best thing.

Hey, asshole, Luke had typed, *call me so I can apologize*.

Trey's mouth twitched in an involuntary grin. It sure

had taken the cantankerous butthead long enough to extend the olive branch. He checked his watch, noting just enough time for a quick call.

Luke picked up on the first ring. "Hello?"

Trey grasped one hip. "Let's hear it then."

"Don't be a dick," Luke recited in their typical fashion. "I'm sorry. We cool?"

"Yeah, we're cool."

"Cool."

Usually, their ritual apology would end there, but Trey needed to say, "I'm sorry too. If it makes you feel any better, she wasn't a fling. I really cared about her."

"Cared? Past tense?"

"No." Not that it mattered, because she didn't feel the same about him. "Present."

"Well, if it makes *you* feel any better, you broke two of my fingers. The splint I'm wearing makes it look like I'm flipping people off."

"Which you probably are, on the inside."

Luke chuckled. "You know me well." Then he turned the subject from rude gestures to a matter Trey didn't want to discuss. "You gonna come to your senses now and take your house off the market?"

Trey exhaled a puff of air into the phone. "No."

"Why not?"

Because wherever you are, your sister will turn up. "It's time to move on."

"Not good enough." When Trey couldn't provide a better reason for leaving town, Luke threatened, "I'll make sure the place doesn't sell. Hell, I'll pay a computer geek to hack the sex offender registry so it looks like you're located smack-dab in the middle of Pervert City."

"I'll bet the neighbors will appreciate that."

"Did you even think about the kid?" Luke's voice darkened, taking Trey's mood along for the ride. "When Carlo asked why you're selling the house, I told him it's because you want to build new when you come back. He said he wants to help."

"Oh, shit." Trey's stomach clenched. "Tell me you're making that up."

"You should've seen his face. He thinks Rainbow Skittles shoot out your ass! What was I supposed to say?"

"Damn it." Trey pressed the heel of his hand over one eye. But he couldn't really blame his best friend. While Luke shouldn't have lied to Carlo, Trey shouldn't have left him with the impossible task of breaking the news to the boy.

"Let's talk about the real reason you won't come home, you wussy," Luke said. "You're afraid of running into my sister."

As usual, Luke nailed it. Trey remained silent, not bothering to deny the truth.

"Well, you got nothin' to worry about," Luke continued, "'cause she's a wussy too. I'm gonna have to fly to California to visit her from now on."

"Good to know she's avoiding me," Trey said sarcastically. But if he moved back home, he'd still see her ghost in Sultry Springs. He'd never be able to pass the coffee shop without thinking of her, or use her old guest room without remembering how he'd tied her to the bed with that silky black scarf and made her come so hard she'd cried. He'd never be free of her. "How about this," he offered. "I'll sleep on it."

"Fine. But don't wake up till you change your mind."

Trey snickered. "Can't live without me, huh? Who's the wussy now?"

Luke told him to do something anatomically impossible, then ordered him to stay safe and keep in touch. They disconnected, and Trey stowed his phone safely inside his footlocker, feeling lighter than he had in a month.

After donning his bulletproof vest and weapons holster, Trey clipped a small communications device to his shoulder and set out for his morning inspection of the property, a five-acre, private residence of Dubai's wealthiest resort mogul. The guy had two other local homes—a penthouse in the heart of the city and a beachfront condo—but Trey hadn't left the main house since his arrival last month. According to rumor, the whole security staff would accompany their employer to the beach in a couple of weeks. Trey looked forward to the change in scenery. He couldn't deny this job was boring as hell.

Still, he needed to be vigilant. His boss had made a lot of enemies when he'd sold townhomes to foreign investors without disclosing one crucial bit of information: the development bordered a reeking sewage plant. And not just any foreign investors, either—members of the Russian mafia. To make matters worse, his boss had spilled secrets to the American military to aid their operations in the Middle East, something local terrorists wouldn't appreciate if they knew. The U.S. government wanted to keep this man alive and snitching, and they'd paid Trey's contractor top dollar to guarantee his safety.

Pushing open the back door, Trey slipped on his Oakleys and shielded his eyes from the nuclear sun. It was only eight in the morning and already hotter than two minks screwing inside a wool sock. The lawn beneath his boots was unnaturally green in this barren land, one of the clear indications of wealth, announcing to all that passed, *Blow me, suckers! I'm watering something I can't even eat!* Seemed like a waste of sparse resources to Trey.

He'd just reached the wrought iron fence that bordered the property when the speaker affixed to his shoulder squawked, "Give me your status, Lewis."

Sounded like his supervisor, a gruff man of few words. Trey muttered in the receiver, "Lewis reporting from the southeast border. All's well."

"Roger that. Report to the front gate. We've got a disruption."

"On my way." Trey double-timed it and prepared to draw his weapon. "Disruption" usually meant a persistent salesman trying to get past security, but casual assumptions could cost lives in this line of work.

However, once he approached the guard station and recognized two of the alleged disruptors, he stumbled over his own feet and released his Glock in a dumbfounded stupor. He reached down to retrieve his fallen weapon, so worthless that a Girl Scout could've taken him out with a peashooter.

It was Bobbi's motley crew—that mammoth, bluehaired Asian dude and the blond stoner who looked like Shaggy from *Scooby Doo*. They stood outside the gate, filming him through the iron bars as if nothing had changed. A long, fishing pole microphone drooped over the spires to capture Trey's stammers of, "What the hell?"

His gaze moved to a third figure, a woman dressed in a long, loose turquoise tunic over white linen pants. In the local custom, she'd used a white silk scarf to cover her hair, but one glimpse at her green eyes told him this was no native. Though it took several seconds for him to believe it, he was gawking at Bobbi.

His heart went south as his eyes continued to absorb the graceful curve of Bo's cheeks, her lush lips, and the pert nose she'd just begun scrubbing with the back of her hand. Good God, she was even more stunning than he remembered, so gorgeous his ribs ached.

Trey's supervisor jerked him back to reality. "You know these clowns? I keep telling 'em they can't film on private property."

"Yeah," Trey managed, "they're—"

Bobbi cut him off, pointing a folded document at the guard. "And I told *you* it's public domain out here. Besides, we've got a permit!"

Trey couldn't stop his lips from twitching in a grin. Typical Bobbi. "Buzz me out," he told his supervisor, "and I'll handle it."

"Fine," came the terse response, "but I don't want them filming the house."

After Trey stepped onto the driveway and shut the gate behind him, he took a few steps behind the camera crew, forcing them to turn away from the main house if they wanted to keep filming him. Out of habit, he scanned the area for suspicious activity before settling his gaze on Bobbi, who stood close enough to touch. He folded his arms to keep from reaching out and stroking her face.

"So," he said to her, trying his best to fake a

disinterested tone, "what's with all this?" He hitched a thumb at the camera.

Bobbi's tanned cheeks drained of color. She quit scratching her nose only long enough to wring her hands and wipe her palms on her tunic. Tiny beads of perspiration popped to the surface of her skin, while her eyes darted back and forth between him and the lens. Trey knew it wasn't the heat that had her sweating bullets. A sick, heavy feeling uncurled in his gut as he wondered what awful news she was about to dump on him.

He didn't expect her to say, "Our story isn't over." While he stood rooted to the pavement, she inched forward and cleared her throat. "*Sex in the Sticks* needs a happy ending."

A happy ending? Could that mean—no, he was too afraid to think it. He couldn't get his hopes up. "More drama for the show?" he asked, squeezing his own biceps for strength. "Is that what you're after?"

She shook her head and swallowed so hard her throat bobbed. When she opened her mouth to speak, it took a few tries before she managed to choke out, "I love you. I'm your pot, and you're my lid, and I love you."

His lungs filled with a thousand fluttering moths. Did she mean it? Closing his eyes, he asked God for a quick favor. *Please let her mean it. Please. I'll never ask for anything, ever again—not even for the Cubs to win the World Series.* Okay, well, maybe he'd still ask for that, but nothing else. For good measure, he promised not to touch Bobbi until their wedding night, even if it took years to get her to the altar. *Please let her love me.*

———∿∿∿———

Bobbi's pulse sprinted painfully inside her veins as she tried to read Trey's guarded expression. He closed his eyes as if the sight of her might turn him into a pillar of salt. Was she too late? Had she hurt him too deeply? Or worse yet, had he moved on with another woman?

She'd felt so emboldened on the way over, but seeing him now, transformed into this fierce warrior in black—armed to the teeth and clearly angry with her for coming—her courage began to wane. Bong made an encouraging *keep going* motion with his free hand, but what could she say to change Trey's mind?

"I'm sorry," she offered, figuring it was a good place to start. "I'm sorry I let you think our relationship didn't mean anything to me. It did. I loved you, and I didn't want you to go. But I couldn't let you stay in Sultry Springs and miss your chance to start over."

He opened his eyes and stared at her a long moment before answering. "Why didn't you tell me the truth?"

"Because you were so adamant about staying." She splayed her hands, pleading for understanding. "You didn't trust me to wait for you."

He unfolded his muscled arms and gripped his waist. "Trust's got nothing to do with it. When you find the love of your life, you don't wanna wait two years to start living it."

"The love of your life?" Her tummy quivered, and she dared another step, moving close enough to savor Trey's scent. It was all she could do not to bury her nose at the base of his throat and breathe him in. "Does that mean you don't hate me?"

His stoic mask fell, blue fire flickering behind his gaze. "How could you even say that?"

"Because I hurt you—"

"Dammit, Bo, come here." Before she had time to gasp, he'd snaked one arm around her waist and yanked her hard against him. She smacked a solid wall of Kevlar with an *oof*, but wasted no time in locking her fingers behind his neck.

Their lips met in a fierce kiss that went from zero to blazing in under a second. His tongue darted inside her, tasting and claiming her, while the rough pads of his fingertips branded each exposed inch of her face. He nipped and suckled her lips until they throbbed, but it still wasn't enough. She could spend hours absorbing his sweetness and never feel sated.

Abruptly, he broke the kiss and tipped their foreheads together. "This isn't the States," he reminded her.

"Right," she panted, fighting for her oxygen. Like it or not, they'd committed to spending the next couple of years in a country that banned public displays of affection. She'd respect the culture, even if she disagreed with it. "Still love me?"

He didn't hesitate. "Completely."

"Do you have to live in your boss's house?"

"No. Why? Looking for a roommate?"

"As a matter of fact, I am. But if we're going to live together here, we should probably get married. I'm pretty sure it's a crime otherwise. We don't want to wind up in a foreign prison, do we?"

His eyes went wide, mouth spread into a smile that tugged both dimples to the surface of his cheeks. "Is that a proposal, Bo Peep?"

"I guess it is."

"Don't you wanna go home? To Inglewood or Sultry Springs? I'll follow you anywhere."

"No way." Rising to her tiptoes, she straightened his black beret. "I've got important work to do right here in Dubai."

"And what's that?"

"My new project for Garry Goldblatt, *Sinful Saudi Nights*. I'll be shooting drunk heiresses while they stumble around making idiots of themselves." In the privacy of their all-inclusive resorts, of course. Garry had loved the idea so much, he'd offered a bonus so Bobbi could film a documentary on the side—on civilian contractors. But unlike Derek's project, hers would focus on the positive.

Trey pulled back and searched her face. "But you hate making that trash."

"Not as much as I love you." She held up one hand and smiled into his sea-blue eyes. "So, when're you going to put a ring on this finger?"

He glanced at the camera and lowered his mouth to her ear. "The sooner the better," he whispered, "because I'm not givin' it up until you make an honest man out of me."

"Well, then," she said, "lucky for us, I happen to know a licensed minister." Years ago, Bong had become ordained through the Mother Earth Commune of Sunshine and Light. "You free tonight?"

"I get off at six." Trey took her cheeks between his delightfully rough palms. "But you're marrying into a hot mess of a family. Don't say I didn't warn you."

She brushed her thumb across the bruise her brother had left near Trey's ear. Her family tree had a few gnarled branches too. "It's okay. If they give us a hard time, we'll just start one of our own."

"What do you say we spend a few years practicing first?"

Bobbi pulled off his beret and ran her fingers through his cropped hair. By the end of the day, this Adonis would belong to her, and she to him. They'd share life's triumphs and trials, spend each night in the refuge of each other's arms. She didn't know what she'd done to deserve such a blessing, but she'd spend the rest of her days making Trey deliriously happy.

Motioning to the silk covering her hair, she whispered, "I'd say I brought lots of scarves, and I can't wait to use them."

"I like the way you think, darlin'." He tapped one finger against her temple, then used it to tip her chin upward. "I love you, Bo. I promise I'm gonna take good care of you."

"I love you too, Golden Boy." She rested one hand over his Kevlar-covered heart, imagining its strong and steady beat. "And we're going to take care of *each other*." Turning to face the camera, she smiled with all the joy in her soul, not the least bit ashamed. She glanced at the tear-streaked faces of her beaming crew and announced, "That's a wrap!"

About the Author

Macy Beckett is an unrepentant escapist who left teaching to write hot and humorous romances. No offense to her former students, but her new career is way more fun! She lives just outside Cincinnati in the appropriately named town of Loveland, Ohio, with her husband and three children.

For sneak peeks and giveaways, please visit her on the Web at macybeckett.com, and don't forget to say "hello" on Facebook, Goodreads, and Twitter.

Available in August, Colton's story:
Surrender to Sultry

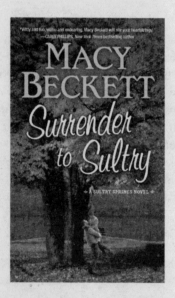

Leah McMahon is back in Sultry Springs, Texas, to help her dad recover from surgery. But there's a new sheriff in town and he's none other than Colton Bea, the wild-as-weeds boy who stole her heart a decade earlier. Colt's a changed man now, and the feelings between these high school sweethearts are stronger than ever. But Leah's got a secret so devastating that he may never forgive her. Can she find a way to earn absolution and build a future with the Sultry man she's loved half her life?

Ben grinned

"You're a beautiful woman, Sunny Outlaw Payton, both inside and out, and I'm a lucky man to be with you."

Electricity seemed to crackle and hiss between them as his eyes caressed her face. She had no idea about any long-term relationship with Ben, but she didn't want to think about that now.

She wanted only to savor tonight.

She wanted to feel the warmth and comfort and passion of a man again.

Of Ben.

Dear Reader,

So many folks who have enjoyed the Outlaw family stories have asked if there aren't any more Outlaws around. Well, I investigated and, by golly, found that Uncle Butch Cassidy Outlaw, who was a Texas State senator, had a couple of secrets, including twin daughters none of his family knew about. *The Twin* is the first of two stories about these sisters, who run Chili Witches Café in Austin.

Naturally it's Sam Bass Outlaw from *The Texas Ranger* (AR, May 2007) who first meets his cousin Sunny, and, wouldn't you know, he happens to stop in to have a bowl of chili with another Texas Ranger, Ben McKee. (I've told you before that I'm a sucker for tall, handsome Texas Ranger heroes.) Sunny and Ben are perfect together, but even with the senator's help, it takes a while for them to realize that.

Austin is a wonderful town, laid-back and mellow, and rich in history as the state's capital. It's also famous for its music scene, and I've added some of that flavor for you to sample, as well.

Now, I'm not allowed to share Chili Witches' recipe, but for those of you who like Texas chili, the recipe is quite similar to several recent winners of the Terlingua International Chili Championship. TICC 2008 winner Susan Dean's entry would give you a good approximation. www.chili.org/terlingua.html.

Enjoy!

Jan Hudson

The Twin
JAN HUDSON

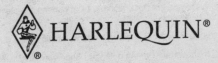

TORONTO • NEW YORK • LONDON
AMSTERDAM • PARIS • SYDNEY • HAMBURG
STOCKHOLM • ATHENS • TOKYO • MILAN • MADRID
PRAGUE • WARSAW • BUDAPEST • AUCKLAND

Recycling programs
for this product may
not exist in your area.

ISBN-13: 978-0-373-75294-2

THE TWIN

Copyright © 2010 by Janece O. Hudson.

This edition published by arrangement with Harlequin Books S.A.

® and TM are trademarks of the publisher. Trademarks indicated with
® are registered in the United States Patent and Trademark Office, the
Canadian Trade Marks Office and in other countries.

www.eHarlequin.com

Printed in U.S.A.

ABOUT THE AUTHOR

Jan Hudson, a former college psychology teacher, is a RITA® Award-winning author of thirty books, a crackerjack hypnotist, a dream expert, a blue-ribbon flower arranger and a fairly decent bridge player. Her most memorable experience was riding a camel to visit the Sphinx and climbing the Great Pyramid in Egypt. A native Texan whose ancestors settled in Nacogdoches when Texas was a republic, she loves to write about the variety of colorful characters who populate the Lone Star State, unique individuals who celebrate life with a "howdy" and "y'all come." Jan and her husband currently reside in Austin, and she loves to hear from readers. E-mail her at JanHudsonBooks@gmail.com.

Books by Jan Hudson

HARLEQUIN AMERICAN ROMANCE
1017—THE SHERIFF*
1021—THE JUDGE*
1025—THE COP*
1135—THE REBEL*
1162—THE TEXAS RANGER*

SILHOUETTE DESIRE
1035—IN ROARED FLINT
1071—ONE TICKET TO TEXAS
1229—PLAIN JANE'S TEXAN
1425—WILD ABOUT A TEXAN
1432—HER TEXAN TYCOON

*Texas Outlaws

For my own Ben,
a hero in the making, and
with special thanks to Jan Yonkin,
Tracy Wolff, Lexi Connor and April Kihlstrom

Chapter One

Ten-thirty on Monday night, and it was past closing time at Texas Chili Witches Café. Sunny Payton closed out the register while the late staff, dressed in their jeans and red Chili Witches T-shirts, bussed the tables and cleaned the kitchen. Coming off a twelve-hour shift, she was bone tired, her feet ached and she was ready to go upstairs and soak in an herbal-scented bath for about a week and a half.

After she stowed the receipts in the office safe, she let her employees out the back door, calling good-night and seeing they all got in their cars safely.

"Jeff, I want to hear that you aced your chem test," she said to a tall, lanky blond.

He grinned. "You're as bad as my mama."

"Worse," she said, grinning back. "A million times worse."

Most of the staff were students from the University of Texas, working flex hours to pay for those cars or buy books, which were outrageous these days, even more costly than when she was in school nearly a dozen years ago. The cooks had left earlier, one of the perks of their job. The students came and went, but the cooks and a couple of others were longtime employees. Many of them had worked for her mother and Aunt Min when they ran the place.

Sunny checked the kitchen, then made a last trip through the two dining areas with the scarred, red-topped tables and rough cedar walls filled with Texas memorabilia, funny signs and assorted collectibles. The kitschy wall decor was swapped out occasionally, and the computer and register were state-of-the-art, but not much else had changed for as long as she could remember.

She was reaching for the light switch when she saw him.

Her heart lurched as it always did. He sat at his usual corner table, a cup of coffee near his hand.

"Hello, Senator."

"Hello, Sunny." He smiled. "Busy day?"

She nodded and sat down beside him. "Very. We had a little cold snap today, and everybody in Austin was in the mood for chili. It's supposed to be back up to ninety by the weekend, so things will be manageable again. I haven't seen you for a while."

He smiled. "Miss me?"

"I always miss you, Senator."

"How's your sister?"

"Cass is settling in and doing well. It's good to have her home. Now she and I can share the work, and Mom has finally been able to retire completely."

"That's good. I'll have to drop in on Cassidy."

Sunny laughed. "You do, and you'll scare the pants off her."

He smiled. "It's good to hear you laugh again."

"Oh, I laugh a lot these days."

"Glad to hear it. Maybe now you're ready to meet a special fellow."

She shook her head. "I already did. Brian. He was special. I don't need anyone else." And she didn't. Brian was the love of her life. When he'd died, a part of her had died, as well.

"Honey, it's been three years since—"

"Sunny!" her sister yelled from the back.

"Sounds like Cassidy," the Senator said, tenderness filling his eyes.

"Ignore her." Sunny absently reached to touch his arm. As usual, her hand only touched the table.

"Your sister is tough to ignore."

"Who are you talking to?" Cassidy asked as she charged into the room.

"The Senator."

Cass rolled her eyes. "Oh, gawd! Not that again. I just got home from the play and decided I want a beer." She walked behind the small bar and grabbed a mug. "Want one?"

"You know I hate beer."

Cass drew a draft and joined Sunny at the table.

"How was the play?"

"Fantastic!"

"How was the date?"

"Abysmal. He had an ego the size of Texas and a brain the size of Rhode Island. If I ever agree to another blind date, tie me to a chair."

Sunny laughed and glanced toward the Senator.

He was gone.

And so was his cup.

Wonder what had prompted his visit? With him, one never knew.

Chapter Two

At noon on Wednesday, Sunny was helping clear a couple of empty tables when she spotted two very tall guys hanging their white ten-gallons on the hat rack by the door. When they turned around, she sucked in a little gasp—and she rarely did that, but these two were unusually good-looking men. Texas Rangers by the looks of the silver badges on their dress shirts and the narrowed cop eyes that quickly scanned the room.

As she approached, the dark-haired one grinned and said, "Boy howdy, it smells good in here."

The sandy-haired one only smiled slightly, dipped his head and stared at her with the greenest eyes she'd ever seen. Taken aback by their color and the intensity of his look, an odd feeling flashed over her.

She forced herself to break eye contact. "And everything tastes as good as it smells. First time at Chili Witches?"

"Yes, ma'am," the dark-haired one said, "but I 'spect it won't be the last if your chili is as good as I've heard it is."

"Count on it," Sunny said. "It's an old family recipe we've been making here for over forty years. We have mild, medium and 'hotter than hell,' as well as a vegetarian version. Don't try the 'hotter than hell' unless you have a well-seasoned mouth and a cast-iron belly. Grab any table that suits you. The one in the corner is free."

The men looked at each other. "Anywhere you want is fine with me," the sandy-haired one said. "You like to keep your back to the wall, Outlaw?"

"You betcha."

The men started for the corner table, but Sunny stopped in her tracks. *Outlaw?* It was not a common name, but not that unusual, either. Although she rarely heard it. Was it possible…? Nah.

She followed them to the table as they sat down. Picking up two menus wedged between the sugar dispenser and a black minicaldron of saltine packets, she handed them to the Rangers. "Your server will be with you in a minute. May I get you something to drink?"

"Iced tea would be mighty nice," the dark-haired one said. He was a charmer. A married charmer by the looks of his shiny gold ring.

"Iced tea for me, too," said Green Eyes as he gave her the once-over.

His left hand was bare. Not that his marital state mattered to Sunny one way or another. She wasn't in the market for a man. But she had to admit his slow perusal revved her motor just a little. Just her pesky hormones acting up, she decided as she hurried to the drink station. She ignored the ominous tingle rising along her spine, the one that usually warned of some momentous or unusual happening.

The Senator suddenly materialized behind the bar. "Mighty nice-looking young fellow," he said.

"Which one?" she asked, being careful to keep her back to the room.

"Both of them, but I was thinking of the green-eyed one for you."

She made a snort. "Forget that," she muttered out of the side of her mouth. "Don't meddle in my love life."

He smiled. "What love life?"

When she headed back to the table with their tea, the one called Outlaw was staring at her and frowning.

"Is something wrong?" Sunny asked.

"No, no. Everything's just fine, but I'm trying to remember where I know you from. Have we met before?"

"I don't think so," Sunny said.

"You sure look familiar."

"Maybe I just have one of those faces." She ought to let it drop and leave, but a funny little feeling tickled the back of her neck. She just had to ask. "Did I hear you're called Outlaw?"

"Yes, ma'am," he said. "Sam Bass Outlaw at your service."

What felt like a five-pound rock hit her stomach and bounced. "*Sam Bass* Outlaw?"

"That's me. My granddaddy was big on all his descendants having the names of famous outlaws. He claimed it was good name recognition for anyone in business or politics—or law enforcement. I've got three brothers and a sister all named for shady characters and all in some kind of law enforcement—except my sister, and she used to be an FBI agent before she quit and bought a newspaper. There's Cole Younger Outlaw, Jesse James Outlaw, Frank James Outlaw, and Belle Starr Outlaw. My daddy was John Wesley Hardin Outlaw, and his brother was—"

"Butch Cassidy Outlaw," Sunny finished before she could stop herself.

Sam's eyebrows went up. "How'd you know that?"

She sighed. Had the Senator engineered this whole thing? "My name is Sunny Outlaw Payton—or more accurately, Sundance Outlaw Payton. Butch Cassidy Outlaw was my father."

Sam looked puzzled. "But Uncle Butch and his—"

"I know. But he was my father."

"Are you sure?"

"Very."

She turned and hurried away.

"WHAT WAS THAT ALL ABOUT?" Ben McKee asked Sam.

"I'm not quite sure, but I think I just met my cousin. Now I remember why she looks familiar. She reminds me of my sister, Belle. Both tall, brunette. Same eyes. Same nose. Well, I'll be damned."

"And you never knew you had a cousin?"

"Nope, not by Uncle Butch. I don't even remember him, but I know he and Aunt Iris never had children."

"Aunt Iris?"

"His wife in Naconiche. I never liked her much. She was a sour-faced old prune who put the fear of God into us kids if we so much as spilled a cookie crumb on her settee. I hated to go visit her."

"I take it your uncle is dead," Ben said.

Sam nodded. "Somebody shot him thirty years ago. Right on the steps of the capitol building. Be funny if it was Aunt Iris. Well, not funny, but ironic."

"They didn't catch his killer?"

"Nope. Never did."

"She's a beautiful woman," Ben said.

"Who?"

"Your cousin."

"You interested?" Sam asked.

"Oh, yeah."

"Me, too," Sam said. "But in a different way than you are. I've got to call my folks. They're not going to believe this."

"I don't imagine your aunt Iris is going to be happy about it."

"Aunt Iris is long gone."

"Dead?"

"May be, for all I know. She married a preacher about fifteen or twenty years ago and moved to Des Moines. We haven't heard from her since. Not even a Christmas card."

Their chili came, served by the young man who was their waiter. He also delivered a cauldron of the oyster crackers they'd ordered along with chopped onions and a couple of kinds of grated cheese. They both dug in. This was good chili. No, it was *great* chili. But hot. Real hot.

"Are you sure we ordered the medium?" Ben asked.

"Hoo-wee," Sam said, "this stuff is hotter than a three-dollar pistol. But good. I'll bet the hottest kind would blister the paint off a butane tank. Dump some of those oyster crackers in it. And some of that cheese. Cuts down on the fire."

Ben doctored up his bowl and ate the whole thing. His forehead was a little damp when he finished, but he'd enjoyed it. A girl came by and refilled their iced tea glasses. He chugged the second glass and looked around for Sunny, but she still hadn't reappeared. Where had she gone?

Sam must have read his mind. "Wonder where Sunny ran off to?"

Ben shrugged. "I was wondering the same thing."

When the waiter came to get dessert orders, Sam asked him about Sunny.

"She must be in the office."

"The office? She the manager?" Ben asked.

"Owner and manager. One of them. How about some peach cobbler with ice cream? Or pecan pie?"

They both ordered cobbler.

"How long has Sunny been the owner and manager of this place?" Sam asked the waiter before he could leave.

"Couple of years, I think. She took over from her mother and her aunt before I started working here."

"From her mother?"

The waiter nodded. "Her mother and aunt started the café. My grandfather says he's been coming here since it opened back in the seventies. That was way before Austin built up so much downtown. I'll get your cobbler."

SUNNY SAT IN HER OFFICE for a long time, staring out the window at the courtyard and fighting the urge to go back and ask Sam Bass Outlaw about his family. Her family. Her family and Cassidy's. She'd always longed to meet them, but her mother would have been mortified if she'd tried. Probably still would be.

Should she tell Cass who had just dropped into Chili Witches? Knowing her twin, Cass would go charging to his table and demand answers. She picked up the phone to call upstairs, then put it back down again.

Maybe it was best to let sleeping dogs lie.

Chapter Three

A couple of days later, Ben McKee managed to shake loose from a case he'd been working on by lunchtime. He'd had a hankering for some more chili ever since he and Sam had visited Chili Witches. He'd had a hankering to see Sunny again, as well. She was a good-looking woman with a warm smile, and he'd been thinking about her a good bit. He hadn't been in Austin long and hadn't had much time to meet any ladies.

Oh, his sister Tracy had been trying to fix him up with this one and that, but he'd sidestepped her efforts at matchmaking. He wasn't interested in the type of women she wanted to introduce him to—the picket fence and happily-ever-after kind. He'd tried that, and he was still paying the price for it. Only thing good that had come from his marriage was his son, Jay.

He grinned at the thought of his five-year-old towhead as he pulled into a parking spot by the café. God, he loved that little boy. No way in hell was his ex getting her hands on him again. Marla had never wanted Jay; she was a party girl and having a kid cramped her style. Having a husband had cramped it, too.

Ben spotted Sunny the moment he walked in the door. Her back was to him, but he'd recognize the curve of her jeans anywhere. When she turned and spotted him, she grinned.

"Well, hello, Ranger," she said, walking toward him. "Ben, isn't it?"

He felt himself grinning back at her. "Right. And you're Sunny."

"That's me. Where's your running buddy?"

"Who? Sam?"

She nodded.

"He's based in San Antonio. He's only in Austin occasionally."

She glanced around the restaurant. "I see that same corner table is available. Seat yourself, and I'll get your drink. Iced tea okay?"

"Tea is fine." Ben made his way to the table and sat with his back to the wall so that he could watch Sunny.

On her way to the bar, she spoke to several people as she passed, including a group of three Austin police officers. They all laughed at something she said to them. A fourth cop came in before she moved on, looped his arm around her neck and kissed her cheek. She grinned and bumped her hip against his.

Ben watched the interplay. Boyfriend? Lover? Or was she just a flirt? He picked up the menu and studied it.

He didn't get very far with his studying before Sunny was back with his tea.

"Here you go," she said. "Your waiter will be right with you."

"You seem to draw a lot of cops." He glanced to the table of four.

She laughed. "Yep. It's because they get a twenty percent discount on Monday, Wednesday and Friday."

"Really?"

"Uh-huh. You get one, too."

"And why is that?"

"You're a cop, aren't you?"

"Well, sure, but I meant why the discount?"

She grinned. "Because I'm civic-minded. And because I used to be one."

"You? A police officer?"

The surprise must have registered on his face, because she laughed. "Is that so hard to believe?"

"I just can't picture you with a gun on your belt."

She sobered. "I wore one for a lot of years. Oh, here's Pete to take your order. Enjoy your lunch, Ben." Sunny turned and was gone before he could say another word.

Ben ordered his meal and ate without speaking to Sunny again. The place was busy, and he watched her move around all over the rooms, smiling and talking to this one and that. He lingered a bit after he was done, but she never approached him again. Finally, he rose and started for the door.

"Everything to your liking, Ben?" she asked, suddenly appearing by the hat rack. She handed him his Stetson.

"Yes, ma'am. It was."

She smiled. "Come back soon, and bring your friends."

"I'll do that." He hesitated a couple of beats, trying to think of something more to say, but he was tongue-tied and nothing came out. He nodded, crammed his hat on and left.

What the hell had gotten into him? He'd never been shy around women. He'd hoped to flirt a little bit with her, maybe ask her out for coffee or something, but he'd felt like a damn teenager all of a sudden. Crazy.

He was still trying to figure it out when his cell phone rang and his thoughts switched to business.

SUNNY STOOD AT THE DOOR and watched Ben talking on his phone. He was one fine-looking man.

"Fine-looking man," the Senator said.

She glared at the Senator and strode to bar. Grabbing a

pitcher of iced tea, she made the rounds refilling glasses. What she didn't need in her life was a man. Fine-looking or not.

When the lunch-hour crowd died down, she went into the kitchen and started filling a dozen plastic containers with chili, labeling the mild and medium lids. She saved the "hotter than hell" stuff for the café's few adventurous paying customers. These were for some of Austin's homeless. By the time the bowls were boxed up with spoons, napkins and crackers, Marge was there to pick them up.

The plump, gray-haired woman was all smiles as usual and wagging the insulated box from the previous day. "Thank you so much, Sunny. This means more than you know."

"You always say that, Marge, and it is I who should be thanking you for all your work. A few cups of chili is nothing."

"Oh, but it is. Chili is one of our favorite items. We have to make the guys take turns."

"Need any salad today?"

Marge shook her head. "We have plenty from the restaurant next door, but thanks anyway."

Sunny insisted on carrying the box outside to the mission's vehicle. A myriad of good food smells flowed from the van when Marge opened the door.

"Looks like you hit the jackpot today," Sunny said. "Reminds me that I haven't eaten."

"The restaurants in Austin are very kind to us. I collected all this in only half an hour. If you're not in the mood for chili, the catfish at Hooks looked very good today," Marge said, winking.

"Sounds like a winner to me."

Marge waved as she roared off to serve the hungry folks who would be waiting for what might be their one decent meal of the day.

On cue, Sunny's stomach growled, reminding her again that

she hadn't eaten anything since the cup of yogurt she had for breakfast many hours ago. She decided to take Marge's suggestion and headed for Hooks, the seafood restaurant next door to Chili Witches. She and Cass often traded meals with Sid and Foster, the owners who'd also been tenants of the building for years.

Sid, a slightly plump man with thinning rusty hair, bustled over when she opened the door. "Hello, baby doll," he said, giving her an air kiss. "Where have you been keeping yourself? Your sister just dropped in a few minutes ago. Want to join her or do you have a yen for some privacy?"

Sunny glanced around the room and spotted Cass, who grinned and waved her over. "I'll join my sister. What's good today?"

"Oh, my dear, we have some pecan-crusted catfish that's to die for. Foster has outdone himself."

"I'll have that. Tell Foster hi for me."

"I will," Sid said as he held out her chair. After she was seated, Sid bustled off to get her drink. Sid bustled everywhere.

"Hey, sis," Cass said. "How's it going? I haven't seen you in a couple of days. Avoiding me?"

She almost laughed off the question, but a funny little hitch in her breath stopped her. Had she been avoiding Cass? Not consciously, of course, but maybe she had. Why?

"You *have,*" Cass said, leaning forward. "Why? Is it a man?" She grinned. "Give, sis."

"Don't do your lawyer bit with me. You know that I don't respond well to grilling."

Cass laughed. "Look who's talking. The grill queen. You're like a pit bull, but don't sidestep the question. What's been going on with you? You know we always tell each other everything."

Sunny thought for a moment. What *was* she avoiding? Not

wanting to stir up old feelings, she deliberately hadn't mentioned Sam Outlaw's visit to the café. "Oh, I had to run a million errands yesterday, and the band practiced last night."

Cass lifted one eyebrow and waited.

"Something sort of interesting happened Wednesday. A guy, a Texas Ranger to be exact, dropped in for lunch. His name was Sam Outlaw."

Both of Cass's brows went up. "Sam Bass Outlaw?"

"Yep." She took a sip of the iced mint tea that Sid had left for her. "The very one." Leaving out anything but a general mention of Sam's being with another Ranger, she related the entire conversation with their relative.

"Interesting," Cass said.

"I thought so."

"Do you think he knew about us before he came in?" Cass asked.

"I don't think he had a clue. It was pure coincidence."

"I don't believe in coincidences."

"Well, whether you believe in them or not, I can assure you that this was," Sunny said. "He seemed genuinely surprised. How could he have known about us to come looking? And why would he care about his illegitimate cousins? Trust me, it was a coincidence."

Cass narrowed her eyes and peered into Sunny's. "Is there something you left out?"

Sunny put on her best innocent face. "I've told you everything that I can remember about my conversation with Sam." No way was she going to mention Ben. Cass would blow it all out of proportion and start to nag her. She was worse than the Senator. Sometimes being a twin with those special connections could be a real pain.

"Why don't I believe you?"

"You must miss being a lawyer. There you go again with the grilling. I feel like I'm in the witness box."

"Sunny, sweetie, I can't hold a candle to you when it comes to interrogation. Must be all those years as a detective that honed your skills. You were great at it. Do you miss being a cop?"

Sunny hesitated. A year ago she wouldn't have hesitated a beat in saying no, but now and again she wondered if she didn't miss some things—not that she would admit it to Cass. "No. Not at all."

"Are you sure?"

"Positive."

Cass studied her for a minute; Sunny resisted squirming. "Running Chili Witches isn't much of a challenge after being one of Austin's finest."

"Maybe not, but it suits me fine. Besides, I wouldn't be much of a cop without a gun, and I never want to pick up one again."

Cass obviously sensed Sunny's discomfort and changed the subject. "Tell me about the other Ranger with Sam."

Sunny squirmed, but only a hair. A hair was enough. Cass let out a hoot of laughter.

"I knew it," Cass said. "I knew it. Tell me about him."

"There's nothing to tell."

Cass rolled her eyes. "Come on, sis. This is me. What's his name? What does he look like?"

"I think his name was Ben."

"You *think?*"

"Okay. His name was Ben. I don't even remember his last name. McSomething, I think. He was tall and kind of nice-looking. I didn't pay much attention. I doubt that I'll ever see him again."

"You're lying. Did he ask you out?"

"Of course not. I mostly talked to Sam, and we were busy in the café."

Cass waited, that look on her face that said she wasn't letting it go.

"And all right, he came back for lunch today."

"Aha! I'd say that he's interested. Was Sam with him?"

"No. He was alone."

"That definitely means he's interested."

"It only means that he likes our chili. We barely spoke."

"And why was that? Did you go hide in the kitchen?"

"Why would I hide in the kitchen?"

"Aha!" Cass said again. "I knew it. Listen to me, sis. It's past time you put aside that shroud you've wrapped yourself in and rejoin the world. You're too young to molder in widows' weeds with your plants and cats."

"Are you nuts? I'm not moldering, and I only have one cat."

"How long since you've gone out with a man? How long since you've even considered going out with a man?"

"Would you stop with the goading? I'm simply not interested in dating. Not yet, in any case."

"How long are you going to wait? Five years? Ten? Twenty?"

Thank goodness Sid appeared with their food, and Sunny was saved from answering Cass's question. But she couldn't help asking herself the same question. How long was she going to wait?

The whole subject gave her a headache. And for no reason. Ben might have revved her motor a little bit, but he hadn't shown any particular interest in asking her out. Anyhow, just because he didn't wear a wedding ring didn't mean a thing. He could be very married. Or he could be in a committed relationship of some sort. It was unlikely that a hunk like him was available. Case closed.

Chapter Four

Sunny was just walking into Chili Witches after her lunch with Cass when the phone near the register rang. Melanie, a short blonde who was the assistant manager, grabbed it, then put her hand over the phone receiver and said, "Sunny, a call for you on line one."

"Who is it?"

"Beats me. Some guy. Are you in?"

"Sure. I'll take it." She reached for the receiver. "Hi, this is Sunny. May I help you?"

There was a pause, then a deep voice said, "Hello. This is Ben McKee."

Her breath caught and an odd rush spread over her. "Ben?"

"Yes. I'm the Ranger who came in with Sam Outlaw on Wednesday. I was there at noon today for chili."

"Oh, yes, of course. Ben. Did you forget something?"

He chuckled and the sound seemed to resonate in her belly. How very odd.

"No, I think I got out with everything I came in with. I wanted to ask you to have dinner with me tomorrow night."

"Din-dinner?" she said, stammering in spite of her efforts at control. "Tomorrow night?" Panic clawed its way up from her stomach to her throat. She wasn't ready to deal with this.

"Yes. Tomorrow. Saturday night. If you're free. That is, if you're not involved with anyone. I didn't even think to ask that. Are you?"

Her mouth went August dry. She finally managed to say, "No. I'm a widow."

"Good," he said quickly. "Oh, God, I didn't mean it was good you were a widow. Sorry about that. I meant it was good you weren't—"

"I know what you meant." She almost smiled. He seemed as nervous as she felt. "And I really appreciate the invitation, but I have a previous commitment tomorrow night."

There was a moment of silence, then Ben said, "Oh. Well, maybe another time. I'll catch you later."

And he was gone. She was left with a dial tone and a minor shock. What was that all about? His invitation had surprised her. True, she'd noticed a bit of interest on his part, but she hadn't expected him to ask her on a date. She really did have a commitment tomorrow night. Her band, the Copper Pistols, played somewhere almost every Saturday night. Made up of police officers, the Pistols had been a garage band formed when Brian was still alive. She played drums, and Brian had played bass. Two other friends played guitar and keyboard and a third sang lead. They'd first started playing together as a stress reliever, and then realized they were pretty darned good and started accepting gigs now and then. After Brian's death, the members of the group had helped her keep her sanity. And although she was no longer employed by Austin PD, the guys hadn't kicked her out. Sometimes the band seemed like her last connection to Brian. They'd had so much fun playing together.

She hadn't even had a chance to explain to Ben that she was working tomorrow night, that her excuse wasn't a brush-off. He must not have been too interested or he would have asked her about another night. She wasn't doing anything Sunday. Or Tuesday. Or Thursday.

It was just as well. She really wasn't ready to date. It had been so long since she'd dated anyone, she wasn't sure she'd know how to act. The whole business was awkward.

When she turned around the Senator stood there, shaking his head.

"What?"

He sighed and disappeared.

"It wasn't my fault," she said to the empty space. "I really am busy tomorrow night."

"I believe you," Melanie said.

"Believe what?" Sunny asked.

Melanie grinned. "I believe you're busy tomorrow night. I'm coming to see you at the Spotted Cow. Remember?"

"Uh, great." It took Sunny a few beats to catch up with the conversation. Melanie, who dated the keyboard player, had thought Sunny's remarks to the Senator were aimed at her. "Listen, did that new supply of napkins come in yet?"

"Sure did. Not ten minutes ago. Jimmy put them in the supply room. Was the guy on the phone asking you for a date?"

"Uh, no. It was something else. Some committee he wanted me to serve on." Sunny didn't like lying, but she didn't want everybody in the place buzzing about her love life—or lack of one. She adored Melanie, and she was an excellent employee, but she was a terrible gossip.

During the afternoon lull, Sunny sat behind the bar, where she could keep an eye on the door, dispensing an occasional beer and rolling utensils in napkins and placing them in a bin.

She glanced up and saw a tall, dark-haired woman enter. Dressed in a blue silk blouse, a gray pencil skirt and killer gray heels, the attractive woman sported a rock on her left hand roughly the size of a large ice cube. She stood by the door and scanned the room as if looking for someone. When her eyes met Sunny's, both of them stared. Sunny had the odd sense she knew the woman, but nothing registered.

Leaving the bar, Sunny approached her. "May I help you?"

A bright smile spread across the woman's face that transformed her from merely attractive to a real beauty. "I'll bet my bottom dollar you're Sunny Outlaw."

"I am. Sunny Outlaw Payton. Have we met?"

"Not yet." The woman threw open her arms. "I'm Belle Outlaw Burrell. I'm your cousin."

"You're kidding!"

"Nope."

Sunny was stunned for a moment, then elation filled her. "My cousin? I can't believe it! You're Sam's sister." Sunny fell into her arms, and the two of them hugged as if they were long-lost buddies.

"I am," Belle said, laughing. "And Colt's and Frank's and J.J.'s. I also come with a husband, two parents, assorted sisters-in-law and a growing number of nieces and nephews. Welcome to the family."

Sunny hugged her again. This was better than Christmas. "I want to know all about everybody. But wait. I've got to call Cass. She'll kill me if she misses this."

"Cass?"

"Cassidy Outlaw, my sister."

"Uncle Butch had *two* daughters?"

"That's right." Sunny grabbed her cell phone from her pocket and punched Cass's code. When she discovered her sister was upstairs, she said, "Drop everything and get down here right away. I have a surprise!"

"I can't believe he had two daughters. We didn't even know he had one."

"He didn't, either. We were born after he…died."

When Cass rushed into the room, Belle looked from her to Sunny, then back again. "You're…twins."

"Yep." Sunny introduced Cass and Belle and they hugged, as well.

"I can't believe we've finally met," Cass said, hugging her again. "It's awful being the family pariahs."

"Pariahs?" Belle said. "Good Lord, why would you be pariahs?"

"Well, our father was married to someone else when we were conceived."

Belle made a dismissing motion. "Aunt Iris never counted for much. My mother said they were married in name only. She wouldn't give him a divorce. She and Daddy were tickled to death when they heard they have a new niece—*nieces* now. They'll be doubly pleased. They can't wait to meet you. In fact the whole family wants to meet you. They're hoping we can all get together for Thanksgiving in Naconiche. Can you arrange it?"

"Sure we can," Cass said.

"We'll manage somehow," Sunny said. She ordered drinks for everyone, and they talked for two hours, mostly with Belle catching them up on the Outlaw family.

They were captivated by learning Belle was a former FBI agent.

"Why on earth did you ever leave?" Sunny asked. "Sounds like a dream job for an Outlaw."

"I discovered I wasn't cut out for being an agent. I'm much happier running a newspaper in Wimberley. I love it."

"I hear that," Cass said. "I got sick of lawyering, too. Boring. And too dog-eat-dog for me."

"My brother Frank is a lawyer…well, a judge now," Belle said. "And his wife, Carrie, is a lawyer. But she was a landman before she went back to practicing law in Naconiche. It might be boring, but there's not much dog-eat-dog dynamics in Naconiche."

"Actually, I think Cass just missed Austin," Sunny said.

"True," Cass admitted. "I love this place. Always have."

"I do, too," Belle said. "And Wimberley isn't that far away. I can't believe we've been living so close all this time. I even went to school at UT here in Austin."

"So did I," Cass said. "Law school. Unbelievable we could have passed each other on the street and not known it."

"Isn't it? Listen, my husband, Gabe, and I are coming up tomorrow with Sam and his wife to Sam's place on Lake Travis. Why don't you two join us? We might even do a little fishing."

"Oh, rats," Cass said, "I can't make it tomorrow. It's my day to run the place, and we're going to be shorthanded, but Sunny can go. She loves to fish."

"Count me in," Sunny said. "I haven't been fishing in ages. But I'll have to make an early day of it. I have a gig tomorrow night."

"A gig?"

"Sunny's a drummer in a band on Saturday nights."

"How fun! I want to come hear you sometime." Belle glanced around. "It looks like the early dinner crowd is beginning to arrive, and I'd better leave and meet Gabe. He's probably through with his business by now, and he'll be chomping at the bit to get home." She gave Sunny directions to Sam's lake house, then rose and hugged them both warmly. "I'm so excited to have met you and have you as part of the Outlaw clan."

Sunny was flying as Belle handed her card to each of them and they exchanged cell phone numbers. For as long as she could remember, she'd yearned for a big family. Having Cass and her mom and Aunt Min had been great, but she'd always envied families with fathers and brothers and kids running around.

"Cass," Belle said, "do you work on Sundays?"

"Nope. We're closed on Sunday."

"Great. I want you both to plan on coming to Wimberley on Sunday of next week. We'll have a barbecue or something."

They walked Belle to the door, hesitant to let her go. Funny, Sunny thought, as she waved goodbye to her newfound cousin. It felt as if they had been friends and cousins forever.

"She looks like us," Cass said. "Did you notice?"

"I did."

"I like her."

"Me, too."

They looked at each other, connecting as they always did, grinned and hugged. "Hot damn!" they said in unison.

"You know what this means?" Cass said.

"Yeah. We've just acquired a humongous family."

"Besides that."

Sunny heaved a big sigh. "We've got to figure out how to tell Mama."

"I vote we table telling her until she and Aunt Min get home from their grand adventure."

Mama and Aunt Min had rented a cottage in France and were making excursions to various places in Europe—the dream of a lifetime. "But they won't be home for another six months."

Cass grinned. "Yeah. I know. But we wouldn't want to spoil their trip now, would we?"

Chapter Five

Saturday was one of those perfect Texas days that come most often in the spring or the fall. The colors on the hills toward the lake seemed brighter than usual. Because most of the trees were evergreen, and the climate didn't generate many autumn colors, this was a rarity. She'd heard something about an especially dry summer and a number of cool nights turning the deciduous trees into a lovely palette of reds and golds against the blue sky.

Sunny followed a winding, blacktopped road toward the place where she was meeting Belle and the others. She hated that Cass wasn't along and had tried to convince her sister to come in her place, but Cass wouldn't hear of it.

"You know I'm not much on fishing," Cass had said. "Go on. Go. Go."

And truthfully Cass didn't know one end of a rod from another. Brian had taught Sunny to fish, and she'd learned to love it. They'd spent many an hour on Lake Travis. She hadn't wet a hook since he'd died. In fact, she'd had to do some digging in her storage unit to find a rod and reel and her tackle box.

After checking the number on the mailbox, she pulled into the driveway of a ranch house at nine on the dot. It was a rather ordinary place except that its backyard abutted the gorgeous panorama of the lake, and a helicopter rested in a large clearing beside the house. Who on earth did that belong to?

She pulled up behind a black SUV and got out. By the time she had retrieved her fishing gear, Belle had appeared from behind the house, and a willowy, short-haired blonde was with her.

"Hey," Belle said, waving. "You found us. Great. Sunny, this is Sam's wife, Skye. She's a veterinarian, a vegetarian, my double sister-in-law and my best friend."

Skye stuck out her hand and laughed. "Sounds ominous, doesn't it? Welcome to our branch of the Outlaw gang. I'm sort of new myself."

"How are you a double sister-in-law?" Sunny asked.

"Well, Belle married my brother Gabe, and I married her brother Sam. Seems like we were destined to be sisters one way or another. I'm sorry your sister couldn't come, but I look forward to meeting her next weekend. Sorry I don't eat chili because Sam says yours is fabulous."

"We have a vegetarian version," Sunny said.

"You do? Sweet!"

Belle grabbed the tackle box, hooked her arm with Sunny's and said, "Come on out back. The guys have the boat about ready to shove off."

In the back, they walked down a flight of steps to a pier where a boat was docked. Sunny was surprised to see three men instead of the two she expected. She immediately recognized Sam, who looked up and smiled. A handsome blond guy she didn't know also turned and smiled. When the third turned around, she almost dropped her rod.

It was Ben McKee. He'd traded his Stetson for a blue ball cap and his dress shirt and tie for a jersey faded from red to almost pink.

"Sunny," Belle said, "the blond hunk in the sunglasses is my husband, Gabe Burrell, and I think you've met the other hunk, Ben McKee."

"Good to meet you, Sunny," Gabe said. "I see you've brought your own rod. It looks custom-made."

"Whoo-ee," Sam said. "We'd better watch out, guys. She looks like she takes fishing seriously."

"Sunny," Ben said, simply smiling and touching the brim of his cap. "Closest thing I have to a custom-made rig is a cane pole I cut myself."

Sunny felt her face blaze, and she felt an irrational urge to slap the silly smile off his face. "It was a Christmas gift from my husband."

There was a sudden silence. Her comment had gone over like a toad in a punch bowl.

"Sorry about the crack," Ben said, and he held out his hand to help her aboard. "It's a fine-looking rod. Was it made locally?"

Sunny accepted his hand, and everybody started talking at once as they climbed onto the large boat.

"The biggest fish of the morning," Sam said, "is exempt from cleaning the catch or cooking lunch. Except for Skye. She's not included in the contest."

"Because you're vegetarian?" Sunny asked her.

"No," Belle said. "Because she'd probably catch a whale. Fish jump on her hook."

"You fish," Skye said, pulling a paperback from her tote, "and I read."

"Why is it fish jump on your hook?" Ben asked.

She shrugged. "Just one of those odd things."

"She's enchanted," Belle said. "Critters of every kind adore her. Who's got the worms?"

"Ben brought the worms," Sam shouted as he pulled the boat away from the pier.

They spent the rest of the morning fishing and laughing and talking. Sunny thoroughly enjoyed herself. She couldn't remember when she'd laughed or talked so much. Sam and Belle were natural cutups, and they were in fine form. A shame she'd only met them now.

Shortly before they were due to go in, Sunny cast her line near where someone had left a milk jug marker. Immediately, a fish struck, a big one by the feel of it. She played it, praying she wouldn't lose what she hoped was a whopping-size black bass. When she finally pulled in the fish, Ben helped her get the huge black bass in the boat.

Ben held it up and said, "Unless I miss my guess, this looks like the day's winner. At least seven pounds."

"Or eight," Gabe said. "Only fitting, Sunny, that you're our winner."

"I agree," Skye said.

Sam looked at Skye and frowned.

"Don't look at me like that," Skye said. "I had nothing to do with it. I've been reading about the latest treatment for mange."

They headed back to the lake house, where the guys lit the grill and cleaned the fish while Belle and Skye retrieved containers of side dishes from the fridge. Sunny tried to help, but they wouldn't hear of it.

"You won, fair and square," Skye said.

"Do you really attract critters?" Sunny asked. Although the thought of such a thing seemed a little odd, who was she to say? She talked to a ghost.

"Umm. Sometimes. When you're a veterinarian, it's helpful to have a good rapport with animals."

"Do you treat many fish?"

Skye chuckled. "Not many. In fact the only patient I can recall was a goldfish, and I wasn't able to revive him. We had a funeral service instead."

"Seriously?"

"Yep. With songs and prayers and the whole shebang." Skye picked up a plastic container. "I'm going to take these veggies out for the guys to put on the grill. Want to bring the paper plates?"

LUNCH HAD BEEN SO MUCH FUN that before she knew it, it was midafternoon. "Oh, wow," Sunny said, jumping up. "I didn't realize it was so late. I have to get back to town."

"Big date?" Sam asked.

Sunny almost laughed when she saw Skye kick him under the table.

"No. I have to work tonight. Most Saturday nights are full. Let me help with this real quick."

She picked up the empty bowls from the patio table, and Skye picked up the ice-cream maker. Belle got the rest of the remnants, and the women carried the things inside to the kitchen.

"Are you working tonight at the café?" Skye asked.

"No, I play with a band on most Saturday nights."

"A band?" Skye said, her eyebrows going up. "Like with instruments?"

"Guitars, drums, keyboard. Real instruments. We're the Copper Pistols."

"What fun!" Skye said. "How did you come up with the name?"

"Seemed like a logical one for police officers—and everybody in the group is a working cop. They let me stay in the band after I left the force."

"I forgot Belle told me you were in law enforcement," Skye

said as they walked back outside. "What did you do on the police force?"

Hearing Skye's question, Gabe asked, "Sunny, were you really a cop?"

"Sure was. For several years. I was in uniform for a while, working traffic, and later I became a detective. Listen, everybody, today has been wonderful. I'm so glad you invited me, and Cass and I are looking forward to next Sunday. In the meantime, if you drop by Chili Witches, your next meal is on the house. Now, I've got to run."

After goodbyes were said, Ben picked up her rod and reel and tackle box and followed Sunny to her car.

"You really did have a previous engagement," he said.

"Did you think I didn't?"

"I wasn't sure if it was a brush-off."

"It wasn't."

He stowed her things in the backseat, then turned to her. "How about tomorrow night?"

"For what?"

"For dinner. With me."

That clawing panic was back. She tamped it down. "I'd like that."

"Where do I pick you up?"

"I live over the café. There are stairs around back. I'm A."

"A what?"

She smiled. "I'm apartment A. My sister is apartment B."

SUNNY WORKED HERSELF INTO a lather trying to find something to wear. She didn't have any dating clothes, especially when she didn't know where they were going. Of course Austin was a super casual town, but she really didn't have much besides jeans and church clothes.

Her wardrobe, like her apartment walls, was pretty plain and boring. Her walls were beige; her carpet was beige; even the countertops in the kitchen were beige. The only spot of color in the living room was her light blue couch with the grape juice stain, and that was old—both the couch and the stain. If she was expecting company, which was rare, she draped a beige throw over the stain.

She'd never gotten around to hanging drapes or pictures. She kept meaning to, but she just couldn't muster up the interest. The wooden blinds were nice and they provided privacy.

Finally, after she'd tried on every stitch she owned, Sunny gave up and called the clotheshorse for help. In less than two minutes Cass was at her door with a pair of black pants and a fussy blue-patterned blouse with fluttery sleeves.

Sunny frowned. "Cass, that's not me."

"Yes, I know. That's why you don't have anything appropriate in your closet. It's perfect. Try it on before you decide. Have you got any heels?"

"Of course I have heels."

"Let me see them."

Sunny pulled out her best black pumps, and Cass groaned. "Those are old-lady shoes. Try these." She pulled off the spike-heel peep-toes she wore and held them out.

"But they're red."

"Duh."

"Okay, okay. I'll try them." Sunny strode to her bedroom with Cass trailing after.

She stripped off her best jeans and was about to step into the black pants when Cass said, "Oh, gawd! You're not going to wear those are you?"

Confused, Sunny said, "I thought you brought them over for me to wear."

"I meant those panties. They look like Aunt Min's."

"Forget it." Sunny zipped the pants. "Nobody is going to see my underwear."

"Well, you never know."

"I know. Trust me. Nobody is going to see it." She put on the blouse and the ankle-buster shoes. As she stood in front of the mirror, she had to admit she looked very nice. Not clownish as she feared. In fact, she looked—and felt—a little sexy.

"See?" Cass said. "I told you. You look terrific."

"I look like you."

"Is that so bad?"

Sunny grinned. "Actually, no. I look pretty darned good."

Cass took off her dangling gold earrings. "Try these."

They were perfect.

"Know what you need?" Cass asked.

"What now?"

"You need to go shopping if you're planning to date this guy again."

"Why?" Sunny gave her a kiss on the cheek. "I can borrow everything I need from my sister."

"You wish. Buy your own clothes, sweetie. I hope you were planning to put on some eye shadow and liner."

"I'm not sure if I even have any."

Cass rolled her eyes. "Now I know you're going shopping. Be right back."

Twenty minutes later, after Cass had worked her magic and left, Sunny leaned close to the bathroom mirror and checked her makeup. She had to admit the difference was amazing and not overdone at all. Mostly she'd made do with lipstick and a little blush. Live and learn.

The doorbell rang and she startled. Was Ben here already? She took a deep breath and walked slowly toward the front door.

Why was she feel so guilty doing this? Was she dishonoring Brian's memory?

Just as she put her hand on the knob, the Senator appeared for just a second. He shook his head, smiled and vanished.

Chapter Six

Sunny almost let out a whistle when she opened her door. Ben stood there in dark brown slacks, a green shirt that matched his eyes and a killer leather jacket that looked butter soft. His dress Western boots were some exotic skin. Snake? Eel? She wasn't up on such things.

Ben grinned, then *he* whistled. "You look beautiful. Turn around." He made a circle with his finger.

She complied, feeling a bit silly and smug at the same time. "Thank you. I wasn't quite sure where we were going. Will this do?"

"Oh, yeah."

She picked up her wrap and they went downstairs to his waiting SUV. While it wasn't a carriage, she noticed it had been washed since she'd seen it yesterday, and she felt as special as any princess.

They went to an upscale Italian restaurant downtown. While it was only a few blocks away, it was a world apart from Chili Witches. The tables were set with fine linen, and a plant-laden room filled with rustic antiques and shimmering candlelight created an inviting atmosphere.

When they were seated Sunny said, "How lovely this place is."

Ben glanced around. "My sister recommended it. I'll have

to tell her you approved. Or maybe we should wait until we taste the food."

"I'm sure it's wonderful. I've heard great things about it, but I've never been here before."

After they'd studied the menu and ordered, she said, "Tell me about your sister. Does she live here?"

"Yes. Tracy and her husband and my two nieces. That's one of the reasons we moved here."

"We?" Her heart must have skipped a half-dozen beats. Dear Lord, surely he wasn't married. Surely he wouldn't have asked her out if he was married. Although, these days, who knew what men would do?

"My son, Jay, and me. I'm divorced." He grinned. "You thought for a minute I was married, didn't you?"

She fiddled with her water glass, then looked up and grinned. "What was your first clue?"

"The bug-eyed gape."

She laughed. "Busted. You Texas Ranger types are sharp. I was always known for my poker face. Guess I'm out of practice."

"Use it or lose it. How long have you been off the force?"

"About three years. Tell me about your son."

"His name is Jay. He's five and in kindergarten. Montessori. Right now he's torn between becoming a fireman and a pilot."

"Not interested in becoming a Ranger like his dad?"

"He's not old enough to be impressed by the Rangers. Their class visited the fire station last month, and he thinks running the siren on a fire engine is much more exciting than what I do. My brother-in-law is a pilot for one of the major airlines, and Jay is very impressed by that—especially since he got to fly on a short hop to Dallas with Uncle Rick."

"You know, I've always wanted to learn to fly. I've thought about taking lessons many times."

"Then why don't you?"

She started to give one of her stock answers, like she didn't have the time or it was too expensive, then stopped herself. "I don't know," she said honestly. "It seems as if I always have one excuse or another, but I don't think any of them are valid. I may look into it."

"Good for you."

Their lobster bisque was served—which was out-of-this-world delicious—and they chatted in a first-date way about inconsequential things. Neither his ex-wife nor Brian was mentioned. Politics was alluded to only briefly, and she could tell by his comment that they had similar leanings, which was good but not a critical factor in a relationship as far as she was concerned. She and Brian had been polar opposites politically, and it had been no big deal; it had simply been an accepted difference, not something they argued about.

The pasta was as good as the bisque, and the wine delicious. Ben was easy to talk to—and easy to look at. She loved the way his eyes crinkled when he smiled. She liked the strong planes of his face and jaw, his thick, short-cropped hair and the way his eyebrows rose when he was listening. He was a good listener.

Their conversation flowed easily, and there were no awkward pauses as they talked. She was surprised so much time had passed, when, as they lingered over coffee, she glanced down at her watch.

"I can't believe the time," Sunny said. "I need to get home."

Ben glanced at his watch, too. "Sorry about that. Do you have an early workday?"

"Not too early, but I usually go to the gym first thing."

He motioned for the check. "I used to do that, too. B.J."

"B.J.?"

"Before Jay. Now he keeps me hopping in the mornings."

After the check was paid and they were leaving, Ben put his hand to her back to guide her out. And left it there. It was a casual touch, but she was totally aware of his hand, of its warmth, of his closeness. His smell even tantalized her senses. He smelled nothing like Brian; his was a new scent, masculine, yet with an undertone of freshness and the vaguest hint of citrus and spice.

His touch made her nervous, but when his hand left her back to help her into the SUV, she missed the feel of it.

"Is Jay with a sitter?" she asked as they drove home.

"No, he's spending the night with Tracy and his cousins. Rick's out of town a lot, and my sister loves having the extra company. I think it was pizza and a Disney movie tonight. Tell me, is Sunny your real name or a nickname?"

Sighing, she said, "Both, sort of. It's not something I tell everyone, because it doesn't often come up, but the name on my birth certificate is Sundance. How's that for a name?"

"I think it's very…interesting."

She laughed. "Diplomatic response."

"No, actually, I kind of like it. Goes with the whole outlaw theme Sam was telling me about."

"Exactly. My father was Butch Cassidy. It's harder to come up with good women's names. I'm just lucky I wasn't named Blue Nose Sally."

Ben hooted. "I'll say."

"My mother did it only because she thought it was what my father would have wanted. She's always just called me Sunny."

The drive home didn't take very long. Ben parked, and when she started to reach for the door handle, he said, "Wait."

"For what?" Was he going to kiss her? It seemed like forever since she'd been kissed. Her heart picked up its pace and sounded an alarm. Did she want him to?

Yes. Yes, she did.

No. No, she didn't.

Yes, she did.

But she wasn't supposed to want him to. There was the guilt again. Oh, Lord, what a mess.

"For me to come around and help you out."

"For heaven's sake, why? I'm perfectly able to open a door."

"Call me old-fashioned."

She smiled. "You are, aren't you?"

"Yes, ma'am."

Wouldn't some of her old buddies on the force carry her high if they could see her now? She'd fought hard to be treated as an equal. She had to. There was no place in law enforcement for fan-fluttering females. Being treated like one felt odd.

"Well, I'm not." She opened her own door and stepped down.

She forgot she was wearing stilettos, stumbled and nearly fell on her keister.

Ben grabbed her elbow. "Gotcha."

"Now I'm embarrassed."

"No need to be. I know you're an independent female, but I doubt if you wear those stilts on the job."

"Have I been teetering?"

He smiled. "Not at all."

As they walked up the stairs, Ben walked beside her, his hand on her back again. It felt warm and solid and…tantalizing. Should she invite him inside?

No. Definitely no. She wasn't ready for that.

When they reached her door, she retrieved her key, turned the lock and pushed the door ajar. She turned and said, "Ben, I had a wonderful time tonight. Thank you."

"You're welcome. I enjoyed it, too."

He gently gripped her shoulders and lowered his face to hers. *Here it comes,* she thought, her knees turning a little wobbly.

But his kiss was so brief she almost missed it.

"Good night," he said.

"Good night." She went inside, closed the door and leaned against it. She heard his boots taking the wooden stairs as he hurried down and the sound of his engine as it roared to life. Then he was gone.

When the last echo died, a tap on the door beneath her head startled her. She checked the spy hole, almost hoping it was Ben returning.

Instead she saw Cass and opened the door.

"Tell me everything!"

"DAMN!" BEN SAID AS HE drove home. This wasn't turning out at all the way he'd planned. He'd been looking for a simple, no-strings relationship. A casual affair to fill his needs. This was going to be more complicated. He felt it in his bones.

First off, Sunny's being part of Sam Outlaw's family made things awkward. Second, she didn't seem the casual-affair type. Oh, she might play the independent woman, and truth was, she *was* an independent woman. No one, man or woman, who was a wimp got to be a detective. Still, he could tell she wasn't cut out for an occasional romp in the sack. He sensed an underlying vulnerability in Sunny that brought out his protective streak. Did he still want to get involved with her and chance being played for a sucker again? Did he want to take things any further?

He was still paying for the mess Marla had made in his life. His and Jay's. He wasn't ready to jump back into something serious. Jay was his first priority.

But something about Sunny Outlaw Payton—

Oh, hell, McKee. You'd better cut and run while you have the chance.

ON TUESDAY MORNING, SUNNY followed her usual routine: a quick breakfast, paperwork, then a visit to the nearby animal shelter. She loved animals, but with her schedule, she'd never felt comfortable having more than Sadie, her nine-year-old cat. Sadie had been a feral kitten she'd saved from euthanasia, and the small Siamese mix still spent most of her time under Sunny's bed or in some other secret hiding spot. Sometimes the only way she was sure she really had a cat was when the food and water disappeared. She'd tried to adopt another cat, hoping Sadie would adjust better with a companion. It had been a disaster, and the second cat had ended up with a friend to prevent it from being totally traumatized.

Sunny loved dogs. She always had, but living in the apartment above the café, combined with dreadful working hours and Sadie's temperament, wasn't conducive to having a dog. She'd tried that once, too. Sadie had terrified the poor little mutt and had shredded her couch, so Sunny re-covered the couch and found another home for the pup. Now she volunteered at the animal shelter for a couple of hours a week. She walked dogs and played with them and tried not to get too attached. Dogs that were there on one Tuesday often were gone by the next.

Annabelle, a permanent employee, gave her a new dog to walk. A beautiful, mostly German shepherd about three years old, he was extremely well behaved.

Sunny squatted down and scratched his ruff. "You're a beauty, sir. How did you come to be here?"

"Somebody was moving out of the country and couldn't take him," Annabelle said. "A real shame."

"We need to find you a good home, boy."

Maybe Ben's son would like to have a dog. Or maybe he already had one. She'd have to ask. If she ever saw Ben again.

He hadn't called or dropped by for lunch the day before, but he'd probably been busy.

Had he been disappointed in their date?

No, she told herself. *Don't go there.* If he asked her out again, fine. If not, that was fine, too. No big deal.

BEN HELD OUT UNTIL THURSDAY. Sunny had been on his mind most of the time. And a sudden cold snap made it a great day for chili. He stopped by about half past twelve, and it seemed as if half the people in town had the same idea. The place was packed.

He didn't even see Sunny. He looked around the crowd, trying to spot an empty place. Some lanky college kid in a red shirt pointed him at a table for two behind a post, and another one brought tea and took his order. He finally glimpsed her behind the bar pulling a tray of drafts. He tried to catch her attention. Tried, hell, he practically stood on the table and flagged her. She smiled and nodded toward him, then said something to a waitress and motioned his way before she hoisted the tray and went off to deliver the beer to the other room. The waitress came over and filled his tea glass, and that was the last he saw of Sunny except for a fleeting glance of her back now and then.

Damn.

Against his better judgment, Ben had planned on asking her out again. He spent a long time over his lunch, but he was finally forced to pay up and leave. He had to get back to work. Once the crowd had thinned out, he'd been tempted to ask for her, but his pride had gotten in his way.

Guess he wasn't the only one who had reservations about their getting involved. He'd thought their date had turned out well. She'd seemed to be enjoying herself, but maybe he'd misread the situation because for sure she was treating him like a leper today. Marla had called him a loser more than once. Maybe Sunny was looking for somebody more exciting than he was.

  Damn.

Chapter Seven

"Have you heard from the hunk?" Cass asked as they drove to Wimberley.

"Which hunk?" Sunny asked, wishing Cass would stop quizzing her every day.

"Ben the hunk."

"How do you know he's a hunk?"

"Because I peeped through my spy hole when he came to pick you up last weekend. Looked like a hunk to me. Has he called?"

"Nope."

"Bummer," Cass said, flipping down the mirrored visor to apply lip gloss.

"Don't do that! Keep your eyes on the road or you're going to end up in a cow pasture." Cass wasn't really a bad driver, but she was a speed demon in her fancy little convertible, and the two-lane highway had a lot of twists and turns.

"I haven't seen a cow for miles, and you're not a cop anymore, so ease up, sis. Have you got the map and directions?"

"I do." Sunny unfolded the directions Belle had dictated as well as a map she'd printed from the Internet. "I think the turn should be about a mile ahead. On the right."

They started looking for landmarks and soon saw their turn.

The road wound and dipped some more before they spotted the entrance to Belle and Gabe's place. It even had a guardhouse, and they pulled to a stop.

A burly-looking guy glanced back and forth between them. "You must be the twins. Go straight ahead and hang a left at the fork. If they don't answer the bell at the big house, try the pool area around back." He touched his hand to the bill of his cap.

"The *big* house?" Cass said as she drove on. "How many houses are there? And how big is the *big* house?"

"Don't ask me. I get the impression Gabe's loaded. The monster helicopter was my first clue."

The house was huge, but not ostentatious. They parked beside several cars and walked up the steps to the large porch stretched across the front. Sunny rang the bell.

A little bit of a woman with sharp features answered the door. "You must be the Outlaw twins. I'm Suki. Come on in. Most everybody's out back in the pool or sittin' around shootin' the…breeze and drinkin' beer. You bring swimsuits or do you need to borrow one?"

"I'm Sunny, and she's Cass, and, yes, we brought our suits. Should we change first?"

"Suit yourself. It's a mite chilly for me, but the pool's heated so you won't freeze your tokus off."

"I think I'll take a dip," Cass said. "It's in the seventies, and I haven't been swimming in ages. Where can we change?"

"Up them stairs," Suki said. "First door on your right. There's extra robes in the closet. When you're done, just go straight through the house to the outside. There's a bunch of windows and doors back there, and you can't miss it. I'll let Belle know you're here."

"Thanks, Suki," Sunny said.

The little woman scurried off, and they went upstairs.

"This place is gorgeous," Cass said as she opened the door to a suite. "Wonder who their decorator was?"

"Beats me. Ask Belle."

After they'd changed and were selecting robes from the closet, there was a tap on the door. "It's Belle."

Sunny opened the door. "Hello. We were just about to come outside. Your house is gorgeous."

"Thanks. We like it. Especially after I redecorated."

"I was admiring your choices," Cass said. "Beautiful."

"Thanks. It's sort of Belle eclectic. I figured if I liked it, it went together."

"A woman after my own heart," Sunny said. "What was it before?"

"Country French from top to bottom and designed by a former fiancé who was also a decorator."

"I don't see a stick of Country French now."

Belle grinned. "Nope. Not a stick. I unloaded most of it on Skye and my mother-in-law for their new places. The rest I gave to the Salvation Army. Come on down. The party's grown and we have a backyard full of people."

"Who's the hottie on the diving board?" Cass whispered to Sunny.

Sunny stopped in her tracks, and her heart bounced. Dear Lord, it was Ben poised on his toes. She didn't realize he'd been invited, and things were bound to be awkward between them. Leaving wasn't an option, although the thought was tempting.

"Back off. That's Ben McKee," she muttered to Cass. "I thought you said you'd seen him through your spy hole."

"It was dark, and I couldn't see much more than his back. His butt was awfully cute, though. You know, he looks familiar," Cass said, gawking at him as he performed a perfect dive.

"His butt?"

"No, his face. I'm almost sure he came into the café one day last week."

"Last week? When? Why didn't you say something?"

"I think it was Thursday," Cass told her, "and I didn't mention it because I didn't recognize him."

"Did you talk to him?"

"Nope. We were packed, and I didn't get a chance."

Sunny groaned. "He probably thought you were me and that I was ignoring him."

"Is something wrong?" Belle asked.

"No," Sunny said, "not a thing. Beautiful pool."

"Isn't it? It's heated with solar power, and we can swim any day of the year, except when it's storming."

"Now there," Cass said, "is a real hottie. The tall one in the red shirt. He looks like a movie star."

Belle laughed. "Don't get too excited over him, though I'll grant you he is good-looking. He's my brother Frank, and your cousin. He's married and has three kids."

"Frank James Outlaw?"

"The very one," Belle said, catching his eye and waving him over to where they stood near the back door. "He's a judge in the County Court at Law in Naconiche."

Frank smiled as he approached. "You must be the newfound family. It's good to meet you," he added as he was introduced and shook hands with both of them. "The rest of the Naconiche bunch wanted to come, but everyone was tied up this weekend except my wife, Carrie and me. We drove down yesterday with our twins. We left the youngest with J.J. and Mary Beth."

"You have twins?" Sunny asked.

He nodded. "Janey and Jimmy. Fraternal, of course, not like the two of you. Come meet Carrie."

"She's the lawyer?" Cass asked.

"That she is," Frank said. "Are you the one who's a lawyer, too?"

"Used to be."

"Once a lawyer, always a lawyer," Frank said.

"I'm not sure I agree. Let's just say I'm a recovering lawyer."

Frank laughed, and the four of them joined a group sitting near the shallow end of the pool and watching children splashing around.

When Skye spotted them approaching, she jumped up and hugged them both. "It's so good to see you again, Sunny, and I know you must be Cass." Sunny was surprised Skye got it right. "Come meet everybody."

"This is Gabe's and my mother, Flora," Skye said. "She's a painter and owns a local art gallery."

Flora, an older woman in a dazzling magenta muumuu and full makeup was effusive in her greeting.

"And this," Frank said, "is my wife, Carrie."

"Lawyer and former landman," Carrie said, standing and hugging them both. "And stepmother to two of those kiddos in the pool. The dark-haired ones."

"What exactly is a landman?" Sunny asked.

"Basically, it's someone who acquires land leases for oil and gas companies. That's how I came to Naconiche and met Frank and the other Outlaws."

They also met the Ballards, neighbors of Belle and Gabe and parents to two other children in the group. The last of the adults was John Oates, a nice-looking guy who was mayor of Wimberley.

A big German shepherd came to stand beside Skye, and she scratched his head. "This big fellow is Gus."

"He's beautiful," Sunny said.

"Isn't he?"

"He reminds me a bit of a dog I was walking at the shelter the other day. I volunteer there."

"How wonderful. A woman after my own heart. Do you think he would be a good service dog?"

"You know, I hadn't thought of that. Possibly. Thanks for the suggestion."

"And, Sunny, you know Ben McKee," Belle said.

The twins turned to Ben, who was hoisting himself from the pool. He looked back and forth between the two of them as if totally bewildered.

"You're *twins?*"

Sunny smiled. "Is that so odd?"

He picked up a towel, dried his face and ran the cloth over his well-muscled chest, which looked even better up close. "You said you had a sister. You didn't mention she was a twin." He frowned and glanced from one to the other again until he zeroed in on her. "Sunny?"

"Yes," she said. "And this is Cass. Cassidy Outlaw, my baby sister."

Cass snorted. "By two and a half minutes. Sorry I didn't recognize you when you were in Chili Witches the other day. Thursday, wasn't it?"

He nodded, then smiled at Sunny. "I thought she was you and that you were ignoring me."

"We're comanagers on flextime. She runs things on Tuesday, Thursday and Saturday, and I'm boss on Monday, Wednesday and Friday."

"What a marvelous idea!" Flora said. "You must let me paint the two of you. I don't think I've ever done twins before, and your bone structure is superb!"

"You ought to let her," Sam said, coming up behind Flora and hugging her against him. "She's terrific."

Flora patted his cheek, obviously adoring him. "You're a dear boy to say so, even if you did move my daughter all the way to San Antonio."

"San Antonio isn't Lubbock. It's just down the road a piece." He kissed the pouf of curls atop her head. "And you know we've always got an extra room for you." He stuck out his hand toward the twins. "I'm your cousin Sam," he said. "Who's Cass?"

"I am," Cass said, shaking his hand.

"Welcome to the family. Hey, Sunny, good to see you again." He gave her a hug. "This is Pookie." He held out a small mop of a dog which had been tucked under his arm. Sunny took her, and Pookie licked her face and wiggled all over. "You're a friendly one."

"She seems to like you," Sam said. "Want a dog?"

"Oh, Sam," Skye said. "Stop that. You know you wouldn't part with Pookie for any amount of money."

He grinned. "Make an offer."

"I have a demon cat that won't share space." Sunny handed the dog back to Sam and glanced around. "Where's Gabe?"

"Here I am," he called, coming in the back gate. He kissed Belle on the cheek. "Sorry I'm late, but I had to show some property to an out-of-town client. You must be Cass." He offered his hand.

"Nope. I'm Sunny."

"Oops. Sorry about that. How does anyone ever tell you apart?"

"They're just different to me," Belle said.

"Me, too," Ben added. "And Sunny has a little scar on the right side of her chin."

She smiled, pleased Ben could tell the difference between them. "Bike accident when we were eight."

They chatted with the members of the group for a few minutes, then several people decided to go in the pool.

"Coming?" Ben asked Sunny.

She put her hand to her long hair. "Yes, but I need to find a rubber band first."

"I'm always prepared," Belle said. Digging a couple from her robe pocket, she handed one to Sunny and one to Cass.

"Thanks." She caught her hair in a ponytail, then shed her robe and ran for the pool with Ben right behind her.

She dived into the deep end and popped up to race across the width in a fast crawl. The water felt wonderful. She loved swimming, but didn't get a chance to go in often. Or, rather, she'd gotten out of the habit.

"You're a regular otter," Ben said as he grabbed on to the edge beside her.

"I love it. I was on the swim team in high school and college."

"Me, too," Ben said. "But only in high school, not college. Where did you go to college?"

"We went to Texas State University in San Marcos. Just far enough away to live in the dorm, but close enough so our mom didn't have a fit. Cass went on to law school at the University of Texas, and I joined the Austin PD. What about you?"

"I went straight into the army and became an MP. Went to junior college after that, majored in criminal justice, then joined the Department of Public Safety. I was a Texas highway patrolman in the Dallas area for several years, then applied to be a Ranger."

"And here you are."

He grinned. "And here I am."

His grin did things to her that made her nervous. And things she couldn't act on, given where they were. "Race you," she said, and struck out across the pool.

After a couple more laps, Sunny climbed from the pool and grabbed a big towel from a stack on a nearby table. Ben grabbed the one under it, and they both dried off. The smell of grilling food reminded her that her bowl of cereal was long gone, and her stomach growled.

"Hungry?" Ben asked.

"Obviously, unless there's a bear around here somewhere."

"There's someone I want you to meet first."

"Oh, who?"

"My son, Jay—if I can drag him out of the pool and away from the other kids for a few seconds."

The idea of meeting his son made Sunny super nervous. She knew zip about kids. What if he was a brat? She'd seen plenty of those in the café, and they'd set her teeth on edge. She crossed her fingers and hoped he wasn't one of those little stinkers.

Chapter Eight

Ben's son was a doll. Jay looked up at Sunny and grinned with the same engaging grin his father used—except that one front tooth was missing.

"Are you enjoying yourself?" Sunny asked the towhead.

"Yes, ma'am. The pool is awesome. And did you know they have *horses* here? Janey and Jimmy have ponies of their own at home. *Awesome!*" He glanced up at his dad. "I don't have a pony."

"And not likely to have one as long as we're living in an apartment."

"Maybe I can get a dog," Jay said. "Or even a cat."

"'Fraid not," his dad told him. "Remember, they're not allowed."

"Have you thought about a fish or a turtle?" Sunny asked.

"I've got a fish, but they're not much fun. They can't play with you like a dog or a cat can."

"That's true," Sunny said, "but I have a cat that never plays with me. She hides under the bed most of the time."

"Why? Is she scared?"

"Maybe, but I've had Sadie for several years. She was a wild kitten when I got her, and she's always been very shy."

"I'll bet she wouldn't be scared of me. Animals like me." Jay pointed to Skye's dog. "That's Gus. He's a German shepherd. Isn't he something? He goes everywhere with Dr. Skye. I wish I had a dog like him." He sighed. "He's really something."

Ben didn't comment, but Sunny could tell he was bothered by Jay's wistful longing for a pet.

"Say, sport, it's almost time to eat. How about you dry off and wrap up?"

"Do I have to?"

Ben nodded.

"Yes, sir. Can I swim some more later?"

"Maybe."

Cass walked up, a towel slung over her shoulder and said, "Hi, there, young man."

Jay looked up at her, then he glanced at Sunny, who smiled at him.

"She looks just like you. Are you twins?"

"Yes, she's my sister. Her name is Cassidy Outlaw."

"Wow. Jimmy and Janey are twins, but they don't look alike much. He's a boy and she's a girl. Their name is Outlaw, too. We have twins in our class, and sometimes they try to fool everybody. Do you do that?" His teeth were starting to chatter.

Sunny grabbed another towel from the stack and wrapped it around him. "Once in a while, when we were younger, but not in a long, long time."

Ben dried Jay's hair and face with his own towel, and gave him a brisk rubdown. Wrapping the towel around him sarong-style, he said, "Keep that on until after we eat."

"Yes, sir." Jay started to bolt for the other kids who were getting out of the pool until his father stopped him.

"What do you say?" Ben asked him, glancing toward Sunny and Cass.

He thought for a minute, then said, "You're very pretty."

They held their laughter until he had scampered away.

"Sorry," Ben said, "he hasn't quite gotten the hang of his manners yet."

"Don't apologize," Sunny said. "His answer was much better than 'excuse me.' He's adorable."

"He's a charmer," Cass said. "Must take after his daddy." She practically fluttered her eyelashes.

Sunny could have brained her sister for flirting with Ben. Though she honestly didn't know why it bothered her. She certainly had no claim to him, and the more she thought about it, the more she reminded herself she didn't want any sort of claim to him. He was fun and attractive, period. No long-term relationships for her. And for sure she wouldn't pick someone in law enforcement. She'd be better off with an accountant or a teacher. They weren't likely to get shot at. Too bad she hadn't met one who revved her motor like Ben McKee.

AT THE TAIL END OF THE LUNCH hour on Monday, Ben showed up at Chili Witches. He could have called, but he wanted to see Sunny again. Not Cass. Sunny. Strange that while the two of them were spitting images, he wasn't particularly attracted to Cass. Their personalities were different, and Cass didn't stir his hormones the way her sister did.

By the time he hung his hat on the rack, Sunny was there.

"Well, hello. Come on in and let me find you a table."

"I was hoping that you might have a few minutes to talk— if you're not too busy."

"Sure thing. The place will slow down in about five minutes. Let me get you some tea."

He watched her go, watched the gentle sway of her hips and remembered her in that bathing suit the day before. Talk about hormones getting stirred up. He hadn't slept worth a damn the night before. Between his guilt about Jay not being able to have a dog, which his son had run on about all the way home from Wimberley, and his yen for Sunny, which didn't stray far from his mind, he'd had the wide-awakes. He couldn't do anything about getting a dog. He couldn't afford a house with a yard, not with this damned trouble Marla was stirring up. Attorney fees were eating him alive.

And private investigators didn't come cheap, either—even with a discount.

His ex hadn't wanted Jay to begin with, and she hadn't wanted him when they divorced. She hadn't even tried to get custody—having a kid interfered with her lifestyle. Oh, she claimed she'd been through rehab and was a changed woman. He didn't believe her tale any more than he believed in little green men from Mars.

Marla was a pro when it came to hoodwinking people. He hadn't had a clue there was anything wrong until the Dallas cops had called him one night when he was out working. Child Welfare had picked up Jay, and Marla was in jail. Seems Jay had woken up scared and alone. His mother had gone out clubbing and hadn't come home until after one in the morning, drunker than a stewed owl. He found out she often left Jay alone. She could have rotted in jail for all he cared, but somebody bailed her out. Ben changed the locks on the doors and divorced her ass. He was still paying off the debts she'd run up.

Not long after that, Ben was accepted into the Rangers and applied for a job in Austin to be near his sister and as far away from Marla as possible. He could feel his blood pressure rise just thinking about the hell she'd put him through. Was still putting him through. No way was she getting her hands on his son again.

"Why the big frown?" Sunny asked.

"Was I frowning? Just deep in thought about a case I'm investigating." Which was true. He was investigating Marla big-time.

Somebody had brought two glasses of iced tea to the table, and he didn't even remember it. Some vigilant Ranger he was.

"What would you like for lunch?" Sunny asked. "If you're burned out on chili, we serve other things. We make a mean hamburger here, and we have a great salad bar."

"A hamburger made on an old-fashioned grill?"

"Yep. About as old-fashioned as you can get. We've had the same grill for as long as I can remember. It's been refurbished a couple of times, but it still works great."

He ordered a cheeseburger and fries, and Sunny helped herself to the salad bar.

When she returned to the table, she said, "Did you just want to talk in general or about something in particular?"

"Both. I lucked into some tickets to the ZACH Theater on Saturday night, and I was hoping you might like to go with me. My sister tells me the play is getting great reviews."

Sunny's face fell. "Oh, shoot. I can't make it on Saturday night. Pretty much all my Saturdays are full. I'm sooo sorry. I wish it were another night."

She really did look disappointed. What was it she did on Saturday nights?

"What if I can get the tickets changed to another night? How about Friday?"

"I'm manager here on Fridays, and we don't close until late."

"Sunday?"

She brightened. "I could make it on Sunday."

"Let me see what I can do." He bit into his hamburger, which was excellent. Every bit as good as their chili.

When their server dropped off the check after they had eaten, he reached for it, but Sunny got it first. "For a chance to go to the theater, at least I can spring for your lunch."

His hand covered hers. "That's not necessary. You have a business to run."

"I know, but I want to treat you."

His hand stayed where it was, and his thumb rubbed slowly across her knuckles. He glanced up and caught her staring at him. What was it he saw in her eyes? Was it a flash of desire or a moment of fear?

Fear? What did she have to be afraid of? He wouldn't hurt her, not in a million years.

As quickly as it came, the expression was gone, and she withdrew her hand.

He glanced down at his watch. "I've got to get back to work."

"Catch any bad guys lately?"

"Trying to put a few away."

She walked him to the door. "Let me give you my cell phone number in case you want to call on my off day." She picked up one of the advertising cards from the bar and scribbled a number on the back.

"And here's mine." He fished a business card from his shirt pocket and wrote down his number, as well.

He tried to think of a reason to linger, but he did need to get back to work. He had an appointment in a few minutes, and he didn't want to be late.

Just as he was walking out the door, another guy walked in. The big, muscled guy had three inches on Ben.

"Sunny! Babe! Come here and give us a hug." He grinned and held open his arms.

Sunny squealed, "Steve!" and threw herself at him.

Ben flinched. Well, damnation!

SUNNY WAS SO THRILLED about seeing Steve that she momentarily forgot Ben. When she looked behind her old partner, Ben was gone.

She hooked her arm through Steve's and said, "Get in here and tell me what's been going on. How are Suzi and the kids?"

"Same old, same old. Everyone's doing fine. Can you believe Jason is in the third grade already, and Paul is in the first?"

"You're kidding? They were just born a couple of years ago."

"Seems like it, doesn't it?" Steve said. "I'm starving. You got any food left?"

"For you? Always. We'll kill the fatted calf if necessary."

She led him to a table, chatting about this one and that. Steve had been her mentor when she was fresh out of the academy. She and Brian had spent a lot of time with Steve and Suzi, but she hadn't seen them in the past while.

She motioned a waiter over, and after he had taken Steve's order, she said, "Where have you been keeping yourself?"

"I feel bad that I haven't stopped by for a while, but we had a little scare with Suzi."

Her heart skipped a beat. "What?"

"Breast cancer."

"Steve! That's not a little scare. It's a big one. What happened? Is she okay?"

"I was truthful when I said she was doing fine. It was a small lump, early stage, and they got everything with surgery, but she had chemo just to be sure."

"You should have called me. I would have helped you. Is there anything I can do now?"

He shook his head. "We're slick. Her mother and sister

came, and I took some time off. She's back to her old speed again—full throttle."

"I'll call her later. Listen, I've got a question for you. Is your brother still with the canine unit?"

"Still there. And loving it. Getting that transfer was the best thing that ever happened to him."

"Tell me, where do they get their dogs?"

"From various sources I suspect. I can ask him."

"Will you? I may have a good prospect for the unit."

Chapter Nine

The following morning, Sunny was both happy and sad to see Leo, the German shepherd at the shelter. He was such a beautiful and well-behaved dog she was sure he would make a great service dog, if he wasn't adopted as a family pet. Steve had checked with his brother, and the K-9 unit had all the dogs they needed. Scratch that idea. There were other groups that trained service dogs, and she vowed to contact them that day.

After she leashed Leo, they walked out in an open area near the building. Obviously he'd been through obedience training because he obeyed her commands perfectly, both verbal and gestured.

She wished she could take him home with her, but it just wasn't practical. Leo needed room to romp around. Again she thought he would be ideal for Jay, if only he and Ben had a yard.

She hadn't heard from Ben about the tickets. It would be great if he could swap them. She'd love to see the musical at the ZACH. The community theater's productions were always top-notch.

Her cell phone rang, and she checked the caller ID. Speak of the devil. It was Ben, and he could swap the tickets for either Thursday night or for a Sunday matinee. She opted for Thursday.

She trotted along the path with Leo, sure there was a silly smile on her face. She was much happier at the thought of going out with Ben than she had any right to be. Her next thoughts were about what to wear. Her wardrobe hadn't improved since the last time they went out, and she didn't want to keep borrowing from Cass. Since she rarely spent any money on herself and had few expenses, her bank accounts had swelled to healthy amounts, especially when she considered the sale of her and Brian's house and the insurance settlements she'd stashed away.

As soon as she left the shelter she stopped by Whole Foods for a quick lunch, then trotted across the street to Chico's to work on her lack of new and appropriate clothing.

She'd forgotten how much fun shopping could be. She got a really good salesperson who helped her build a new mix-and-match wardrobe so she had really cute stuff for every occasion, including the proper jewelry and accessories. The salesperson even made suggestions for shoes and told her about a great place down the block that was having a sale.

Now, Sunny had never been much of a shoe person, and certainly not one to spend wads of money on fancy-schmancy stilettos with two straps and a sole, but things changed. She bought six pairs and left with a spring in her step and new, more fashionable sneakers on her feet. She kept the old ones in case she went fishing again.

On her way back to the car, Sunny passed an upscale hair salon she'd often heard about but never patronized. She hesitated a moment, then thought, *Why not?*

Luckily, one of the stylists had a last-minute cancellation, so an hour later, Sunny walked out with a gorgeous new cut, still long but with half bangs and hair framing her face in a flattering way. Cass, who was always nagging her to update her

hairdo, would have a fit when she saw it. She smiled. She
hoped Ben liked it, too.

He did. Or at least it seemed so in man-speak.

"Did you do something to your hair?" he asked when he
picked her up on Thursday evening.

"New haircut."

"Looks nice. You look nice all over."

"Thanks. So do you." He wore a navy sport coat with gray
slacks and a patterned blue shirt. A subdued pattern, of course.

She wore gray slacks, as well, but there was nothing subdued
about the rest of her outfit. Her lightweight jacket shouted a host
of colorful designs, mostly reds, and she wore it over a red
T-shirt and with pewter kitten heels and felt like a fashion
model. Better than a fashion model. Those gals always looked
as though they'd kill for a good steak and a baked potato
dripping butter and sour cream.

They'd decided to go directly to the theater and have dessert
somewhere afterward, so she'd had a quick sandwich downstairs after she dressed. Cass, in woman-speak, had raved about
her new outfit, so Sunny knew she looked good.

As they walked down the stairs with his hand resting on her
shoulder, she could smell his cologne and feel the heat from
his body next to hers. That light-headed, giddy sensation stole
over her. She wanted to wrap her arm around his waist, but she
hesitated, even though it would be a natural and casual gesture.

Brian's face popped into her head, but she shook off the
image. And she kept her arm at her side.

"I'm really eager to see this show," she said as they drove
to the theater. "I'm glad you could exchange the tickets."

"Me, too," Ben said. "That was my sister's doing. She and
Rick have season tickets, and Tracy and one of her friends
switched nights."

"I'm glad. Thank Tracy for me. She and Rick aren't going?"

"He's flying."

"Is she babysitting again?"

He nodded, then chuckled. "We had dinner at Jack in the Box. My treat."

Sunny tried to think of something to say, but she, who was ordinarily quite glib, felt at a total loss. All she could focus on were the male pheromones bouncing around the cab, pinging off every surface like ricochets and making her skin tingle. Ben McKee was a very sexy man. The scent of him, which was even more pronounced in the vehicle, seemed to reach out and caress her. Oh, Lord, this wasn't good.

Or maybe it was *too* good.

Guilt rose up inside her like a tiger set to devour its prey. She had vowed her everlasting love to Brian and promised to be true to him. She had adored Brian and had experienced the wildest of passions with him. Brian had been sexy. Powerfully potent. There hadn't been a thing wrong with their sex life.

Maybe that was the problem. It had been too good. She missed him; she missed those feelings. She missed the wild nights.

And she missed the tenderness.

Oh, Brian, damn you! Why did you have to go and get yourself killed and leave me alone?

She shifted in her seat. Thankfully, the theater was less than a dozen blocks away, and they soon reached their destination.

SUNNY COULDN'T REMEMBER when she'd laughed so much— or had an urge to sing and dance in the aisles. The musical comedy was beyond great. The house was packed, and the performers seemed energized by the crowd and belted out their songs with gusto.

There were half a dozen curtain calls.

"Oh, I loved this," Sunny said as they stood, clapping vigorously. She clapped until her hands stung. "Bravo!" she shouted.

"I'm glad we came," Ben said next to her ear.

"I wish it would go on and on," she said. But the houselights came up, and she was forced to gather up her program and handbag and leave the theater with the flow of the crowd.

They drove up MoPac to a late-night restaurant that had some of the most scrumptious desserts in town. A hostess seated them in a quiet alcove with soft lighting and a flickering votive.

Ben chose coconut cream pie and coffee.

"Coconut cream pie?" Sunny asked. "With all those decadent chocolate concoctions and killer cheesecakes?"

"I like coconut pie."

"To each his own." Sunny went for broke and ordered the mocha fudge torte. It was to die for.

When she savored her first bite, eyes closed, salivary glands doing their thing, she tried not to moan with delight. Glancing across the table, she saw that Ben was watching her. Mesmerized.

"Good?" he asked.

"You have no idea." She scooped up a bite on her fork and held it out to him. "Try it."

Taking hold of her hand, he pulled her closer, let her feed him, then licked the fork. His eyes didn't leave hers. Nor did his hand move. Never had such a simple act seemed so...intimate. She couldn't seem to tear her stare from his mouth.

He swallowed; she swallowed.

He licked his lips; she licked her lips.

"Very...nice," he said, his deep voice rumbling.

"Nice? That's like calling the *Mona Lisa* 'nice.'"

"I'm not much into art."

"Me, either." *But I'm into mouths,* she thought, her eyes still riveted to the most exciting one she'd run across in a long time. Why hadn't she noticed before how full and sexy his lips were?

His thumb stroked along the side of her hand that still held her fork. Goose bumps traveled over her skin in the same rhythm.

"Want another bite?" she asked, her voice sounding more sultry than the question warranted.

"Not right now. Thanks." His hand didn't move. His thumb kept stroking.

She had a death grip on her fork. "Wrong response."

His brows rose, questioning.

"You're supposed to say, 'Want a bite of mine?'"

"Oh. Well, help yourself."

"Thanks. I'd like to try it, but I'll need my hand."

He glanced down at the hand he still held and smiled. "Use your other hand. Or better yet, I'll feed you."

"I prefer to feed myself." She tugged at her hand; he held firm.

He offered his fork and pushed his pie toward her.

Since she wasn't as adept at using her left hand as he apparently was, it took her three stabs to get a small piece of pie on her fork, and it fell off twice before she could get it to her mouth. She hoped the tablecloth was clean as she mooshed it onto her fork again.

"This isn't working," she said, her fingers shaking.

"Here, let me help." He took the fork, whacked off a giant-size bite and held it to her lips. The meringue alone must have been three inches high.

"You overestimate my mouth."

He smiled, a lazy, suggestive smile that sent new chills running amok. "Oh, I don't think so. I've been studying it."

Enough already! This was driving her nuts.

She yanked her hand free. "I'm not a largemouth bass!"

He gave a bark of laughter. "I wasn't intimating you were."

He popped the bite of pie into his own mouth. A dab of meringue lingered at the corner.

She politely tapped at the spot on her own mouth, but he didn't pick up her signal. Or maybe he deliberately ignored it. She was beginning to suspect Ben McKee had a bit of the devil in him.

"You have some pie at the corner. Here." She tapped the spot on her mouth again.

"I do?" He licked the wrong corner.

"No, the other side."

"Show me," he said.

She reached out and swept the bit away with her index finger. Quick as a snake strike, he caught her hand and licked her finger.

She almost went boneless and slithered to the floor.

A waiter approached with a coffeepot, but Ben shot him a look, and the waiter made a quick U-turn and hightailed it back to his station.

"What are you *doing?*" she asked, trying not to squeal.

"Licking your finger."

"Didn't your mother ever tell you that wasn't proper?"

He grinned. "If she did, I didn't pay much attention."

"Behave yourself, Ben. I want to eat my torte."

"Yes, ma'am. Want some more coffee?"

"I haven't finished this yet. Besides, I doubt if we'll ever see our waiter again."

Somehow she managed to finish most of her dessert, and Ben polished off every crumb of his pie. But she was breathing hard when they walked out of the place. He hadn't touched her again, but she had been thoroughly seduced by his looks, his smiles. Everything, no matter how innocent the comment from either of them, seemed rife with innuendo.

Was she ready for more?

Yes.

No.

Maybe.

They seemed to fly to her apartment. Well, maybe not fly, but they arrived more quickly than she wanted. She was still trying to decide if she wanted to kick things up a notch.

When they reached her front door, Ben lifted her chin. "Are you nervous?"

"What was your first clue?"

"Dropping your keys three times. Don't be nervous. I'm in no hurry."

"You're not?"

"No," he said, kissing the tip of her nose.

"Oh, thank God." She sagged against him. "I'm new at this. Well, not new-new, but it's been a long time since—"

"I understand. Relax. I'm just going to kiss you good-night."

She relaxed. Sort of. And he took her lips in a kiss that was slow and gentle and exploratory. It escalated until she wanted to climb into his pocket. Her bones melted; her brain turned to tapioca. Every cell in her body went on high alert.

A scuffling noise penetrated her scrambled senses, and Ben pulled away. Sunny clung to his lapels for support.

"Oops," Cass said. "Sorry. Continue what you were doing, and don't mind me. I didn't realize you were here."

"Hello, Cass," Ben said.

"Hello, Ben. Goodbye, Ben. Let me get my door unlocked, and I'm gone. Carry on." Cass's door slammed.

A part of her wanted to strangle her sister; another part wanted to thank her. Sunny figured if she'd carried on, she would have gotten totally carried away, and who knew what would have happened. Actually, she knew what would have happened—or at least she had a pretty good idea.

Easy, Sunny. Easy.

But she loved the way he kissed. She lifted her face to him, ready for more of the delicious sensations and heard a male throat-clearing sound at Ben's back.

Glancing over his shoulder, she spotted the Senator standing there, arms crossed and looking stern.

She could have strangled him, too. But how did one strangle a ghost?

She sighed. "Good night, Ben. I had a wonderful time."

"So did I. I'll call you." He kissed her nose again and waited until she went inside.

Chapter Ten

The following morning, Sunny was downstairs getting things ready to open the café when Cass came in the back way.

Dressed in her running clothes and mopping her face, Cass said, "Water for a dying woman."

"What on earth have you been doing?" Sunny asked, pouring her a glass of water.

"Running. I'm training for the marathon."

"The marathon? Good grief! Which one?"

"Whichever one is next. There are always marathons in Austin."

"I think you're nuts. We're not kids anymore."

"That's the truth. I think I'll make it a short one." Cass took another swig of water.

"A short marathon. Isn't that an oxymoron? How short?"

"Maybe two or three blocks."

Sunny laughed. "That's more your speed. When did you become so fitness motivated? I thought you were a dedicated couch potato."

"Since I saw some really good-looking guys on the trail beside the lake. Listen, I'm sorry about last night. I'd just closed up and was coming upstairs to fall into bed. I didn't even see you until it was too late."

"Not a problem," Sunny said. "I'm glad you interrupted. Things were moving a little too fast for me. I'm still not sure how I feel about dating, much less…the other. Want a cup of coffee?"

"Coffee? Surely you jest. I'll take another glass of water, though. With ice. Lots of ice."

Cass plopped down at a table while Sunny brought the water pitcher and a cup of coffee for herself.

"I thought you liked Ben."

"I do, but…"

"Sweetie, you can't grieve for Brian forever. Is that what has you hung up?"

"Partly. There was only Brian for so long that I don't know exactly how to act with another man. I thought when Brian and I married I was through with the dating scene. Now I find myself flung into alien territory without a road map."

"Looked to me as if you were finding your way just fine."

"Well, yes, in some ways, but I'm not sure Ben is the right person for me to get involved with."

"How so?"

"Being in law enforcement, for one thing. I suppose I'm drawn to that kind of man, but…"

"You're afraid he might get killed like Brian?"

"I haven't thought that far ahead, but maybe so."

"Sweetie, Texas Rangers aren't as likely to get shot at as SWAT members."

"True, but—"

"No more buts. Stop borrowing trouble, Sunny. You've done that all your life. Why don't you just go with the flow? Enjoy yourself. He hasn't proposed yet, has he?"

Sunny chuckled. "You're right. Thanks for the reality check."

"You're welcome." Cass stood. "I'm going up to take a shower. I have an appointment to get a haircut."

"At the new place where I got mine done?"

"Yep. I like that style on you, which means it would look good on me. Nice thing about having a twin to model stuff. You don't mind, do you?"

"Not a bit—as long as you don't want to start dressing alike."

Cass laughed. "Now there I draw the line. You're much too conservative for my taste."

BY THE TIME LUNCH-HOUR RUSH was over, Sunny was already tired. She hadn't slept well the night before. Tossing and turning and "borrowing trouble," as Cass had said. As much alike as she and her twin were, in some ways they were very different. She'd always been the more serious of the two, more apt to worry. Well, that was going to stop.

Carpe diem was her new catchphrase word. Seize the day!

She pasted a smile on her face and turned to the front door just as it opened. There stood Ben, tall and handsome and wearing his white hat.

Her smile went real and wider. She had the strangest urge to run and hug him right in front of God and all the waitstaff. She restrained herself. "Well, hello there, Ranger. Come for some chili?"

"I did. Can you join me?"

"Sure. Things have quieted down enough so I can be spared." She motioned for a waiter and sat with him at his favorite corner table.

After they ordered, she said, "What new and exciting cases have you been working on today?"

"I don't know how exciting it is, but I've been doing some footwork on one of Sam's cases."

"A cold case?"

He nodded. "Five-year-old murder." He swigged down

half a glass of iced tea that had discreetly appeared on the table. "You know, you have the best iced tea in town. How do you make it?"

"From scratch with the best ingredients. Austin water helps. Tell me," she said, nodding to the holstered Sig Sauer he wore, "do you use that often?"

"Rarely have to draw it. Rangers intimidate by reputation, you know," he said, winking. "I imagine you've heard the 'one riot, one Ranger' story."

Sunny grinned and rolled her eyes. "Which tale is that? I've heard a lot of tall ones."

"There are a couple of versions of the story, but, in one rendering, it seems that back over a hundred years ago, a town in the middle of a riot wired for outside help from the Rangers. When the train arrived, a single Ranger got off. The mayor went bug-eyed and said, 'They only sent one Ranger?' And the Ranger said, 'You only got one riot, don't you?'"

She laughed. "And you believe that?"

"What's not to believe?" He looked decidedly smug.

Sunny had just bitten into her BLT when she saw Marge from the mission come in. "Excuse me just a minute. I have to get something from the kitchen for Marge."

"Who's Marge?"

"The gray-haired lady who just came in. She helps run one of the homeless missions in town. Be right back."

As soon as she had Marge fixed up with containers of chili to take with her, Sunny returned to the table, bringing along a tea pitcher for refills.

"What exciting activities do you have planned for the weekend?" she asked.

"I promised Jay a rousing game of miniature golf tomorrow afternoon."

"Miniature golf? I haven't played in ages. Not since I was in elementary school at least."

Ben said. "There's a pretty good course just south of the river. Want to join us?"

"I wouldn't want to interfere with father-son activities."

"You wouldn't be interfering. Come on and go with us."

She thought for a moment, then said, "Why not? But I need to be home before six."

"Or will you turn into a pumpkin?"

"A pumpkin?" she said, not understanding for a moment. "Oh, if you're talking about Cinderella, I think it was her coach that turned back into a pumpkin. And no, I just need to get back because I have to work Saturday nights."

"Oh," Ben said, looking pensive. "Busy time, I guess. How about we pick you up about two tomorrow afternoon?"

"Great."

She saw a movement by the bar and glanced over. The Senator stood there. He smiled and touched a finger to his forehead in greeting, then disappeared.

JAY CHOSE A RED BALL, Ben a blue, so Sunny opted for yellow.

"Suits you," Ben said, nodding to her ball.

"How so?"

"Sunny. Yellow. Logical."

She shrugged, having heard that before. Actually red was her favorite color, but she hadn't wanted to wrestle a five-year-old over a golf ball. "Jay, where's the first hole?"

"Right over here," the towhead said, running to it.

"Think we can trust your dad to keep score?"

Jay looked up at his father. "I think so. He's pretty honest, being a Ranger and all."

Ben winked at her over his son's head. "You can trust me."

"I was hoping I could bribe you. I haven't played miniature golf in about twenty years, and I wasn't very good at it then. Jay, why don't you show me how it's done?"

"Yes, ma'am," Jay said. "I'm really good." He set his ball on the pad and whacked it. A red blur caromed around the boards surrounding the hole and stopped two inches from the cup. "See. That's the way you do it. Only it's better when it goes in. That's called a hole in one."

She wiped her hands on her jeans, dug in and gave it a try, but her club only clipped the top of her ball, and it rolled about a foot.

"I think that's a do-over," Ben said. "Don't you think, Jay?"

"It's a do-over for sure."

"What's a do-over?" Sunny asked Jay.

"It's kinda when you make a mistake and don't do your best," he said earnestly. "It doesn't count, and you try again. You probably just aren't used to playing this. Me and my dad play a lot."

She wanted to hug the boy. His comment told a lot about Ben's parenting skills, and she could imagine those very words coming from his mouth. "I see. Thank you." Sunny picked up her ball, and tried it again. She whacked it more soundly that time. It jumped the rail and landed in the bushes by the third hole.

"Whoops," Ben said.

"Oh, no!" Sunny dramatically slapped her forehead. "I'm toast."

Jay laughed. "Do-over!"

With Jay and Ben instructing, she finally got the hang of it. The score for the first two holes was Jay, four; Ben, four; Sunny, eleven. At least she was entertaining. Jay and Ben were starting to yell "Do-over!" before she even hit the ball. She improved vastly by the ninth hole, and during the last nine her score went down considerably.

"That was fun," she said as her ball dropped into the last cup and disappeared.

"Want to play another game? Me and my dad sometimes play two."

She checked her watch and saw there was plenty of time. It was a beautiful day for being outside, sunny and back up in the seventies after a cool front midweek, typical of the seesaw weather of late fall in Austin. "Sure, if you guys don't mind me holding up the play."

"We don't mind, do we, Dad? And you're getting lots better. My aunt Tracy sucks."

Ben cleared his throat.

"Uh, I mean, she's…not as good as you are. Your shot, Dad. Can I have a snow cone?"

Ben sank the last hole in one shot, and they all had snow cones before they started the next round. She got better at it. At least she didn't suck, and she even made a hole in one on the seventh, the one with the chipped gorilla standing guard.

"Got time for a burrito with us?" Ben asked.

Sunny checked her watch again. "I'd love to, but I need to get home and get dressed."

"Oh, please, please," Jay begged. "Don't you like burritos?"

"I *love* burritos. And enchiladas. And tamales. And nachos." She poked Jay in the tummy. "And fajitas."

"And queso?"

"Especially queso. And tacos. And flautas. And guacamole."

"Ewww. I hate guacamole."

"Of course you do," she said. "You're a boy, and it's greeeen." She drilled her finger into his tummy again and made a face. Jay bent over to get away and burst into peals of laughter.

"It's greeeen. Ewww."

"I like guacamole," Ben said.

"But it's greeeen." Still laughing, Jay drilled his finger into his dad's belly.

"So is Shrek, and you like him." Ben swung Jay up onto his shoulders. "Let's get along, pardner. If we don't hurry, Sunny will turn into a pumpkin."

"A pumpkin? Ewww."

They returned their clubs and walked to the parking lot.

On the way home, Jay, who was strapped into his safety seat in the back, said, "Tomorrow we're going canoeing on that lake down there." He pointed to his left as they crossed the bridge joining the two halves of Austin.

"That's part of the Colorado River, and it used to be called Town Lake," Sunny told him, "but now it's called Lady Bird Lake."

"What's a Lady Bird?"

"It's not a what, it's a who," Ben said. "She was an Austin lady who was married to a president of the United States and was very interested in plants and nature."

"And the bridge we just crossed is where the bats live," Sunny added.

"Bats?" Jay twisted around in his seat. "Can we see them?"

"Nope. They've left already, but they'll return next spring."

"Are they scary? Do they suck *blood?*"

Sunny smiled. "They're not the blood-sucking kind. They fly around at night and eat little bugs, mostly mosquitoes. Next summer you can come down here just before it starts to get dark and watch them fly out from under the bridge and go bug-hunting. There are hundreds and hundreds of them."

"Cool. Can we do that, Dad?"

"Absolutely. I wouldn't mind seeing them myself."

"Can Sunny come canoeing with us on Lady Bird Lake tomorrow, Dad?"

"If she wants." Ben glanced at her. "Want to come?"

"Sure. If the weather holds. I'm a better paddler than I am a golfer."

"What's the weather supposed to do?"

"Another cool front, maybe some rain, but I don't think it's due until tomorrow night."

"It better not rain!" Jay said.

When they arrived at the parking lot in back of the café and her apartment, Jay said, "Can I come see your cat?"

"I don't think so," Sunny told him. "I haven't seen her all day myself. Sometimes I don't see her for a whole week."

"Where is she?"

"I'm not always sure. Sadie has a bunch of hiding places."

"Sadie is a funny cat."

"That she is, Jay. Listen, guys, I had a great time. Thanks for taking me along."

"You're welcome," Jay said. "Be sure to bring a jacket tomorrow. Dad says it may be chilly on the lake."

Sunny hid a smile. "I'll do that. Thanks for the tip. Bye." She reached for the door handle, but Ben was already out of the car and opening it for her.

"I'll walk you upstairs."

"I can manage."

"I know you can, but I want to walk you upstairs."

Surely he didn't mean to kiss her again, not in front of his son and with customers coming and going.

"Thanks for putting up with Jay. He's usually shy around strangers, but he was on a roll today."

"Not a problem. I really did have fun—after I got the hang of it."

"And don't feel obligated to come along with us tomorrow."

She cocked her head at him. "Are you trying to talk me out of it?"

"No way. Jay put you on the spot, and I wanted to give you an out. You're more than welcome."

"Good. I'll bring snacks. What time?"

"Two?"

"Perfect."

And it was. Having Jay along was a perfect buffer between them while she sorted things out.

BEN HAD WANTED TO KISS SUNNY, wanted it in the worst way, but with Jay staring after them and customers getting in and out of their cars, he decided he'd better pass. He'd settled on running a knuckle along her cheek and hustling back down the stairs before he gave Jay an education in the birds and the bees.

Was she really going to work tonight? He could have sworn she'd told him she worked Monday, Wednesday, Friday, and Cass worked Tuesday, Thursday and Saturday. Surely she wasn't lying about working tonight. Surely she didn't have a date. But, then again, she seemed very popular with men and seemed extra friendly with a lot of them. It was logical to assume she went out on dates with other guys.

For some reason, the thought of her with another man irritated the crap out of him. God, was he *jealous?*

No. No way. No skin off his nose what she did with her time.

Maybe she and Cass switched work nights for some reason or she was helping out on a busy night. Sunny didn't seem the type to lie.

But then he'd never caught on to Marla. Maybe he didn't understand women at all. Maybe, hell. What man understood women?

He started the SUV and backed out of the lot.

"I like Sunny, Dad."

"Good. I like her, too."

"It's neat she has a twin."

"Yes, it is."

"Are you going to marry her?"

Stunned by the question, Ben waited a moment to answer. "No, we're just friends."

"I wish you would marry her. Then I could have a mom, and we could get a house with a big backyard and a dog."

Chapter Eleven

Sunny took a quick shower, why, she didn't know. In less than an hour, she'd be setting up her drums and sweating like a horse, but old habits died hard. She dressed in frayed cutoffs, a white tank top and well-worn black sneakers. After slapping on a little makeup, she twisted her hair up and clipped it in place. The police uniform shirt she pulled on was black, oversize and had the sleeves ripped out. She pinned a huge phoney badge on her pocket, grabbed her bag and one of Brian's old SWAT caps and was out the door.

She was locking up when she remembered Sadie. Rats. Opening the door again, she filled the cat's food and water bowls and made another quick exit.

Of all the instruments in a band, drums were the most trouble. She sometimes wondered why she hadn't taken up the flute. Times like this, she really missed Brian's help, but she'd devised a method that made setup easier. She drove to the nearby storage unit she rented and backed her car up to the door. After she unlocked and rolled up the door, she backed the car up farther so she could hitch the small trailer to the back. It was a good system. The guys would help her unload and set up, then help with the breakdown and reloading. When the gig was over, all she had to do was drop the trailer in the storage unit until next time. Piece of cake.

One of the perks of playing together was getting to share a meal with her friends beforehand and catch up on all the news. Of course she saw most of them at the café sometime during the week, but this was different. The Copper Pistols had a special comradery.

Bright outside lights cast shadows inside the dim interior of the unit and outlined the boxes she stored there. She meant to go through those sometime, but she never quite got around to it. Some of her extra furniture was covered and lining the perimeter. After Brian had been killed, she'd sold their house. She just couldn't bear to live there without him, and the apartment over Chili Witches was vacant and convenient. She'd fixed up the apartment and moved, stashing here the things that wouldn't fit—or that she couldn't part with.

She went to one box and read the index card taped to it. *Keepsakes,* it said, listing various photo albums and other memorabilia inside. Though many of the pictures were stored on computer disks, some were not. She'd meant to scan those and save them, as well. Ripping the tape with her fingernail, she opened the box and found their wedding and honeymoon trip albums on top. She reached for them, then drew back. Another time, she thought. Another time. Why torture herself with the past? Turning to walk away, she had second thoughts and went back for them. She put the albums in the backseat and pulled the trailer out of the unit.

WHEN SUNNY PULLED INTO the loading zone of the Spotted Cow Bar and Grill just off Sixth Street, she saw Hank Wisda, the keyboard player, and John Elrod, the guitarist, were already there unloading their amps and instruments.

"Hey, sweetcheeks," Hank said, giving a wave. "Ready to rock?"

"You bet."

John ambled over to the rear of the trailer and waited while she unlocked it. "Hey, babe. Gets old, doesn't it?"

"What?"

"Unloading all this stuff. You know what we need? Roadies."

Sunny grinned. "We can't afford roadies to tote our stuff."

"True. This gig doesn't pay as much as I could make doing some private security jobs."

A sudden panic clutched her. "You're not thinking of leaving the Pistols are you?"

"Nah, hon." The lanky guy grabbed her in a phony headlock and kissed the top of her head. "No need to worry about that." John had been Brian's best friend and was still part of SWAT.

The three of them had started the Copper Pistols partly to earn a little extra money, but mostly as a way to blow off steam. Their love of music was one of the things she and Brian had shared. They'd hung a sign on the bulletin board at work to recruit other players and had been surprised at the response they had—everything from saxophonists to fiddlers. One guy even played spoons. Trish Perkins, an attractive redhead who now worked in the sex crimes unit, was picked for lead singer. Not only did she have a strong and versatile voice, but also she played fiddle. Hank, who was lady-killer good-looking and now in the motorcycle unit, rounded out their group on keyboards and was a darned good singer himself. He was the one engaged to Melanie, Sunny's assistant manager at Chili Witches.

Hank pitched in and they soon had her gear and theirs unloaded and set up. As they were finishing up, Trish and Mike Martinez walked in with their stuff. Mike, a member of the bomb squad, had taken Brian's place on bass. At first it was hard for Sunny to watch Mike playing and not resent his being there instead of Brian. The feeling soon faded as Mike blended into the band as if he'd always been there. He was a quiet, soft-spoken man and a heck of a bass player.

There were others who filled in from time to time, and the Pistols played an eclectic range of music from soft rock to contemporary country. They even threw in a little R & B from time to time. Over the years, they'd built up a local following with a lot of law enforcement people but also a surprising number who weren't.

Things weren't jumping at the Spotted Cow yet, so they congregated at a quiet table in the rear to await their dinner and review the playlist John had made up. Part of their payment in places that served food was a meal and endless drinks, and this grill served the best steaks in town. Everybody ordered beer except Sunny, and she had a Diet Sprite with a splash of grenadine and a lime twist, her drink of choice when she played, that and water with lemon.

"Say," John said, "I've got some bad news. Duke Ford died this morning. Heart attack."

"Oh, no," Sunny said as the rest of the group expressed their surprise and concern. "I can't believe it. I was sure Duke would live forever. He gave us our first job."

"I know," John said. "It's hard to believe, but he was getting up in years. His wife had been after him to retire for a long time."

"Any idea when the funeral is?" Trish asked.

"Not yet. They're waiting for his son to arrive from Oregon."

"What's going to happen with Duke's Joint?" Hank asked.

John shrugged. "Don't know, but for now it's closed. The assistant manager called me this afternoon to cancel our gig there next Saturday and said they may shutter for good. They're sitting on a prime piece of real estate, and I imagine they'll sell it. The land grabbers are probably already circling like buzzards."

"I hate to see the old landmark places go," Sunny said. "Duke's has been on South Congress for as long as I can remember."

"I know," Hank said. "Damned shame."

"Want me to line up another gig for next week?" John asked.

"I don't know about everybody else," Trish said, "but I wouldn't mind having an extra Saturday off for a change."

"Fine by me," Mike said.

Hank and John both looked at Sunny.

"I'm okay with that," she said.

"What do you want me to do if they don't reopen?" John asked.

Everybody was quiet for a moment. They'd always played Duke's Joint on the first Saturday night of the month, other spots on the second through the fourth Saturdays, then any fifth Saturdays were free.

Nobody said anything.

Finally Sunny said, "Why don't we just play it by ear and not make any decisions until we find out what's going to happen with Duke's."

"Good idea," Hank said, taking a swig of his beer.

Everyone else agreed as their steaks arrived. They ate and swapped department gossip. A lot of the people they talked about Sunny knew, but she'd noticed in recent weeks that a lot of the people they mentioned, she didn't know. APD, like everything else, was changing with time.

By the time they'd finished eating, the Spotted Cow was filling up. A large, bald man yelled, "Hey, Copper Pistols, when are you going to start?"

Sunny recognized Sergeant McDonald and grinned as John yelled back, "Right now, Curly. Keep your britches on."

The wooden floor screeched as the band's chairs scraped back and they stood. Curly led a smattering of applause as they took their places.

When everybody was set, Sunny clicked her sticks: One, two. One, two, three. And they cut down on an up-tempo Sugarland hit. Trish could give Jennifer Nettles a run for her money.

Curly stood up and whooped.

SUNNY WAS BOTH PUMPED AND exhausted when she finally got home. She took a long shower and washed her hair, then pulled on boxers and one of the oversize SWAT T-shirts she slept in. Knowing she was too wired to sleep, she turned on the TV and dished up a bowl of Blue Bell ice cream and drizzled chocolate syrup over it.

She curled up on the couch with a pillow in her lap to steady the bowl and flicked the remote until she found something besides infomercials. An old romantic comedy had just started, so she settled in to watch while her hair dried.

In the old days, she hadn't needed ice cream and old movies to soothe her after a gig. She and Brian had always used that energy to make love.

She wondered if Ben played an instrument. Or what his hands would feel like on her skin. Or how it would feel to make love with him.

Shivering at the thought of Ben and playing instruments and making love, she stirred the ice cream and chocolate into a soft goop and spooned it into her mouth as fast as she could. It didn't distract her. Nor did the movie. All she could see was Ben's face. All she could taste was his lips.

Oh, Brian, I'm sorry. I'm sorry.

THE WEATHER HELD. It was a perfect day for canoeing on the lake. While Ben was making arrangements for a boat, Jay said, "Dad says the day is perfect, and we probably won't even need a jacket."

"I was just thinking," Sunny told him, "that our guardian angels must have arranged for such a perfect day."

Jay nodded. "What's in the box?"

"A special treat for later."

"What kind of treat?"

"Do you like brownies?"

Jay's face lit up. "I *love* brownies. Brownies and pizza and spaghetti are my favorite things in the whole world."

"And burritos?"

"And burritos. And hamburgers. And hot dogs. And peas."

"Peas?" Sunny asked, surprised.

"I was joking," Jay said. "I hate peas. They're greeeen." He bored his finger into her belly.

"I'll get you for that," she said, scooping him up, throwing him over her shoulder like a sack and holding his feet. "Into the lake you go."

"Noooo," he cried, laughing and kicking. "Not that. It's cold and has germs. Daddy! Save me!"

She grabbed his feet and hung him upside down in front of her. "Nobody can save you now. You're due for a dunking."

Still laughing, he said, "Don't dunk me, please."

"Please? Did I hear a magic word? Ah, I believe I did. No more belly-boring?"

"No more. I promise. And I'm a man of my word."

Sunny glanced at Ben and winked. "Well, okay then." She turned Jay upright and set him on the ground. "I guess I can trust you."

"Would you really have dunked me?" Jay asked, his eyes wide, laughter gone.

"You betcha. Only your magic words stopped me."

"My dad said you used to be a policeman."

"Nope. I was a police officer."

Jay cocked his head. "What's the difference?"

Ben ruffled his son's hair. "Does she look like a police-*man* to you?"

Jay studied her for a minute. "Nope. She looks like a police-lady to me."

"Officer covers men and ladies both," Ben said.

"Oh. Did you catch people for speeding and direct traffic and stuff?"

"I did for a while. Then I became a detective in the homicide unit."

"Homicide!" Jay said. "I know what that is. Did you ever catch any murderers?"

"Yep."

"*Cool.* Why don't you catch bad guys anymore?"

"Because now I run a café called Chili Witches, which makes the best chili and the most scrumptious hamburgers in Austin—maybe in the entire state. Maybe in the entire world."

"Wow!" Jay said. "Dad, can we go get a hamburger there later?"

"Not today," Ben said. "The café is closed on Sunday, but maybe we can go tomorrow. Put your life jackets on, crew. The canoe is rented, and we're burning daylight."

"Can I paddle?" Jay asked.

"Sure. *Everybody* paddles."

After an hour, Sunny was getting tired, mostly from compensating for Jay's enthusiastic, if inaccurate, style of paddling. They had explored a good portion of the lake and watched the swans swimming around. Jay was as excited about the swans as he'd been about the bats.

They stopped by the bank to have a brownie from the stash she'd brought, and Sunny said, "There's a barbecue place on the outskirts of town—"

"What's an outskirt?"

"It means a place not in the main part of town." She brushed a chocolate crumb from Jay's chin. "Anyhow, the restaurant has very good food, plus it backs up to a big creek where several ducks live. After people have their dinner, many of them go outside and feed the ducks with their leftover bread."

"Can we go there, Dad? Please, please, please?"

"I thought we were going to grill hot dogs."

"We can grill hot dogs any old time. This place has ducks! And I'll bet Sunny would love to feed the ducks." He flashed his dimples at Sunny. "And I'm getting kind of hungry."

Ben raised an eyebrow. "You just ate two brownies."

"That was just a snack, not a real meal with meat and stuff."

"We'll see," Ben said.

"We'll see," Jay explained to Sunny, "usually means 'probably not.' Is it too expensive, Dad?"

There was an awkward silence, then Ben chuckled and glanced at Sunny and shook his head. "Kids."

HE WOULDN'T SAY ANYTHING to Jay at all, but damn if his kid didn't make him feel lower than a cow chip. His son's comment was bound to make Sunny wonder if he was a deadbeat. True, Texas Rangers didn't make big bucks, and for sure money was tight right now because of this mess with Marla, his ex, but he wasn't so broke he couldn't buy dinner.

Sunny hadn't acted as if it bothered her. In fact, she ignored the comment, and they canoed around the lake a while longer, then went by Zilker Park to let Jay attack the playscape and burn off some energy.

"Would you like to go to dinner with us at the place you mentioned? I know Jay would be thrilled, and I'd enjoy your company even more."

"I'd love to, but I've already made other plans," she said, smiling sweetly. "Maybe another time."

He loved her smile. It lit up her whole face and nearly convinced him she was telling the truth. She was concerned about the extra expense. Dammit! He wanted to turn the air blue, but instead he said, "Sounds good. Maybe one night next week."

"Great."

She looked tired, and Jay, despite his protests, was flagging fast. Ben motioned him in. "Come on, buddy. Tomorrow's a schoolday, and you look pooped. Have fun?"

"Lots." On the way to the car, Jay walked between them, slipping his hands into theirs.

After they dropped off Sunny and were on their way home, Jay yawned and said, "She likes us. I can tell. I think she'd make a really, really good mom."

"Don't rush things, son. Sunny's just a good friend." And he wasn't looking for a wife or a mother for Jay. He was still smarting from the mess his last one had made of his life.

Chapter Twelve

Sunny wasn't surprised when Ben and Jay walked into Chili Witches on Monday evening just before six. She was a bit surprised by the two adorable little girls with them. The redhead looked about Jay's age and the blonde was a year or two older.

"Hi, Sunny!" Jay said, beaming. "We came to have the best hamburger in town."

"Well, I'm glad you did. Come in, come in, and let's find you a special table." She winked at Ben over the children's heads, then seated them at a spot set for four.

"Are you too busy to join us?" Ben asked.

"I'll have to pop in and out. Who are these lovely ladies?"

"These are my nieces. April," he said, touching the blonde's head, "and Lexi."

They both grinned up at her and said hello.

"Aunt Tracy had to go to a meeting tonight, so my dad is babysitting."

"I'm not a baby," the redhead said, "but I *love* hamburgers. And I like chili, too. My daddy says my mouth is 'bestos-lined.'"

"Do you have fries here?" April asked.

"We surely do. We have lots of things you might like, and a menu just for kids." Sunny handed the children the kids' menus that were printed on paper place mats along with a cauldron of crayons. "What may I get you to drink while you're looking over the menus?"

Sunny heard a cacophony of choices, but the deep one vetoed choices with, "Three milks, iced tea and four waters."

Lexi sighed. "I was hoping for a Dr. Pepper."

"I know you were, sweetheart," Ben said, "but it's too late in the day for caffeine. You know the rule."

She sighed again, loudly, but she didn't argue. Sunny bit her lip to keep from laughing at the drama. This one must be a handful. "Be right back."

Fixing up the milk and water in plastic kids' cups with straws, she added an iced tea and carried it back to the table while Jeff took their order. As she passed Jeff on the way, she whispered, "These are special friends, and everything is on the house."

The waiter nodded, and she knew there wouldn't be any glitches.

"Four waters," Sunny said, distributing the cups all around. "Notice it has a *W* on the red lid. Three milks with a white lid and an iced tea." She set down three cups of milk and a regular glass of iced tea.

Lexi giggled. "Uncle Ben has a kids' cup, too."

Jay and April joined in the giggling, and Sunny again grinned and winked at Ben.

"I'm just a kid at heart," he said.

"I'm going to have chili," Lexi said.

"Only a little one," Jay said. "With her junior hamburger. I'm having a big hamburger with no onions and no green stuff. Onions make your breath smell bad."

"I'm having fries," April said. "And Uncle Ben is having a hamburger all the way."

"That's with the green stuff *and* the onions," Jay said.

"A man after my own heart."

"What does that mean?" Lexi asked.

"It means," Sunny said, "that's the way I like my hamburgers, too."

"Are you going to have a hamburger?" Jay asked.

"Not right now. I have to tend to customers, but I'll be back from time to time."

Sunny got busy and by the time she dropped back by their table, they were eating. "How's the food?"

"It's delicious!" Lexi said. "This is the best chili I've ever eaten in the whole world. My mommy would love it. She's got a 'bestos mouth, too."

Lexi might brag about her asbestos mouth, but Chili Witches was always careful to serve the mild version to children.

"Mine's really, really good," Jay said, ketchup dribbling down his chin.

"I love the fries!"

"You win the blue ribbon," Ben said.

"What does that mean?" Lexi asked.

"It means the chili and the hamburgers win the prize as the very best."

"Is there a prize? I want to see."

"Don't forget the fries! They win, too."

Ben shushed the kids, and Sunny hurried off to tend to new customers and check the kitchen.

By the time she returned, they were finishing up. "Do you have room for dessert?"

"Yes!" all the kids said.

"Uncle Ben said the peach cobbler is *larrupin'*," Lexi said. "What's larrupin'? Does it have raisins? I don't like raisins."

"No raisins," Sunny said, "and I believe *larrupin'* means delicious."

She waved Jeff over. "Bring us four kid-size peach cobblers and a regular size. Anybody need any more milk?" Nobody did.

Jay giggled. "There are only three kids. See. One. Two. And I'm three."

"But I'm four. Mind if I join you?" She pulled up a chair to the corner of the table and sat down.

"You're not a kid," Lexi said, giggling again.

"Do you really own this place?" Jay asked.

"My family and I do. My mother and my aunt started Chili Witches years and years ago before my sister and I were born. My mother and aunt have retired, so my sister and I run things now."

"Jay said you live upstairs over the café," April said. "Do you?"

"Yes, that's true. There are two apartments on the second floor, and my sister and I live there."

"I think it's neat you can eat chili anytime you want," Lexi said. "I wish I lived upstairs. I'd have chili for breakfast. Do you have chili for breakfast?"

Sunny smiled. "No. I usually have cereal or scrambled eggs or something like that."

Their cobbler came, and everybody dug in.

"This is larrupin'," Jay said.

"Yes, larrupin'," Lexi added.

"Almost as good as the fries," April said.

Ben laughed. "I think I can safely say the meal was a hit. I have a feeling we'll be back."

"Oh, yes!" the kids said.

"Tomorrow," Lexi added.

"Maybe not tomorrow," Ben said, "but soon. Now I've got to get these three home and ready for bed." He motioned to Jeff for the check.

When Jeff ignored him, Sunny said, "No check. This is my treat."

"No way. You can't make a living giving away your food."

"Think of it as my asking you over for dinner."

"But you didn't ask," Ben said. "We just fell in on you."

"I distinctly remember inviting you to drop by anytime. I've loved having you. Come back soon, everybody."

The kids were enthusiastic in their response.

Ben said, "Thanks, but next time I pay."

"It's a deal."

When she walked them to the door, all the children hugged her, and Ben put one arm around her shoulders and squeezed. "Thanks again. This has been a big success."

"Can we go upstairs and see your apartment?" Lexi asked.

"No," Ben said. "Now scoot, Red."

"My name is Lexi, not Red."

Ben laughed. "I stand corrected."

Lexi nodded curtly and marched out the door.

"They're adorable," Sunny said.

"They're a handful," Ben countered. "I'll call you. Good night." He squeezed her shoulder again and left.

Watching them through the window, Sunny saw Ben buckle up everyone, then pull away. The thought crossed her mind that having a house again would be nice. Her apartment wasn't meant for entertaining.

Cass was always grumbling about living upstairs and their lack of privacy, but the convenience had overridden the privacy issue for Sunny. Now she was beginning to rethink the idea.

ON TUESDAY MORNING, SUNNY arrived at the animal shelter, hoping Leo was still there, yet hoping he'd been adopted. "Leo, the shepherd, still here?" she asked Annabelle.

"Yes. I think he's been looking for you."

"Don't try to con me, Annabelle. He's only seen me twice."

"Leo's a smart dog."

They retrieved him from the kennel, and Leo truly did seem glad to see her, Sunny thought as she snapped on his leash. She could have sworn he was grinning. She squatted in front of him and scratched his ruff. "Are you glad to see me, boy, or are you just glad to have some special attention from anybody?"

His tail went crazy, and she could tell that with a little bit of encouragement, he would lick her face. She laughed and stood, before his urge got the better of his manners.

"Come on, Leo. Let's go for a run."

Or rather she ran, and he trotted beside her. She had a soft spot for all the dogs she'd helped with, but there was something special about this one. She desperately wanted to take him home with her, she thought as she slowed to a walk. Not sensible, she knew. Sadie would have a fit, for one thing. And her hours wouldn't be fair to Leo.

Though, now that she thought about it, he'd have more human interaction with her than he had now. What if he wasn't adopted? She couldn't bear the idea. Maybe she could adopt him, or maybe even foster him until she could find him a home.

She stopped and scratched his head. "Would you like to live with me for a while, boy?"

He sniffed her jacket pocket, then licked her hand.

"Does that mean yes or does it mean you smell the treats in my pocket?"

Leo gave a quiet "woof" and wagged his tail. Was he grinning again?

She gave him a treat, then unhooked his leash and threw the tennis ball she'd brought along. Leo raced after it and brought it back to her in his mouth.

"Good dog!" She patted his head, then threw the ball again.

Leo loved playing ball, but Sunny finally stopped. "I'm pooped, buddy, and I have errands to run. Sit."

He sat.

She attached his leash and led him from the field to the shelter, hating to leave him. If she had a house, she'd take him in a minute. On the other hand, people in apartments had dogs all the time. Even big dogs like Leo.

But then there was Sadie, the neurotic cat. Sadie would make his life miserable. Hers, too. And she couldn't just toss Sadie out on the street or dump her into a shelter. She knew what would happen.

Sunny sighed and turned Leo over to Annabelle. Reluctant to leave him, she squatted down and ruffled his coat again. "Goodbye, buddy."

Leo nuzzled her ear, and she nearly cried. "If I had a house with a yard, I'd take you in a minute."

She patted him again and hurried out before she started blubbering big-time.

No more than three blocks away, she jammed on her brakes. "Well, hell! I've got plenty of money. I can buy a house."

Quickly she circled the block and went back to the shelter.

"Annabelle, I'm going to adopt Leo. Can I make some arrangements and pick him up Thursday?"

"Sure."

Sunny tried to whistle as she strode back to her car, but she was grinning too wide to pucker. Before she pulled away, she made two calls on her cell phone. The first was to Hank Wisda's sister Diane, who was a real estate agent. The second call was to Cass.

SUNNY POURED HERSELF A CUP of coffee and sat down in the empty café with Cass. The cooks were busy in the kitchen and the waitstaff was beginning to arrive.

"What did you want to discuss with me?" Cass asked. "You sounded serious. Are you getting married again?"

"Good Lord, no! I'm going to buy a house."

"Well, halle-damn-lujah!"

"You don't mind if I move and leave you alone here?"

"Why would I mind?" Cass asked. "I'm thrilled for you. I've had my eye on a town house for a while myself."

"I didn't want you living here by yourself. Security."

"We've got state-of-the-art security systems, and I've never been a 'fraidy-cat. Also, it wouldn't be hard to rent out your apartment. What fun to have a new place to decorate!"

"Decorate? Me? You're the decorating half of this duo."

"Tell me you're not going to put that blue bomb of a couch in a new place," Cass said.

"Okay, I won't tell you."

"Sunny, my gawd. Is it a matter of money? I've got some socked away if it would help."

"Thanks, sis, but money isn't my problem. I've still got the insurance settlement I haven't touched, plus profit from the sale of our house, plus what I've saved since I've been living upstairs. My expenses are practically nothing."

"Tell me about it. I'll bet those clothes you bought the other day are the first things you've bought in five years. Tell you what, I'll let you move off and leave me if you'll let me help decorate the new house."

"You'll *let* me?" Sunny felt old history and her hackles rise.

"Oops. Bad word choice. I meant I won't bitch about it. How's that?"

"Better. Much better. It's a deal."

"When are you planning to move?"

"By Thursday."

Chapter Thirteen

Sunny didn't stay around to listen to Cass sputter. In reality, she doubted she could be in a new house by Thursday, but it would be nice. She'd told Diane Wisda she wanted to move ASAP and preferred to see houses that were move-in ready with nice backyards, two or three bedrooms and close to Chili Witches. She'd given her a price range, too. Austin real estate was cheap compared to other places around the country, but she didn't want to get carried away. If she could find something at the lower end of her budget range, she could pay cash. If not, she'd have to get a mortgage for part of it—something she wanted to avoid. Debt made her nervous.

Diane, a cute redhead with a big smile, was waiting when Sunny walked into her office.

"Sunny!" Diane said, holding out her arms for a hug. "It's so good to see you. I'm glad you called. You're super lucky it's been a buyer's market lately, and I've lined up some great houses to show you on short notice."

"Fantastic, Diane. It's good to see you, too. Hank tells me you're engaged."

Diane held out her left hand and fluttered her fingers so that her ring flashed. "Kurt and I just decided."

"That's wonderful."

Diane grabbed her oversize bag and her keys. "Come on. My car's out back. Or do you want a cup of coffee first?"

"No coffee, thanks. I'm eager to look at houses."

They drove to an area within a couple of miles or so of Chili Witches and pulled to a stop in front of a cottage that was painted a golden tan with white trim, black shutters and a red door.

"Nice," Sunny said, noting the lush lawn and mature landscaping.

"It's adorable inside," Diane told her. "Newly remodeled with wood floors and granite countertops in the kitchen. Two bedrooms, two baths. Best of all, the owners are being transferred overseas and are motivated to sell. They've just lowered the price. You're going to love it."

"Is it vacant?"

"Almost," Diane said as she unlocked the front door. "They've already packed and shipped things they're taking with them. All the kitchen appliances stay with the house, and some of their larger items of furniture, the wife's sister is going to sell for them."

Sunny stepped inside the foyer and fell instantly in love. A feeling of coming home settled over her like a warm comforter. A sense akin to déjà vu, but not quite, sent chill bumps over her skin. Even the smell of the house seemed familiar and welcoming.

The doorways were arched and the walls were painted a soft yellow. On the right was a dining room with a long table and six chairs. Brightly patterned draperies hung at the windows. The foyer led to a great room with high ceilings and one deep red wall. A couch of the same color faced the fireplace and a dark brown leather easy chair and ottoman sat in the corner. The coffee table, void of the knickknacks Sunny imagined had been there, was large and rough-hewn.

And there was a fireplace.

"Wood or gas?" Sunny asked, pointing.

"Both, but the gas logs stay. And over here is the kitchen and breakfast room."

"Beautiful!"

"Isn't it? I love the copper accents," Diane said, touching the stove vent. "Five-burner gas cooktop and self-cleaning electric double oven."

"I rarely cook these days except for nuking stuff, but I might be tempted to make a few meals in here. What about the backyard?" She bent down to look out the back bank of windows, but the shutters were closed.

Diane chuckled. "We'll get to that. Let's look at the bedrooms first."

A nice-size bedroom and bath were down a short hall off the foyer.

"Okay," Sunny said. "What about the backyard?"

"Patience, patience."

Diane led her back through the great room to the large master bedroom and showed her the walk-in closet and huge jetted tub in the spalike bath. Only a king-size four-poster bed was left in the bedroom.

"Very nice. Backyard?"

Diane walked to the French doors and opened them wide. "Ta-da!"

"Oh…my…God."

The fenced backyard was huge for this part of town. Mature oaks shaded part of the grassy expanse as well as the large flag-stone patio stretching along the back of the house. Flower beds lined with Austin limestone flanked the patio, and some meandered along the fence. Sunny knew zip about flowers, but the ones planted there were gorgeous clusters of purple, pink, gold and red, some compact, others tall and feathery. It wasn't so much a yard as a garden. There was even a birdbath and a either a huge doghouse—or a small playhouse.

Laughing, Diane said, "Fantastic, no?"

"Fantastic, yes."

"There's plenty of room for a pool if you wanted to put one in. Let me lock these doors, and we'll go outside through the breakfast room."

On the way, Diane stopped to open the shutters and let in light as well as the lovely outside view.

"I love it!" Sunny said. "But I don't think I can afford this. How much is it?"

"Just wait. There's more."

If Diane wouldn't tell her, the price must be astronomical. She'd better not get her hopes up.

They went through a laundry room off the breakfast nook area and out a back door to a breezeway leading left to the patio and right to the garage.

"And look," Diane said, ducking into the garage and pointing to a stairway going up the side of a wall. "Garage apartment. Come on." She flipped on a light and led the way upstairs.

The moment the door was opened, familiar smells of paint and linseed oil hit Sunny.

"The wife is an artist. This was her studio."

"I can tell," Sunny said. "My mother paints. Our house always smelled like this. Brings back memories."

"Do you paint?"

"Not a lick."

"Then you won't need a studio, and you can rent out the apartment for extra cash."

The businesswoman in Sunny nodded. "Good idea."

Back downstairs, she wandered around the perimeter of the

yard and looked back at the patio where Diane waited. She could imagine Leo romping around here, fetching a ball Jay had thrown, and Ben cooking steaks on a patio grill.

Whoa! Where had that come from? She erased that image and put herself in front of the grill with Leo curled up at her feet. There. That was better. Much better.

She ambled to where Diane stood. "How much?" She held her breath, waiting for the bad news.

When Diane named the price, Sunny was floored. Floored in a good way. "You're kidding."

"Nope."

It was at the top of her price range and a wee bit over, but not nearly what she had expected. "Is something wrong with it? Termites? Leaky roof?"

"Nothing's wrong with the house. It's the market. It's way down, and these people really, really want to sell soon. I understand the husband's company will pick up any loss they have to take. I think they'll accept an offer of less than the asking price, especially if it means a quick sale."

"Wow."

"Exactly."

"I'll take it," Sunny said. "This is my house. I knew it the moment we walked in the door."

"Don't be so quick to decide," Diane said. "I have a couple of other places to show you first. You may like one of them even better."

She didn't. They looked at five other houses. In and out in less than five minutes each. None of them measured up to the first one on Etta Place. Sunny had laughed when she learned the name of the street. Etta Place had been the Sundance Kid's lady love—and may have cavorted a bit with Butch Cassidy, as well—and had hightailed it to South America with Butch and Sundance when things got hot. Seemed like destiny—or a very strange co-incidence at least. Had the Senator somehow finagled all this?

Nah. That was reaching.

AFTER SUNNY SIGNED THE PAPERS for her contract offer, which included a lower price, immediate closing plus closing costs and the furniture thrown in, she hurried back to Chili Witches to tell Cass the news.

"Are you nuts?" Cass said. "You can't simply buy the first house you see."

"Why not? It's perfect. You'll love it."

Cass rolled her eyes. "I can't wait."

"Okay. Get Diane to take you by tomorrow. See if I'm not right."

"I may do that."

"Do it. I dare you. Just because I didn't go to law school doesn't mean I'm a complete idiot."

"Now, girls," the Senator said. "Play nice."

"Buzz off," Sunny said and stomped out of the café.

SUNNY'S CELL PHONE RANG as she was clattering up the stairs to her apartment. She figured it was Cass wanting to get in the last word, and she almost didn't answer it.

When she relented and did answer, Ben said, "Hello. I was about to hang up. Did I call at a bad time?"

"No, not at all. I was going upstairs to my apartment. Are you at work?"

"Just got home. I wanted to tell you again how much we enjoyed last night. Jay and the girls haven't stopped talking about it. Tracy's sorry she missed it. I suspect she and her husband and the girls will be in one night. Depends on Rick's schedule."

"Rick the pilot?"

"Yes. How do things look for the weekend? You going to be busy?"

"Very. I'm moving."

"Moving?" She could hear the shock in his voice. "Where?"

"Not far from here. If I get the house. I made an offer on one today."

There was silence for a moment, then he said. "I didn't know you were looking for a house. No reason why I should, I guess."

"I only decided to look for one this morning."

"And you've already bought one?"

"Why is everybody so surprised about that? I saw it. I liked it. I bought it. Simple."

"Ah, darlin', who's been giving you a hard time?"

Her toes curled at the way he called her "darlin'," and she sank down on the top step. "Nobody really. Cass thought I was a little nuts."

"Little sis. I see. It's amazing you can move in this weekend."

"Actually, I'm hoping Leo and I can move in on Thursday— if the sellers accept my offer."

More silence.

"Leo?" he asked.

"My dog."

"I didn't know you had a dog."

"I don't yet. I'm adopting him on Thursday. He's a great dog, mostly German shepherd. He looks a lot like Skye's Gus. Which reminds me, I have to go to the pet store tonight and stock up on supplies. I have nothing to tend to a dog."

"What if you don't get the house?" he asked.

"Bite your tongue. I'll get the house. It's on Etta Place. It's fated."

"Fated? Etta Place? The street?"

"Yes. You know, Etta Place, the mistress of—"

"The Sundance Kid," he finished. "Got it. You know, I think that street is only a couple of blocks over from where my sister lives. Small world. Need any help moving?"

"I wouldn't turn down the offer."

"I'll take off early on Thursday and come tote boxes. I'll see if I can borrow Rick's pickup. Would that help?"

"Enormously. I'm not taking much in the way of furniture, but no way can I get a dresser and a breakfast table in my car."

"I'll call you on Thursday when I'm leaving work."

"You're a sweetheart. Thanks, Ben."

"Glad to help, darlin'. Good night."

Darlin'. He called her darlin' again. She loved the way that sounded, loved the deep rumble of his drawl. "Good night," she whispered, wishing he were sitting on the step beside her. She'd love to snuggle up and have his strong arms around her, telling her everything was going to be all right.

"It is, you know." The Senator was sitting on the steps beside her.

"What?"

"Everything is going to be all right. Ben McKee is a fine man."

"Of course he's a fine man. He's a Texas Ranger for gosh sakes, but what does that have to do with anything?"

He only smiled. "You'll be very happy on Etta Place. Interesting coincidence, don't you think?" He chuckled and was gone.

Chapter Fourteen

Sunny's cell phone rang about twelve-thirty on Wednesday, right in the middle of the lunch rush. When she answered, Diane said, "Guess what?"

There was no need to guess when she heard the excitement in her real estate agent's voice. "I got the house."

"Yes! They jumped on the offer. It's all yours."

Sunny let out a rebel yell.

The noisy café suddenly became funereally quiet, and everybody turned to stare at her.

She grinned. "It's okay, folks. It's good news. I just bought a house."

There was a smattering of laughter and several people started clapping and more joined in with congratulations. After all, she knew most of the patrons to some degree or another.

"Sorry, Diane. Give me the details. When can I move in?"

Diane related the particulars of the closing, then said, "The owners said you could move in today if you want. You'll have to sign some stuff as a formality. I can bring the papers by this afternoon if that's okay."

"Thanks. I'm in Chili Witches today. Cass said she wanted to see the place. Can you take her by?"

"Sure. I'll see you about two. I wish all my sales were this simple."

John Elrod, the guitar player from the Copper Pistols, and one of his buddies were having lunch at the time. Both were dressed in black SWAT T-shirts. He motioned her over and pulled her down into his lap.

"What's this about a house?"

"Oh, John, I'm so excited." She looped her arms around his neck.

"I'm getting a new dog tomorrow, and he needed a backyard, so I bought a house."

"Let me get this straight. You bought a house for a dog?"

She grinned. "Sounds crazy, doesn't it? No, I'd been thinking about a house so I could have some privacy and do some entertaining."

"So when's the housewarming?"

"Soon. I have to get moved in first. Some furniture comes with the house, and I hope to be completely moved by the weekend. Good thing our gig was canceled, huh? Have you heard any more about Duke's funeral?"

"It's tomorrow morning at ten. St. Mary's. You going to make it?"

"Of course," she said. "I'll see you there."

"Unless—"

"Some nutcase takes his mother-in-law hostage. I understand."

"Babe," John said, "I'd love to have you sit here in my lap a while, but there's a big guy with a white hat and Ranger badge over by the door who looks like he could chew ten-penny nails and spit them at me."

"Ben!" She waved. "I want you to meet him, John." She hopped up and hurried to where Ben stood.

He wasn't smiling. "Lap dance?"

She snickered. "With John? Hardly. He's one of my best friends. Come meet him."

He hung his hat on the rack and walked with her to the table. He still wasn't smiling. When she introduced him to John and his buddy, Ed, he nodded curtly and shook hands with both men, who were standing.

John said, "Sunny, if you need help moving this weekend, let me know."

"I'm helping her," Ben said.

John's brows went up. "Call if you need me."

"I will. Thanks, John." She tiptoed to kiss his cheek, then turned to Ben. "You having lunch?"

"Thought I would."

"Good." She led him to a table. "I'll have a quick glass of tea with you to celebrate." She motioned to a waiter for two teas.

"What are we celebrating?" He still didn't flash that grin she adored.

"I definitely got the house. Isn't that terrific? I can go ahead and move in if I pay them a nominal amount for rent until the closing—which won't be for two or three weeks. My agent has lined up an inspector to go through everything this afternoon."

"That's good. You date him?"

"Who? The agent? My agent is a woman."

"No. Him. The SWAT guy. John."

"John?"

"Is there an echo in here?"

Sunny went dead still. "Why are you being such a smart-ass?"

"Are you?"

His green eyes lacked the sparkle she usually saw in them. They looked cold and hard. She started to mouth off a snappy reply, but settled for a calmer approach. "I told you John is a friend. He was my husband's best friend, and I've known him for years. We play in the band together."

"What band?"

"The Copper Pistols. Haven't I mentioned the band? I was sure I had."

He shook his head. "First I've heard of it."

"The group's made up of local cops—and me. I was on the force when we formed the Pistols. We play at different places around town on most Saturday nights."

"*You* play in a band?" He looked skeptical.

"I do, and we're darned good."

"Well, I'll be damned."

"You very well might be." She took a swallow of the tea Jeff had brought and then looked Ben directly in the eye. "Ben, let's get something straight right now. I can't abide controlling, possessive men. I saw too much of that kind of thing when I was on patrol—and later in Homicide—and I saw where it can lead. I have lots of friends, men and women, and I won't be cut off from *any* of them. I hadn't dated anyone since my husband was killed until you came along, but that can be remedied easily enough. Decide now if you're interested in the package that I am."

He took a deep breath. "Was I being a jerk?"

"You were."

"Sorry." He turned his tea glass around on the table, leaving wet circles, then looked back up at her. "I got pretty well burned my last time out of the chute."

"Your ex?"

He nodded. "We'll talk about it sometime."

"I've got to get back to work. What would you like for lunch?"

After he decided, she went to the kitchen to turn in his order, patting John's shoulder on her way past him.

When she had a minute to spare, she called Cass and told her about the house.

"Well, I'll be a cross-eyed monkey," Cass said. "You really did it."

"Of course. I can do almost anything I set my mind to, sister dear. Diane is coming over after a while, and she'll take you to see the house if you want. Take your notebook and make notes on stuff I'll need to do the place up, but for gosh sakes, don't get carried away."

SUNNY THOUGHT THURSDAY would never come. When it finally arrived, she got up early and started packing kitchen stuff in moving boxes Cass had picked up the afternoon before. She stopped only to dress and go to Duke's funeral at St. Mary's downtown. On her way home, she stopped by the shelter to pick up Leo.

"You certainly look spiffy," Annabelle said.

"Thanks, but I had to go to a funeral. Leo ready to go?"

"Ready and waiting. I even gave him a bath."

Sunny took care of the paperwork and wrote a check to the shelter.

"Thanks," Annabelle said. "Looks like you have a dog."

"Or he has me. I bought him a new collar and leash." Sunny pulled the items from the bag she brought while Annabelle re-trieved Leo from his pen.

"I think he knows something is up," Annabelle said. "Look at that tail."

It was doing some serious wagging. And Leo was grinning.

"Hey, boy. Ready to go home with me?"

He made a soft "woof" and looked up expectantly. They changed out his collar, and Sunny attached the new leash.

"Come on, fella. Let's go finish packing. You want to wrap or tape?"

Sunny was halfway home before she thought about Sadie. Sometimes it was easy to forget her when, for days at a time, only empty bowls and used kitty litter gave any indication she was around.

"Leo, I have a cat named Sadie. She's shy, and she can be cantankerous. Please be patient with her. We'll work something out about territory if we have to."

Leo hung his head over her seat and nuzzled her ear.

"Good dog."

BY MIDAFTERNOON, SUNNY HAD most everything packed—not that she had much. Leo hadn't ventured far from her side, and she hadn't seen Sadie, nor heard her. Cass had come upstairs and helped after the lunch rush, which made things go faster. Instead of messing with wardrobe boxes, they carried her hanging clothes downstairs and dumped them in the backseat of her car. Her shoes went into a laundry basket, then in the trunk.

"What's this?" Cass asked, picking up one of the photo albums Sunny had stashed in the trunk.

"Wedding and honeymoon pictures. I'd forgotten I left them in the backseat until I picked up Leo. I moved them to the trunk for safekeeping. Just leave them there."

No sooner had she closed the trunk than a big blue Ford pickup pulled into the parking lot, and Ben climbed out wearing his jeans and a T-shirt.

"Need some help, ladies?"

"You betcha, big guy," Cass said. "Glad to see we've got some muscle."

"Thanks for coming," Sunny said. "We've got some boxes and a few pieces of furniture I think will fit in the truck bed perfectly."

"I'm not toting that muncher of a dresser down these stairs," Cass said. "Let me go get a couple of guys from inside to help bring it down."

"I've brought a dolly and a ramp for loading any heavy stuff," Ben told Sunny.

"The heaviest thing is the dresser, and if I take out all the drawers, it won't be so bad."

"Who is this guy?" Ben asked, scratching Leo's head.

"This is Leo, the newest member of the family. He hasn't budged from my side all day."

Ben winked. "I understand the feeling."

That warm glow she was getting used to slithered over her body, and she smiled.

One of the cooks and one of the waiters, both burly guys, came out of the back of the café. "What do you need moved, Sunny?" one of them asked.

"The dresser in my bedroom and the breakfast table and chairs. I think we can manage the rest okay."

Ben grabbed the dolly, and the three men took off upstairs with Leo and her behind them. In no time the furniture and several boxes filled the truck. Sunny slipped the guys from the café a tip before they went back to work, then she hurried upstairs to get her purse.

"You want to take this litter box over?" Ben asked.

"No, I'll have to coax Sadie out first, and with all the commotion around, she's never going to come out. I'll leave food and water for her and try to cage her tomorrow."

"Are you sure you have a cat?"

She laughed. "Positive."

"Are you really going to try to stay in the new place tonight? It will be dark soon."

"Then we'd better hurry." She gave him the address and directions. "You can follow me, but in case we get separated, you'll know where you're going." She grabbed her purse and a sweater and locked up. Leo sat in the passenger seat on the way over to the new house.

Ben didn't lose her, and he backed into the driveway after she pulled in. She unlocked the door and they started unloading, which was a bigger chore than when they had help. They were both sweating by the time they had everything inside. She was really going to enjoy soaking in her lovely huge tub tonight.

While they'd unloaded, Leo had run around the house, sniffing everything, exploring every corner and acting very excited. He seemed to be happy about the new house, as well.

"I like your new place," Ben said as he carried in the chairs to the breakfast table. "Really nice."

"Thanks. I fell in love with it the minute I walked inside." She flopped down on the couch, and Ben stretched out beside her. "I'm pooped," she said, swiping her damp forehead. "And thirsty. I'll get us some water."

She started to rise, but he stopped her. "I'll get it. Where are the glasses?"

"In one of those boxes marked Kitchen. I think I know which one." She hopped up, and they made for the sink. "Leo's probably thirsty, too."

Leo woofed and his toenails clicked on the wooden floor as he followed them. Sunny found glasses and a bowl while Ben checked the fridge for ice.

"Ice maker's empty."

Sunny turned on the faucet and groaned. "So's the faucet. Rats! The water's off. I meant to call today and make sure everything got switched over. I can't stay here without water. I could just cry."

Ben seemed to sense how disappointed she was, and he

pulled her into his arms. "I'm sorry, darlin'. I know you had your heart set on spending the night here."

"I did. Cass even bought new bed linens for me. Well, shoot!"

Being comforted in his arms felt so good that Sunny didn't move, couldn't move. She just closed her eyes and went with the warmth of sensation flowing over her.

For long moments, neither of them moved, then his hand began to slowly stroke her back. She snuggled closer. Nothing more happened for a while, then he lifted her chin with his finger and gave her a gentle, nibbling kiss. "Have I told you I like your house?" He brushed his lips across hers.

"Yes," she murmured against his mouth. "I like it, too."

"Have I told you I like your lips?"

"I don't think so."

"I do. I like everything about you."

His kiss deepened and a jolt of longing shot through her as he lifted her onto the kitchen counter and, never moving his mouth, stepped between her legs. Her arms went around him and their tongues met. She nearly came unglued. His hand went under her T-shirt and stroked her breast.

Lord, was she sitting on the stove? Was it on? She was on fire.

He moaned. She moaned. Leo barked and started growling.

Ben drew away and looked down. "What's your problem, dog?"

"Maybe he thinks you're hurting me."

"Am I hurting you?"

"Not hardly. Where am I sitting?"

"On the counter by the sink."

"Good. I was afraid I was on the stove."

"On the stove?" he asked, looking puzzled.

"Never mind. He's probably thirsty. I know I am."

Ben looked at his watch and frowned. "As much as I'd like

to continue this, I need to take Rick's truck back and pick up Jay. He has an early bedtime."

"I understand. I have to go back to the apartment and take a shower. I'm sweaty and stinky."

"I didn't notice. You smell nice to me."

She laughed. "That answer is good for an extra ten points." She put her hands on his cheeks and kissed him quickly. "I have to get a few things if I'm not going to stay here tonight. You go ahead and pick up your son."

"Want some help on Saturday? Jay and I can come over."

"Sure, but don't make it early. I need to hit a few garage sales first."

"Garage sales? If you're moving, isn't the timing a little off to go shopping?"

"You're obviously not a woman."

"I'll grant you that."

After Ben left, Sunny let Leo out into the backyard for a few minutes while she packed a bag to take with her as well as a few doggie items she'd need. When she let him back in, he was grinning again.

"You like it here, huh? Me, too, but we can't stay tonight. Sorry. You're going to have to bunk at the apartment tonight and tomorrow while I work. But I'll do everything I can to protect you from Sadie. She's not so bad really."

Chapter Fifteen

Friday seemed to go on forever. Not only did Sunny spend half the morning on hold, trying to get the utilities straightened out, but the phone company couldn't get to her until Monday, which meant that the security system couldn't be activated until after that. At least her new flat-screen TV was being delivered on Saturday afternoon, and the cable was hooked up and ready.

Cass had taken Sunny's credit card and gone shopping for a rug for the den and "a couple" of other things Cass insisted she needed.

"Don't get carried away," she'd warned.

Cass had only laughed, which made Sunny very nervous, but she hated to fuss at her sister too much because Cass had promised to start unpacking all the boxes.

During the afternoon lull at the café, Sunny went upstairs to check on the animals. Even though she'd left Leo in the living room and closed off her bedroom and bathroom, Sadie had obviously not been happy with the arrangement. Sometime during the night she'd been awakened by a gosh-awful yowling at the bedroom door. She'd turned on the light and found Sadie sitting there and heard Leo scratching and whining on the other side.

Thinking it was the perfect time to coax Sadie into the cat

carrier, Sunny had gotten out of bed and tiptoed over. But capturing Sadie was like chasing lightning bolts. After she climbed the draperies and jumped onto the ceiling fan, which, luckily, wasn't on, Sunny gave up and went back to bed.

When she awoke, she found the shower curtain shredded, panties she'd hung over the rod in tatters and a hair ball on her bra.

"Gee, thanks, Sadie. I get the message," she'd said to the room.

Now, no telling what she'd find. She was tempted to hotfoot it back to the café and not even open the door, but when she did, she found Leo waiting for her, tail wagging and looking ready to play. She'd left the TV on the home improvement channel to keep him entertained.

"Want to go for a quick walk, boy?"

Leo woofed.

"Let me check on Sadie first." She peeked into the bedroom, but the only sign she saw of the cat was another hair ball on her sleep shirt. "Brat!" She'd clean it up later.

She took Leo for a quick walk, then made sure he had food and water in the kitchen, left him in the living room and went back to work. During a breather in the evening, she went back upstairs to check on Leo again, feeling guilty about his having to stay cooped up rather than having a backyard to run in. When she opened the door and turned on the lamp, Sunny could only stand there in shock. Leo was curled up on the floor in front of the TV, and he looked up at her but didn't stand. Curled up beside him was Sadie, sound asleep and looking like a furry angel.

"Amazing, isn't it?" the Senator asked. "They seem to have hit it off."

Sunny could only gape at the pair, absolutely stunned. "Did you have something to do with this?"

He only smiled and disappeared.

Why did she have the feeling that the Senator had his finger in several pies lately? And exactly how was that possible?

WHEN SUNNY AWOKE ON SATURDAY morning, she was glad she'd decided to stay in the apartment one more night instead of taking the animals to a strange place late Friday night. She stretched, feeling really rested and ready to tackle all the tasks of the day.

She chuckled when she saw Leo and Sadie sleeping together on an old bath mat beside her bed. As soon as her feet hit the floor, both animals rose. Expecting Sadie to zip under the bed, she was surprised when she didn't.

"Are you becoming socialized, Sadie?"

Sadie didn't purr or wind herself around Sunny's ankles, but she didn't run and hide, either. It was a miracle.

Sunny dressed quickly, slapped on a little makeup and carried her bags and the pet items down to her car. After taking Leo for a quick walk to the alley bushes, they went back upstairs for the task she dreaded: getting Sadie in the cat carrier.

Oddly enough, she went in without much of a fuss. Sunny only got a very small scratch and hiss. Leo must have made the difference. The cat wasn't happy about the car ride—that hadn't changed—but when the yowling got too loud, Leo woofed, and, wonder of wonders, Sadie hushed.

At the new house, she lugged in all the pet supplies, then came back for the cat. Once inside, Sunny opened the carrier door, and Sadie shot out as if her tail was on fire. Where she went was anybody's guess. Sunny and Leo went out into the backyard, and she checked to make sure the gate was locked and there were no holes in the fence.

She squatted down in front of Leo and scratched his ears.

"Say, buddy, I have some errands to run, but I won't be gone long. Want to stay outside while I'm gone?"

The shepherd ran away a bit, then circled back, wagging his tail.

"I'm going to take that as a yes. I'll see you later."

He followed her to the back door, then when she went inside, he bounded off. It was good to see him run.

She hadn't noticed the new rug in the den until then. It was very attractive and cheerful. And expensive-looking. She didn't even want to think about that, nor did she go scouting to find the other purchases her sister had made. "Just a few bath towels and stuff," Cass had said. It was the "stuff" she was worried about.

After checking to make sure the gas, water and electricity were working, she decided to forgo the garage sales until next weekend. Instead, she went to the pet store and bought a padded window ledge and a scratching post for Sadie and stocked up on pet food and treats. Next, she went to the grocery store and bought a cartful of people food and treats. She even found a tall green potted plant for what seemed like a bargain, and bought it, as well.

On her way home, she stopped by the storage unit and picked up several lamps and an end table she barely got wedged into the backseat. She didn't have room in her small car for anything else, though she saw several pieces of furniture she thought would be perfect for certain spots in the house—but she'd better talk to Cass first.

A quick call confirmed that the red Chinese armoire would be perfect in the master bedroom, and the bookcases were exactly right for the den.

She also managed to wrestle one box labeled Decorative Items into the passenger seat. She didn't even remember what was inside except that they were probably things Cass had helped her select for her previous house.

Her cell phone rang as she was locking the unit. "Hey, babe," John said. "Hank and I find ourselves at loose ends. Need some help moving?"

"Don't ask if you don't mean it."

"I mean it."

John had a key to her storage unit, so she described the things she wanted from there. "And I need the bed from my apartment knocked down and brought over. Cass can let you in."

"You got it. Where do you want this stuff delivered?"

She gave him the address, then drove back to the new neighborhood where she saw people out doing Saturday chores and kids playing. When she pulled into the driveway, she just sat there for a minute and studied the house and the yard with its sweeping oaks and colorful flowers. This beautiful spot was hers, really, really hers. A lump came in her throat and her heart swelled. This was home now, the perfect place for a new beginning.

Just as she started to haul stuff inside, Ben and Jay pulled up in his SUV. "Need some help?" Ben called.

"Sure do. You guys willing to provide some muscle?"

"I am," Jay said, straining to flex his biceps.

"Great. You can carry this lamp inside." She loaded Ben's arms with grocery sacks and carried the plant and items from the pet store in hers.

Once they were inside, Jay made a beeline to the back windows. "Wow! Look, Dad, a dog! Is he yours, Sunny?"

"Yes, he is. As soon as we unload the car, I'll take you out to meet him."

"Come on, Dad. Let's hurry," he yelled as he ran to the front door.

By the time they got to the car, Jay was already on his way back with a sack of groceries.

"Is that too heavy for you?" Sunny asked.

"Nope," Jay said, but she noticed he stopped twice to readjust the weight.

"You and Jay go on in the backyard," Ben said after they deposited the second load. "I'll get the rest."

"Aw-right!" Jay ran to the back door but waited for Sunny to unlock it.

She grabbed a tennis ball on the way out, and Leo came loping up to meet them, tail wagging. "Jay, this is Leo. He's a very polite dog. Why don't you hold out the back of your hand and let him get acquainted with you."

"I know how to do it. My dad showed me once." He held out his hand and let Leo sniff, then lick it. Jay went into an ecstasy of giggles. "He likes me. See, he likes me!"

Sunny handed Jay the ball. "He likes to play ball. Want to throw it for him?"

Jay took the ball and hurled it. Leo took off in a flurry of muscle, grabbed it in his mouth and bounded back. Jay laughed and threw it again.

Ben came out the back door. "I think it's love at first sight."

"Absolutely."

"I brought everything in. What shall I do next?"

"Mind watching Jay and Leo for a minute? I want to make sure they're all right together. I'll go put up the groceries."

In the kitchen, she put the beer, wine and soft drinks in the fridge along with milk, eggs and other perishables. The rest she stowed in the pantry or under the sink. Bless Cass, who'd unpacked her dishes and staples. Even the tableware was neatly stacked in a holder and placed in the top drawer beside the dishwasher. Another drawer beside the stove held cooking spoons and gadgets and another was filled with new, and coordinating, dish towels. Cass again.

She hadn't had a chance to check out the master bedroom, but when she walked in, it was obvious Cass had been at work here, as well. Another exquisite rug lent warmth and color to the room, and the bed was covered with a magnificent, but simple, coverlet in heathery blue and coordinating pillows. They were perfect with the custom draperies that had been left behind. There wasn't a speck of beige in the room. And in the bathroom, new towels hung on the rods instead of her old worn and mismatched ones. They were beautifully coordinated, of course, as were the fat candles and bowls of scented soaps.

Tears rose into her eyes. "Ah, Cass, you are a piece of work," she whispered. "It's beautiful, but I only hope you haven't ruined my credit completely."

Plucking a color-coordinated tissue from its fancy holder, she blew her nose and started back to the kitchen. She met Ben on the way.

"Something wrong?" Ben asked, studying her face.

"No, I just got a little weepy. Good weepy. Cass must have worked her butt off yesterday. She's a great sister."

Ben took her into his arms. "I'll bet you're a great sister, too."

The back door slammed, and Ben stepped away.

"We're thirsty," Jay said as he and the shepherd came inside. "Me and Leo have been running and running."

"Is it okay for the dog to be inside?" Ben asked.

"Sure. He's part of the family. He's even socializing Sadie." She told them the story of the new alliance the animals had formed while she fixed glasses of water as well as a pitcher of lemonade. She didn't mention the Senator, but she jazzed up the story until they were both laughing.

A moment later, the doorbell rang. First time she'd heard the sound of the chimes, and she loved their mellow tone—so much better than the *blaaat* of her old buzzer.

When she opened the door, Hank said, "Hey, sweet-cheeks. Where do you want us to park?"

She went outside with him. "There is fine. You can bring stuff through here." She waved to John, who was in the driver's seat of his truck.

She didn't realize Ben had followed her until he stuck out his hand to Hank. "Ben McKee."

"Hank Wisda. Pardon the sweat."

"No problem. Need some help?"

"I wouldn't turn it down. That red son of a gun is *heavy*."

"Would a dolly help?" Ben asked. "I've got a dolly and a ramp in my SUV."

"Get it, man. It'll keep me from getting a hernia."

Sunny laughed. "A hernia? Tell me again, Hank, how much do you bench-press?"

Hank grinned. "Melanie and Amy are on their way over. They stopped to get some Chinese food. You like Chinese?"

"I love Chinese," Sunny said.

"Me, too," Ben said as they walked away.

In a short time, the men had unloaded the furniture and set up the bed. Sunny didn't spot Sadie during the commotion, suspecting she was either under the couch or the king-size bed or in some closet or cubby. She set the dining-room table, adding an extra chair from the breakfast room for Jay. By the time the men washed up, Amy and Melanie arrived with bags of food.

She introduced Amy, John's tall brunette wife, and Melanie, Hank's fiancée, to Ben and Jay. Hank and John got beers and everyone else chose either soft drinks or lemonade and took places at the table.

"I adore your new place, Sunny," Amy said, passing the rice.

"Me, too," Melanie said. "I can hardly wait to see the rest."

Everyone passed food and dug in. Sunny noticed that Jay

tried to sneak a piece of chicken to Leo, who sat politely beside him. She shook her head, and Jay popped it in his mouth instead.

They had a great time, and the group easily drew Ben into their conversation. Even Jay got his share of attention.

After cleanup, Hank and John got another beer, Ben got a Coke, and the men went out to explore the backyard and watch Jay and Leo romp. She took Amy and Melanie on a tour of the house, which they oohed and aahed over.

"It's gorgeous," Amy said. "Only needs one thing to make it absolutely perfect."

"What's that?"

Melanie grinned. "The right guy, of course." She winked at Amy. "I think she's working on it. Isn't that Ranger a hunk?"

"Whoa, whoa," Sunny said. "We're just friends. Don't go starting rumors, you two romantics."

"Who, me?" Melanie said, her eyes wide and innocent. "Why, I wouldn't dream of it, hon."

"Me, either," Amy said. "But if you ask me, I think he's ideal for you. Why, the man looks at you like he's itching to lick your toes."

Chapter Sixteen

"Say," John asked when the guys walked back in, "did you want us to bring the TV from the apartment? And what about the couch?"

"The couch has seen better days," Sunny said, "and Cass threatened me with dire consequences if I brought it over here. The TV is old, so I thought I'd leave it there, as well. At least for the time being."

"Are you going to rent out the apartment?" Hank asked.

"Eventually, I imagine. I haven't had time to think much about it."

"Don't, until you talk to me."

"Okay. You know someone who may be interested?"

"Yeah." He grinned. "Me. If the price is right. My lease is about up, and my unit is full of college kids who carry on at all hours and drive me nuts."

"Getting to be an old man, Hank," John said, socking him on the shoulder.

"That's the truth."

"Anything else we can do other than get out of your hair?" John asked.

"Not a thing. Sorry the new TV isn't here or y'all could watch the football game."

"He's having a fit to get home and watch the Longhorns play," Amy said, "so I guess we'd better hit the road."

"Us, too," Melanie said. "Sunny, your new place is fabulous." She hugged her boss. "I'll see you Monday."

"Thanks for helping and for lunch." Everybody walked out into the front yard for goodbyes.

When the two couples had left, Ben said, "I like your friends."

"Thanks. So do I. We've been through some tough times together, and they mean a lot to me. Are you going home to watch football, too?"

"Hadn't planned to. I don't have any particular ties to the University of Texas or the Longhorns. Now, if we're talking professional football and the Cowboys, that's another story. You wanting to kick us out?"

"Not at all," she said. "I was hoping you'd help me put up Sadie's new window ledge. And as soon as the TV is delivered, I'm going shopping for a new patio grill. There's a big sale at Home Depot."

"Do you have a lawn mower?"

Sunny stopped dead. "I hadn't even thought about a lawn mower. There may be one in my storage unit, but I seem to remember Brian saying that ours was on its last leg."

"Brian? Your husband?"

She nodded. "He always loved working in the yard." Memories flashed of Brian in shorts and a sweaty, ragged T-shirt mowing the lawn and clipping hedges while he listened to music through his ear buds. The memory didn't hurt as much as it used to. "The growing season is about over. I'll use a lawn service until I figure something out."

"What kind of a guy was he?" Ben asked as they went inside.

"Brian? A nice guy. Strong, brave, fun. You would have liked him."

"I'm sure I would have. I like his wife and his friends."

As tears stung her eyes, she turned away.

"How did he die?"

"He was SWAT, like John." She stared out the back windows to where Jay and Leo played. "They were in a hostage situation against three armed prison escapees holed up in a warehouse on the east side of town. Despite all the body armor he wore, a bullet hit a vulnerable spot, and he went down. Nobody could get to him for a while, and he bled out before John found him." The tears came despite all her efforts to control them.

Ben gathered her into his arms. "I'm sorry, Sunny. So, so sorry. That must have been hell for you."

"It was bad for me. Worse for him. They gave me a medal. I didn't want their damned medal."

He held her close while she cried for another man.

AFTER THE NEW PLASMA TV was finally delivered, hooked up and tested, Sunny was honestly too pooped to go look for a grill, and poor Jay was curled up asleep on the end of the couch.

They decided to table the trip to Home Depot. Ben took Jay home to bed, and Sunny tried out her new bathtub. It was heavenly, but when she found herself dozing, she got out before she drowned and had a glorious night's sleep in her big new four-poster.

Cass woke her at the crack of nine.

When Sunny mumbled "hello" into her cell phone, Cass said, "Don't tell me you're still asleep."

"Not now. Why are you calling so early?"

"Because I'm coming to see everything. Let me in."

"Where are you?"

"Walking up to your front door."

In about ten seconds, the chimes sounded. Sunny threw back the covers and trudged through the great room. The chimes rang again. "I'm coming, I'm coming," she yelled. Leo barked and trotted alongside her. She opened the door, barely glanced at Cass, then headed for the back door to let Leo out.

"I've brought doughnuts, and I'll make the coffee," Cass said. "You go wash your face while the coffee drips. Say, I love that painting of Mom's over there."

"I forgot I had it until I found it yesterday in some stuff," she said as she left the room. "Ben helped me hang it."

By the time Sunny threw on some clothes and quickly made her bed, Cass was pouring their coffee and putting out napkins on the breakfast table. The coffee was nectar from the gods. And the doughnuts were ambrosia.

"Want to go help me pick out a patio grill?" Sunny asked.

"It's at the very top of things I'm dying to do," Cass said, rolling her eyes.

"I get the message. I love the rugs and the other stuff you got."

"Thanks, and before you ask, I found the rugs at a super colossal sale price, and I got all the other stuff at an outlet store for almost nothing. Here's your credit card." Cass handed her the tickets, as well.

Sunny looked over the receipts and was pleasantly surprised. "You're a genius, sister dear."

"Naturally. Let's take a tour and see all the stuff you've added and what you still need. We can make a list, then drive down to San Marcos and go shopping."

San Marcos, a smaller town several miles south of Austin's city limits, was home not only to Sunny and Cass's alma mater, Texas State University, but also boasted a humongous complex of outlet stores.

"Great," Sunny said. "I need some new socks."

"Sweetie, socks are the least of what you need. Let's make a day of it."

SUNNY WAS LOOKING THROUGH some really sweet deals in the Pottery Barn Outlet when her cell rang.

"Still interested in shopping for the patio grill?" Ben asked.

"Sorry, but I'm in San Marcos with Cass. We've hit half the outlet stores in the place. I wish we had your SUV. I'm not sure how much more stuff we can cram in her car."

"Want me to drive down there?"

"Oh, no. We're wrapping up soon because of the space limitations and my attention span."

"Are you busy for dinner tonight?"

"I don't have any plans. Want to come by, and I'll broil a couple of steaks for us? I'd say grill, but I don't have the grill yet."

"Sounds good. I'll bring the steaks."

"I already have steaks. Just bring yourself about six-thirty. Does Jay like steak?"

"He does, but he's staying with Tracy and the girls tonight to watch a special on the Disney Channel."

Sunny's heart gave a little skip. She had a feeling that tonight might be the night.

"I take it that was Ben," Cass said when Sunny ended the call.

"Mmm."

"You going to get those pillows?"

Sunny tossed the pillows back on the shelf. "We've got enough stuff for now."

"And you're eager to get home and get ready for Ben."

"Does it show?"

Cass smiled. "Sweetie, you positively glow."

Sunny paid for the items she'd chosen, and they lugged the bags to where they were parked in the sea of vehicles. They even managed to find nooks and crannies in the backseat and trunk to stow everything.

Only problem was the car wouldn't start. Cass ground and ground. The blasted thing was deader than a doornail.

Cass muttered several colorful phrases, and Sunny muttered even more. Ben was going to be at her house in two and a half hours expecting to be fed.

Sunny heaved a huge sigh. "What are we going to do now?"

"The same thing I always do when I'm in this kind of mess. Act helpless." Cass fluffed her hair, got out of the car, opened the hood and stood peering at the motor and wringing her hands.

Not to be outdone, Sunny joined her, looking equally mystified. She figured they needed a jump and would have called security herself, but, hey, Cass's way might be quicker.

Sure enough, some kind soul with jumper cables came along in less than a minute with an offer to help. Thank God. Now she could make it home in time—not only for dinner but also for…any other developments later in the evening.

Problem was jumping the battery didn't help. Not the first try nor the second. An interested group began to gather. Another passerby tried his cables.

Nada.

Sunny was getting really nervous.

"Bet it's your alternator," said a bull-necked guy in a gimmie cap.

"What can we do about that?" Cass asked.

He suggested calling a wrecker and having it towed to a nearby car dealership service center. Sounded like a reasonable plan. And it worked well until they arrived at their destination in the wrecker, Cass's car in tow. Seemed that the dealership was open to sell cars, but the service center was closed on Sundays.

Rats!

A salesman there was very nice, and helped them locate a local rental company that was open and had a full-size car available—not easy on a Sunday afternoon. The whole process, which ended in renting a car and unloading and reloading all their purchases, took time. A lot of time.

It was after six when they finally got on the road home. But the problem was they were at least forty-five minutes from their destination. She called Ben and told him their dilemma.

"Don't worry about it," he said. "I'll meet you at your place and help you unload. We can go out and eat or order a pizza for that matter."

Double rats! She'd planned to take a relaxing bubble bath and dress in something sexy, then fix a lovely dinner with wine…and maybe candlelight. So much for her plans.

"Poor Leo has been inside all day," she said to Cass. "I need to install a doggie door for him. Why haven't I thought of that sooner?"

"A doggie door? Leo's huge. Aren't you afraid a burglar can get in the house? Or a raccoon or a coyote? How would you like to come home and find your silver stolen or the house trashed?"

"In the first place, sister dear, it would take a very small burglar to get in a doggie door, even one in Leo's size, but you're right about the critters. They have electronic gizmos now that you can attach to your pet's collar to unlock the door when the pet approaches and lock it behind him after he goes through. That way Sadie stays in and other animals, including two-legged ones, stay out."

"Amazing," Cass said.

"Yep. Live and learn."

Traffic seemed to crawl, and when they finally arrived home, Sunny was a frazzled mess. Bless his dear heart, Ben sat in his SUV waiting for them.

He smiled when he got out. "Buy the stores out?" he called as he walked across the yard.

"Almost. Sorry we're so late."

"One of those things," he said. "How are you, Cass?"

"Doing fine. I'm glad you're around to help us tote this stuff inside."

The three of them carried all the purchases into the guest room and dumped them, then Sunny let Leo out into the backyard.

"I'm off, you guys," Cass said, fluttering her fingers. "I'm going to go home and soak my tootsies."

When she left, Ben said, "You need to soak your tootsies, too?"

"I need to soak more than my feet. I'd planned to take a nice long bubble bath before I fixed us a lovely dinner. So much for plans. I must look a sight."

He smiled and locked his arms around her waist. "You look fine. More than fine. You look beautiful. You always look beautiful."

"Do I really?"

"Are you fishing?"

"Shamelessly."

He grinned. "Yes, you always do. You're a beautiful woman, Sunny Outlaw Payton, both inside and out, and I'm a lucky man to be with you."

Electricity seemed to crackle and hiss between them as his eyes caressed her face. She had no idea about any long-term relationship with Ben, but she didn't want to think about that now. She only wanted to savor tonight. She wanted to feel the warmth and comfort and passion of a man again. Of Ben.

She would have jumped his bones right then except she felt so grungy, and he smelled so much better. Ben must have read her mind because he said, "Tell you what, why don't you go take that bubble bath, and let me worry about our dinner."

"Are you serious?"

"I'm very serious. And take your time." He rubbed the tip of her nose with his. "I'll be here when you get back."

"Help yourself to some munchies from the kitchen. Anything you find is fair game."

He gave her a quick kiss and let her go.

Sunny felt guilty, but only a little. She needed a nice soak and some aromatherapy to dissipate the stress of their car ordeal and refocus on Ben.

She wanted tonight to be perfect.

THE SCENTED BATH DID the trick. Stress melted away as she lolled in the water and let the jets pulsate against her tight muscles. By the time she stepped out and dried off, she was feeling very mellow. She slipped into lacy lingerie, silky black pants and a frothy top of the palest butter yellow. After she applied her makeup and brushed her hair, she touched perfume to her wrists and behind her ears and stepped into soft black flats.

To heck with dinner. She was hungry for something else. It had been too long. Much too long. Yearning unfurled deep inside, and her skin tingled in anticipation. *Hold on to your hat, Ben McKee,* she thought as she walked from her bedroom. Tonight was definitely the night. Her libido was straining at the reins, and she planned to finally let it run wild.

Chapter Seventeen

A lovely smell drifted from the kitchen, and Sunny's stomach responded. Maybe dinner first would be a good idea. She hadn't eaten anything since doughnuts and coffee that morning. She and Cass had been so busy shopping they hadn't stopped for lunch—only a Coke and a bag of chips.

The first thing she noticed was that the TV was on but turned to a music station with soft mood music and a candle on the coffee table was lit.

"Something smells really good in here," she said as she walked in the kitchen. Another candle burned on the breakfast table.

"Your timing is perfect. The steaks are almost done."

"Steaks? You cooked?"

"I did. The potatoes are in the microwave, the salad's in the refrigerator and the steaks are in the broiler. If you'll set the table, we'll be ready to eat."

"Ben McKee, you're a wonder among men. You can actually cook."

He grinned. "My mama said every man needs to learn to cook and sew on buttons. I'm not bad in the kitchen. How do you like your steak?"

"Medium."

"I guessed that. Better hurry with the table setting."

She hurried, and soon they were cutting into perfectly cooked steaks. He'd even picked out a wine from among those she'd bought, a nice red to complement their meal.

"Fantastic!" she said as she savored her first bite. "My compliments to the chef."

"Thanks, darlin', but there's not much to baking potatoes and broiling a steak. Just about any fool can do that. Sometime I'll make you a meat loaf. I make a mean meat loaf."

She laughed and held up her wineglass. "Here's to a mean meat loaf."

He clicked his glass against hers and sipped from it, as did she.

"I've been meaning to ask if you're a semiteetotaler," she said. "I've rarely seen you drink anything alcoholic."

"I'm not much of a drinker these days, and I don't like to drink around Jay at all. His mother— Well, I just don't."

"She had a problem?"

He nodded. "Still does as far as I know. A bad one."

"I'm sorry."

"Me, too. What all did you get on your shopping trip?"

Recognizing his deliberate change of subject, she briefly recounted their excursion to San Marcos, making it into a funny story.

When they finished dinner, she said, "I'm sorry I don't have any dessert. I did get some fudge on our shopping trip. There's a place there that makes the very best in the world. I kid you not, it's to die for."

"Fudge is one of my favorite things," he said.

She went to find the bag among the booty in the guest room, and when she returned she found that Ben had cleared the meal and loaded the dishwasher. Their wineglasses were sitting on the coffee table.

"You're a nice guy to have around."

"Hold that thought. Think it's cool enough for a fire tonight?"

"It's about sixty or so. That should qualify. I don't even know how the fireplace works."

"I'm pretty good at starting fires," Ben said, walking over to the mantel.

Sunny bit her tongue to keep from blurting out, "You can say that again, babe."

He picked up a gizmo from atop the mantel and punched a button. A bright fire sprang to life.

"How did you do that?"

He flexed his muscles. "Fire starter," he said in a phony bass.

She laughed. "A remote control, I presume."

He winked. "We used to have one just like it." He adjusted the flame until the gas logs settled to a warm glow with a gentle lick of flames.

"We?" she asked, sinking into the couch in front of the hearth.

He hesitated a moment. "My mom and dad."

"Ah. Are your parents still living?"

He sat down beside her. "My mother died several years ago, but my dad is still going strong. He retired a couple of years ago and moved from the panhandle to the valley. Said the weather was better for his arthritis. And he has a brother there. He grows grapefruit and oranges in his backyard now and has a big time playing forty-two at the Harlingen Senior Center. Say, did you find the fudge?"

"I did." She held up the sack. "Do you like pecans in yours?"

"Darlin', I like it any way I can get it."

She stifled a snort. Was everything he said a double entendre, or was it just her mind on one track?

He chuckled as if he'd read her mind—and as if his mind was on the same track. She broke off a piece of the rich chocolate confection and held it to his lips. "Prepare yourself for an unbelievable sensation."

He took a deep breath. "I'm prepared…in every way." He nibbled the piece from her hand. "Umm."

She sat mesmerized by his mouth, watched his Adam's apple as he swallowed.

"Don't you want some?" he asked.

"I do," she whispered, her eyes still on his lips. She leaned closer to him, drawn by a powerful force aching inside her.

"Tell me what you want."

"I want you to kiss me."

"I can do that." He pulled her into his lap and kissed her eyelids, her cheeks, her nose, and he nibbled and teased her lips with his tongue.

Her insides turned over, and her breasts swelled. She strained to get closer to him and growled to have the mouth she craved. When he kissed her fully, she sighed and gave in to the lovely sensation of his mouth on hers. Gentle at first, the kiss became deeper, more urgent. Their tongues touched and probed. Her arms tightened around him.

His hand stroked the length of her body, his touch warm, hot, scorching.

"Oh, Ben," she murmured.

"Yes, darlin'?"

"I love it when you touch me."

He brushed her lips with his. "I love touching you."

He cupped her breast, and his thumb circled the nipple made hard by her desire. His tongue thrust as his mouth tried to consume her with his own brand of fire. Yearning for more, she ground herself against him.

"Oh, Ben," she moaned.

"Tell me what you want, love."

She whispered in his ear, and he went wild, stripping off her blouse and bra and burying his face against her breasts. He flicked her nipple with his tongue, then he stopped abruptly.

Sunny tried to pull his mouth back to the delicious sensation, but he moved her from his lap. "What's wrong?" she asked.

"Nothing's wrong. Not a single thing, but let's take this to that big bed of yours. I'm going to need lots of room."

She laughed, and they both hurried to the bedroom, strewing clothes along the way.

Ben was a magnificent lover, demanding yet considerate, taking what he wanted and giving her anything she desired. There wasn't a place he didn't touch or kiss or murmur against until he came to know her body better than she did. When she was so aroused she didn't think she could stand another second, he took her to new levels until she was begging for release.

At last, he rolled on a condom and slipped into her, his entry eased by her heat and wetness. As soon as he was inside her, she felt her release coming and stiffened. Sucking in a gasp, she whispered, "Ohhhhh, no," and sensation broke over her in rolling waves that went on and on.

Ben held her until the throbbing stopped. "You okay?"

She nodded. "Sorry."

"Nothing to be sorry about. I'm right behind you." Two thrusts, and she felt his shudder. His back bowed, and he let out a long, deep groan. After a moment, his tension eased, and he rolled over and took his weight off her.

She laid her face against his chest and listened to his heartbeat. He stroked her back with his fingertips. "I wanted it to last longer," she said.

"We just took the edge off," Ben said. "Next time it will."

And it did. Much, much longer.

SOMETIME IN THE MIDDLE of the night, Sunny woke up in Ben's arms and remembered she'd left Leo outside. She eased out of bed, grabbed Ben's shirt to put on and hurried to the back door. Some proper pet owner she was, she thought, irritated by her behavior.

Whistling softly and calling, "Leo," she waited at the door, peering into the darkness. Leo crawled out of the doghouse and loped to her. She could swear he was grinning again. "Sorry, boy." She gave him an extra pat and rub.

Like the good-mannered dog he was, Leo didn't even sulk. He wisely strolled over to the fireplace and curled up in front.

Strong arms encircled her from behind. "Where'd you go?" Ben asked. "I missed you."

"I forgot to let Leo back in."

"I'm sure he didn't mind." He kissed the nape of her neck and led her back to the bedroom.

Ben left a half hour later. "Tomorrow's a workday, and you need some sleep," he'd told her when he kissed her forehead and left her drowsy and sated.

She had lovely dreams.

"HOLY HELL," BEN SAID AS HE stood in the shower the next morning. Making love with Sunny was beyond his wildest dreams. He'd never had anybody who'd turned him on and tied him up the way she did. And sometime during their night together, he'd realized she'd become a lot more than just a ticket to a casual lay. Not five minutes in a day went by that thoughts of her didn't pop into his head. He would be able to recognize the smell of her if he were blindfolded in a ballroom full of women.

Sometime while he was prepping her to crawl in her bed, she'd crawled into his heart. His and Jay's. Jay couldn't stop talking about her. What had happened to the "friends with benefits" idea the kids were always talking about these days? Furthermore, what was he going to do about his feelings for her? Back off a notch? Let it play out and see where things led?

On his way to work, he was still mulling over his dilemma when his lawyer called. The conversation was short, but his blood pressure must have gone off the charts. A court appearance was scheduled in Dallas on Friday. Marla and the shyster she'd hired must have really pulled some strings. He didn't really think she stood a chance in hell of getting custody of Jay, but still he got chills just entertaining the possibility.

At least the lawyer's news had pushed his worries about Sunny onto the back burner. He was more worried about getting in touch with the private detective he'd hired to dig up dirt on Marla. It made him sick to think she might get her hands on Jay—even for a few hours now and then. He wondered again what her game was. He might have suspected she was after money, except he didn't have any. What was she after?

On Monday night after Chili Witches was closed, Sunny let the last of the employees out the back and watched them safely to their cars. Then she locked up and went upstairs to collect Leo. There had been a forty percent chance of rain, and she hadn't wanted to leave him in the backyard, even with the doghouse, so she'd brought him to work with her. She'd taken him out for a walk between the spell of drizzle just after lunch and the dinner hour. He'd seemed content to stay in her old apartment and watch the home improvement channel.

Maybe he would learn to build a doggie door. She chuckled at the idea as she opened the apartment.

Leo met her, tail wagging and obviously glad to see her. "Hello, boy. Miss me?"

"Not too much, he didn't. We've been keeping each other company."

The Senator smiled from where he sat on the couch.

"I've been wondering where you go between visits," Sunny said. "All this time you've been watching TV."

The Senator chuckled. "Not usually. I merely dropped by to see how things were going between you and your young man."

"*My* young man? And which one would that be?"

"Why, the Ranger, of course. I like the cut of him."

Sunny noticed Leo glancing toward the couch when the Senator spoke. "Can he see and hear you?"

"The Ranger?"

"No," she said. "The dog."

"Animals are more sensitive than humans about such things, you know," the Senator said. "He's a fine dog."

"Yes, he is, and we'd better be going home. Want to ride with us?" she asked, half joking.

"Thank you for the invitation, but I'd better hang around here and see after Cassidy."

"Do you think she's in danger here alone?"

"No, no. She'll be fine. I'll see to it. Good night, dear."

As she and Leo drove home, her thoughts strayed to Ben. She'd been surprised not to hear from him that day, but he hadn't dropped by for lunch nor had he phoned. Was there a problem?

Chapter Eighteen

By Tuesday afternoon, Sunny still hadn't heard from Ben, and she was beginning to feel deserted—the old "Wham-Bam, Thank-You-Ma'am" routine. Or was that simply her insecurity talking? If she wanted to talk with Ben, no reason why she couldn't instigate a call. No reason at all.

Yet she found herself reluctant to pick up the phone.

Don't be such a wuss! she told herself. Snatching the phone, she quickly punched in his number.

Caller ID must have given her away because Ben answered with, "Hello, darlin'. I was just thinking about you."

"Something good I hope."

"Something terrific. I was going to see if you were going to be working this Saturday night."

"Yes, I am. Sorry."

"No way to get out of it?" he asked.

"Not really. What did you have in mind?"

He chuckled. "I hadn't gotten that far yet. I have to go out of town Thursday for a couple of days, and I'm covered up with work here so I can leave. How about Sunday?"

"Sunday's good. Give me a call when you get back, and we'll plan something."

When they hung up, Sunny felt there was something wrong. Oh, Ben was polite and said all the right words, but he seemed…distracted. Maybe he was just focusing on one of his cases.

After she got a drink of water, she grabbed her screwdriver and the directions and went back to work on the doggie door.

DRIVING BACK FROM DALLAS on Saturday morning, Ben felt totally wrung out. He'd been through the week from hell—after months of hell—but he hoped the worst of it was finally over. All he wanted to do was go home and hug his boy and get his head back together. And see Sunny. Thoughts of her had helped keep him going.

Thank God for his attorney and for the private detective he'd hired. Turned out they were both worth every penny he'd paid them. Marla had sued for custody of Jay, claiming she'd been rehabilitated, had seen the light and wanted to claim her parental rights again. She'd joined A.A., had a good job and was able to take care of her son. She'd shown up in court looking like a librarian in a buttoned-up shirtwaist dress and very subdued makeup, which was totally out of character for her. Usually she favored dresses that barely covered her ass, were cut down to her navel and looked painted onto her body. Her makeup always looked as if she'd troweled it on. Why he had ever been attracted to her eluded him. Well, maybe that wasn't exactly true. She oozed raw sex appeal, and the part of him without any brains went panting after her. If she hadn't gotten pregnant, he never would have married her. But he had, and he'd tried to make the best of it.

As it turned out, Marla didn't have a chance. His P.I. had filmed her knocking back booze in at least six different joints—three in Dallas, two in Fort Worth and one in Arlington. In one she was so drunk, she was literally dancing on a table and stripping until a bouncer intervened. The P.I. had sworn statements from bartenders, bouncers and various patrons that painted an ugly picture of her drunken behavior. There were also photos of her going home with various men and a particularly disturbing one of her snorting something in a dark corner. All this was in the past two months.

She'd had a screaming, cursing meltdown in court after the damning evidence was shown and put the final nail in her coffin.

She hadn't changed.

A shame for Jay that his mother was the way she was.

Determined to put the whole thing out of his mind, Ben focused on more pleasant things. And, as always, Sunny's smile popped into his thoughts. He'd missed her.

When he stopped to get gas and a Coke, he called her.

"Well, hello, stranger," she said. "How are you?"

He could hear the smile in her voice, and he ached to see her.

"Right as rain. I'm on my way home from Dallas. I sure would like to see you tonight. You haven't had a cancelation, have you?"

"No, sorry. We're still playing tonight at the Fiery Pit. We'll have to make it tomorrow."

"How about brunch?"

"Sounds good," she said. "What time?"

They settled on eleven, and Ben hit the road again. Tempting as it was to drive straight to Sunny's, he needed to see Jay and spend time with his son. Jay hadn't stayed more than one night away from Ben since he and Marla had split. Jay loved his aunt and cousins and always enjoyed his time with them, but Ben was his anchor. Jay had to come first.

Things would be simple if Ben and Sunny could move in together. Jay would love it. He was crazy about Sunny and being able to play with Leo all the time would be icing on the cake. Unfortunately, that wasn't an option. Wouldn't Marla love to catch him in that sort of arrangement? She'd have him back in court in a flash.

No, living together wouldn't work.

Unless they got married.

No, he wasn't ready to jump into that lake of fire again.

Still, it might be something to think about some more. Jay did need a mother.

"DADDY!" JAY SAID. "Don't squeeze me so tight."

"Sorry, buddy. I missed you. Ready to go home? I thought I might drop off my stuff and we can go play miniature golf or something. Maybe we can get a hot dog for lunch."

"Can April and Lexi come? And Aunt Tracy and Uncle Rick?"

"Sure, if they'd like to."

Tracy laughed. "I think Rick and I will pass."

Ben winked at her over Jay's head. "Maybe another time."

"Maybe Sunny could go with us, too," Jay said. "And Leo."

"I'm pretty sure Leo doesn't play miniature golf," Ben said.

"But Sunny does," Jay said.

"Is she the chili lady?" Lexi asked, looking up from her coloring book.

"I like her. She's nice."

"Ask her, ask her," Jay said, jumping up and down.

Ben didn't need much prodding to call Sunny and make the invitation.

Problem was, she was on her way out the door for an early lunch and a movie with a friend named Suzi.

"Have I met her?" Ben asked.

"I don't think so. You might have met her husband, Steve."

"Steve? Big muscled-up guy?"

"Yes, we were on the force together. He was my mentor when I was fresh out of the academy."

"Well, have fun." After they hung up, he told Jay that Sunny couldn't make it, and Jay's mouth turned down. Ben ruffled his son's hair, knowing exactly how he felt.

He loaded all the kids into the safety seats and took off to the fast-food place Jay declared had the best hot dogs. "Their French fries are very good, too," April assured him.

Ben wisely tucked about a dozen napkins into the necks of their clothes and kept the smears down to a minimum.

Later, miniature golf with those three was a challenge. Balls were going all over the place, and he finally gave up on keeping an accurate score. Scores aside, the kids had a fantastic time, but by the time he delivered the girls back home, he was about out of gas.

"You look exhausted," Tracy said.

"Did the bags under my eyes give me away?" Ben asked.

"No, it was your knuckles dragging the floor." His sister kissed his cheek. "I know you've been stressed out."

Ben had called the night before and had given Tracy and Rick a recap of the court events. He nodded.

"Why don't you go home, put your feet up and relax?" Rick said. "Let Jay spend another night with us. I promised the girls we would camp out in the backyard. The tent's big enough for an extra sleeping bag."

"Oh, Dad, could I please? That would be so cool!"

"We're going to tell ghost stories," Lexi said.

"Not me," April said. "I'm going to listen to my iPod."

"Scaredy-cat," Lexi said.

"I prefer music to silly stories," April said. "I'm going to take a flashlight with me, too."

"We're all going to take flashlights," Rick said. "Let him stay."

Ben glanced at Jay, whose eyes pleaded to stay for the big adventure.

"Okay. I'll pick you up in the morning."

"Yipppeee!" Jay grabbed Ben around the legs. "Thanks, Dad."

His sister walked him to the door, her arm around his waist. "I'm so glad everything turned out well in court. I know you've been worried."

"I've tried to stay positive and not think about it much, but I tell you the past few days have been hard on me. I'm whipped, and I have a hell of a headache."

"I know. I can see the frown lines. Go home, take a couple of aspirin and relax."

"Sounds like a fine idea," he said as he left.

When he arrived at his apartment, he unloaded his bag and unpacked. Stripped down to his shorts and T-shirt, he washed down a couple of aspirin with a swallow of Coke before he reared back in his recliner and flipped on the remote control.

That was the last thing he remembered until he woke up at nine o'clock. Was it night or morning? Disoriented for a moment, he glanced around, noting it was dark. His headache was gone. He got up and took a shower to get rid of the muzzy feeling he always had after a nap. As he was toweling off, he thought about Sunny. Her little band was probably playing by now. Where had she said they were going to be?

The Fiery Pit, that was it. Sounded like a barbecue place. Wonder how long they played? Maybe if he hurried he could catch part of their performance and grab a late supper.

SUNNY HIT THE CYMBALS in a final crash and half her drumstick went flying. The Pit was really rockin' that night, even more so than usual. It was the wildest spot of all the gigs they played—and not her favorite. The crowds sometimes got a bit too rambunctious, and only knowing the Pistols were a bunch of cops kept the patrons from getting downright unruly. A friend of John's was one of the owners, and they paid very well, so they put up with the mob scene a few times a year.

Red, orange and yellow lights flickered like flames against glittery streamers and flashed along the gray-and-black walls which were plastered to look like a rocky cave. You could barely see your hand in front of your face. The dance floor was minuscule, the joint was packed, and the place was stifling hot. It lived up to its name. She wiped sweat off her face with a towel she kept handy and gladly took the drink the waitress handed her. It was her usual Diet Sprite with a splash of grenadine and a lime twist, and she downed half of it in one gulp.

"Thanks, Monica," she yelled over the crowd. "Keep 'em coming."

"You got it!" Monica yelled back.

They wouldn't be playing any ballads tonight, and they would earn every penny of their pay. She grabbed fresh drumsticks and clicked them together. "One, two. One, two, three!"

BEN FINALLY FOUND A PARKING place three blocks from the address he'd found on the Internet. He could hear the throb of music as he got out of the car and walked. The Fiery Pit was on Sixth Street in the area of downtown known for its bars and music and partying. It rivaled the old Bourbon Street in New Orleans and boasted some of the best live music in the country. Or so they said. Tourists, university students and other locals flocked to what used to be named Pecan Street in the old days. He'd never visited the area at night himself, but it appeared to be well patrolled.

He began to get a funny feeling about the Fiery Pit as he got closer and doubted it was a barbecue joint. The only supper he was likely to get would be from one of the pushcarts he saw here and there along the street.

Sure enough, he arrived at a windowless black storefront with neon flames flashing around the door and a sizzling sign proclaiming the Fiery Pit. He opened the door, and the noise damn near knocked him down. The people were loud and the band was louder.

He pushed his way to the bar where he could see the stage. Between the writhing bodies on the dance floor, he caught a glimpse of Sunny beating hell out of a big set of drums.

"Well, I'll be damned," he muttered to himself, not quite believing what he saw.

"What'll it be, cowboy?" the bartender yelled.

"Beer."

"What brand?"

Ben named the first one that came to mind and slapped money on the bar when it was delivered. He didn't even pick up the bottle; he stared, dumbfounded, at the Copper Pistols and their drummer. He recognized John and Hank, but he didn't know the keyboard player or the singer who was belting out a song he'd never heard.

Two women hit on him before he took his first swallow of beer. This was Marla's kind of place, not his. Half the people in there were drunker than Cooter Brown. Now, he didn't mind folks cutting up and having a good time, but this was ridiculous. After the round he'd just been through with Marla, being in a dive like this and seeing Sunny working here didn't sit well with him.

He'd made the assumption that Sunny and her friends, who were police officers for God's sake, probably played at local restaurants like the bands he saw everywhere in Austin. There were as many bands in this town as there were panhandlers or grackles—and that was saying something.

But this place didn't fit the Sunny he thought he knew.

His eyebrows went up when he watched Sunny beating a

drum with one hand and swigging down a drink with another. Of course it could be water for all he knew. That notion was shot down when he heard a waitress yell, "Give me another Sunny's Special!"

He turned around as the bartender mixed something from a dispenser and a bottle, then added lime peel. It didn't look like water. He watched the waitress deliver it to Sunny's side and take away an empty glass.

After half an hour of being assaulted by the god-awful racket and watching Sunny knocking back drinks like a lush, Ben's headache was back worse than before. He'd had all this crap he could take. Feeling somewhere between ticked off and heart-sick, he left his warm beer on the bar and left.

Chapter Nineteen

Sunny was exhausted when they finished playing the Fiery Pit. "I must be getting old," she told John and Hank as they helped her load her drums in the trailer. "Gigs like this one wear me out."

"Ain't it the truth?" Hank said. "If it were up to me, we wouldn't play this joint again. I'm looking for less stress, not more."

"Just say the word," John said, "and we'll cross them off our list."

"I thought you were friends with one of the owners," Hank said.

"We went to school together. We're not best pals. Won't bother me to cancel our schedule at the Pit, especially not with the number of bands in Austin. There'll be a dozen lined up begging for the spot."

"You can say that again." Hank loaded the last of Sunny's equipment and closed the trailer door. "Mike and I were talking the other day about cutting back some more, maybe just playing a couple of times a month. What do y'all think of the idea?"

John glanced at Sunny as if waiting for her to speak first.

"I'm cool with it," she said, "if that's what everybody wants to do. How does Trish feel about it?"

"I got the idea she and Mike had already talked it over," Hank said. "I think they'd like the extra time off—at least for a while, maybe until after the first of the year. Things are be-ginning to get hectic with the holidays coming up. Give us a breather."

"It's okay with me," John said. "I'll talk to everybody this week, and see what I can work out. Any preferences about which gigs to cut and which to keep?"

"I'll go along with the majority," Sunny said. "My only request is cutting the Fiery Pit. I have a monster headache from that room, and I'd just as soon not have to set foot in it again."

"I hear that," Hank said. "Night, babe."

"Good night, guys," Sunny said. "Or rather, good morning. Thanks for the help."

They waited on the curb until she got into her car and pulled away. The guys looked as worn-out as she felt. It was true what Hank had said about the stress. The band was supposed to relieve the tension of the job, not add to it. Playing together used to be more fun. Sometimes it was beginning to feel like a grind. Still, she loved these people, and the idea of not getting together with them to play made her heart hurt.

She was just tired. More than tired. She felt as though she'd been yanked through a knothole backward, and she didn't even go by the rental unit to leave the trailer. All she could think of was getting something to relieve her headache. Driving straight home, she parked the trailer in one side of the garage. It fit fine and leaving it there was certainly more convenient. Another plus for buying the house.

Inside she found Leo waiting for her at the back door. It was good to have someone waiting—even if it was a dog.

A bigger surprise was to see Sadie sound asleep on the rug in front of the hearth. Leo followed Sunny into the den, then curled up beside the cat.

"Amazing," she whispered. "Things are really changing."

WHEN THE PHONE RANG the next morning, Sunny had to fight her way out of a sound, dead-to-the-world sleep.

"'Lo," she croaked, not opening her eyes.

"Did I wake you?" Ben asked.

Her first reaction was to say, "No, I've been up for hours," but why lie when somebody had deliberately interrupted your sleep? Instead of saying the latter, she took a more neutral approach. "What time is it?"

"Ten-thirty."

She popped straight up in bed. "Ten-thirty!" Ben was supposed to be here in a half hour, and she still had to shower, wash her hair and dress. She'd been too tired the night before to do more than take a couple of Tylenol and fall into bed in only her panties.

"You sound like you might have the mother of all hangovers," Ben said.

"Me? No. Just a hard night."

"Rough night at the Fiery Pit?"

Was it her imagination or was there an edge to his words? "Yes. Listen, Ben, I'm sorry I overslept. I guess I forgot to set my alarm. Could we change our time for brunch and make it lunch?"

"That's what I was calling about. Jay has been talking about the restaurant with the ducks since you mentioned it, and he's been begging to go there for lunch. Is that okay with you?"

"Sure." She'd assumed she and Ben were going to be alone, but she understood he had a child and needed to spend time with his son. "Give me an hour or so to get dressed."

"I'll give you two. Take your time and have a cup of coffee. The caffeine will help."

There was that tone again. What was wrong with him?

She staggered to the kitchen and made coffee. While it dripped, she tended to the animals who seemed to be happy as best buds. Sadie sat on her window ledge and watched Leo running around in the backyard. "Sadie, dear, I guess all it took was a good man."

GOD MIGHT GET HIM FOR LYING, Ben thought, but he was still stung about last night. He wouldn't have believed Sunny was the type. Watching her at that dive on Sixth Street had knocked the props from under him. Sunny had been tossing back those "Specials" at a pretty good clip, and he'd watched men ogling her as she played those drums in nothing but a damp white tank top and shorts. She'd looked sexy as hell with her hair pinned up and long sweaty strands plastered to her face and neck. How could they not ogle?

He tried a dozen times to make excuses for her, tell himself things might not be as they appeared, but it didn't work. He'd seen her with his own eyes. No way could he take a chance on getting in any deeper. That was why he'd used Jay as an excuse not to be alone with her. True, Jay had wanted to go to the place with the ducks, but he hadn't mentioned it in a while. And, in fact, all he could talk about this morning was camping out with Rick and the girls. Make that girl. April had gone inside about midnight, but Jay and Lexi had stayed with it.

Jay would probably talk Sunny's ear off about his adventure, and Ben wouldn't have to say much. He had to decide if he even wanted to see Sunny again. One thing for sure: she wasn't mother material.

SUNNY FELT PRETTY MUCH HUMAN again a couple of hours later. When she answered the door, a grinning Jay flung himself at her, hugging her legs.

"Hi, Sunny! How's Leo?"

"Hi, yourself, pardner. Leo's fine. I think he might be in the backyard."

"I'm gonna go see." He started to take off for the back, but Ben grabbed his shirt.

"Whoa, buddy. Let's go eat first while you're still reasonably clean."

"Can I play with him later?"

Ben hesitated, then said, "Sure." Barely glancing her way, Ben asked, "Ready?"

At least Jay seemed glad to see her; Ben, not so much. What in the world was wrong? Her first inclination was to simply ask him, but with Jay there, she hesitated to say anything. "I'm ready." She ruffled Jay's hair. "It's a perfect day to feed the ducks."

Jay skipped and hopped alongside her as they walked to the SUV. "Guess what I did last night?"

"You rode on a spaceship."

"No," Jay said, laughing. "I camped out with Uncle Rick and Lexi."

"You did? What fun! What about April?"

"She just stayed a while and went inside. She said stuff was itching her. Itchy stuff didn't bother me." He began a blow-by-blow description of the adventure as they drove.

Sunny interrupted only long enough to ask Ben if he needed directions.

"No, I know where I'm going."

Thank heavens for Jay, since he seemed to be the only one interested in talking to her. Something was definitely bothering Ben, but she didn't have a clue as to what it was—nor did he seem interested in explaining. If Jay hadn't been there, she would have demanded an explanation. As it was, she could only bide her time before confronting him. She'd never believed in letting things fester. So she and Jay talked, and Ben and the GPS device conversed until they arrived at the County Line.

The smoky barbecue smell filled the air as they got out and walked to the lodgelike building on Bull Creek.

"Where are the ducks?" Jay asked.

"In the creek behind the building," Sunny told him. "We can watch them while we eat. Feeding them comes later."

They had to wait a few minutes for a table, and, as luck would have it, they were seated next to the bank of windows creekside.

"By the way," Sunny said, leaning across the table toward Ben, "I have a coupon for half off our meal."

"I can afford to pay for it," he said brusquely.

She bit her tongue again to keep from laying into him or dumping a glass of water over his head.

"Do you like ribs?" she asked Jay. "They're great here. Messy, but great."

Everybody had ribs. Good thing there were plenty of napkins and a roll of paper toweling at every table, because there was no way to eat barbecue ribs neatly. Sunny also was sure to order extra bread to bag for the ducks.

When they were finished, they went out onto the back deck, then down the steps to the creek where several ducks paddled. Sunny showed Jay how to break off pieces and toss them. He scampered along the bank, throwing hunks of bread and laughing as the ducks gobbled them down.

Ben stood aside watching.

Sunny walked up to him. "Ben, what's wrong?"

"Not a thing."

"Then why are you acting as if you have a burr up your butt?"

"It's been a rough week."

He didn't offer any more explanation, which irritated her to no end. "We all have rough weeks now and then," she said.

"What happened? Did it have something to do with your out-of-town trip?"

"Yes."

"Dammit, Ben, talk to me. I'm struggling here."

He sighed. "My ex-wife was trying to get custody of Ben."

Her heart lurched. "And?"

"She didn't. Thank God. She's not fit to be a mother."

Sunny touched his arm. "Ben, I'm so sorry. That must have been terribly stressful. You've never told me much about your ex-wife."

"Not much to tell. She was a lush and a lousy mother. Still is. I didn't know she was leaving Jay alone at night to go out drinking and partying until a neighbor called Child Welfare to report her."

"How atrocious! Where were you?"

"Working."

Jay ran up just then. "Did you see? Did you see? They ate all the bread. Daddy, can I have a duck?"

Ben laughed for the first time since they'd picked her up. "No, you can't have a duck. But we'll come back again so you can visit these."

"I liked those ducks," Jay said. "And I saw a frog. I wish we lived by a creek."

Creeks and ducks and frogs were the main topic of conversation all the way home.

BEN ALMOST HATED TO GET to Sunny's house. He'd promised Jay he could play with the dog, which meant Sunny would corner him again. She was like a pit bull when she got hold of something. He'd learned that about her for sure. And he'd also learned she was big on honesty. So was he. Usually he was a plainspoken man.

Being around her again, he had to admit she wasn't much like Marla, if he hadn't seen it with his own eyes, he wouldn't have figured she was the type to hang out at places like the Fiery Pit, either. But he *had* seen her. It wasn't her twin. He ought to tell her about it, but, truth was, he was scared to. He was angry, and, deep down, afraid of how things might turn out. He wasn't ready to let go of her just yet—which pissed him off, too.

Sure enough, the minute Jay went running out in the yard to play with Leo, Sunny was at him again.

"Tell me," Sunny said simply.

"Tell you what?"

She rolled her eyes. "Is it something in the Y chromosome that prevents men from talking about things? You know what. You've just been through a serious event in your life that has affected you deeply. I'd like to think we're…close enough for you to discuss something like that." She led him over to the couch, and they sat down.

He didn't want to rehash things, but for some reason he laid his head back, and the whole mess came tumbling out of him. He told her about his fear of losing Jay and about the dirt the P.I. had dug up and the videos he'd seen. Everything.

She took his hand and kissed it. "Oh, Ben, I'm so sorry. Jay doesn't deserve that. *You* don't deserve that. It must have been like a sword over your head. Be glad it's over and you can move on."

Her words were so tender and sincere he wanted to take her into his arms, but he didn't. "I am glad. I think the woman is nuts. I know she's a lush who frequents dives like—" He caught himself.

"Like what?"

"Like the Fiery Pit." He debated with himself for a few seconds, then decided to get it all out. "I was there last night."

"Where? The Pit? You were there? I didn't see you. Why didn't you say something?"

"I didn't stay long. It's not my kind of place."

"Lord, I can believe that," she said, chuckling. "It's not my kind of place, either. I hate that joint. It's awful. We're not going to play there anymore."

"You're not?"

"No, definitely not. Playing in a crowded, overheated hellhole to a bunch of noisy, rowdy drunks isn't my idea of fun."

"You looked like you enjoyed beating the devil out of those drums."

She grinned. "I was taking out my frustrations and trying to be heard over the racket. Things have gotten much worse since we started there. I broke three drumsticks last night and ended up with a splitting headache. We decided after the gig to forget about the good money we make at The Pit and cross them off our list. We haven't played there much anyhow—maybe two or three times."

"Good." Ben felt considerably relieved. He didn't bring up her drinking right then. For all he knew, she could have been chugging pink lemonade. Best wait and make sure of his facts. Do a little more investigating before he decided what to do about Sunny. He needed time, a lot more time to make sure of not only his feelings for her but also what kind of person she was. "I don't like to see you in dives like that."

She stroked his cheek and smiled at him so sweetly he wanted to take her in his arms and kiss the dickens out of her. But he didn't. He ground his molars instead.

"I understand," she said. "And I appreciate your concern. Ben, you're a wonderful, considerate and caring man. You're also a terrific father." Her thumb brushed across his lips.

Right then he didn't feel like all those things. He felt like a horny bastard. He glanced out the window and saw Jay having a high time with the dog, so he forgot about all his reservations and kissed her.

Her lips were so soft and her mouth was so warm and she felt so good that he went rock-hard. He wanted to strip her naked and carry her off to bed.

"Oh, darlin'," he whispered. "You are sinfully addictive. Do you know how bad I want you?"

"I have some idea. I didn't think that was your belt buckle."

He laughed. "Woman, you are something else. I just wish I could figure you out."

"What's to figure? I'm not a complicated person."

He laughed again. It felt good to laugh.

Chapter Twenty

About six o'clock on Monday evening, Sunny saw a couple and two little girls enter Chili Witches. She recognized the children immediately: Ben's nieces, Lexi and April. And she would have probably figured out who the red-haired woman was as soon as she got a look at her beautiful eyes. Only once before had she seen eyes so green. Ben's. She was an attractive woman, and the blond man with her was no slouch.

"Hello, April and Lexi," she said to the children. "And you must be Tracy and Rick."

"In the flesh," Tracy said. "The girls have been begging to come back, and I've been eager to meet you. If you're Sunny."

"I am. Sunny Outlaw Payton." Smiling, she shook hands with Tracy and Rick. "Welcome to Chili Witches."

"She's the chili lady," Lexi said. "She makes the bestest chili in the world. And hamburgers, too. And she's not really a witch."

"Best chili," April said to her sister.

"That's what I said," Lexi told her.

"You said bestest," April said smugly.

"Well, it's very, very, very good. Daddy is going to have some just so he can see if it isn't true."

Rick grinned and bowed. "Rick Nolan, taste-tester."

"I hope we pass," Sunny said, seating them at a table near the window. "Menus are here on the table, and your waiter will be here in a moment to take your orders. As I tell my new customers, the mild chili is well spiced and tasty, the medium chili is hot, and the hottest one will sear the skin off your mouth. So beware."

"Remember I got a 'bestos mouth," Lexi said.

"I remember," Sunny said, winking. "What may I get you to drink?"

She took their drink orders, then sent Jeff over to be their waiter. He was her best and great with kids.

When she delivered the drinks, the girls remembered the code for the kids' cups. "White lids are for milk," April said.

"And a *W* on the red lids are for water," Lexi added. "Grown-ups can tell what is iced tea because you can see what's in the glass."

Rick nodded. "Excellent idea."

"I wish you could join us," Tracy said, "but I know it might be a bad time for you." She glanced to where people stood waiting at the door.

"I'll drop by from time to time. Jeff, your waiter, can help you with any questions. Our salad bar is quite good if you're not in the mood for chili."

"Bite your tongue," Lexi said. "My mother *loves* chili."

Sunny laughed out loud.

"Guess where she got that?" Rick asked.

Sunny grinned at Tracy. "I can't imagine." She left to greet two tables of customers waiting to be seated.

Occasionally she stopped by the Nolans' table to chat briefly. Tracy and Rick seemed like really nice people and great parents. When Sunny mentioned she'd gotten the dog Jay was so crazy about at the shelter where she volunteered, Tracy wanted to know more.

"I love animals," Tracy said, "and I'd enjoy helping out."

"You're welcome to come along with me in the morning, and I can show you the ropes."

"That would be great." Tracy gave her their address and directions. "Rick's flying off to Singapore or somewhere tomorrow."

"London, actually," he said, smiling as if he knew that she knew very well exactly where he was going.

"I'll pick you up at nine-thirty," Sunny said as they left. "Good night, everybody. Come again soon."

She stayed very busy the rest of the night. Closing time couldn't come soon enough. And when it did, she made her final rounds of the café and found the Senator sitting at his usual table, a coffee cup by his hand.

"Well, hello, Senator. How are you this evening?"

"I'm well, thank you. And you, my dear?"

"I'm tired. I'm not sure I've completely recovered from the band's last gig."

"Gig?"

"A performance date," she explained. "We played Saturday night at the Fiery Pit."

"Ah, a most disreputable venue."

"You can say that again. The place sucks."

He laughed. "I trust you're not going back there."

"You're right."

"How is your relationship with young Ben coming along?"

"I'm not sure it's to the 'relationship' stage," Sunny told him. "We enjoy each other's company I think. That's enough."

"I hear he's a bit conflicted right now," the Senator said.

"Conflicted? How?"

"I'm not quite clear on that part. But his mother told me he was conflicted, and mothers seem to know about these things."

Her eyebrows went up. "His mother? But Ben said she was dead."

The Senator smiled. "So I understand. She looks in on him fairly often. We happened upon one another recently. She's a lovely woman and quite approves of you. Alta says you're good for him."

"Alta?"

"Yes, I believe I understood her name to be Alta, though I could be mistaken. We're not as much into names here."

"Why does she think I'm good for him?" Sunny asked.

"We didn't get into specifics. I suspect it has to do with balance. Most every relationship does," he said. "Good night, dear."

He disappeared before she could question him further. She didn't have any idea what he was talking about, and now she couldn't ask, so she locked up and went home.

SUNNY COULDN'T BELIEVE Tracy lived only three blocks away from her. She was a couple of minutes early, so she waited in the car until their appointed time. She liked the house. Built of white Austin stone, it was two storied with dark green trim and a well-landscaped yard.

She was getting out of her car when the front door opened, and Tracy came out. "I'm sorry," Tracy said. "I didn't realize you were here."

"Just drove up and was admiring your house. Who does your yard?"

"We have a great landscape service. Rick used to, but it's not his thing, and he complained something awful. I like to putter with the flowers, but I'm not into pruning and mowing and fertilizing grass, either. I figured not learning how to start the lawn mower was a smart move."

Chuckling, Sunny said, "I hear that." When Tracy told her

what the service charged, she said, "Sounds like a bargain. Give me their number if you don't mind, and I'll have them out. Did you know I live only three blocks away from you?"

"Ben told me," Tracy said. "Isn't that amazing? Let me lock up, and we can get going."

When they were on their way, something popped into her head from her conversation with the Senator. She wanted to ask Tracy about it, but couldn't quite figure out how to bring it up. Maybe she could back into the subject some way.

"It's great that Ben could move near you," Sunny said. "It's good to have family to count on, especially when you're a single parent."

"We're happy to have him here. I'm glad to be of help with Jay, and he's great to have around, especially with Rick being away so much. I don't know diddley-doo about cars or anything mechanical, and Ben can do all that kind of stuff. Just last week he fixed the dishwasher—which was a lifesaver."

"He told me your mother died a few years ago and your father lives in the valley. Now what did he say their names were? Was it Alta and…?"

"Alta and Jim McKee."

Sunny felt the blood drain from her face. "Ah, yes," she managed to say. Their mother actually *was* named Alta. It wasn't the sort of name she would have forgotten if Ben had mentioned it to her. Sometimes she wondered if she imagined the Senator—the same way kids have imaginary playmates, but this was another example of his veracity. She had a dozen more questions she wanted to ask about Ben, but she didn't want to act as if she were pumping Tracy for the skinny on her brother.

Until they reached the shelter, they chatted about animals they had owned, past and present. Tracy hooted over Sadie stories, particularly her retributive hair balls around moving time.

"In your bra?" Tracy asked, laughing.

"I kid you not. I had to toss it and the shower curtain she shredded."

Once at the shelter, she introduced Tracy to Annabelle, who was happy to have another pair of hands to help out. They each received new dogs to exercise—female corgi mixes that were littermates and about six months old.

"Aren't they just precious?" Tracy said as she cuddled and petted her charge. "I can see the corgi in them. I believe the queen of England has corgis."

"Does she? I didn't know that."

They took the two pups for a romp along the trail to the field, giving them a long lead to chase bugs and puff balls from the weeds. A cool front had moved through the night before, leaving sweater weather and just enough nip in the air to make the dogs frisky.

"I think we ought to give them names," Tracy said. "Something British in honor of Queen Elizabeth."

"I'm not sure they'll stick, but I'm game. Any ideas?"

"I suppose Fergie and Di are out."

"They don't look like a Fergie or a Di to me," Sunny said.

"How about Emma and Jane from Austen's novels?"

"Which one is Emma?"

Tracy studied the pair for a moment. "Yours, I think. This one is definitely a Jane. My girls would love these dogs. We lost ours last spring. Fannie was eleven."

"I'm sorry. What kind of dog was she?"

"Mostly sheltie. Sweetest thing you ever met. We all miss her. Even Rick cried when she died."

"If you're serious, you'll have to fill out an application, but I'm sure there won't be any problem," Sunny told her. "The biggest difficulty might be having to housebreak them."

"Ugh. I'd forgotten that part, but I wouldn't mind. Do I need to take them home today? It would be better if I got the house ready and the girls prepared first. You know I believe it's providence that I came with you today."

"You believe in providence?" Sunny asked.

"I've learned to believe a lot of things," Tracy said. "I discount nothing. Rick tolerates me, and Ben thinks I may be a little wacky." She chuckled.

"Speaking of Ben, do you think he seems a little odd lately? Maybe…sort of…conflicted?"

A "ha!" burst from Tracy. "That's exactly what my mother says—said. Uh, what she used to say I mean. For when we were troubled. She'd say we were conflicted."

Why was Tracy acting so nervous all of a sudden? "Is he?"

"Is who what?"

"Is Ben conflicted about something?" Sunny asked. "I'm not trying to be nosy, but I'm concerned."

"Ben's not much of a talker about some stuff. Rick's the same way. I guess it's a man thing. I'm not sure how much he's told you about his previous marriage."

"He's told me a little," Sunny said. "I know about her trying to get custody of Jay. I know that's been stressful for him."

"Very. I assume the whole situation is what's been eating at him."

"Is she as bad as Ben paints her?"

"Worse," Tracy said. "She was a lush who went out partying with her drinking, drugging friends and left a three-and-a-half-year-old child alone while Ben was working nights. He woke up one night, sick and scared and alone. He went next door to the neighbor's house. They found him ringing the doorbell at one o'clock and crying."

"Oh, dear God." Sunny's breath left her at the thought of little Jay sick and terrified. "What if the house had caught on fire?"

"I know. And this wasn't a onetime thing. She'd been doing it several times a week for months. Ben tried to help her, begged her to go into rehabilitation for alcoholism and drug abuse. She refused, so Ben kicked her out and filed for divorce. It's a long, ugly story, one Ben doesn't like to discuss much. Like most men, he mostly grunts and cusses instead of talking about his feelings."

"I hear that. It was traumatic for him I know. And he probably wouldn't like us discussing his private business, either."

Tracy winced. "You're right. I won't tell if you won't."

"My lips are sealed."

"You're very good for him, you know," Tracy said. "I thought he'd pretty much sworn off women after his divorce. I've seen a new light in his eyes in these past few weeks."

"Don't make this more than it is, Tracy. We're just friends. I don't think either of us is looking for anything serious right now."

"If you say so." Tracy smiled and tossed a rubber bone for Jane to catch.

BEN CALLED THURSDAY MORNING about ten. She turned off the vacuum and answered.

"What are you doing?" he asked.

"Nothing exciting. Ridding the house of animal hair and dust."

"Say, I'm taking a long lunch hour today, and I wondered if you're free."

She felt the grin creep across her face. "I might be. What did you have in mind?"

"A quick bite somewhere and a trip to an indoor shooting range. I need some practice. Think you can beat me?"

Bile rose up in her throat so quickly she was afraid she might vomit. Her muscles tightened and she trembled. Taking several deep breaths, she closed her eyes, tried to relax and fight back the sour taste. "I hate being around guns."

"And how long were you a cop?" He sounded incredulous. "You're around guns all the time, Sunny. Cops are always in the café, and I'm almost always armed."

"I don't see holstered guns. I've learned to ignore them. But I can't stand to see weapons being fired, hear the noise, smell the gunpowder." Her voice grew more shrill as she spoke. "I can't. I can't," she screamed. "I have to go. I'm sick."

She ran to the bathroom and threw up.

Chapter Twenty-One

Ben knew immediately that something was wrong with Sunny, and it scared the crap out of him. He grabbed his hat and flew out of the office. Cursing the distance to her house, he drove as if his tail was on fire. He'd never heard her talk like that. He couldn't stand it if something serious had happened to her.

Despite all the doubts he'd had about her recently and no matter how much he'd tried to tell himself otherwise, it had only taken something like this to convince him that he cared about her. Really cared. Loved? He wasn't ready to go that far, but his feelings bordered on the edge of something mighty like love.

Oh, hell. He didn't even want to think about love, but there it was.

He'd called with an offer of a quick lunch and some target practice with the idea of a nooner filling up the rest of the time. Right now, sex was the furthest thing from his mind.

Getting to her place seemed to take forever, but, in fact, it only took about fifteen or twenty minutes at the speed he traveled. He bolted out of his SUV and up the walk. He rang the doorbell and began knocking and calling her name.

When she didn't answer right away, he was tempted to break

a window or bust down the door. He pushed the button over and over and kept banging.

"I'm coming, dammit!" he heard her yell.

She flung open the door and stood there staring at him, looking pale and a little green around the gills.

"Are you okay?" he asked, searching her face, then wrapping her in his arms.

"No, I'm not okay. I just vomited up my toenails." She pushed against him. "Let me go. I have to wash my face." She turned and left him standing in the open doorway.

Ben closed the door and strode after her to the master bathroom. When she looked up from where she splashed her face and caught his reflection in the mirror, she said, "This is embarrassing," and closed the door in his face.

He opened it again. "To hell with embarrassing. Are you sick? Do I need to call a doctor?"

She shook her head, grabbed a towel and buried her face in it. "Give me a minute."

He led her to the bed and sat down with her in his lap. "Take your time."

She took several deep shuddering breaths while he held her close. Her body still trembled. After a few minutes, she said, "I need to brush my teeth and get a drink of water."

"Okay."

"You have to let me up first."

Ben didn't want to move his arms from around her, but he let her go. "Need any help?"

She shook her head again, but she didn't look at him as she got up, walked into the bathroom and closed the door. This time he waited for her. When she came out a while later, her color was better. She had on fresh lipstick and smells like mint, watermelon and honeydew followed her out.

"Sorry about that."

"Nothing to be sorry about. Have you got some kind of bug?"

Sunny sighed. "No, I had a panic attack. Worst one I've had in a while."

Puzzled, he said, "What caused it?"

"Talking about going to the firing range. If you don't mind, I'd rather not discuss particulars right now. Since Brian died—"

"I get it. We don't have to talk about it. Can I get you something to eat or drink?"

Giving him a "you've got to be kidding look," she said, "Definitely not. No, I take that back. A Diet Sprite with lots of ice would be good."

"I'll get it for you." He headed for the kitchen.

"I can get it, thanks," she said from behind him.

After he waited for her to catch up, he walked beside her into the kitchen. "Let me do it."

"Ben, I'm okay now. Just a tiny bit queasy."

He lifted her onto the counter. "Humor me, darlin'. I like to feel useful." He fixed a glass for each of them and handed her one.

She took a sip, then closed her eyes and sighed. "That's good. Thanks." She took another sip. "You must think I'm nuts."

"Not at all." He didn't push for any sort of explanation. Leaning against the counter beside her, he sipped from his own glass.

"That's one reason I quit the force after Brian died. What good is a cop who freaks about guns?"

"Have you seen a psychologist or a counselor about it?"

Sunny nodded. "I went to a therapist for a long time. It helped a lot. At least I stopped going ballistic just looking at a gun. I'm not sure why I reacted like I did today. That was totally out of left field."

"You know, Sam was telling me that his wife, Skye, had a

serious mess of phobias for a long time. Seems a hypnotist here in Austin cured her. You might talk to Skye about it."

"I might do that." Something in her tone of voice made him think it would be a cold day in hell before that happened.

"You look a lot better. How about I fix you a grilled cheese sandwich and a bowl of soup?"

"I feel a lot better. How about I fix *you* a grilled cheese sandwich. Or, better yet, I have some super chicken salad in the fridge. And some fresh fruit, all from Central Market. What sounds good?"

"All of it sounds good."

He watched her bop around the kitchen a few minutes, and she ended up with two plates that looked like something from a five-star restaurant. She'd fixed everything they'd mentioned and some things they hadn't. It tasted even better than it looked.

He liked sitting across the table from her and watching her nibble on a bit of her food. He liked just watching her, period. Maybe, he thought, he ought to ask her about what he'd seen the other night, about the drinking. No, now wasn't a good time, but it was obvious they needed to do some earnest talking. Since he'd realized his feelings for her were more serious than he'd ever intended, he had to know if she had a drinking problem and an attraction to the party life before he got in any deeper.

"Is the band going to play this Saturday night?" he asked, hoping the question sounded innocent. Truth was, he wanted to check out her behavior, see if he'd jumped to the wrong conclusions. It might sound like a sleazy thing to do, but he had a kid to think of.

"Yes, and at a much better place than the Fiery Pit. It's a dance club on Lamar. We alternate sets with another band. You ought to come. Do you like to dance?"

"I've been told I have two left feet."

. She looked under the table and smiled. "Nope. Looks like you have one of each."

He laughed. Damn, she could melt his heart faster than a blowtorch on a Popsicle. Was he destined to fall for the wrong women? Why couldn't life be simple?

AFTER BEN LEFT, SUNNY finished the vacuuming and sat down to read the newspaper, which she hadn't gotten around to that morning. Her new cousin Belle called while she was working the crossword puzzle.

"I wanted to finalize plans for Thanksgiving next week," Belle said. "The family is so eager to meet you and Cass. Are you both going to be able to come?"

"We are," Sunny told her. "Cass and I mulled over a dozen different scenarios, and we finally decided to close the café for the holidays. Because we're usually closed on Thanksgiving Day anyhow, and because so many of our staff are students who'll be going home, we decided to give ourselves a vacation. We're going to close after the noon hour rush on Wednesday and go to Naconiche. The signs are already up announcing our holiday closing."

"Oh, wonderful! Do you want to fly up with Gabe and me in the helicopter?"

"That would be fun, but I think Cass and I would like to drive. We might want to take a side trip. Is there a hotel in Naconiche?"

"No hotel, but J.J.'s wife, Mary Beth, has a really cute motel called the Twilight Inn. Do you and Cass mind sharing a room? The accommodations are limited. Gabe and I, as well as Sam and Skye, will be staying there, too. We could all stay with various of my brothers' families, but they're wall-to-wall kids, and we like to have a little downtime to ourselves."

"Sounds good to me, too. Shall we make a reservation for Wednesday and Thursday nights?"

"No need. I'll take care of it," Belle told her. "We're going to have such a great time. If you'll give me your fax number or e-mail address, I'll send maps and directions and phone numbers for everybody in the family."

Sunny gave her the information, and they chatted a moment more before they hung up. She was so excited she could hardly wait, and she called Cass immediately to tell her about Belle's call.

"What does one wear to meet long-lost relatives?" Cass asked. "We need to go shopping."

"Shopping? What to wear hadn't even crossed my mind."

Cass sighed. "Sis, sometimes I worry about you."

"Tell you what. Since you love to shop, pick up something for me while you're out. How's that?"

"You think I *won't*?"

Sunny laughed. "No, I think you *will*. Enjoy!"

ON SATURDAY EVENING, SUNNY dressed in her usual drummer garb, except as a nod to cooler weather, she traded her shorts for black cargo pants with zip-off legs if she got too hot playing. She tended the animals, grabbed her bag and hooked 'em to Sidewinder's to set up.

Sidewinder's was a big barn sort of place that served fried catfish baskets, steak fingers and lots of beer. They sold other stuff, too, but those three items were the most popular. The dance floor was huge and the crowd more polite—and a little older—than the bunch they'd played for last time. They came there more for the dancing than the drinking—though they did plenty of both and had a good time doing it. Because they alternated with a straight country band, the gig wasn't as tiring as some others.

She had a sneaking feeling that Ben might show up. He'd hinted at it that afternoon when they had taken his nieces and

Jay kite-flying at Zilker Park. She'd also heard about the girls' new dogs, Muffin and Lulu. So much for the good British names. Emma and Jane had been rechristened.

After the band set up, they got food and gathered at a large round table for their usual conversation.

"I've talked to everybody, and it sounds like we're in agreement to cut back some more on gigs. the Fiery Pit is definitely out. Unanimous decision. Duke's isn't going to reopen. The family sold the property. That leaves us with The Spotted Cow and Sidewinder's. How's that for now?"

"Good for me," Mike said. "We can try it for a couple of months and reevaluate. Trish and I are going to be taking one or two night classes this spring, so we can use a lighter load for sure."

Everybody agreed with the plan, and they switched to discussing their playlist. Here they played less rock and more contemporary country, R & B and ballads. They left the waltzes, line dances and two-steps to the other band, who played all country.

A crowd was gathering as the Pistols played the first set of the night. Amy, John's wife, and Melanie, Hank's fiancée, dropped by about halfway through. They often came to Sidewinder's and made their guys dance with them while the other band played. John and Hank and even Mike always asked Sunny to dance—and she did occasionally, but she missed not having her own fellow. Brian had enjoyed dancing as much as she did.

Did Ben really have two left feet? She'd gotten the definite impression that he didn't care much for dancing or dance halls or any place that was even slightly rowdy. He didn't seem that staid otherwise. Certainly not in the bedroom. Maybe his experience with his ex-wife and all her carousing had soured him. A shame if that was true. She loved music and dancing.

Sunny kept a lookout for Ben, but he didn't show up for their first set. When the Pistols finished their last song, they left the stage to the second band and moved to the double table Amy and Melanie had set up and reserved for them.

She hugged both women.

"You were really jammin' tonight," Amy said. "Sounded great."

"Thanks," Sunny said. She held up the empty glass she'd brought with her and said to the waitress who appeared, "Water and another Sunny's Special, please, Bitsy."

Everybody else ordered beer, and John ate what was left from his wife's French fries.

Amy slapped his hand. "Order your own fries. Those are mine."

John kissed her cheek. "Don't beat me, honey. I need to keep up my strength to dance with you. Come on, babe. Let's boogie." He grabbed her hand and pulled her onto the floor.

Hank and Melanie joined them. Mike and Trish stayed at the table with her. Sunny knew better than to urge them to dance, as well. They would come up with a dozen plausible excuses, but she knew there was a tacit understanding that Sunny wouldn't be left sitting alone.

When they had a line dance later, Sunny joined in, and near the end of the country band's set, she did a fast two-step with John.

Before the Pistols went on again, she made a quick trip to the ladies' room to freshen up. As she was coming out, she spotted Ben coming in the door. Catching up with him, she said, "Hi there, Ranger."

"Hi there, yourself," he said. "Aren't you supposed to be playing?"

"In just a minute. We have two alternating bands here. We're about to start our second set. You can come over and sit with Amy and Melanie if you'd like. If you haven't eaten, the catfish is good."

Ben didn't seem at all happy to be there. He looked as though he'd rather be passing a kidney stone.

BEN HAD TO ADMIT THIS PLACE wasn't as bad as the last one Sunny's band had played. Still, it wasn't much better than a plain old honky-tonk of the kind he'd gone to in his younger days, the kind where he'd met Marla. At least he could hear the music and could talk to Amy and Melanie if he leaned close and talked loud.

When the waitress came by, he ordered the catfish basket.

"And to drink?" the waitress asked.

"How about a Sunny's Special? You know what that is?"

She grinned. "Sure do. I keep Sunny supplied when she plays. Diet Sprite with a splash of grenadine and a lime twist."

"Grenadine?" Ben said.

"Pomegranate syrup."

"Well, I'll be damned," he said.

"Probably not for drinking grenadine," she said. "Pome-granates are full of antioxidants. Virgin pome-ritas are good, too. I like the frozen ones myself, but they may be a little sissy for a Texas Ranger." She laughed and hustled off.

Ben's mouth was still hanging open. He felt like a damned fool.

He ate his catfish when it came, listened to the Copper Pistols play and thanked all that was holy that he hadn't confronted Sunny in anger and accused her of being a lush. He could have ruined something fine. Still not happy about her playing in booze joints, he was at least glad to know she wasn't a boozer herself.

Surprised at how good the band was, he watched Sunny closely. Obviously she was enjoying herself. She caught him watching her and winked. He found himself grinning like a proud papa. Damn, she was something else. Those drums she beat stirred up primitive feelings in him. He wondered if they affected her the same way.

In a few minutes, the band broke and left the stage. The members made for the table and the water pitcher the waitress had left there. He spoke to John and Hank, and Sunny introduced him to Mike and Trish.

Sunny was a little out of breath when she sat down next to him. "Tired?" he asked.

"Just a little," she said. "Playing drums is hard work. And good exercise." She gulped a glass of water. "Enjoying yourself?"

"It's interesting watching you play. You're very good."

"Thanks," she said. "I've been playing since I was in sixth grade."

"I played the triangle when I was in first grade."

She smiled. "I'll bet you were cute."

"My music teacher said what I lacked in talent, I made up for in enthusiasm."

The band on stage started a fast two-step, and their table emptied, leaving only Sunny and Ben.

"Want to dance?" he asked her.

"You told me you couldn't dance."

"I told you I'd been told I had two left feet. I can dance."

She jumped up. "Then what are we waiting for? Come on." She pulled him to the dance floor.

After they'd circled the floor once, and he'd made a few fancy moves, she said, "Whoever told you that you had two left feet was nuts. You're terrific."

He twirled her around. "I took lessons."

"You got your money's worth."

He chuckled and twirled her again. Damned if he wasn't having a good time. Originally, he hadn't planned on staying the whole evening, but he did, and they danced some more.

By the time the place was ready to close, he could tell Sunny was tired out. He and the guys helped her load her trailer. "I'll follow you home," he told her.

She looked as if she were about to say something, but she just nodded and got into her car.

Chapter Twenty-Two

Sunny was bone tired. She was getting too old for this stuff. She couldn't chase kites all over the park for hours, then play a gig *and* kick up her heels on the dance floor. She wasn't eighteen anymore.

Praying she didn't hit anything, she backed the trailer into the garage. By the time she got out of her car, Ben was there to disconnect the trailer and position it. "Thank you," she said as he walked to her. "I owe you big-time. I'm too tired to even move my car, and at the same time I'm wound tighter than Trish's fiddle strings. Every muscle in me is complaining." She leaned against him and tucked her head under his chin.

He put his arms around her and held her close. His strength seemed to draw some of the weariness from her. "I'll take care of it. Go inside and draw yourself a warm bath."

"But—"

"Go ahead. I'll bring your keys in."

She didn't try to argue anymore. Trudging inside, she managed a few pats for Leo before she headed for her bathroom, shedding clothes as she went. She dumped a handful of lavender crystals into the tub and turned the water on full force. Tossing the last of her underwear aside, she climbed into the tub before it was filled.

"Ahhh." She wiggled her toes in the water. It was heaven, pure heaven. She closed her eyes and reveled in the sensation as the tub level rose and cradled her in its lovely warm scent.

"Don't go to sleep and drown."

Sunny opened her eyes to see Ben turning off the water.

"Ben! I'm in the tub."

"I see that." He started unbuckling his belt.

"What are you *doing?*"

"Taking off my clothes. I'm going to wash your back and massage your shoulders, and I don't want to get wet. These are my best boots."

Sunny was simply too tired for modesty, and he'd seen it all anyhow. By the time he stripped down to his boxer briefs, a new jolt of energy came to her from out of the blue. Well, not exactly out of the blue. She had a good idea where it had come from, and when he'd shed everything, she was sure. He seemed to have received a considerable jolt himself.

"I know you're tired, darlin'," he said, "and despite appearances, I'm not after my own pleasure. I want to help you work out the kinks and relax." He climbed into the big tub behind her, his legs bracketing hers.

Sunny didn't know when the relaxation part was supposed to start. Right then she felt anything except relaxed. But when he soaped her back with the creamy bar and began to knead her shoulders and neck with his strong hands, she turned boneless. He took his time and worked out every knot.

"Oh, Ben. That feels won-der-ful." His thumbs walked their way down her spine, and she moaned. They walked their way back up, and she arched her back as a writhing sensation kindled a deep longing inside. He squeezed water from a washcloth over her shoulders so that it trickled down her back and over her breasts.

Settling her back against him, he slowly lifted and massaged her left foot, her calf, her thigh. Next he did the same with the right foot and leg, going slowly until her muscles were relaxed, but her senses were on high alert. When his hands moved between her legs to stroke there, she gasped.

"Feel good?" he murmured in her ear.

She could only nod.

The gentle strokes continued until she felt fingers easing inside her. She pressed against his hand and magic happened. She stilled and let the throbbing release wash over her. "Oh…my…word."

"I like to feel you come against my hand."

"But you—"

"Shh," he whispered against her ear. "This was for you. Relaxed now?"

"Beyond relaxed. Way, way beyond. I could stay here forever."

He chuckled, and she felt his hardness against her. "You'd turn into a prune for sure. Come on, darlin'. Let's get out and put you into bed."

"Fine idea."

He helped her from the tub, grabbed a towel and quickly wrapped it around his waist. Taking another big towel, he carefully dried her, then lifted her and carried her to bed.

Sunny opened her mouth to protest but didn't. She'd never felt so pampered in her life. And she loved it. Resting her against his knee, he yanked back the covers and laid her on the sheets.

Ben kissed her forehead and pulled up the cover. "Sleep tight, darlin'."

As he turned away, she jerked his towel. "Where are you going?"

"Babe, you're tired, and—"

"I'm not tired anymore. Come to bed with me."

She didn't have to ask him twice.

THEY MADE LOVE MORE THAN once that night, slept late and ate French toast at the breakfast table.

"Oh, I forgot to mention it yesterday, but Tracy wanted me to invite you and Cass to have Thanksgiving dinner with us on Thursday. That is, if you don't have other plans."

"I'm sorry, but we do. We're going up to meet all the Outlaw clan and have Thanksgiving there. We're closing for the holidays so we can both go."

"It's strange you have family so close and you've never met them."

"Isn't it? Cass and I are excited. The problem is going to be explaining all this to Mom. She's going to have a fit when she hears about us visiting with the entire Outlaw family."

"Do you have to tell her?"

"I think so. She's old-fashioned, and being unmarried when we were born was shameful to my mother. Since he was a married man, she assumed that our father's family would be embarrassed by our existence. Mom didn't tell us the truth about our father until we confronted her when we were grown. Even now, she gets upset when we mention wanting to meet the Outlaws."

"A shame, but I understand her feelings." He stood. "Babe, I hate to eat and run, but I need to pick up Jay at Tracy's. Want to mess around with us later?"

"If you don't mind, I think I'll pass. I have a mound of paperwork to catch up on. The two of you feel free to drop by later if you'd like."

She walked him to the door, and he gave her a kiss to remember him by. Not that she could forget. Ben McKee was one of the sexiest men walking. He was right up there with George Clooney and Brad Pitt. Merely catching a scent of him could set her pulse racing. Not only was he a fantastic lover, but he was a considerate man, a caring father and a tough Texas Ranger to boot. Three out of four wasn't bad. It was the Texas Ranger part that bothered her. Why couldn't he have been an accountant, a salesman or even a baseball player? she wondered for the umpteenth time. If she ever married again, which was extremely doubtful, it wouldn't be to another lawman.

She got another cup of coffee and went to her computer desk in the guest room. The family not only owned Chili Witches and the building it and Hooks Restaurant were in, but also other rental property on the block as well as various additional parcels around town. Her mom and aunt were astute businesswomen, and they had bought Austin real estate when prices were considerably cheaper. Sunny and Cass split overseeing property management, too. Juggling everything took time and effort.

She began opening a stack of mail she'd picked up from the post office box Saturday morning. One particular letter caught her attention. She frowned. This was something she needed to talk with Cass about. This guy was beginning to be a pain.

THE DAYS SEEMED TO SPEED BY. Sunny had a million things to do getting ready to leave town, everything from having her car serviced to going in for a manicure and pedicure, the latter being at Cass's insistence. Then of course there was packing and finding a pet sitter. Ben and Jay volunteered to tend to the animals, and she was relieved by their offer.

At last Wednesday afternoon came. The car was packed, so she and Cass closed the café at three, gave all the leftover food to the mission, locked up and headed for East Texas.

"Nervous?" Sunny asked her sister.

"Nope. Excited. But I'm trying to remember who's who and which kids belong to which brother."

"I'm sure we'll get it sorted out," Sunny said. "J.J. is the sheriff, and he's younger than Cole and Frank and older than Sam and Belle. He's married to Mary Beth, who owns the Twilight Inn and the Twilight Tearoom. Mary Beth has a daughter, Katy, by a previous marriage, and they have a son named John, named after J.J.'s father, John Wesley Hardin Outlaw, known as Wes, who was the sheriff before he retired and J.J. was elected. Wes is married to Nonie, who was a teacher for many years and now runs the Double Dip, an ice-cream parlor."

"How did you learn all this?" Cass asked.

"Picking up things here and there. I made a cheat sheet. It's in my purse. Get it out and you can quiz me."

Cass dug through the bag and pulled out two typewritten pages. "All this?" she asked, glancing through the material.

"Yep. The second page is a genealogy chart someone in the family made. We've already met Frank, the judge, and his wife, Carrie, the lawyer. Their twins, Janey and Jimmy, are from Frank's first marriage. His wife died, I think. Their daughter is named…"

"Lily," Cass supplied.

"Right. I keep getting her mixed up with Cole and Kelly's daughter whose name is Elizabeth. Cole, who's the oldest son, used to be with the Houston Police Department—in Homicide. Now he teaches criminal justice at a community college."

"And Kelly is a doctor."

"She's the redhead," Sunny added. "Have we missed any Outlaws?"

"Only Sam and Skye and Belle and Gabe, but we know them. Glad they don't have any kids yet."

"Ain't it the truth? By the way, Cass, did you get a chance to look at the letter I gave you?"

"The one offering us an indecent amount for Chili Witches

and the building? I did. That bunch doesn't know when to quit, do they? I drafted a very lawyerly reply telling them to stuff it."

"What do you mean by lawyerly?"

"Businesslike with a bunch of big words."

Sunny laughed.

For over four hours they yakked and observed the scenery and listened to the radio between pit stops.

"Aren't we getting close?" Cass said.

"I hope so. My butt's about worn-out. Look for a sign."

"A sign?" Cass said, peering out into the darkness. "I haven't seen anything but trees for miles. Tall ones. I wish there were a few streetlights. This is creepy around here."

"I think it's a national forest."

Suddenly, a loud noise jarred the car, and the steering wheel shimmied and jerked in Sunny's hands.

"What was that?" Cass yelled.

"A blowout, I think." Sunny pulled over to the side of the road. "We've got a flat."

"A flat? How can we have a flat? We're miles from nowhere. Do you have triple A?"

"Nope."

"Well, I do," Cass said. "I'll call them." She dug out her cell phone. "Oh, crap. No bars."

"Probably the hills and the trees. Don't worry about it. I can change the tire if you'll hold the flashlight."

"I can hold a flashlight. Where is it?"

"Glove compartment."

They got out and surveyed the situation. Sunny unloaded their bags from the trunk and pulled out the spare and a jack. In no time, the tire was changed, and Sunny lowered the jack.

"I'm impressed, sis," Cass said.

"Uh-oh."

"What?"

"The spare's flat."

Cass shone the light on the tire. "It's flat all right. What now?"

"We can either walk, spend the night here or wait for a Good Samaritan to come along."

Cass ran the light around the woods and up the two-lane highway. "Are you up for walking twelve miles? There's a sign just ahead that says it's twelve miles to Naconiche."

Sunny's mother would have washed her mouth out with soap if she'd heard her daughter's comment. "Where is the Senator when I need him?" Exasperated, she sat down on the fender.

"Would you stop with the Senator stuff?" Cass said. "He's not going to help us. The man's been dead and buried for over thirty years."

Chapter Twenty-Three

Sunny didn't want to argue with Cass about the existence of the Senator, but stuck out here in the middle of nowhere, she seriously wanted help from any realm she could get it. The sooner, the better.

About that time, lights topped the hill and a pickup pulled to a stop behind their car. Gripping the tire iron, she waited.

"I wish you still carried a gun," Cass whispered. "Does this remind you of a spooky movie?"

All she could see was a very large man in a big cowboy hat stepping down from the truck and walking toward them. "You ladies need some help?"

He sounded like an older man. Sunny wondered if she could take him if she had to. "Yes, sir. We had a blowout and the spare's flat. If you could send somebody from the next town to help, we'd appreciate it."

With the glare of his headlights, she could only see his silhouette, but obviously he could see her clearly. "Don't I know you?" he asked. "You look mighty familiar." He glanced back and forth between Cass and her. "Why, you're twins."

"Yes, sir."

He suddenly laughed. "I'll bet dollars to doughnuts I've

stumbled onto Butch's girls. Frank said you favored Belle. I'm Wes Outlaw."

Sunny felt her tension leave, and Cass said, "Oh, thank God! You're Uncle Wes."

"That's me. Let's get you ladies to town, and I'll rustle up Royce Jenkins to come tow your car. Have you been here long?"

"It seems like forever," Cass said, "but I think it was more like twenty or thirty minutes."

"Lucky thing I had to deliver a clock to Emma Yonkin," Wes said. "Bet you're tired and hungry. Mary Beth left plates for everybody in the refrigerator at the inn."

After they loaded their bags into the pickup bed, the three of them squeezed into the truck's cab and headed for Naconiche and the Twilight Inn.

"Thank you, Senator," Sunny said silently. Whether Cass believed in him or not, guardian angels were handy to have around.

BELLE MUST HAVE HEARD THEM drive up because she poked her head out the unit next door, and watched them dismount from the big pickup.

"What in the world?" Belle said.

"We've had a grand adventure," Sunny said. "Your dad rescued us from a night in the woods. Let us get unpacked, and we'll tell you all about it."

About ten minutes after Wes left, they were unpacked and sprawled on the double beds when there was a knock at the door.

When Sunny opened it, Belle, Gabe, Skye and Sam trooped in. "What happened?" Belle said. "You can't just leave us hanging. Have you eaten? Mary Beth made plates from today's lunch in the tearoom. Shall I warm them for you?"

"Sure," Cass said. "I could eat a table leg."

Everybody exchanged greetings and took a chair or a corner of a bed while Belle fixed food in the room's kitchenette.

"Actually," Sunny said, "it wasn't much of an adventure. We had a blowout and the spare was flat."

"We were in the middle of more dark woods than I've ever seen, twelve miles from Naconiche," Cass added. "I was sure Leatherface of *Texas Chainsaw Massacre* was going to appear at any minute."

"Why didn't you call one of us?" Sam said.

"Dead zone. No bars," Cass said. "And then Wes came riding up on his white charger."

"More accurately, it was a black pickup," Sunny said.

They all laughed and talked while Sunny and Cass ate. After an hour or so, the visitors left them to rest.

"I can hardly wait until tomorrow," Sunny said. "Carrie said their house is the one Wes and our father grew up in. Isn't that something? It's going to be a wonderful day."

THE DAY STARTED OFF GREAT. They made coffee and breakfast from the bounty of stuff stocked in the kitchenette, and, while Cass took a shower, Sunny went outside to find the car fixed and parked in the carport beside their room. There was a nice chill in the air, and she found Gabe and Sam playing Frisbee in sweatshirts.

Belle and Skye, dressed in jeans and sweaters, were coming out the door. "Good morning," Belle said. "Are you two ready for the Outlaw gathering?"

Sunny looked down at her sweat suit. "Not quite. We'll have to dress."

"Trust me, you look fine," Belle said. "We're not formal around here."

"This is what we're wearing," Skye said. "Layering is a

good idea, too. It will likely get warm later. We may even go horseback riding this afternoon while the guys watch football."

Clothes were the least of her concerns, but she knew Cass would croak if Sunny wore her stretched-out sweats with coffee stains down the front.

"I barely know one end of a horse from another, but thanks for the tips. I was just getting some air while Cass steams up the bathroom. What time is lunch?"

"Whenever we get stuff together. Usually about one, but we start congregating early to get all the dishes coordinated. Everybody pitches in."

"Oh, by the way, we weren't sure what to contribute, so we brought a mixed case of wine. We left it in Uncle Wes's truck last night. Some will need to be chilled."

"Super," Belle said. "I'll get Gabe to make sure it gets inside and tended to. Sam said somebody fixed your tire and delivered the car last night late. I gather that the blowout is a lost cause, but I imagine J.J. can rustle up a spare for you before you start home. He's very enterprising."

"Thanks. I can't wait to meet the sheriff. And Mary Beth and everybody. Tell me which way to go."

Belle gave Sunny directions on how to find Frank and Carrie's house from the inn. "We'll be leaving in a few minutes. Come on anytime you're ready."

By ten Sunny and Cass were dressed in their casual, but chic, new attire and on the road to the old home place for the most memorable Thanksgiving either of them could remember.

"Oh, look, Cass," Sunny said as they pulled up to the big Victorian on the country road. "Can you believe our father used to play in that yard?" Her throat tightened, and she got teary-eyed thinking about the Senator as a little boy.

Cass seemed to be feeling it, too. She was very quiet for a few minutes. "We have a heritage."

By the time they got to the big porch, Frank and Carrie were standing there waiting for them.

"Welcome to Bedlam," Carrie said, smiling. "Come in."

Janey and Jimmy came tearing out of the house with another girl about their age. "It's the twins!" Janey yelled. "Look, Katy! I told you. They look just alike. This is my cousin Katy, and my other cousins are inside. And so is my baby sister."

"They're all littler than us," Katy added.

Sunny and Cass greeted everyone, and went inside.

"Something smells heavenly," Sunny said.

"Nonie just put the corn bread dressing in the oven," Carrie said. "This year the guys are frying our turkeys outside. So lunch will depend on their skill with the fryers."

A beautiful redhead with a toddler on her hip came out of the kitchen. "Hi," she said. "I'm Kelly, Cole's wife."

"Is this Elizabeth?" Cass asked.

"No, this is Lily. If you see a little red-haired ball of fire running after Skye, that's Elizabeth. She adores Skye. They're probably out in the barn or with an animal somewhere."

In the kitchen they met Mary Beth, a pretty blonde, who stopped stirring a pot long enough to hug both of them. "Welcome to the Outlaw gang. I'm J.J.'s wife, Katy and John's mother and your innkeeper. It's great to have you here."

"And I'm Nonie, mother, mother-in-law and grandmother," an older white-haired lady said, offering the sweetest smile Sunny had ever seen. She grasped Sunny's and Cass's hands. "And now I'm a new aunt, too. I remember your father fondly. He would have been so proud of you two."

Sunny hugged Nonie, who was nearly a head shorter than she. "Thank you, Aunt Nonie."

Cass hugged Nonie, as well, and both sisters were sniffling when she was done.

"Where are your brothers?" Nonie asked Frank, who had relieved Kelly of Lily.

"Outside discussing turkey-cooking strategy," Frank said. "Come out to the patio, ladies, and I'll introduce you to some of the rowdier members of the family."

"Is J.J. watching John?" Mary Beth asked.

"I'll check," Frank said, leading the way through the huge den to the back doors.

Outside stood four very tall men and Belle. A boy, a bit bigger than Lily, rode the shoulders of one of them.

"Belle and Gabe brought the cookers, the oil and the turkeys," Frank said. "Unfortunately, the cookers came unassembled. I think they finally turned the assembly over to Dad."

Wes looked up from screwing a nut onto a rod. "Good morning, ladies. I guess you found your car."

"We did," Sunny said. "Thanks. You saved us."

He smiled. "Glad to help. Don't think you've met Cole, our oldest."

The man with the child on his shoulders nodded and smiled. "Ladies. Which one of you is the cop?"

"Ex-cop," Sunny said. "That's me. I was in Homicide. I understand you were, too."

"I was. Now I teach. This rascal beside me is brother J.J., the local sheriff, and I never cease to be amazed that he recently got elected again."

J.J. grinned. "Don't pay Cole any attention. He's just jealous."

"And this little rascal on my shoulders," Cole said, "is John, J.J. and Mary Beth's son." He tugged on his nephew's feet. "Say hello to the ladies, John."

"Hellooo, ladies," John said, laughing. "Hellooo, ladies. Got to *pee*."

"Not on me, buddy."

"Peee!" Lily squealed, clapping her hands.

J.J. lifted him off Cole's shoulders. "Go over behind that bush, John."

"J.J.!" Belle said. "Act civilized. We have guests."

"Be sure to turn your back politely," J.J. called after his son, who was headed for the bush as fast as his little legs would churn.

"J.J.!" Belle said again. "Cole, do something with him."

Sunny and Cass both started laughing.

"Growing up here must have been fun," Sunny said.

Belle rolled her eyes.

"It was never dull," Sam said. "Anyone want to shoot some hoops?"

"We'd better get the oil in these fryers," Gabe said, "and start it heating if we want turkey for Thanksgiving. I hope those birds are thawed good."

"Does it matter?" J.J. asked.

"Frozen turkeys tend to explode when you fry them."

"Sam, get the fire extinguisher."

THE TURKEYS DIDN'T EXPLODE. They were perfectly cooked, and Wes and Frank carved them and added the heaping platter to the enormous amount of food that had been prepared and laid out on the kitchen island. Both the large dining table and the breakfast table had been set as well as a card table in the den.

After Wes said the Thanksgiving prayer, everybody grabbed a big paper platter and heaped it high with turkey and dressing with giblet gravy as well as sweet potatoes, cranberry sauce, green beans, peas, mac and cheese, three kinds of salads and yeast rolls.

People grabbed the first seat they came to, and Sunny ended

up at the breakfast table with Nonie, Mary Beth, Cole, J.J. and the high chairs for John and Elizabeth. The food was fabulous, and the company even better.

She talked with Cole more about his career change. "I'd never thought of going into teaching," Sunny said, "but it sounds very interesting."

"Turns out I love it, and my background as a police officer in a metropolitan area gives me credibility with my students and gives me real 'on the street' experiences to share with them."

Soon everyone was groaning from their second—and sometimes third—helpings. Desserts would wait until later. The whole clan, even the older kids, pitched in with cleanup and had fun doing it.

"Ready for some football?" J.J. yelled, heading for the big-screen TV with all the men following.

"I don't know why they even bother," Kelly said, covering the potato salad and storing it in the fridge. "They'll all be sound asleep in fifteen minutes."

Nonie laughed. "That hasn't changed in years and years."

The younger children were put down for naps, the older kids scattered and the women poured themselves another glass of wine and went out on the patio to sit in the sunshine and avoid the inevitable snores.

Sunny stretched out on a chaise, rested her wineglass on her tummy and listened to the rustling sway of wind high in the trees. "I love it here," she said. "It's so peaceful."

"Isn't it?" Carrie said. "I spend lots of time out here."

The French doors opened, and Sunny craned her neck to see Sam coming out. He squatted down beside Skye. "Honey, I've got a problem," he said. "I just now had a call from the captain, and we have a situation. Five prisoners, badass ones, escaped sometime during the night. They hit a pawnshop in Bastrop before dawn this morning, so now they're armed and holed up in the area—with hostages. They're calling in Rangers from the nearby counties to help."

Sunny felt the blood drain from her face, and she started to shake. "Does that mean Ben?"

"I imagine he's already there," Sam said.

Oh, dear God, please, please not again.

Chapter Twenty-Four

Kelly was immediately at Sunny's side. "What's wrong?"

"Panic attack," Sunny managed to say.

Skye knelt on the other side, her hand on Sunny's chest. "Breathe slowly through your nose," she said in the softest, gentlest voice. "This will pass. We're with you. Just lie back and breathe slowly. Imagine that you're floating on a cloud."

Sunny heard other talking, other commotion going on, but it was Skye's voice and her touch that captivated her. Everything else seemed to fade away as she listened to Skye whispering near her ear. She closed her eyes and drifted. Tension melted and feelings of peace filled the empty spaces. Skye's words and her touch had a soothing, healing effect that brought an unbelievable calmness moving through her.

When Sunny opened her eyes again, Kelly and Skye still knelt beside her, and Cass stood at the foot of the chaise looking worried.

"How are you feeling?" Kelly asked.

"I'm okay." Sunny looked at Skye. "What did you do?"

"In my humble medical opinion," Kelly said, "she worked a miracle."

Skye smiled. "Not quite. I've had lots of experience with panic and anxiety attacks. Just lie there quietly for a while."

"I'll go tell everybody you're all right," Cass said. "You're sure you are?"

"I'm fine, Cass. Cross my heart."

"Do you have these often?" Kelly asked.

"Not much anymore," Sunny said. "They were frequent after my husband was killed in a gun battle. He was a police officer. SWAT."

"Ahhh," Skye said. "And you were afraid for Ben in a similar situation."

Sunny didn't reply. Her answer was obvious. "I feel like such an idiot. I'm sorry."

Skye chuckled. "You say this to the queen of panic attacks? My dear, I used to be a screaming mess with a list of phobias longer than my arm. I'll give you the name of my psychologist, who is an excellent hypnotist. I'm living proof of her ability. Trust me, I know about these things."

"She's right," Kelly said.

Sunny started to get up. "I think we'd better leave and get back to Austin."

"I think you'd better stay here with us," Kelly said. "Sam will keep us posted."

"I'm ready for dessert," Skye said. "Sunny, Kelly makes the world's best pecan pies. Think you could handle a little piece?"

"With ice cream?"

"Naturally."

THE WHOLE OUTLAW BUNCH rallied around Sunny, and that afternoon she learned the true meaning of family. It was an awesome feeling. Her spirits soared even higher when Sam and Gabe returned two hours later. Gabe had left to fly Sam to Bastrop.

"We didn't even make it for the shooting," Sam said. "Ouch, J.J.! Why'd you elbow me? Anyhow, the whole brouhaha was settled before we got there, and we turned around and came back. The prisoners surrendered pretty quick, so nobody got hurt. Seems as though the dumb bastards stole a bunch of guns but no ammunition."

"Sam!" Nonie said.

Sunny was the first one to laugh.

"Ben's fine," Sam said to her. "In case you were wondering."

"The thought crossed my mind." Her tension eased considerably.

The rest of the afternoon passed in a variety of activities. Cass even got on Carrie's horse for a slow walk around the corral, and, not to be outdone, Sunny tried it, as well. She probably wouldn't take up horseback riding anytime soon, but it was fun.

After a supper of leftovers for adults and grilled hot dogs for the kiddos and anyone else who wanted one, the group broke up. After warm goodbyes to everyone, Sunny and Cass drove back to the Twilight Inn.

Soon after they arrived in their room, there was a soft knock on the door. It was Skye.

She handed Sunny a piece of paper and her business card. "That's the name and number of the psychologist I mentioned, and this is my number."

"Thanks, Skye," Sunny said. "I'll give her a call."

"Promise?"

"Yes."

Skye hugged her. "Good. My cell number is on the back of my card. I'm available to you any time of the day or night."

Sunny was so touched, tears came to her eyes. "Thank you so much, Skye, and thanks for today, too. I sense that you're a very special person."

Smiling, Skye said, "I sense some things about you, too. Good luck."

After Skye left, Cass said, "What was she talking about?"

"I'm not exactly sure, but there's more to Dr. Skye than one might expect. I've never felt anything quite like I did when she put a hand on my chest."

"Some of that woo-woo stuff?"

Sunny chuckled. "Maybe."

Cass rolled her eyes. Sunny threw a pillow at her.

J.J. APPEARED AT THE INN the next morning with a tire. It looked new.

"Let me get my checkbook," Sunny said. "I really appreciate your getting this for us."

"Oh, you don't have to pay me. It was an extra one I located. I'll put it in your trunk if you'll give me your keys."

She wasn't quite sure she believed him, but Belle said he was enterprising, so she let it go with a thank-you and helped him stow it in her car.

A similar thing happened when they went to check out. One of two elderly men in the office said, "You don't owe anything. Your bill has been taken care of already."

"Say, I knew your daddy, Butch," the other old man said. "Knew him well. He was our senator, you know. We were awful proud of him in these parts. Good to meet his girls."

"Thank you," Cass said.

"And thank our benefactor," Sunny added.

They took their time getting home, stopping at interesting places, including a couple of antique shops. They browsed and bought and replayed their time in Naconiche and their new family.

"You seem awfully quiet," Cass said on the last leg of their drive back to Austin. "Did the sign for the Bastrop turnoff have anything to do with it?"

"Maybe. I think I'm going to have to stop seeing Ben McKee."

"For gosh sakes, why? He's such a hottie."

"Because I'm very afraid I'm falling in love with him. And I'm very afraid…"

AFTER SUNNY DROPPED OFF CASS at her apartment, she called Ben on her cell to tell him she was home. "You don't have to feed the animals this evening."

"Jay will be disappointed. He's taken to pet-sitting. Sadie almost let him touch her."

"Now that's a miracle."

"Want to go out tonight?" he asked.

"I don't think so. We've had a long drive, and I need to unpack and do stuff around the house."

"How about tomorrow?" he asked.

"I have a ton of paperwork to do, and we're playing to-morrow night. Anything exciting happen while I was gone?"

"Not much. Same old, same old. Tracy cooked a great dinner. Sunny, is something wrong?"

She hesitated, and the silence hung like a curtain between them. "I'm pulling up into the driveway, and my phone's about out of juice. I'll talk to you later. Bye."

Chicken, she told herself. She was going to have to talk to him sooner or later and probably break things off. She chose later. Right then she needed to be alone, to be quiet and have time to think and decide what she really wanted. At the moment, self-preservation was leading.

She was miffed with Ben that worries about him had cast a pall over her phenomenal holiday with the Outlaws. Irrational? Probably, but she felt it nonetheless.

And she would not, under any circumstances, marry anyone in law enforcement again. Never, ever again. Of course mar-riage hadn't been mentioned, or even hinted at, but she knew how these things worked. If people fell in love, sooner or later marriage would come up.

But then, Ben hadn't hinted at being in love with her, either.

Oh, hells bells! She was getting a headache thinking about the whole dilemma. She unpacked and headed for her favorite spot: the bathtub.

Hydrotherapy for the body; aromatherapy for the spirit.

With jets going full blast and lavender wafting in the air, Sunny leaned back on her new bath pillow and closed her eyes. Ahhh.

Pounding on the door set Sunny's heart racing, and she bolted up from the water. Casting about for a weapon, she grabbed the lid from the back of the toilet with both hands, raising it high, ready to attack the intruder.

"Sunny! Dammit, answer me!"

"Ben?"

"Are you okay?"

"Of course I'm okay. I'm in the tub."

The door opened, and he came in.

"Ben, I'm taking a bath."

"So you said. What's with the toilet lid?"

"It's for coldcocking an intruder, which I'm about to do if you don't get out of my bathroom this very minute."

"I'm not leaving."

"What is it with you, McKee? Do you have some sort of bathroom fetish? And how did you get in the house?"

"I have a key."

"Well, leave it on the coffee table on your way out."

"You really want me to leave?"

He looked so woebegone, feigned she was sure, that she started to laugh.

Ben grinned and reached for his belt buckle. "I'll wash your back."

"You'll do no such thing!" She waved the toilet lid. "I know where back-washing leads."

He grinned wider.

"Out! Now!"

Heaving a big sigh, he retreated.

"And close the door!"

The door didn't move.

Sunny replaced the porcelain lid, turned off the jets and took her time drying off. Grabbing her robe from a hook, she put it on and belted it tightly before she walked out.

Ben was sitting on the corner of her bed with a big grin on his face.

"What's so amusing?" she asked.

"Not a thing."

She looked behind her to see the large vanity mirror, which provided an excellent view of the entire bathroom. "You dirty dog."

"Oh, darlin', don't be mad." He pulled her into his lap and kissed her.

Sunny meant to push him away. She tried to push him away, but she didn't try very hard. She couldn't. Her arms were weak, and she was melting. Dear Lord, she loved this man.

"I missed you," he said as he nibbled on her neck and slipped his hand inside her robe. His hand suddenly stilled. "Oh, crap!" He jerked his hand away and set her on her feet. "I have to go. I left Jay in the car. Don't move. I'll take him to Tracy's and be right back. Now don't move."

Stunned, Sunny watched him hotfoot it from her bedroom. *Oh, dear. This may be harder than I thought.*

Chapter Twenty-Five

The minute he unlocked the door, Ben knew something was wrong. The television was on, tuned to a news station. He found Sunny, not in the bedroom as he'd hoped, but in the den, on the couch, fully dressed.

"You moved," he said.

"I did."

"Why?"

"We need to have a talk," she said. "A serious talk."

Everything from her having cancer to finding another man flashed through his mind. "What's wrong?"

"Come sit down." She patted the couch beside her.

He sat down and, slinging his arm over the couch back, turned to her. He didn't like the look on her face. "Talk." That came out harsher than he'd intended, but his guts were tied in a knot.

She sighed. "Ben, I think it's best if we stop seeing each other."

He felt as if he'd been poleaxed. Stunned, he said, "Why?"

"I just think it would be best. I don't think we're well suited."

"You've got to be kidding. We practically set the bed on fire."

She shook her head. "I don't mean the sex. The sex is great, better than great. I'm talking about other things. You've made it clear that you don't approve of my playing in the band, and I have some issues—" She choked.

Ben could only gawk at her. Not that long ago, he'd thought she was another version of Marla and was ready to end it. Now her words stabbed him in the heart. Now he'd fallen head over heels in love with her, and he couldn't stand the notion of never seeing Sunny again.

"You're not making any sense, Sunny."

"Dammit, Ben McKee, I'm falling in love with you, and I can't—"

A big grin spread over his face. "Oh, darlin', I—"

Putting two fingers over his lips, she said, "Shhh. You don't have to say anything, and that's not the point. I can't get into this relationship any deeper. I just can't."

"Is it because of Brian?"

"Yes. No. Partly. I've told you how he died, and his death screwed me up pretty badly. I promised myself I'd never get involved with another cop, and here I'm getting involved with another one. I don't want that."

"You want me to give up the Rangers? Sunny, being a Texas Ranger is who I am. How would you like it if I told you to sell Chili Witches or get out of that damned band and stop playing those sleazy dives?"

She winced. "Ben, I would never ask you to leave the Rangers. I know how much it means to you, but I can't handle it. Emotionally, it would wreck me." She told him about what had happened in Naconiche when Sam had told them about the escaped prisoners. "I freaked, Ben. Totally freaked. And if you and I stay together, it will happen again."

"Dammit, Sunny, people can work out differences. They do it every day. You're not the only one falling in love here. What about me? What about Jay?"

He was scared, and he was mad. They both said things they shouldn't have, and soon they were arguing heatedly. She called him a hardheaded stick-in-the-mud, and he practically called her a slut who flirted with anything in pants.

He should have kept his mouth shut, but he felt as though he was fighting for his life. Finally, before he said anything worse, he banged her key on the coffee table and strode from the room.

"I hate chili!" he shouted and slammed the door.

IF SUNNY HADN'T BEEN CRYING, she would have laughed. She hated arguing, and she'd handled things badly. Ben didn't understand how real and debilitating her attacks were. He couldn't imagine how long and hard she'd worked to come as far as she had. After Brian had been killed, she was a total mess, nonfunctional. The thought of having to go through that again was unthinkable. She couldn't do it. She couldn't.

She turned the TV back on and stared at the screen until she fell asleep.

She woke up Saturday morning with a crick in her neck and Leo licking her hand. "Hello, buddy. You hungry?"

He licked her hand again and sat down with his muzzle on the edge of the couch where she lay. She scratched his ears. "Life with you is certainly less complicated than with that other guy."

In the light of a new day, she wondered if she'd been too quick to throw in the towel. Would she have traded all the wonderful years with Brian to avoid the pain she'd endured after his death? No. Never.

She had another chance at happiness with a fine man. What was it worth to her? How strong was she?

After putting out fresh food and water for Leo and Sadie, Sunny dug out the piece of paper Skye had given her. She called Dr. Gossett and made an appointment for the following Tuesday.

And then she thought about the band.

THE SPOTTED COW WAS HAVING two bands Saturday night, and the Pistols were playing the early half of the evening. "I hope this means we're not getting just half a steak," she said to Hank as he helped her unload her drums.

He laughed. "Me, too. The steak's the best part about playing here."

"Hank," she said, leaning back against her trailer, "you've always been honest and up-front with me, and I want to ask you something."

"Sure, babe. Shoot."

"Do you and the other members of the Pistols want to disband? Is everybody tired?"

He hesitated, and she knew.

"Why didn't you guys say something, Hank?"

"Aw, I don't know. I think everybody's on the fence. We enjoy playing, but it's getting to be a grind. And, face it, babe, we were a lot younger when we started. Now, we're getting to be a bunch of old farts with hemorrhoids and corns."

Sunny laughed. "The Stones are still rolling."

"If I made their kind of money, I'd still be rolling, too."

"Have people been reluctant to talk about disbanding because of me?"

Hank hesitated again.

"Got it. I think we need to have a heart-to-heart over our steaks tonight."

Getting people to discuss the situation honestly wasn't easy, especially with John glaring at anybody who tried to say anything about disbanding. John had always been protective of her, and she figured he'd been the force behind keeping the Pistols together. For her. But one by one, and little by little, everybody reluctantly admitted that it was time for the Copper Pistols to retire.

"We can play at the APD picnic every year, and maybe we can get together and jam once a month or so," Sunny said. "I have an empty apartment over the garage, and I've been thinking it would make a great music studio."

"Excellent!" Trish said. "I'd love that."

The mood became lighter, as if a weight had been removed from their shoulders. Sunny had to admit the same sense of relief. She was tired of the grind, too. That night a new sense of joy returned to their playing, and they had fun.

The crowd seemed to sense it, as well, and the applause was louder.

BEN SAT IN A DARK CORNER where he could watch Sunny, but where she couldn't see him. The place was only a few blocks from the Fiery Pit, but it was worlds apart in atmosphere. He could tell from the T-shirts and comments dropped here and there that a lot of cops were among the patrons of the Spotted Cow. Everybody seemed to be having a good time, including Sunny. If he were honest, he'd have to admit that before Marla had soured him, this was the kind of place he might have enjoyed, too. The kind of spot where you could stop by with your buddies or your wife or girlfriend for a beer and a little music to unwind.

And he had to admit he'd really enjoyed dancing with Sunny at Sidewinder's. He used to love dancing before Marla started drinking too much when they went out and kept making an ass of herself. He'd begun to associate music and dancing and drinking with Marla's excesses. He'd forgotten about moderation. And fun.

Sunny was right. He'd become a hardheaded stick-in-the-mud. Sunny was no more like his ex than he was like Donald Duck. Sunny would never in a million years go off partying and leave a child alone at night. Never.

Ben sat and watched her tossing back Sunny's Specials and beating hell out of those drums, and his heart swelled with a love so big he thought his ribs might crack. He wasn't about to lose that woman. She was the best thing that had ever happened to him. He could almost hear his mama whispering in his ear, "She's the one." He'd do whatever it took to convince her they were perfect for each other. He'd do anything it took to get her back. Anything.

He'd even been thinking about another line of work. The Rangers didn't pay all that well anyhow.

WHEN SUNNY BACKED THE TRAILER into the driveway, another car pulled in after her. Apprehension sharpened her senses, and she waited until someone got out. The tall silhouette and the white hat kicked her pulse into overdrive.

It was Ben.

She punched the remote for the garage door and backed the trailer in.

"Need some help?" he asked.

"Sure."

He unhooked the trailer and positioned it inside. Because she was hemmed in, she couldn't move her car, so she got out and closed the garage.

"Hard night?" he asked.

"No, actually it was a good night. It was our farewell performance."

"How so?"

"The Copper Pistols are retiring."

"But you love playing in the band. I watched you tonight, and you were having the time of your life."

"You were there?"

He nodded. "For the whole thing. I even had a steak. It was larrupin'."

Sunny laughed. "The steaks *are* fantastic. We'll miss the Spotted Cow's food, but we decided that the grind was getting to be too much. We're just going to jam for fun from now on."

"So Saturday nights are going to be free after this?" He leaned against the fender of her car and pulled her close to the juncture of his spread legs. She shivered. "Cold?"

She shook her head. "All my Saturday nights are open."

"Want to go dancing with me next Saturday night?"

Startled, she said, "*Dancing?* Where?"

"Anywhere you want. I liked the floor at Sidewinder's, but I'm open to suggestion."

"Sure. I'd love to."

"Speaking of love," he said, "I don't think I've ever told you how very much I love you, Sunny Outlaw Payton. I don't think I've really loved any woman before—except my mother and sister—and the feeling kind of snuck up on me."

"I see."

"I've been doing a lot of thinking since last night, and it's plain to me that you're more important than any job. I want you, Sunny, and I'd rather wash cars or flip hamburgers than do without you. If my being a Ranger will cause you one minute of pain, I'll resign."

Sunny's heart was filled to overflowing with love for Ben. "You'd do that for me?"

"I would."

"Oh, Ben." She pulled his head down and kissed him. "I know how much being a Texas Ranger means to you, to any Ranger. That's the greatest gift anyone has ever offered me, but I would never ask that of you. I love you too much. We'll work it out without your doing anything so drastic."

"Are you sure?" he asked.

"Positive. I already have an appointment with Skye's psychologist."

"Do you know that right now I feel like I'm the luckiest man in the world?" He picked her up, plunked her on the fender and kissed her breathless.

A male voice harrumphed behind them.

"Don't you believe you ought to take this inside?" the Senator asked.

"Fine idea," Sunny said.

"What?"

"That we should take this inside."

"Darlin', you must have read my mind." He lifted her down from the fender. "But before we do, I have to tell you something. I lied."

Sunny's heart almost stopped. "About what?"

"I love chili."

She hooted with laughter as, arm in arm, they walked to the door.

The Senator and Alta watched them disappear inside, and they smiled and disappeared, as well.

* * * * *

There's one more Outlaw looking for love!
Find out how Cassidy gets her man in
THE MAVERICK,
coming soon, only from Harlequin American Romance

"AREN'T YOU GOING to say 'Fly me' or at least 'Welcome aboard'?"

Amanda Bauer didn't. The softly muttered word that actually came out of her mouth was a lot less welcoming. And had fewer letters. Four, to be exact.

The man shook his head and tsked. "Not exactly the friendly skies. Haven't caught the spirit yet this morning?"

"Make one more airline-slogan crack and you'll be walking to Chicago," she said.

He nodded once, then pushed his sunglasses onto the top of his tousled hair. The move revealed blue eyes that matched the sky above. And yeah. They were twinkling. Damn it.

"Understood. Just, uh, promise me you'll say 'Coffee, tea or me' at least once, okay? Please?"

Amanda tried to glare, but that twinkle sucked the annoyance right out of her.

Coffee and tea they had, and he was welcome to them. But her? Well, she'd never even considered making a move on a customer before. Talk about unprofessional.

And yet...

Something inside her suddenly wanted to take a chance, to be a little outrageous.

How long since she had done indecent things—or

decent ones, for that matter—with a sexy man? She hadn't had time for a lunch date, much less the kind of lust-fest she'd enjoyed in her younger years. The kind that lasted for entire weekends and involved not leaving a bed except to grab the kind of sensuous food that could be smeared onto—and eaten off—someone else's hot, naked, sweat-tinged body.

She closed her eyes, her hand clenching tight on the railing. Her heart fluttered in her chest and she tried to make herself move.

Was she really considering this? She had no idea if he was actually attracted to her or just an irrepressible flirt. Yet something inside was telling her to take a shot with this man.

It was crazy. Something she'd never considered. Yet right now, at this moment, she was definitely considering it. If he was available...could she do it? Seduce a stranger. Have an anonymous fling, like something out of a blue movie on late-night cable?

She didn't know. All she knew was that the flight to Chicago was a short one, so she had to decide quickly. And as she put her foot on the bottom step and began to climb up, Amanda suddenly had to wonder if she was about to embark on the ride of her life.

Look for
PLAY WITH ME
by Leslie Kelly
Available February 2010

Sold, bought, bargained for or bartered

He'll take his…

Bride on Approval

Whether there's a debt to be paid,
a will to be obeyed or a business
to be saved…she has no choice
but to say, "I do"!

PURE PRINCESS, BARTERED BRIDE
by *Caitlin Crews*
#2894

Available February 2010!

REQUEST YOUR FREE BOOKS!
2 FREE NOVELS PLUS 2 FREE GIFTS!

HARLEQUIN®

American ★ Romance®

Love, Home & Happiness!

YES! Please send me 2 FREE Harlequin® American Romance® novels and my 2 FREE gifts (gifts are worth about $10). After receiving them, if I don't wish to receive any more books, I can return the shipping statement marked "cancel." If I don't cancel, I will receive 4 brand-new novels every month and be billed just $4.24 per book in the U.S. or $4.99 per book in Canada. That's a saving of close to 15% off the cover price! It's quite a bargain! Shipping and handling is just 50¢ per book in the U.S. and 75¢ per book in Canada.* I understand that accepting the 2 free books and gifts places me under no obligation to buy anything. I can always return a shipment and cancel at any time. Even if I never buy another book from Harlequin, the two free books and gifts are mine to keep forever.

154 HDN E4CC   354 HDN E4CN

Name _____ (PLEASE PRINT)

Address _____ Apt. #

City _____ State/Prov. _____ Zip/Postal Code

Signature (if under 18, a parent or guardian must sign)

Mail to the Harlequin Reader Service:
IN U.S.A.: P.O. Box 1867, Buffalo, NY 14240-1867
IN CANADA: P.O. Box 609, Fort Erie, Ontario L2A 5X3

Not valid for current subscribers to Harlequin® American Romance® books.

Want to try two free books from another line?
Call 1-800-873-8635 or visit www.morefreebooks.com.

* Terms and prices subject to change without notice. Prices do not include applicable taxes. N.Y. residents add applicable sales tax. Canadian residents will be charged applicable provincial taxes and GST. Offer not valid in Quebec. This offer is limited to one order per household. All orders subject to approval. Credit or debit balances in a customer's account(s) may be offset by any other outstanding balance owed by or to the customer. Please allow 4 to 6 weeks for delivery. Offer available while quantities last.

Your Privacy: Harlequin is committed to protecting your privacy. Our Privacy Policy is available online at www.eHarlequin.com or upon request from the Reader Service. From time to time we make our lists of customers available to reputable third parties who may have a product or service of interest to you. If you would prefer we not share your name and address, please check here. ☐

Help us get it right—We strive for accurate, respectful and relevant communications. To clarify or modify your communication preferences, visit us at www.ReaderService.com/consumerschoice.

HAR10